Midnight in the Snow

Karen Swan is the *Sunday Times* top three bestselling author of twenty-one books, and her novels sell all over the world. She writes two books each year – one for the summer period and one for the Christmas season. Previous winter titles include *Christmas at Tiffany's*, *The Christmas Party* and *Together by Christmas*, and for summer, *The Spanish Promise*, *The Hidden Beach* and *The Secret Path*.

Previously a fashion editor, she lives in Sussex with her husband, three children and two dogs.

Follow Karen on Instagram @swannywrites, on her author page on Facebook, and on Twitter @KarenSwan1.

Also by Karen Swan

Midnight
in the
Snow

KAREN SWAN

PAN BOOKS

First published 2021 by Macmillan

This edition first published 2021 by Pan Books
an imprint of Pan Macmillan
The Smithson, 6 Briset Street, London EC1M 5NR
EU representative: Macmillan Publishers Ireland Ltd, 1st Floor,
The Liffey Trust Centre, 117-126 Sheriff Street Upper,
Dublin 1, D01 YC43
Associated companies throughout the world
www.panmacmillan.com

ISBN 978-1-5290-0614-8

1 3 5 7 9 8 6 4 2

A CIP catalogue record for this book is available from the British Library.

Typeset in Palatino by Palimpsest Book Production Ltd, Falkirk, Stirlingshire
Printed and bound by CPI Group (UK) Ltd, Croydon, CR0 4YY

Visit **www.panmacmillan.com** to read more about all our books
and to buy them. You will also find features, author interviews and
news of any author events, and you can sign up for e-newsletters
so that you're always first to hear about our new releases.

For Caroline Hogg
Who is far more brilliant than she knows

Midnight in the Snow

Prologue

Clover Phillips Tell me what it was like.

Cory Allbright *(Pause)* It was like . . . being inside a washing machine. You're getting thrown about. You don't know which way is up and which is down. The pressure is immense. The wave slams you down and crushes you. Then it sucks you back up again . . . When the wave is on you, everything's dark. It's like the sky is falling.

C. P. How long were you under for?

C. A. From the first one? Two minutes twenty, forty.

C. P. That's a long time to hold your breath.

C. A. We train for it. But it's different when the wave's got you and you're being tossed like a rag doll. You're getting grilled. You're not in control of what your body's doing. All the forces are coming from outside your body.

C. P. Were you able to orientate yourself?

C. A. Not at first. When the wave's on you, it's like an avalanche – weight, pressure, noise. You have to let it extinguish itself before you can even try to get out, you've gotta wait for the trough before the next wave. I had been upside down but I got myself right and when I could see the brightness of the sky, I knew I could kick up. But before I could surface, it got dark again. I felt the water sucking back.

C. P. How far were you from the surface?

C. A. A metre?

C. P. And the second set came?

C. A. *(Nods)*

C. P. What could you see?

C. A. . . . I saw hell. I saw my life being taken from me . . . I could see the wave coming down, it was like watching a building fall on me . . . There was nothing I could do. I couldn't get out of the way. I knew I didn't have the breath to stay down for a double.

C. P. What's the last thing you remember?

C. A. Spreading darkness, and then pressure. The wave crashed down on me and threw me onto the seabed. I was knocked out. Next thing I knew, I was waking up in a hospital bed, a day later, with a broken arm and a TBI.

C. P. By TBI, you mean traumatic brain injury?

C. A. *(Nods)*

C. P. But that isn't the only lasting damage, is it? According to your doctors, you were under the water for four minutes twelve seconds before you were rescued. You suffered hypoxic brain injury as well and as a result of inhaling sea water, you have acute respiratory distress syndrome.

C. A. . . . Yeah.

C. P. What has the impact been on your family?

C. A. *(Hides face in his hands)* They've got it worse than me. I can't provide for them no more. My wife's working two jobs, on top of looking after me. My boys don't know what's happened to their dad cos they're too young to understand. They can't see my injuries so they don't know why I can't get on the boards or why I won't go throw a ball with them.

C. P. So you lost more than just a world title that day.

C. A. I lost the only titles that matter. Father. Husband. I wish I could just . . . go back to that day and do it all different.

C. P. But what could you do differently?

C. A. *(Silence)*

C. P. . . . Cory?

Chapter One

One year later
London, April

'And the winner is . . .'

The lights pooled on the stage, spotlighting the flawless form of the beautiful young actress in the gold lamé dress.

'Clover Phillips, with *Pipe Dreams*!'

The room erupted into jubilant applause and Clover felt Liam's grip tighten around her hand, a rough cheek pressed against her own. 'You did it.'

'*We* did it,' she said generously. Her idea, her graft, her years of research and filming, interviewing, editing, pitching . . . but his money. And money was king in every industry.

The spotlight had found her already, its beams sinking into the thick plush of her emerald velvet tuxedo as hands of the people sitting all around her reached out for a touch, a stroke, a squeeze as she passed by, as if to absorb some of her newly endowed glory.

She walked up the steps and towards the podium, where the distinctive gold mask was being held towards her. It felt surprisingly heavy as ownership was conferred on her, the actress greeting Clover with a delicate air kiss and enveloping her in a subtle scent of rose otto and neroli.

She looked out into the auditorium, recognizable faces from a world that wasn't hers, smiling back at her like old friends, telling her this award – like all the others – was a key that let her into the club; all those famous people knew her name, admired her work. She was twenty-seven years old and, on the inside, one of them.

She allowed a small smile to grow upon her lips, revelling in the moment of glory as still the clapping continued. She was growing accustomed to making these speeches now. 'Thank you,' she nodded. 'Thank you.'

She pressed a hand above her heart as a token of gratitude, waiting for the noise to die down. In the corner of her eye, beside the cameras, she could see a set of numbers spooling down, reminding her she had precisely eighty-four seconds left before the host – a comedian with a cruel wit she would rather not engage – came back on stage to drive the show towards its punctual ending in time for the ten o'clock news.

Eighty-two . . .

'Ladies and gentlemen, the distinguished judges of the BAFTA committee,' she began, debating whether to reach for the speech notes in her jacket pocket. 'On behalf of all the team at Honest Box Films, thank you for this great honour. Thank you for seeing, hearing and recognizing the power of Cory Allbright's story. Thank you for giving it a reach that would not otherwise be possible without your endorsement – for that is, after all, our ultimate aim: to take the message of hope and second chances to the darkest corners, where the light is most needed.

'When I first approached Cory and his family about the idea of doing a documentary, none of us could have envisaged the reception this film has received all over the world. The past few months have been a whirlwind and I know Cory wishes he could have been here tonight to thank you himself.'

She looked out across the sea of faces. 'But sadly it's just not possible, as we all know. Cory Allbright has always been the people's champion, the underdog who fought every disadvantage, kicked down every obstacle thrown his way to scale the heights of the Pro Surf World Tour. For years, he was the nearly man, the runner-up, world number two; so when, finally, he stood on the very brink of having it all, the world was cheering him on. We wanted him to win it. He deserved it; he'd earned it. It was his time to shine.' Clover's smile faltered. 'One single moment; that was what it came down to. One split-second choice, not even his own, and everything changed.' She felt the familiar lump gather in her throat as she looked out and saw the sad furrowed brows among the audience. 'Not just the sponsorships and the competition money vital for supporting his young family, but his health, his strength, his ability to live a life free of pain.' Clover was quiet for a moment, letting her words settle.

'I wish I could say I was in the business of happy endings. I wish I could tell you talent or passion or dogged determination will always overcome adversity; but if that was the case, it would be Cory standing here talking to you. Instead I can offer only this.' Her eyes scanned the room, noticing the numbers still ticking down: *thirty-three, thirty-two* . . .

'An ending doesn't have to be happy for a new beginning to spring up; it will follow anyway, just as surely as the sun chasing the moon. There is always hope. And we must set our gaze ever upwards, ever onwards. We keep fighting for the next chance. Cory is still fighting, even though his life as he knew it ended that day on Supertubos Beach in Peniche, Portugal, October 2017. And he has shown through his fight, his strength and courage that while champions may shine in the light, it is heroes that light up the dark.' She held up the glistening trophy. 'So thank you, BAFTA, for giving us another torch along the path.'

The applause had erupted again, even before she'd finished speaking; several people were on their feet. Then some more. And more.

Four – three – two . . . The spooling numbers stopped at zero but the clapping didn't as she looked out in wonder at the sight before her. Meryl Streep, Emma Thompson, Gillian Anderson, George Clooney, all nodding their heads and holding out their claps towards her in a show of unity. Of course, she knew it wasn't her they were applauding, but Cory. This was their show of support, they were standing beside him. She hoped he was watching.

Clover raised the trophy with triumphant victory as she made for the side of the stage, where a backstage manager in a headset was waiting to usher her off and prepare to shoo the next presenter on. Only as she was squeezing past him did she notice it was Daniel Craig.

'Congratulations, Ms Phillips,' he murmured in that familiar voice. Her mouth parted in surprise that Daniel Craig knew her name but in the next instant, he was announced on stage and had stepped out into the lights. The show must go on, from her moment of glory to the next one.

She was led away from the wings and people began shaking her hand and patting her shoulder again, offering congratulations in low voices. She looked down at the trophy in her arms as she walked through the backstage area towards the exit that would allow her re-entry to the auditorium.

The door was opened and a wave of sound rushed over them. For a moment she stood in the doorway, staring out again at the honed and chiselled profiles of the seated audience. It felt strangely dreamlike.

'Mick will direct you back to your seat,' the backstage manager said, handing her over into someone else's care.

'Follow me please, Ms Phillips,' Mick said, striding quickly up and along the rows. The film excerpts for the nominees in the next category were playing out on the massive stage screens, providing cover as she slid back into her seat at the end of the aisle. Her victory lap had taken all of three minutes.

Liam winked at her. 'I just got a congratulatory text from Steve McQueen,' he whispered as she settled herself. 'And Lewis Hamilton's agent. He's suggesting lunch next week.'

Clover arched an eyebrow, knowing exactly what he was implying: Hamilton could be the subject of their next film. The viral reach of her fresh-out-of-film-school debut – a documentary on the life and tragic death of fashion stylist Isabella Blow – had been followed up with critical acclaim for her gritty and often harrowing account of three Grenfell survivors as they navigated homelessness and trauma following the fire. She was acquiring a reputation for empathy and warmth, and an instinct for championing the underdog.

'Come on. Diversity in F1, a knighthood . . .' Liam whispered. 'You know it's got legs.'

'That's what you said about Angelina Jolie,' she whispered back. Ms Jolie's team had made preliminary contact after their Golden Globes win.

'Well, she's *definitely* got legs,' he grinned.

She looked at him sidelong. A former banker who preferred the excitement and cachet of film finance to investing in big tech stocks, his head was turned by the glamorous world in which he now found himself. He loved staying at the grandest hotels, drinking cocktails in the bars, flirting with actresses at parties and lounging on yachts in Cannes. She couldn't deny the thrill of sharing space with these starry people either, but unlike him, though she might now move among them, she wasn't one of them – and never could be. By the very definition of her job she had to be an outsider, a mere face at the window peering in. She had to ask the difficult questions that peeled back the artifice, film shots that captured the truth of a situation.

'Listen, James Bond knows my name. I can afford to take my time a bit,' she said as the film clips ended. The audience began clapping again, Daniel Craig tearing open the envelope like it was a lace negligee.

'Yeah, but just don't take too long, that's all I'm saying,' he murmured. 'We can't wait another three years before we release another title. The momentum's with us, and you know what I always say: consolidate—'

'Or capitulate. I know,' she sighed. Hardly a day went by when he *didn't* say it.

'We've got to keep swimming with the current. You never know when the tide will turn . . .' He took a deep inhale, as if smelling one of his favourite Montecristo cigars. 'Which is why I want the next title to debut at Cannes.'

'Next year?' she almost yelped. Several heads turned in their direction.

'Of course,' he smiled, his bemused tone suggesting he wasn't so unreasonable as to expect it for this year, three months from now. But even next year was tight . . . It spoke to his naivety about this industry, that he thought it was perfectly reasonable to get their next project fully researched, filmed and edited in eleven months. *Pipe Dreams* had taken two and a half years of solid planning and work.

Her long blonde hair fell forward like a gold satin sheet as she tipped her head towards him. The winner was announced, and everyone began clapping again. So much clapping at these events. 'Liam, that's just not realistic.'

'It's gonna have to be,' he shrugged, clapping along, his eyes on the next winner as she walked up to the stage. 'The other investors want a green light on this. There's a time for cooling your heels – and this isn't it.'

'But—'

He turned to her with a sharklike smile. 'I know you can do it, Clover. Just don't over-think it. Go with your gut. You'll get the right story in time.'

The car pulled away from the kerb, the paparazzi flashlights blinding even through the tinted windows. Luckily, they weren't trained on her but on the beautiful actress in the gold dress, who was now leaving with Timothée Chalamet.

Clover let her head tip back on the headrest and closed her eyes. She felt drained. An after-party spent schmoozing with the stars, while great for her profile – *consolidate!* – had left her exhausted. Liam had 'gone on' with some producers from Helen Mirren's table, trying to get her to string along too, but she wanted her bed and nothing but her bed. They had been on this awards circuit for months now and when they weren't dressing up and clapping by night, they were meeting with distributors by day. Thanks to their efforts – and their first really big win at the Golden Globes – they had sold to over thirty-five territories already, and there were precious few corners of the world still unaware of the Cory Allbright story.

Cory . . . She still hadn't had a chance to call him and share the good news.

What time was it? She calculated quickly. One thirty in the morning here meant . . . five thirty in the afternoon there. She found his number and pressed dial. She rolled her head to the side and, with her phone to her ear, stared out the window. They were coming down Queen's Gate, the museums and embassies dramatically spotlit, a couple late-night exercising their dog before bed.

'Hey!' Even in that one word, rush and busyness were conveyed.

'Mia? It's Clo.'

'Clo!' Mia's voice tilted up with excitement and Clover could practically hear her feet come to a stop. No doubt she had a laundry basket on her hip or was whisking a perinaise sauce, little Brady careening off the walls and wanting to be out on the waves with his brothers. 'How was it?'

'Well, we did it again. Another piece of hardware that says the world frickin' loves your husband!'

'. . . Aaah.' The sound was like an exhale. 'He'll be so stoked.'

Clover frowned. She had spent too much time with this family not to know immediately when something was up. 'Everything okay?'

'Oh, yeah. Yeah.'

But Clover wasn't fooled by her friend's attempts at upbeat. 'Is it a bad day?'

There was a hesitation. 'Well, yeah . . . a bit, I guess.'

'Is he up?'

Another hesitation. 'No.'

'Yesterday?'

'. . . No.'

'Shit,' Clover whispered, feeling the shine come off her night. She looked down at the trophy in her lap – at the laughter and tears on one face, this very situation captured in bronze. She had been celebrating her triumph all night, while Cory and his family continued to live another day with the fallout of his accident. Clover knew she was the only person outside their family who really understood what post-concussion syndrome actually meant; she was the only person who had seen Mia sobbing on the sand, bewailing the fact that the man she had married was gone and she was living with someone fundamentally altered, forever broken. 'I'm sorry.'

'Hey, you know the drill.' Mia's voice was flat, matter-of-fact. 'We roll with the punches.'

'Is it his lungs?' But it could be anything – the headaches, the double vision, the mood swings, panic attacks, anxiety, deep depression.

There was another pause – a longer one this time – and when Mia's voice came back on the line, it was thick with checked emotion. '. . . He's just under one of his black clouds. It'll pass. We just have to sit it out. He'll be up again tomorrow, I bet.'

Not necessarily, Clover knew. She had spent two weeks sitting in a dark room with Cory, listening to his angry silence, his frustrated screams, his moans of pain. Much of that time she had been frightened by his unpredictability, Mia beseeching her to come out – that it was bad enough enduring it on the other side of the wall where the sun still fell in through the shutters – but only by sitting in it with him had Clover been able to earn his trust, pull down his walls and get him to talk. By the time they had both stumbled from that back room, she had lost four pounds and it had taken a day for her eyes to tolerate the daylight again. For Clover, such an episode had been a one-off, but for Cory, these depressions rolled in as regularly as storm clouds. He couldn't function through them, certainly couldn't work.

'Mia, is there anything I can do? . . . Are you okay for money?' It was a blunt question, but their family had become almost her own. For nine months she had lived with them, dined with them, cried with them. She knew the raw reality of their situation.

She heard Mia swallow hard. 'I think it's time. We're going to have to sell the house.'

Clover squeezed her eyes shut. The house was a ramshackle wooden bungalow with peeling aqua paint and yellow shutters. It needed a small fortune spent on it, after years of putting off repairs: it leaked every time it rained and in big storms it very often felt like it might blow over. It had an open-plan kitchen and living area, three bedrooms – the boys all shared – and a wraparound deck. But it wasn't the house a buyer would be buying; nor was it the house that made it their home; it was the plot that was so special – small but perfectly formed at the very head of Half Moon Bay, on a rocky promontory overlooking a small cove. Mavericks, the famous big surf beach, was right around the corner and Cory always said it had one of the best views in California. The entire family spent their lives either in the ocean or sitting looking at it. They could judge the offshore wind directions and swell conditions long before they set foot on the sand. A house was just a house, but if they sold up, they'd never be able to afford a location like this again. The only private property on Pillar Point, with a military reservation otherwise dominating the headland, Cory had bought the tumbledown cottage and plot from a man who'd negotiated the sale of a few acres from the army when the site had sat unused after the Second World War. Even before he and Mia were married, he and his surf buddies used to hang out there, people sleeping on sofas, on the floor, all with sandy feet, ready to race down to the surf again at sun-up.

'There's been a developer sniffing around ever since the

accident. First time he came over, Cory threatened to knock his teeth out if he ever stepped foot on the property again . . . He gave me his card anyway . . . and I kept it.' Shame cut through Mia's words, as though she was confessing to an infidelity.

Clover didn't blame her, but she knew what toll this would take on Cory. It would be the cruellest blow. After everything he had lost following the accident, it had been the only thing left, to still be able to sit on his porch and watch the ocean. They saw dolphins and humpback whales as regularly as Clover saw cockapoos in Battersea Park. What would become of him, staring out into a concrete yard? 'But I thought some work offers had come in?' she said quietly.

'Yeah, some. A couple of endorsements, but they're not enough. And the rest of the stuff coming through, he can't commit to. Motivational speaking's all well and good in theory but he couldn't cope with the travel, or frankly the stress of not knowing whether he's gonna wake up that day with his head feeling like it's splitting open.' Mia gave a soft, contemptuous snort. 'His old sponsors even got back in touch, sounding out if he'd be up for doing some free-surfing work with them.'

'Free-surfing?' Clover was appalled. They might not be competing for money, points or titles but the barrels those surfers were dropping in on for films, shots and promos were no less risky. 'But those guys are effectively stuntmen. The water they have to go in to get the shot—'

'I know. And Cory knows it too. I think that's what got him feeling so bad. It's all just reminded him he can't be part of that world at all, ever. Not in any form.'

'Oh, Mia.'

'The worst thing is, I reckon they already knew one more

wipeout could kill him. It was just good . . . what do they call it? Good optics? With all the hype around the film at the moment, they didn't want to look like they let him go without a backward glance.'

'Which they bloody did!' Clover said hotly. She knew that losing the patronage of his sponsors had hit Cory hard, a seal of confirmation that his old life and everything that came with it – fitness, strength, vitality, success – was gone.

'Yeah. They signed off saying maybe he could do some guest appearances on the tour instead, perhaps some judging. I dunno, it's all just bullshit.' She gave a heavy, angry sigh. 'He's been in bed ever since.'

'Oh god.' Clover stared at the trophy, seeing only the crying face now. She understood now Mia's hesitation at the beginning of their call. The fame that would attach to the film – and Cory – because of this latest high-profile win would produce even more off-beam suggestions that would only drive him deeper into depression. 'Are the die-hards still keeping a vigil?'

The ripple-effect success of the film as it had won at Toronto and Venice film festivals had seen the Allbrights' humble home become something of a pilgrimage site in recent months. Mia gave a weak laugh, the sort that precedes either mania or tears. 'Oh Christ, it's like a shrine out there. All those fucking candles. I swear to god I can't sleep worrying they're gonna burn the house down!' She drew a breath. 'I know they mean well. They're just trying to show their love and support but it makes me feel so . . . mad! I just wanna scream at them, he's not fucking dead! You know?'

'I do,' Clover nodded. For the first time she noticed the car had stopped moving and they were now parked outside her flat. She held up a finger, signalling the driver to please wait. Mia was a woman at the end of her rope; she needed help.

She needed a friend. Three kids, a traumatized, broken husband, two jobs, financial pressures . . . Clover could feel the suppressed rage in her voice. It ran through her words like a hot wire in towels.

'Listen, you know what – I know you've resisted selling up; but maybe moving *wouldn't* be the worst thing to happen?' she said, reaching for positives, some optimism. 'As unlikely as it seems right now, maybe this is the fresh start that's needed. Yes, Cory loves being by the ocean, of course he does, but perhaps that isn't in his best interests anymore? It's maybe even a form of torture surely, like sitting an alcoholic in front of an open bottle of wine? A constant reminder of what he can't be. Or do. Or have.'

There was a long pause. '. . . Yeah. Maybe.'

Clover was no more convinced herself. 'Look, at the very least, taking the financial burden off you would be one less stressor. You've got to find ways to make life easier, and kinder for you all.'

'I know.'

Clover bit her lip. 'Have you mentioned it to him . . . about selling?'

'Not yet. I've been putting it off.' Mia's voice broke. 'Every time I even think about how to raise it with him, my chest gets tight . . . I swear to god, I think it'll kill him.'

'Mia, no. No,' Clover hushed her. 'He'll resist it initially, of course he will, but this could well be the change you need. You're stuck in a half-life at the moment, holding on to what used to be. Maybe this has to happen for you all to move forward.'

There was no reply.

'. . . Mia? Are you there?'

'Yeah.' Her tone was bleak.

'Listen, you know I'm coming out the week after next.' She didn't even want to mention the word *Oscars*. Not right now. What good was glory when they were face-down in the grit? 'I'll come to you straight afterwards and we'll talk then. I can even help you tell him, if you want? He may accept it better if we're both saying it?'

'You'd do that?'

'Of course. If you think it would help.'

'Okay. I'll see how it goes.' A heavy sigh whistled down the line. 'I don't know what to say. You've been so good to us.'

'Mia, you're my friends. You know I'll do anything I can to help. I'm in your corner always, no matter what.'

Chapter Two

'It's a shoo-in now, surely. It's got to be,' Johnny said, sprawled in his chair and puffing on his vape. 'Everyone knows the BAFTAs presage the Oscar wins.'

'Did you really just say "presage"?' Matty quipped, checking her caramel-tinted hair for split ends.

'Hey! Being a cameraman doesn't mean I'm illiterate, you know.'

'Well, why should anyone assume you're not, when you insist upon dressing like a vagrant?' Matty shrugged, eyeing the grubby wash of his torn jeans with particular disdain. Admittedly they didn't look like they'd been washed since . . . well, ever. 'If you want to be taken seriously—'

'Children,' Clover warned, sitting on the worktop beside the kettle. 'Play nice.'

Condensation was dripping down the inside of the windows of her first-floor mansion flat, misting the view onto the mirroring red-brick block opposite. The mornings were still chilly and they relied on the oil-fired heater to send out a rosy heat. It ticked quietly on the floor, the closest thing they had to an office pet. In the minutes of their last meeting, a motion had been put to save up for a fish tank.

'All I'm saying is, everyone knows that what wins in London goes on to win in LA.' Johnny shrugged.

'Not necessarily,' Matty argued. 'Best actors, yes. But best picture, no. And as for Best Documentary Feature—'

'But both academies share five hundred voting members.' He shrugged again, as though that clinched the argument.

'Guys!' Clover said, raising her voice to bring their attention off each other and onto her. She looked at Matty warming her hands around her mug of tea, Johnny dragging on his vape; neither of them looked particularly like they made up two-thirds of an international award-winning documentary filmmaking team. 'It's pointless you bickering over this. It'll be what it is.' The truth was, she could hardly bear to think about it. Her stomach was pickled with nerves, yes, but after her conversation with Mia last night . . . 'Far more pressing is what comes next. How exactly do we follow up on all this?'

She spread her arms wide to indicate the flowers that were on every surface. Florists had been knocking at her door all morning, bringing extravagant displays of white roses, striped buckets of yellow roses, sprays of lilies and freesia, monumental orchids – not to mention a basket of muffins sent over by way of congratulations from Louis Theroux. A clutch of giant, helium-inflated balloons bobbed in one corner of the ceiling, looking like it had escaped a child's hand, or a thank-you card, or the set of *Up*. Johnny had 'taken responsibility' for the case of Bollinger Liam had sent over, and was using it as a footstool.

The trophies they had been winning all year were now lined along the middle of the table among the condiments. The new BAFTA mask took pride of place, positioned between the salt and pepper and a bottle of ketchup. (Old-school glass bottle because Matty was a stickler for 'standards'.)

'What's the rush?' Johnny said. 'Can't we just enjoy this for a bit?'

'You'd think.' Clover sighed. 'But sadly not. Liam sprang it on me last night that he wants to debut the next project at Cannes.'

'What?' Matty looked horrified. As their researcher-slash-PR and marketing person, it was her job to know the international film festival schedules by rote. She dealt with the paperwork, admin and T&C for each one and as such, she immediately knew this meant an eleven-month turnaround. That was possible for bigger production teams, but for Honest Box, with just the three of them . . . they overlapped on duties to such an extent that their job titles were often more honorary than anything. They each made coffee, ran the post office trips, picked up a camera or sat at the edit decks when required.

Which was just how they liked it. Liam had suggested Clover use some of her budget to grow the team, but she was convinced it was the intimacy of their unit that gave their projects such a distinctive, raw voice. The three of them had all been at Leeds Film School together, although they hadn't become friends until the final year when they were put together to collaborate on their graduation project. It had been an inauspicious grouping. They were all so different: Johnny, a grungy tech-head who'd been kicked out of boarding school not for the usual drugs or fighting offences, but 'consistently sleeping in'; Matty, a willowy locksmith's daughter whose ambition had been sharpened to a point after she'd had to fund her degree working behind the bar, while Clover and her trust-fund friends caroused on the other side of it . . . And yet, these two people she wouldn't have chosen as friends had quickly become her closest confidants. Now, they too were almost family.

The girls lived ten minutes apart from each other in Battersea, with Johnny ten minutes away by motorbike in Shepherd's Bush (or 'Shay Boo', as Matty liked to call it).

There wasn't much distinction between a work meeting – such as this – and hanging out. It invariably involved lounging around in Clover's kitchen, sitting on worktops and drawing smiley faces on the misted windowpanes.

'My response exactly,' Clover groaned. 'But he's adamant. No knuckle-dragging. He wants a pitch by the end of the month, or—' She shrugged. It didn't need to be said: no money. They all had a love-hate relationship with their generous but wildly unrealistic executive producer. Had he forgotten it had taken months just to set up the filming agreements with Mia? That Cory wouldn't see anyone at all at that point, could barely even look at his own wife? Not to mention the months then spent living with the Allbrights, the post-production edits?

'Well, if he's going to be a git about it, then we need to simplify the process,' Matty said, rallying. 'Cory was a reluctant subject and that made things so much slower.'

'Yes, but also heartfelt,' Clover interjected, one hand over her own heart.

'Yes. But also slower,' Matty reiterated; she was nothing if not practical. 'And if warp speed is the brief, then we need to find someone who's actually on board with being filmed.' She shrugged. 'Who *wants* us to tell their story?'

Clover frowned. She had a feeling this question already had an answer. 'Are you thinking of anyone specifically?'

'I say we go Angelina,' Matty said without missing a beat. She had been lobbying for this ever since the call had come in from Jolie's LA publicist whilst she was midway through a trying-on session of her latest ASOS order and eating a packet of Percy Pigs. It had taken her several days to recover from the shock and she now spoke of Nancy – the publicist – as though they were old muckers. 'UNICEF, war crimes against women. Being a single mother to thirty kids . . . It's really got it all.'

Clover's eyes narrowed. 'You just want to know what really went down with Brad.' Clover also knew her friend wanted to see inside Angelina's house. According to Matty, it wasn't a person's eyes that were the window to the soul, but their downstairs loo.

'Clo, the whole fricking world wants to know that! That's what makes it compelling.'

'She'll never go there,' Johnny said with a shake of his head. 'She'll just say it's part of the custody agreement or whatever.'

'Then we make it a condition. No Brad, no war crimes!' Matty said, as if she was telling toddlers they couldn't have chips without eating their peas. 'Nancy called us, remember? Angie needs a platform people will engage with. Her image needs to be softened. She knows we can do that for her.'

'I'm just not sure anyone cares about her and Brad that much anymore, do they? Haven't we all moved on?' Clover asked, drumming her socked feet against the plate cupboard. 'Besides, it's just gossip and famous people. We need something with meat. Human interest. A living, breathing tragedy.'

'Michael Jackson's kids?' Johnny suggested after a moment. 'The truth about life with him as a dad, growing up under a blanket, being swung from hotel windows?'

'Ha!' Matty laughed before she could stop herself.

'Liam's pretty keen on doing something on Lewis Hamilton,' Clover said, putting the idea out there. 'We're having lunch with his agent next week.'

'Ooh, get you,' Johnny teased.

'I'm not sure, though.' She wrinkled her nose.

'Why not?' Matty queried, looking immediately thoughtful. 'He's won more world titles than anyone else, he's got that dog he takes everywhere that's Insta-famous. He's a knight of the realm, but it's BLM he bends the knee for . . .' She shrugged. 'And that's just off the top of my pretty head.'

'Hmm. Yeah.'

'What? What's wrong with it?' Johnny asked, knowing she was distinctly unenthused.

'Well, I know he's interesting . . . I've just sort of got that feeling – was it Groucho Marx who said "I don't want to belong to any club that would have me as a member"?'

There was a puzzled pause.

'. . . Is that your way of saying you don't want to do a documentary on anyone who wants you to do a documentary on them?' Johnny asked. 'Because I'm pretty sure Matty's just been explaining that speed-of-light production is only possible with a willing subject.'

Clover wrinkled her nose again. 'I just don't think we can compromise on the integrity of the subject. People coming to us with an agenda . . .' She shook her head. 'The stories most worth telling are sometimes also the best hidden. We've got to really dig.'

Johnny sat forward, his elbows on his thighs. 'Oh. So to be clear, you're now saying the brief is actually a *hidden* story, on someone who doesn't want to be filmed.'

She grinned. 'Basically.'

He looked across at Matty. 'Piece of piss. What are you waiting for?'

Matty slumped back in her chair. 'This is hardly fair.'

'But Mats, you're our chief researcher,' he jibed.

She hitched up an eyebrow. 'I'm the only researcher.'

'You must have a list of Don't Bothers, surely?' Johnny pressed. 'People we wouldn't feature in a million years?'

'Oh yeah! I've definitely got one of those!'

'Well, let's hear it then. Clearly, that's our gold mine.' Johnny shot Clover a thoroughly amused look. She threw him back a silent 'ha-ha' – but didn't argue.

'Ugh.' Matty put down her mug and leaned across the table for her iPad. They watched as she swiped the screen a few times. 'I'm warning you now. It's mainly pariahs, despots and Tom Hanks.'

'What's wrong with Tom Hanks?' Johnny protested.

'He's too damned nice! Why bother? There's more edge on jelly than can be found on that man.'

Clover chuckled as Johnny sat back, appeased, in the chair. 'Okay, so Tom Hanks and despots are no good to us, but pariahs . . . ? Even villains love their mums.'

'Hmm, right. So we've got . . . Roman Polanski. No.' Matty pulled a face.

'Why not?' Johnny countered.

Matty looked back at him as though it was perfectly obvious. 'He's a rapist.'

Johnny sat up. 'And as such, a pariah. But just playing devil's advocate for a second, his wife and unborn child were brutally murdered. He's a villain, yes, but also a victim.'

'Villain and victim is interesting,' Clover agreed.

'But his story has been covered on every true crime episode ever,' Matty countered. 'He's overexposed.'

'That's true too.'

Matty looked back at her list. 'Geldof.'

'*Saint* Bob?' Clover queried.

'Not taking anything away from Live Aid, clearly,' Matty said quickly. 'But it's recognized now that well over half a million people were forcibly resettled in the south-west of Ethiopia; the spotlight on the famine enabled a military campaign to masquerade as a humanitarian effort. And it was paid for with western aid money.'

'I never knew that,' Johnny frowned.

'His personal life too of course – the deaths of Paula and Michael Hutchence, his daughter Peaches . . . It's really sad.'

Clover agreed. It was a life threaded with tragedies. 'Will he talk, though? In the timeframe we've got? It might have to be a slow-burn. Make contact and proceed slowly.'

'Okay. I'll mark it as a possible going forwards.' Matty checked her list and gave a small, startled laugh.

'What?'

'Ha! Right. Well, don't laugh,' she warned. 'But . . . Kit Foley.' She took in their flummoxed expressions. 'Hey! This *is* the Don't Bother list!' she said defensively. 'You asked me to read it to you, and clearly we wouldn't bother with him.'

Clover rolled her eyes. If she never heard Kit Foley's name again, it would still be too soon.

'Well, he's what we would call a very hostile witness,' Johnny murmured. 'I seem to recall that when you wrote asking to interview him for *Pipe Dreams* he got his big-shot lawyers to reply, threatening to sue for defamation?'

'He did. And as I told them, it's only defamation if it ain't true.' Clover smiled gratefully as Matty proudly clapped her; but for all the brave talk now, they'd been shaken at the time by the prospect of being sued by someone with pockets as deep as Kit Foley's.

Matty gave a deep sigh. 'Well, anyway, that was the last we heard from him until an email dropped into my inbox a couple of months ago, asking if we'd like to cover his – and I quote – "return to the international sporting landscape, following the fallout and tragic consequences of Cory Allbright's accident".' She looked at them with a wry expression.

There was a stunned silence.

'. . . I'm sorry, what?' Clover asked. 'He wants us to cover his comeback?'

Matty nodded.

'*Us?*'

Matty nodded again.

'Are you actually telling me he hasn't seen the bloody film? Has it somehow passed him by that there are ninety-eight minutes of film footage, winning trophies around the globe, spelling out the devastating consequences of *his* dangerous and reckless actions?' Clover picked up the BAFTA and shook it. 'The world hates him! In what universe would we *ever* feature Kit Foley – except to assassinate his reputation further?'

'Quite.' Matty looked across at Johnny, bemused by Clover's strong reaction. 'Which is why I didn't mention it to you. There was no point.'

Clover looked at Johnny too, as if he could explain the absurdity of Foley's team getting in touch. Johnny just gave one of his famously lackadaisical shrugs.

'I can't believe he's coming out of retirement,' she mumbled, not quite able to let it go. Kit Foley had been Cory Allbright's nemesis and that meant, at some point during the past couple of years, he had become hers too. 'Well, that lasted long!' she scoffed.

'Well—' Matty began.

'What's it been?' Clover interrupted, looking at Johnny. He was their resident sport nut. 'Three years?'

'About that.'

They all knew Foley had retired the year after Cory's accident, although the jury was out on whether he jumped or was pushed. All his sponsors had dropped him, crowds booed him from the beach and, although he'd gone on to win the world title again, his brand had remained toxic. He was persona non grata everywhere he went, and had dropped off the elite sporting radar altogether.

'I'm amazed anyone's taking him on again,' Johnny shrugged.

'Well, that's the thing,' Matty said in a pointed tone, waiting for them both to look at her again. 'In surfing, they're not. But he's not a surfer anymore. He's moving into snowboarding now.'

'What?' It was Johnny's turn to look stunned.

'Kit Foley – nine-time world surfing champ – is now a *snowboarder*?' Clover echoed.

'Yep. Specializing in Halfpipe. I guess maybe there's . . . transferable skills from one to the other? According to this email, he's going pro next season.'

'I don't believe I'm hearing this.' Clover was confounded. 'He's going to just . . . switch sport?'

'It's all right here. From his new sponsor. A . . . Julian Orsini-Rosenberg, whoever he is. He thinks Kit's going to go all the way. He's invited him to design his own range of clothing and boards . . . Looks like a big-money deal. He'll debut it next winter.'

Clover stared at Johnny as though he had all the answers. 'Does that man's ego know no bounds?'

'I think we already know the answer to that question,' he muttered.

Matty looked troubled. 'Do you think Cory knows?'

Clover fell still. Oh god, did he? Could this be another reason behind his new dip? Or *the* reason? She pressed her fingers to her mouth in concentration. 'I'll have to tell Mia,' she said flatly. But how? How could she tell her friend that the man wholly responsible for her husband's accident was not just moving on with his life but moving forward, switching it up?

There was a silence as they digested the revelation.

'Anyway, I think we can all agree that's a firm no for Foley,' Matty murmured, going back to her list. Her eyes narrowed again. 'Hmm. Edward Snowden. Traitor? Or whistle-blower for exposing unconstitutional spying? Living in Russia now. Obvious difficulties with filming there, not to mention bloody freezing . . .'

Clover looked away distractedly, not listening. She was too rattled by what she'd just learned. She tapped 'Kit Foley snowboarding' into her phone and scanned the few entries, all recent, nothing more than a year old. There were no big articles on his switch in careers, just a few lines showing his name in some competition line-ups in Europe – *Europe*? It was just local, small-scale stuff. Hardly a big splashy launch into a new venture. Perhaps people hadn't connected the dots – they didn't realize he was *that* Kit Foley?

So perhaps Cory didn't know after all? Not yet, anyway.

She put her phone away and stared at the line of trophies running down the centre of the table, feeling some sense of calm return. A little perspective. In two weeks, she would walk the Oscars red carpet and the world's press would do the rest for them, taking Cory's story farther and wider than ever. After more than three years in the wilderness, this was his moment. Everyone loved him and they were rooting for him. They were on his side. Kit Foley, meanwhile, was an international pariah. His name – when it did appear in the press now – was forever attached to what he'd done in the water that day. He would never be forgiven. The surfing community was fiercely tribal and they'd picked their camp. Perhaps Cory wasn't the only one left with an unhappy ending?

Clover looked on blankly as Matty and Johnny began bickering again. For Mia and Cory's sake, she could but hope.

Chapter Three

The phone on the bed buzzed. Clover glanced at it and gave a wail. 'Shit! The driver's here.'

Johnny, who was still – in spite of the commotion – trying to sleep on the sofa in the next room, lifted his head. 'Just get the next flight.'

Not helpful.

Matty dismissed his suggestion with a withering look and moved her arms in a calming motion. 'Okay. Let's not panic. I think we're in pretty good shape.' Clover didn't find that calming, coming from someone whose mascara had migrated onto her cheeks and had a biro stuck in her hair. They were all much the worse for wear.

'Mats, there's two of you! I'm still drunk! I'm not sure they'll even let me on the plane.'

But Matty shook her head, refusing to be panicked. 'We'll do a checklist.' There was nothing in her world that couldn't be solved by a list of some sort. She closed her eyes and compiled a mental inventory. It was like watching someone meditate. 'Passport?'

Clover reached into her bag and pulled it out. 'Yup.'

'Visa?'

'Yep.'

'Purse?'

'Yes.' Clover nodded, her eyes skating towards the window. She was sure she could see the exhaust fumes from her waiting car drifting past the glass. She was so late. How could she have thought 'farewell drinks' at Soho House would end in any way other than how it had?

'Shoes? And that means heels – not trainers.'

Clover thought, reminding herself of the moment of packing them. 'Yep.'

'Tux?'

'Yes.' She definitely remembered that. It was a bugger to pack to avoid getting crease lines in the velvet.

Matty's eyes opened. 'Not that it matters. I've managed to get a couple of dresses sent to your hotel room. Don't ask me how I did it. A few well-placed calls . . .' She took in Clover's underwhelmed expression and rolled her eyes. 'Thank me later. Chargers? Including your toothbrush charger? You always forget that.'

'Yes.'

'Adaptors?' Johnny offered from the next room. His one contribution to getting her to LA on time. He was pushing himself slowly up to a sitting position, his shaggy dirty-blonde hair looking more tangled than ever.

'Oh shit. Adaptors.' Clover caught her hair in her hands, twisting it at the temples. Where had she last seen them?

Matty caught her by the shoulders as she went to tear clothes from yet more drawers. 'No time. You can get them at the airport. I'll WhatsApp you a list while you're in the car. Stay focused. Speech?'

'On my laptop.'

'Okay then. Laptop?'

Clover's eyes widened. 'Shit!'

'Clo!' Matty cried, losing her cool. 'Sort it out! Laptop is basic!'

31

'I know!' Her phone buzzed. It was the driver again.

Matty reached onto the bed and pulled Clover's laptop out from under the twist of clothes and the thick eiderdown. Clover stuffed it into her hand luggage. 'Right, I've gotta go. Anything else I've forgotten, it won't be a disaster, I can get out there.'

'Yes. Good. Go, go!' Matty clutched her hard, her fingertips digging into the back of Clover's shoulders. 'It's going to be incredible.'

Johnny shuffled over and put his arms around them both, leaning on them heavily. In spite of his dishevelled appearance, he smelled good.

Clover pulled back. 'I so wish you guys were coming too. It's so unfair. We're a team.' They had only been issued with two tickets and there was no way Liam was going to pass on the chance to share air with the Hollywood cognoscenti.

'It fucking sucks,' Johnny agreed. 'There's some cinematographers out there I'd give my right arm to meet.'

'I *promise* I'll make sure they all know your name and the things you did. I'll get their cards for you,' she said earnestly.

'Thanks, Clo.'

'If you do happen to meet Nancy . . .' Matty shrugged. 'Send her my best. Tell her I'll be in touch.'

Clover gave a bemused nod.

Johnny picked up her luggage. He gave a surprised look. 'Have you actually got anything in here?'

Matty groaned. She could never understand that 'packing light' was actually a thing. Her guru and queen in most things – packing, jewels, grooming routines – was Elizabeth Taylor. More was more.

'Just the essentials.' Clover blew them both a kiss as she headed for the door. 'I'll buzz you when I get there. In the meantime, Mats, I think there's legs in the Geldof idea, make an approach, see what comes back. Johnny-boy, if you can begin editing that material for the bonus content deal with Netflix. They need eleven minutes on the nose.'

'Got it.'

She started down the stairs. 'Hollywood, here we come!'

'And if you get a chance to snog Liam Hemsworth, I say go for it!' Matty hollered as she disappeared out of sight down the grand winding staircase. 'Do it for me!'

'Will do!' Clover said, getting down to the communal hall and opening the heavy front door. '. . . Sorry, sorry!' she said, seeing the driver in a dark grey suit waiting by the car for her. 'I overslept.'

He was too professional to point out it was gone two in the afternoon.

'There's traffic on the M40, Ms Phillips,' was all he said, reaching for her bags and putting them into the boot.

'Hey Clo!' She looked back to find Matty waving from the sitting-room window. 'You forgot your bloody phone!'

'Fuck!' She was so excited – and hung over – she'd forget her own head right now.

'Johnny's coming down!' Matty yelled, just as the front door burst open and Johnny leaned through, holding it out with an outstretched arm. He had no shoes or socks on and the path was glistening with spring rain. 'Just as well it rang or we wouldn't have noticed in time,' he said as she jogged back to him.

'Rang?'

'Mia's on the line.'

'Oh! Thanks Johnny.' She took it from him, blowing him a kiss and heading for the car again. The driver was standing beside the open door with a look of barely concealed agitation.

'Hey Mia! I'm literally – *literally* – leaving now! I'm so late!' What time was it there? Half six in the morning?

'Clo? Is that you?'

Clover's feet stopped moving at the sound of her friend's voice. It sounded crazy-glazed, as if Mia's very surface was covered in cracks, as if she was breaking apart. 'What is it? What's happened?'

Her own voice sounded peculiar too: it was strangled, inflected with strain. She saw a frown crease Johnny's brow.

'Cory's gone.'

For a moment, the words rang in her head, empty and meaningless, just a swirl of sound. 'What do you mean, gone? Gone where? Like, out?'

'We don't know where he is. He's been sleeping on the sofa the last few nights but when the kids woke up this morning, he wasn't here.' Mia's voice rose in pitch, panic fraying at the edges.

'Well, has he gone for a walk? The fresh air helps his head.'

'No, it's not that. I know it's not.' There was an ominous silence; Clover could hear Mia's breathing was rapid and shallow. 'I told him, Clo, last night . . . I told him we have to sell the house.'

Oh god. 'How did he take it?'

'At first he just stared at me and didn't say a word.' Her voice slipped into the next octave. 'Then he said if I thought it was for the best . . .'

'That was it?'

'I could see he was upset – but I thought he understood that there's no other way.'

Clover swallowed, determined to be optimistic. 'So then he's gone for a walk. He's thinking it all through and processing the news.'

Mia's voice cracked suddenly, the emotion breaking through. 'No. He's not walking. There's a storm blowing in. Offshore wind, swell from the west.'

Clover knew what those conditions meant. Right around the headland from Ross Cove, where their cottage sat, lay Mavericks. Big wave country.

'His board's gone.'

Those three words were like little tombstones. Clover felt the ground drop an inch beneath her feet. She had to step back to balance herself as the reason for this call finally shot across the ocean and down the phone, right into her ear, her brain, her heart.

Mia's voice, when it came back, was tiny, as though curled up inside itself. 'They're out looking for him now. Everyone. There's more people on that beach and in the water than I've ever seen. Guys risking their lives . . .' Her voice broke off.

Clover became aware Johnny had come over and was standing right in front of her, his bare feet on the wet tiles, one hand resting lightly on her arm, looking down at her with a look of open alarm. 'So then they'll find him and bring him home.'

'No . . . you're not hearing me.' Mia crumbled in the face of her stoicism, all her reserves gone. 'It's heavy out there today. The coastguards have told me to prepare myself, Clo. They're looking for a body. Cory's dead.' A sound left her body unlike anything Clover had ever heard. 'My husband is dead!'

The water heaved and sighed beneath them, glittering and tranquil beneath a cloudless sky. The storm had been and gone, blown itself out in a fury that left trees toppled in its wake, power lines down, and a body on the beach.

Giving them closure, at least.

By the time her plane had landed in San Francisco and she had made the journey to Half Moon Bay, the storm had been at full pitch – the wind ferocious, bending the palm trees to its will, whipping the water into mountainous peaks that toppled and crashed every few seconds, deafening, thunderous, terrifying the hundreds of onlookers safe on the shore.

The beaches had become so packed as news of the search spread, police had been forced to close off the local roads and it had taken forty minutes before she could get hold of Mia on the phone and be allowed through to their bungalow at the head of the bay. The two women had hugged in anguished silence. What was there to say? There was no hope to cling to, no comfort to find from this, nothing to counter the sight of Cory's three young sons, standing tense and erect on the scrap of lawn overlooking the ocean, watching the activity on the water as pro surfers and lifeguards, jet ski teams and the coastguard scoured the clear water between the wave sets for their father's body.

By the time the ocean spat him out, the storm had spent itself and now picture-postcard conditions had returned. The surf – though always imposing there – was without snarling menace once more, families back playing on the beach, the familiar line-up of surfers sitting on their boards, waiting their turn.

But today didn't look like any other day Clover had ever seen. Under a cloudless sky, a mile up the coast from the scene of the tragedy, an incredible spectacle was already under way. Word had spread fast about Cory's death, inflamed by the global media coverage and the pathos that he should have been walking the red carpet in LA tonight – Liam was bringing a date along on her ticket; Clover couldn't think of anything less important than attending the awards right now – and now hundreds of surfers were standing on the beach, boards by their sides, ready for the paddle-out memorial. Clover was with Mia and the boys in a traditional Hawaiian outrigger canoe which Cory had brought back with him following his first ever win at Pipe Masters at Oahu. He had loved that thing.

The five of them, plus Eddie 'Razorfish' Kahale – a retired local surfer and long-time buddy of the Allbrights; Clover had interviewed him extensively for the documentary – had paddled out together. Clover had been surprised at just how skilfully and powerfully the young boys paddled, the muscles visible on their skinny brown backs as they did this for their father. To make him proud.

Now, a few hundred metres offshore, they were getting their breath back, allowing the boat to gently drift and watching the gathering crowds watching them. There was press everywhere – TV crews, drones, long-lens cameras on tripods – occasional passing boats hooting their horns in sympathy at the sight. But it was surprisingly quiet on shore, the crowds standing in silent respect.

Gulls wheeled overhead, listing on air currents, spying for fish. Clover could just see the Allbrights' small, battered house above the rocks at Ross Cove. For safety reasons, the memorial was being held the next bay up from Half Moon; the lifeguards wouldn't allow such a large gathering near those breaks. Here, at least, there was no reef, no white water.

The calm was broken. Clover's head jerked up as a bell sounded suddenly, three times, and the mass on the beach moved as one, the multicoloured crowd dispersing into bright fragments as they picked up their boards and raced into the water, leaping belly-first onto their boards and beginning to paddle, long-stemmed flowers held between their teeth.

She couldn't help it – Clover felt the tears begin to flow down her cheeks again as they all headed straight for the small canoe. There had been so many tears in the days since she had arrived here and it was an overwhelming sight, to have that many people heading towards the family in a show of such love. They drew close in minutes, surrounding them protectively, getting to within metres of the boat.

Two girls paddled right up to the *ama* – the outrigger section of the canoe that acted as a counterbalance – and began to decorate the booms with lei garlands.

Brady, the youngest, still only three – Mia had been seven months pregnant with him at the time of Cory's accident – began crying; Mia reached over, lifting him onto her lap and kissing his hair. She was managing to stay strong. Ever since that one animalistic cry down the phone, she had been holding it together, going through the motions for her boys and doing what had to be done. But there was a look in her eyes that hadn't been there before; a blankness, surprise registering whenever a voice carried to her ear. It took several repetitions before she ever heard what Clover said to her and although she fussed over the boys, making sure they finished their meals, Clover was pretty sure Mia herself had scarcely eaten. She looked spectral.

Clover knew from her own experience that this was the shock that came with grief. Years of nursing and caring for a man she loved, but who swung from utter dependency to utter contempt, couldn't be undone in a few days. Mia was used to being needed, rejected, run off her feet, and several times Clover had found her standing in a room just staring at the emptiness, as though confounded that he wasn't in it. There was no longer anything to do. No one to fight with, or for.

The sight around them became ever more wondrous. There were hundreds of people all around them on the water, floating like lily pads, faces turned towards them. Someone pointed to a pod of dolphins further out in the bay. Clover could feel the medley of emotions gathered all around them, sitting within each and every person: loss, shock, sadness, anger. But also gratitude, affection, love.

A man she vaguely recognized as Pipe Rat, the leader of Cory's local surf tribe – his actual name was Wes – stood on his board, as arranged, and began to speak.

'Friends! We've come together today to give thanks for the life of our friend and fellow soul surfer, Cory Allbright. At thirty-six years old, he's gone way too soon. He had so much more to give. Things should have been very different to this . . .'

His words carried over the quiet body of the congregated crowd. All eyes were upon him.

'Cory was our guy. A true local, he was born here, lived here. Died here. He was one of us, even though he was also one of the greats! He was as happy riding with the Half Moon homies or an off-duty dentist as he was screaming through a barrel at Pipe Masters. And he was *never* happier than when he was riding with his three boys.'

Pipe Rat looked over at them, bringing the weight of the crowd's stare with him. 'You boys can be so proud of your dad. All he ever wanted was to make you proud. To be the best for you.' He looked back at the paddlers. 'Forty-eight career victories in twenty years, riding against guys half his age. He was ranking first on the ASP World Tour when he had his accident but before that, he had been world number two for four consecutive years . . . He was consistent, dogged, the best surfer never to make world champ there ever was.'

His words skimmed across the ocean's surface.

'Cory never had it easy. He never quite caught the breaks that mattered. But he was a fighter. He kept going. He was like all of us – a regular guy, not without his demons, just doing his best.'

Clover glanced at the boys. One day – just not today – they would also hear about their father's sporadic drink and drug problems, the half-hearted retirement episodes when he gave up, gained weight and checked out of the sport. But he had always turned things around, gone back. The ocean didn't need mermaids to lure him in, just barrels.

'He didn't grow up in some fancy house. He wasn't no rich kid who got given everything on a plate. What he got, he *earned*. He did it the hard way. Through grit. And resilience. And talent. And self-belief. He wanted to win, not for money, but for love. For his family: Mia and his boys – Hunter, Taylor, Brady. You guys were his world. He wanted to make you proud. Cos he was so damn proud of you.'

Clover saw that Mia's shoulders were hunching up by her ears as she tried to hold back her tears, and she leaned forward, resting a comforting hand upon her shoulder. Brady was still tucked up on his mother's lap but the older boys were stoically looking back at the crowds, peering from behind their long fringes of white-blonde, sun-bleached hair. Their little bodies were rigid with tension as they hung on Pipe Rat's every word about their father, their breath coming in big gulps that inflated their rib cages.

'. . . Cory Allbright was a beautiful soul. This never should have gone down the way it did, we all know that. But there'll be justice down the line. Karma be like that.'

His voice had become hard and brittle; everyone knew to what – or rather, whom – he was referring. Clover realized they were all now holding hands, forming linked chains in concentric circles around the small boat, ten, eleven deep. A short distance away bobbed a solitary surfer. Had he arrived too late? Or was he simply a passing rider, unaware of what he'd come across? He sat, silhouetted, watching, making no attempt to draw closer.

'. . . But that's for the future. Today is about honouring Cory's memory. About blessing his spirit and keeping in our hearts, the good times. He won't be forgotten. And the surf community will make sure his family is loved. Supported. Protected.' He looked at Mia. 'Mia, that is our promise to you. You and the boys are not alone.'

Mia swallowed and nodded her thanks.

'Cory, we love ya, man! Rest in peace, brother!'

A cheer went up, growing in volume and heft as people began splashing and scooping up water into the air in a form of salute. Goosebumps raced up Clover's arms as she watched the cacophony.

Eddie stood and handed Taylor, who was sitting behind him, the urn he had kept safe by his feet. Taylor stared at it for several moments, then kissed it. 'Love you, Dad,' he sobbed. He passed it back to Hunter, who did the same.

Clover didn't think she could bear it. These poor children, their final goodbye . . .

Mia patted Brady and he squirrelled off her lap, understanding it was his turn now. The urn was heavy, heavier than he might have expected, and he had to clutch it to his body to take the weight. He closed his eyes, swinging from side to side with it, like it was a teddy bear. 'Come back, Daddy. We'll be good.'

A cry escaped Mia and she reached over to him, stroking his hair back and kissing his face. 'Daddy loved you so much, baby.' Her voice was thick with tears. 'You were his best boys. All of you. He lives in here now.' And she tapped Brady's chest, by his heart. 'He'll never leave you. He'll always be with you.'

Clover turned away, not wanting the children to see her tears. She knew all about losing a father, but this wasn't her tragedy. Who was she to be so upset? And yet . . . she was intricately woven into the tapestry of their family life now. She had lived with them, seen the truth of their situation behind closed doors. She knew how it felt when a family fell apart.

Mia took the urn and stood. Tears pooled in her eyes and she didn't try to hide them as she stared out at the silent gathering. The crowd stared back at her in common under-standing; they didn't need her to speak. She just nodded slowly and they understood, the connection sparkling in the quietness, like a spiderweb catching the sunlight.

At the far end of the canoe, Eddie stood and began to sing a mournful Hawaiian lament. The circles of floating surfers seemed to draw even more tightly together as Mia unscrewed the lid and carefully, with slender, trembling arms, tipped her husband's ashes into the sea. They slipped into the water, heavy and silent, as though returning to their rightful place. Not so much dust to dust as sand to the beach.

Eddie's song lifted and carried above them all. No one stirred. People were weeping silently but openly. Salt-water tears to a salt-water ocean. As the song ended, everyone threw their garlands, stems and wreaths into the water too and within moments it became thick with colour and scent, a carpet upon the sea's surface, like a minuscule, beautiful scar in the water.

'Mom, look!'

Mia looked down to find Hunter, her eldest boy at age eight, pointing out to sea. The surface was flat, a dead calm in the bay today – except for a single set of waves heading for them.

Everyone turned to look, releasing a collective gasp at the sight. In under a minute, the waves reached them, lifting up beneath each and every one of them and rocking them all. Eddie looked over at Mia and nodded. Clover knew what he was confirming, something that Cory had told her himself: it was Hawaiian belief that the departed would show their presence with a wave passing under the circle, and although Cory had been a California boy through and through, he had long ago adopted the spirituality of the ancient Hawaiian water men. He was telling them he was here, with them.

Leaving.

Mia sobbed in astonishment, in heartbreak, at her husband's final goodbye. He was really gone. A chant suddenly started up, led by Eddie again, and everyone began to splash in unison. It wasn't just an incredible sight, but the sound of it was too – hundreds of hands hitting the water to the same beat, droplets catching the sunlight. A dance on the water, with the water.

Clover watched the set of waves roll towards the shore, preparing to break themselves apart against the land and be gone forever. Her gaze fell again on the lone surfer. He had given up on their strange, private ceremony and was paddling back to shore, looking for an excitement not to be found here. Not today.

From her bed – the bed that had been hers for nine months last year – Clover could see the moon glistening on the water, throwing out a light that made dark dots of passing ships on the horizon. Closer by, she could hear the rhythmic roll and crash of the surf. It underpinned life here, in this bay, in this house. Even the wind let up sometimes but the surf always kept on rolling in, endless, repetitive, dependable. It would never not be here. Cliffs would crumble and mountains fall before those waves stopped.

That was why Cory had walked into a stormy sea. He had been as much a part of this landscape as the cliffs and the ocean itself. He belonged to it. There was no moving on for him. Mia had told her, in the quiet hours since getting here, how she'd pleaded with Cory for them to not just move house, but move state. Start over properly and find somewhere land-locked, with no coastline, no surf to torment him with what could never be. But salt water was his oxygen, that was what he'd told her. He could no sooner 'live in the dry' than a landed fish. In the end, he hadn't even tried.

Throwing the sheets back with a sigh, she got up. Sleep was like a nervous bird tonight, nowhere close to landing on her yet; she could feel the day's high emotions still flickering like dying flames through her veins. Opening her bedroom door a crack, she peered out into the open-plan kitchen-living space, seeing the long shadows across the wooden floor. The tap was dripping. A skateboard was poking out from under the sofa, a wet beach towel bunched on one of the bar stools.

She went over to pick it up and spread it out along the back of a chair to dry, her gaze falling inevitably to the scene outside. The ocean was a midnight ribbon sparkling below a full moon, the trees like cathedral spires, throwing inky spines on the grass.

One shadow in particular – soft and round – caught her eye. She stopped and watched for several seconds, then, grabbing a throw from the sofa, slid open the back door and tiptoed past the rack of surfboards propped against the wall. Mia was sitting on the grass in a vest and knickers, hugging her knees. Her skin was blue-tinted in the moonlight, her blonde hair a regal silver. She looked like an angel.

'Couldn't sleep?' Clover asked quietly, her voice little more than a whisper.

Mia didn't startle. As ever now, it seemed to take several seconds before she registered the question. She turned her head with a sad smile.

Clover put a hand on her shoulder. 'You're cold. Here.' She draped the throw over Mia's bare skin, sinking onto the grass beside her.

Neither of them spoke for several minutes, both watching a container ship bound for . . . who knew? . . . tracking a steady course along the horizon. It was soon out of sight.

'Today was beautiful,' Clover said finally.

'. . . Yes. Yes, it was,' Mia said slowly, like the words were being pulled out of her on a thread. 'He would have loved it.'

'For sure.'

'I think it would have amazed him to see – to actually *see* – how many people loved him.' Mia looked at her as if baffled. Then she looked away again, her gaze fixing upon the reflected moon, its shape flickering and twisting as the waves rippled through it, and Clover remembered again that moment when the set of waves had rolled in under them all this morning. Cory's farewell lap. '. . . Do you think if he'd known . . . ?'

Clover knew what she was asking, but there was no answer to give. 'The important thing was that he knew how much *you* all loved him.'

'Did he, though?'

Clover was surprised. How could Mia even doubt it? Their relationship had been fiery and passionate, but Clover had never once questioned the strength of their bond. 'Mia, of course! You more than anyone. You were his greatest protector.'

Mia blinked at her, shaking her head softly. 'I'm no saint. There were so many times when I wanted it to just be over. When I felt like I couldn't keep going.' Tears shone in her eyes. 'I *wished* for this.'

Clover reached over and clutched her arm. 'Mia, you listen to me. You didn't want him dead. You didn't make this happen . . . Of course you're not a saint. No one is. It would not be humane to expect any one person to deal with everything you've dealt with, for the past few years, and not sometimes lose your shit. You hear me? You did the best you could. Better than anyone else could have done. Certainly better than I ever could have done. You were his wife, right to the end. You're the mother to his kids. He was lucky to have you and he knew it. He told me that himself, so many times. Over and over he'd tell me how he couldn't believe that you had stuck with him. He said you deserved better than him.' Clover swallowed. '*You* are the reason he kept going as long as he did.'

Mia stared back at her with huge, shining eyes. The tears were racing down her cheeks in silent tracks. '. . . I just want to scream. All the time.' The words were softly said, quiet as opening flowers, but the sinews in Mia's neck were strained, the muscles in her arms flexed with repressed rage. 'I want him to see what he's done to us. I want him to see what he's done to me. To my little boys. I want to make him suffer the way we're suffering. Because it's not going to ever stop. This feeling. This pain.'

Clover put a hand on her shoulder. 'Mia, it will. With time—'

Mia jerked her head sharply, pinning her with a wild look. 'Bullshit.' Her voice was still quiet, but savage. 'This isn't the *beginning* for us. We've been living in this nightmare for years already. Brady never knew his father before the accident – he only got the monster. They all did! Hunter and Taylor were too little to remember him before. All they'll remember of him are the rages and the depressions. That's the legacy of what he did. He took their father from them – not once, but twice!'

Clover frowned. 'Mia . . . who are we talking about?'

Mia blinked back at her, as though confused by the question. 'Kit Foley!' she cried, tears streaming down her cheeks. 'Who else? He's the architect of this. Everything that has happened to us . . . *all* of this . . . can be traced back to what he did that day. We know it. He knows it. And he got away with it.'

Clover's mouth opened to protest, to offer words of encour-agement, but what could she possibly say? Knowing what she knew of Foley's latest adventures, it was undeniable that his life was on the up again. It was true – he *had* got away with it.

'We're the ones left living with the fallout. My boys are growing up without their father. I've lost my soulmate. And we have nothing. No money.' Mia gave a small sound of despair, hiding her face in her hands suddenly. '. . . Oh. Did I tell you? The latest kick in the teeth?'

Clover shook her head, mute, dreading to think what other calamity could have befallen her friend.

Mia drew in a deep, slow breath. 'The life insurance is invalidated because it was a suicide.'

'Oh god, Mia.' Clover hadn't even got as far as thinking about what came after Cory's death.

Mia rubbed the heels of her hands against her eyes, exhausted, agitated, defeated. Neither one spoke for several minutes. Mia had no husband. And now no money. 'I've sold the house.'

'Already?'

'What other choice did I have? We're out in five days.'

'But so soon?' Clover was shocked. Then she remembered. 'Oh. That developer?'

Mia nodded. 'He's emailed me every three months since the accident. Regular as clockwork. Did we want to sell? Like all this was inevitable.' Her voice cracked on the last word, as she looked back at Clover with questioning eyes. Had it been? Had there really never been any hope for her husband?

Clover took her hand and squeezed it hard.

Mia shrugged, her head hanging again, her silences saying as much as her words. 'The day after they found Cory, I told him to give me his best offer. It's nothing like what we could have got if we could afford to wait, but he knows we can't. So he wins too and we keep on losing. We just keep on losing.' She stared out to sea, at the black morass which had taken everything from them. Clover could see the tears shining on her cheeks. 'Cory always said this place was where our souls danced, but now it'll just be torn down and some glass holiday home will get built for a tech millionaire who probably doesn't even like getting his feet wet.'

Clover put an arm around her friend's shoulders. 'I'm so, so sorry, Mia,' she whispered. 'This is all so unfair. You don't deserve any of it.'

They sat huddled together, Mia weeping as the moon sketched a tremulous path across the bay.

'I just wish I knew why,' she whispered into the dark. 'How can I ever find any peace when I don't understand why this happened to us? How do I explain to my boys why they lost their dad, and their home . . . ?'

Clover was quiet. In the process of making *Pipe Dreams*, she had watched the footage of the accident thousands of times. In her mind's eye she could easily see Cory paddling for the wave, the turn of Kit Foley's head to check his rival, and then him paddling too . . . Both men standing on their boards within a second of each other. Cory had priority as the outside rider, but Foley deliberately blocked his line, forcing him off the board just as the wave broke. It was an automatic interference penalty for Foley, but by then Cory was under the water.

Cory had needed only one more good run to win the heat, win the event, take the world title. Foley had been running down the clock and he'd burned him to stop him getting the points. The will to win was one thing, gamesmanship another. But to do what Foley had done, in those heavy surf conditions . . . it had been nothing short of reckless endangerment.

They stared out at the midnight horizon together, but as the moon peeped from behind a cloud, Clover felt something, previously hidden, begin to surface within her too. Through the shock and the sadness, the first stirrings of anger shifted inside her – because Mia was right. Her husband was dead. Her family's life in ruins. The very least she deserved was to know why.

Chapter Four

Six months later

The train picked up speed, the scenery melding into a smudge of hesitant greys and greens. Clover looked out over red rooftops, seeing nothing.

'There's hardly any snow!' Johnny complained, looking out at fields that were muddy, not frozen.

'Well, give it a chance. We've only just left Salzburg,' Matty mumbled, not looking up from her phone.

Clover shifted in her seat, refusing to acknowledge the nerves that were tickling her fingertips and toes and making her tummy fizz. She had that feeling she always got when standing at the top of a skyscraper, a sudden fear that she couldn't trust herself not to jump. But this wasn't vertigo and there was nothing imagined about the tension that had crackled through the six months of email correspondence for the pitch, which had come from an idea, born of a promise.

Neither Johnny nor Matty had believed her when she'd unveiled her proposal on her return from California. They'd expected her to come back with an Oscar, not a plan for 'career suicide'. First they'd laughed, then they'd laughed harder. Only her paleness had convinced them she meant every word. Liam too, sitting opposite her in their usual chairs in Soho

House, had looked at her as though he couldn't decide if the proposal was a stroke of genius or entirely mad. Couldn't it be both? she had argued.

Crudely put – in commercial terms – the story had moved on. *Pipe Dreams* had been about life after Cory's injury: loss of identity, loss of health, loss of the dream. Now they had life after Cory's death. Only, she didn't want to come at it from the same angle as before. This wasn't a sequel. She wanted to pivot a full one-eighty and examine how this played out for the antagonist of the story. How did Kit Foley live with what he'd done? How did someone like him sleep at night?

People had loved Cory precisely because he was forever the underdog, always the groomsman, never the groom. They saw themselves in him, especially when pitched against a competitor who wasn't *just* a supreme athlete – Foley had had every advantage: he was six foot one to Cory's five nine; his famously pale blue eyes and chiselled bone structure had made him a second fortune as the sponsorships rolled in; he had seduced a trail of Hollywood actresses. In short, Foley had been winning his whole life. He'd had no idea what it was like to lose – until now.

And now he couldn't win. If his surfing career and reputation had become collateral damage in the fallout from Cory's injuries, Cory's death was the fatal blow to his hopes of any sort of comeback. In the weeks after Cory's suicide, the papers had run features on his tragic decline from every possible angle: should helmets become mandatory in big surf events? What were the long-term concussion risks, not just in surfing but all contact sports? Where did legal culpability begin in the professional sporting arena when safety rules were deliberately breached? Only one fact was taken as fixed – Kit Foley had done this. He had brought the sky falling down on Cory's head. And also his own.

Liam couldn't understand it. 'Everyone's going to expect you to hate him,' he'd said.

'I do hate him. But I can still do my job.'

'But why do it?'

'Because it's the very last thing anyone expects,' she had shrugged.

'But you're crossing enemy lines! It will undo everything you set up in *Pipe Dreams*. You risk dismantling your own work.'

'That's assuming I fall for his spin. But I've lived and breathed this story for three years. He can't justify his actions to me. I know exactly what he did – I just don't know why.'

'Well if Cory would never tell you, why should Kit?'

'Because this is his one shot to publicly restore his reputation. His life's in tatters. Surfing's done with him, he knows that; but if he wants to start a new chapter – and he does – then he's going to have to redeem himself first. He can't just ignore this and hope it'll blow over. It's been four years since Peniche and now, with Cory's suicide blowing up in his face . . . This isn't going to go away. Until he apologizes and fesses up, it's his Kryptonite.'

'So you want him to beg?'

'I want him to own what he's done. People want to see that. Cory's death is on him.'

'And if he doesn't?'

'Then they'll see him for what he really is.'

Liam had stared at her, seeing her anger. 'He won't do it. I don't know much about the guy, but I do know a tell-all isn't his style.'

'His fancy new sponsor with deep pockets is saying otherwise.'

Liam's eyes had narrowed. He had sighed. 'Okay, say he does want to give his side of the story. Why would he collaborate with us, the very people who helped trash him in the first place?'

'Because who better? If he can convince *me* he's a good guy, misunderstood, whatever . . .' She had given an amused, disbelieving laugh. 'He'll convince everyone.'

'Or he could just do Oprah.'

Liam hadn't bought it. Quite literally. They had both left the meeting in shock, Clover unable to believe Liam wouldn't back her and Liam stunned that she'd go ahead without him. For months afterwards they had each believed the other would backtrack but now here she was, on a train winding through the Austrian countryside, gathering speed towards her target.

Her tummy fizzed again. Pitching the idea and actually delivering on it were two different things. Day in, day out for the next six weeks, she, Matty and Johnny were going to be living with the man they had come to loathe – and who loathed them. But if this project was going to work – and the remortgage on her flat meant it had to – she would need to find some neutral ground; show him they were, if not friends, at least not outright enemies either. She had a job to do. There was no place for personal emotion here.

To her surprise, despite Foley's pivotal but off-stage role in *Pipe Dreams*, she had quickly realized she didn't know much about him, beyond the tabloid headlines. Her focus till now had only been on what he'd done and not who he was.

That had all changed. For six months, she and Matty had researched everything there was to know about the man. She had sat through thousands of hours of surf competition footage, watching the heats, the post-comp interviews. She had watched him grow from a pre-teen prodigy to a young gun scooping up trophies like they were sweets. He had gone pro at fourteen and won his first world title at sixteen, but even as a very young man he had been guarded and seemingly old for his years. He was always professional, terse and brief. Difficult to interview.

'You okay?'

Matty was looking over at her from the chair opposite. Her gaze fluttered lightly towards Clover's legs and Clover realized she had been frantically jigging her leg against her seat.

'Yeah, fine.' Clover uncrossed her legs and placed her hands under her thighs instead. She looked out of the window. The distant mountains were gradually drawing closer, their white-capped peaks already beginning to pitch into high relief, revealing steep gullies and glistening glaciers.

'Have you updated our new friends on the delay?' Matty asked her. They had spent two hours on the tarmac at Heathrow, having missed their slot thanks to an errant crew member.

'Of course.' Clover nodded. 'I told them not to hang back for us and that we'd make our own way to the chalet.'

'What did they say?'

'Nothing. They didn't reply.'

Matty's eyebrows shot up. 'Oh. Nice. Great start.'

They all looked at one another apprehensively. Matty was biting her lip. Johnny looked sick.

'Don't look so nervous. It'll be fine,' Clover said, trying to rally them.

'Will it, though?' Johnny asked flatly. 'We've all seen the emails. They're not on board with this.'

'Well, Julian Orsini-Rosenberg is, and he's their pied piper. Where he leads, they follow. Right, Mats?'

Matty shrugged. 'That's what he's saying. He's been very

helpful, practically falling over himself to make sure this happens.'

'Well, of course he is,' Johnny muttered. 'He's relying on us to polish the turd.'

Clover laughed. 'You did not just say that!'

Johnny just grinned. 'All I'm saying is, I'm the one who's going to be in the firing line.'

'Why?' Matty scowled, as though *she* wanted to be in the firing line.

'Because I'm the token bloke! They're not gonna hate on you two, are they?'

'Why not?'

'Duh. Looked in a mirror lately? I'm the only dude. I'm the one they're going to target.'

'Oh, so you mean it's like an alpha male thing?' Matty asked innocently.

'Well, y—' Johnny almost fell for it. 'Sod off, Mats.'

She laughed. 'Come on! What are they going to do to you, Johnny? Challenge you to an arm-wrestle? A plank-off?'

'Maybe!'

'Relax. If it comes to that, I'll step in for you.'

'Oh, you think you could beat me in an arm-wrestle?'

Matty pinned him with a withering look. 'Johnny, I know I could.'

Clover chuckled quietly and Johnny looked between them both. 'I don't think you two quite get what it's going to be like up there. The big guns in surf culture are hard nuts. You've got to be, to do what they do. It's not *Baywatch*! Surfing is tribal. Localism is a thing. They defend their territory like hyenas – and we're out-and-proud Team Cory. I've been telling you for months – this is a bad idea.'

Clover's leg had begun jigging again. 'Look, I know it'll

be a bit awkward for a day or two but we don't have to pretend to be their friends. This is a business proposition for all parties. We stay neutral and professional. There's certainly no need to go in braced for all-out war.'

'Clo's right,' Matty said, flashing them a photo on her phone. 'I've been scoping them out and you can't tell me this guy's not a complete pussycat.' Her grin widened as Johnny took in the image of Kit's manager, Ari Jones, from his own pro surfing days.

Clover rolled her eyes as Johnny whimpered at the sight of Ari roaring victoriously, riding on his board. He was a brick of a man, with aboriginal tattoos and some severe scarring on his face that made Clover worry for the well-being of whoever had done that to him. 'He looks like he could crush my legs just pulling a fist.'

'Well don't irritate him then,' Matty said simply. She swiped the screen. 'And then there's Tipper McKenzie. Now, he's hardly threatening, is he? He looks like my old geography teacher.'

Johnny peered closely at the image of Kit's coach, a tall, narrow white-haired man in a padded jacket. It was true there was less to fear physically – Clover thought he looked like the love child of Ted Danson and Arsène Wenger – but he had a stern, dour look about him. He had worked previously with Shaun White and it was his presence in the Foley camp that had first tipped people off that Foley's intentions might be a bit more serious than first assumed.

'And as for Beau, well, what an overgrown puppy dog. Look at him – he's all shaggy hair and long limbs. He's like Pluto!'

Johnny spluttered. 'He's not like bloody Pluto! Beau Foley's a loose bloody cannon. He got arrested in the summer for being drunk and disorderly. He's a total pothead. He's his brother's wingman and a complete freeloader.'

'You say that like it's a bad thing,' Matty quipped. She arched an eyebrow at his agitation. 'Johnny, chill. There's nothing to worry about. Clover and I will protect you.'

Clover chuckled at her friends' endless banter; it made her feel braver again as she looked back out the window at the soaring mountains. Kit Foley was up there somewhere – and she was coming to get him.

'Well, they obviously took you at your word,' Johnny said as they stood on the street an hour later, bags at their feet. The sun had come out to play and the light was dazzling, reflecting off the snow-tipped mountains that encircled them in a splayed bowl. At the heart, along the valley floor, lay a sapphire lake, and the town of Zell am See clung to the shallow stretch of land between its shores and the Pinzgau mountains. The views approaching by train had been spellbinding and Johnny had done his best to capture them, hastily unpacking his camera and filming from the doors.

It had been a warmer welcome than their hosts had managed. There was very clearly no one here to greet them. After fifteen minutes of standing forlornly on the pavement just in case someone should show, Clover walked over to the bright yellow taxi at the head of the rank, dragging her ski bag behind her and showing the driver the address Ari Jones had reluctantly provided. Matty and Johnny climbed in after her.

'Have they got a Jacuzzi, d'you reckon?' Johnny asked.

'I doubt we'll be allowed in it, if they have,' Clover sighed. This snubbing was a highly inauspicious start.

They looked out of the windows as they were driven through town. It was lively but not crowded, people walking about in jeans and down jackets. It was still a couple of weeks too early for tourists. Zell am See was 700 metres above sea level but the snowline currently stopped 100 metres above the town and although there was a good covering on the upper slopes, the pistes wouldn't open until early December.

It was a pretty town even without the spectacular lakeside setting. Unlike the purpose-built 1970s concrete jungle resorts Clover had visited when skiing in France, the buildings were largely traditional low wooden chalets and rendered apartment blocks in colourful hues of lemon, custard and clay. It was perhaps a little tired-looking in places, but Clover liked that – it made the place feel real and lived-in year-round, rather than somewhere that was a ghost town through the summer months. It all seemed impressively, stubbornly 'normal'.

The taxi soon came to a stop outside a double-height wall and solid gate.

'We're here already?' Clover asked in surprise, climbing out and looking up at the four-storey chalet that rose behind it. It was a large new build, but modestly blended to its environment, with pale grey stone foundations rising to dark, aged timbers above. One gabled wall, facing straight back down to the centre of town and the lake, was fitted with faintly smoke-tinted glass, withholding from the street any glimpse of the interiors within. Clover felt her heart beat a little faster. The whole place spoke quietly, but the quality shone – like Gianni Agnelli in cream cashmere. Foley's fortunes hadn't taken *that* much of a dive, then? It was a world away from the Allbrights' reality; Mia and the boys had moved to a condo in Redwood City, half an hour from the coast, with a concrete backyard. 'Their own bedrooms, though,' Mia had said, grasping for upsides.

'Well, this is disappointing,' Johnny quipped under his breath. 'I hate it already.'

'Same,' Matty breathed, looking awed.

Clover, feeling her resolve stiffen again, stepped forward and pressed the buzzer. They all waited, trying to look relaxed, knowing they were being watched through the intercom system. None of them said a word, just in case.

It was a full minute before anyone responded, and Clover had reached to press the buzzer again when the double-width gate slid open to reveal a cobbled driveway and a series of stepped terraces. A shiny black Range Rover was parked at the far end, beside a jet bike.

'Shit,' Johnny said under his breath. It clearly wasn't intimidating enough that they were hard nuts; they were also rich hard nuts.

Clover looked at him, determined not to panic. 'Johnny. He won the World Tour nine times.' She was speaking in such a low voice, her lips weren't moving. 'We know he's got money. There's no surprise in that.' She pulled herself up to her full five-foot-six height. 'But we've got a Golden Globe and a BAFTA, which is not too shabby either, so we go in as equals. Capiche?'

'Capiche.'

They carried their equipment through before the gate could close again. Johnny in particular had multiple bulky padded bags of camera apparatus to transport, as well as his snowboarding kit; he had been boarding since he was eleven and took it seriously. Clover had skied throughout her childhood, first clipping her boots in as a toddler – although she hadn't skied now in over ten years. Matty had come to the sport late, learning only when a family she nannied for in the university holidays took her to Les Arcs with them. Naturally, she had picked it up within days and was skiing blacks by the end of the first week.

The door to the chalet opened, revealing a muscular bald

man in a white tunic. His austere look completely diminished as he smiled at them. 'Hello there. You must be the film crew?' he asked in a broad Scottish accent, his gaze falling to their luggage.

'Yes,' Clover replied. 'I'm Clover Phillips and this is Martha Marks – Matty – and Johnny Dashwood.'

'A pleasure to meet you at last. I'm Fin Maclennan, the chef.' A small grin played on his lips. 'Everyone's been very excited about your arrival.'

'Excited? Really?' Clover tried to keep her tone free from scepticism. Behind her, she could hear the gate slide back smoothly on its runners.

'Oh yes. Come in, come in. We've been expecting you . . .' He stepped back to allow them into a long hallway with rough stone walls. An antique Spanish table was pushed against the left wall and arranged with some squat black-clay lamps and a contemporary sculpture. '. . . Although I'm afraid they're not in just at the moment. They've gone up to the glacier at Kitzsteinhorn for a training session.'

'That's quite all right. Our flight was delayed, so we're two hours behind schedule anyway. We texted ahead. We didn't want to hold them up.'

'It's Carlotta, the chalet manager's, day off today too – she'll be back on duty from seven – but Ari said to make yourselves at home. They'll be back later.'

'Great.'

'I'll give you a quick tour, shall I? Seeing as we're down here?' he asked, walking to the nearest door and opening it. 'That there's the boot room – heated sticks, racks et cetera. No outdoor ski kit on past this point, I'm afraid. The antique stone floors don't like ski boots.'

'Nor do my feet.' Clover smiled.

'Quite,' Fin agreed. 'Next along is the gym and right at the end, the hammam and spa.' Clover knew Johnny would be wondering what a hammam was.

Fin then pointed to the doorway on the right-hand side at the far end. 'Opposite is the Jacuzzi and pool. And next to it, over there, is the garage.' He pointed to a lift on their right and gave a shrug. 'Self-evident. Useful on big nights when you can't manage the stairs.'

'That's happened, has it then?' Clover asked innocently.

Fin laughed and wagged his finger. 'Ha! Strictly no comment!'

He led them up a winding staircase that was halfway along the hall on the right. It had slate treads and spotlights every third step, a sculpted giant bonsai on a console on the half landing.

'This floor is where the smaller bedrooms are – for staff and guests. Mine is down that end, opposite the lift, Carlotta's is next to mine. There's an empty room at the end there,' he said, pointing to the door in the right-hand corner. 'Ari's got the big corner room opposite and there's a twin next to him, here.' He opened the door onto a bedroom with two single beds draped with charcoal-grey throws edged with red blanket stitch. A medley of soft toys was arranged on a shelf, along with some jigsaws and board games. Fin raised an eyebrow. 'Sorry, we're a full house now. This room is usually used by the kids.'

So there were three beds but only two bedrooms?

'Well then, I guess that's us in here,' Clover said, looking at Matty . It wasn't like Johnny and Mats could share; they'd kill each other.

'Sleepover time.' Matty gave an easy shrug.

'Lucky me,' Johnny murmured as Fin began leading them

up to the next floor. 'So I get to sleep directly opposite Ari "Killer" Jones?'

Matty guffawed loudly. 'I told you. I'll protect you,' she sniggered as Fin brought them up to the next level.

'And here's what we call the fun palace.' He stood back and waited as they trooped up behind him, their jaws dropping open one by one.

'Yeah. I know,' he nodded. 'Pretty amazing. It takes some getting used to.'

The space was vast: double height, double width, double . . . everything. At the far end, beside the smoky floor-to-ceiling picture window, were two banks of vintage burnt-orange velvet Camaleonda sofas, arranged either side of a giant 'onion bulb' hanging fireplace. Sheepskin beanbags were dotted around the floor. On the left-hand wall was a huge colour-soaked canvas of abstract art above a four-metre-long Shou Sugi Ban dining table and fourteen chairs. At the near end, at a perpendicular angle, was a billiards table and a fully stocked butler's bar set into a wall that was shelved and stacked with books – as was the entire wall opposite. An oak pole ran across at three metres high, with a ladder perched against it. At a guess, there had to be over a thousand books in this one room alone.

Clover looked up, seeing a mezzanine upstairs. She realized her mouth was hanging open and made a conscious move to close it.

'Through there's the cinema and games room.' Fin pointed to a door at the opposite end. 'Fifty-two-inch plasma, Playstation, Xbox, you name it.'

'Scrabble?' Matty enquired, poker-faced.

Fin grinned. 'Naturally.'

'Uh . . . where's the kitchen?' Clover asked, noticing the chalet was set up for all play and no work.

'Ah-ha.' Fin walked over to the library wall to their right and pushed lightly against a book. With a faint click, a jib door opened to reveal a bright and beautiful ode to stainless steel, with long, pristine workstations and super-scaled Wolf and Sub-Zero appliances. Beautifully arranged fruit was visible in glass-fronted chillers and there was an industrial juicer in the corner.

'Kit takes his smoothies pretty seriously,' Fin said, seeing Clover's amazement at the size of a metre-wide bowl beside it, piled high with oranges.

'Everything here's so . . . extra,' Matty murmured, stepping back into the living space again.

'To match the scenery,' Fin shrugged. 'The light's beginning to go now but you can see the view's pretty sensational over the lake.'

'D'you know what?' Johnny turned to face them. 'Maybe we don't even need to interview Kit. Let's just film this place! It'll be a hit just doing that. Talk's cheap, we all know that.'

Clover gave him a smile and a look. 'What time will they be back, do you know?'

'They didn't say, but Ari did ask that I have dinner ready for you for seven, if that suits?'

'Yes, fantastic,' Clover said, relieved to have a short reprieve before the formal introductions. 'Thanks.'

'As I said, Carlotta will be back on duty at seven. I'll leave you to unpack and settle in. Everything's pretty self-explanatory but let me know if you have any queries. I'll be in the kitchen if you need me.'

'Uh . . . which book do we press to open the door?' Matty asked, with a thoroughly bemused expression.

Fin chuckled again. 'I know. It's a bit nuts. Here.' He showed them a small run of burgundy leather folios on a shelf at eye height. 'They're dummy books. Just press anywhere on these spines and it'll activate the panel.'

'Do you never worry about getting locked in?' Matty asked.

'No. I dream of it!'

'Uh, Fin?' Clover asked, as he went to go back into the kitchen behind the library.

'Yuh-huh?'

'. . . Where's Kit's bedroom?'

Fin pointed upstairs. 'Up there. He's got the master suite and his brother Beau is in the other one. But I can't take you up there, I'm afraid. Strictly off limits.'

Clover smiled. 'Of course, yes. That's fine. I was just wondering.'

Fin disappeared back into his shiny refuge, the door closing automatically behind him. Clover followed the others downstairs again; they were beginning to babble with excitement, but her mind was already on other things.

They pulled their bags out of the hall and up to their rooms. Matty and Clover's room was pretty small for two grown women to share, even without Matty's overpacking tendencies. Clover was done within five minutes and she looked on in reluctant wonder as packing pods and organization cubes were laid on Matty's bed and the wardrobes and drawers steadily filled.

Leaving her friend to it, she went across the hall and popped her head into Johnny's room.

'How are you getting on in here? Slumming it?' His bags were untouched and he was lounging on the double bed, a shearling throw draped over his legs as he worked out the remote on his TV. 'Ha! Make yourself at home, why don't you!'

'What?' he protested. 'We had an early start and we've been travelling all day. They're not back yet and like you said, we've got six weeks here. It's not like every single minute counts. I just wanna chill before Ari "Evil Eye" Jones murders me in my sleep.'

'He's not going to murder you in your sleep,' she grinned, but he refused to look consoled. 'Listen, I came over to see if you wanted to . . .' She jerked her head towards the ceiling. 'Come and check out upstairs?'

Johnny looked panicky as he immediately realized she didn't mean the living room. 'You mean the bedrooms?'

She nodded.

'Clo! That's breaking and entering!'

She rolled her eyes. 'How can it be breaking in if we're already in?'

'And if Fin catches us? He specifically said no and that would be so awkward.'

'Yes, but he's locked away in the kitchen. And if he did catch us, we would just say curiosity got the better of us. No biggie. I mean, where's the harm in just having a peek?'

Johnny cocked an eyebrow, looking distinctly unconvinced. As far as he was concerned, there was harm all around.

Clover sighed. 'Listen, this isn't exactly planned and I appreciate it may not be my wisest idea ever . . . On the other hand, the housekeeper's got her day off and they're all out . . . We might not get another opportunity like this.'

'But what do you want to do up there?'

'Nothing. I just want to look.'

'You mean snoop.'

'Fine. Snoop, then . . . I want to get a sense of him before we meet. You can tell a lot about someone from their private spaces.'

Johnny smirked.

'Bedrooms! You know I meant bedrooms!' she groaned. 'I'm not going to do anything or take anything. I just want

65

to get a glimpse of how he lives when no one's watching. He gives practically nothing away in public; he's like a machine in press interviews. This is just a chance to have a peep behind the curtain.'

'What about Matty? Why can't she go?'

'Because apparently she lives here now and she's still got the kitchen sink to unpack.' She pressed her hands together in prayer. 'Please, Johnny. Don't make me go on my own.'

'Ugh,' he groaned, kicking off the shearling throw. 'Well, can we at least take the lift?'

'You're not five!' she grinned. 'And we can't – it might ping.'

They crept like pantomime burglars, hunched and on tiptoe, up to the living room, and straight up from there to the mezzanine. The décor on the top floor became immediately softer and more sumptuous. Gone were the rough stone walls and antique flagged floors, deployed to withstand higher footfall; instead a thick cream carpet closed over their socked feet. A pale charcoal mural of a mountain scene was etched in pen and ink on the walls and offset by a pair of oxblood linen side chairs. There were only two doors on the whole floor, one on each side of the hall.

They opened the door on the left first, peering in tentatively. It was empty but they still held their breath as they stepped in.

'Oh yes,' Clover whispered, pleased by what she saw. The room was large – at least twice the size of her bedroom – with huge windows looking up the valley towards the mountains, the rising cables for the Schmittenhöhebahn ski lift visible; it felt even bigger on account of the vaulted ceiling and exposed timbers. The walls were linen-lined in dark moss, with a buttoned headboard as high as the bed was long.

But if the room's concept and design were refined, the

person inhabiting it was not. The bedsheets were a twisted tangle, a pillow on the floor, a laptop left charging in the middle of the mattress. The wardrobe doors were hanging open but it seemed to be superfluous, for there were clothes everywhere: jackets, jumpers and jeans piled high on chairs, bunched-up boxers and single socks on the floor, snow base layers inside out on the radiators. Vape cartridges and Rizla papers had been left on the desk, some magazines – car, surf, porn – slowly sliding off a chair.

'Huh. So he's forever fifteen, then,' Johnny muttered. 'This looks like he had a party in his parents' room.'

'He's certainly a slob,' she said slowly, following Johnny into the bathroom.

There were wet towels on the floor; a stale urine smell told them the loo hadn't been flushed. More vapes. A shampoo bottle upside down in the shower.

'Ah. This is Pluto's room,' Johnny murmured, reading the name on the label of a white pill bottle in the wall cabinet above the basin.

'What?' She walked over and stared at it. *'Beau Foley.'* Dammit. 'Alprazolam. What is that?'

He gave a disdainful snort. 'It's a street benzo . . . Benzodiazepine? . . . Treats anxiety.'

'He's got anxiety?'

'Oh, I sincerely doubt it. Uses it as a downer, most likely.' He reached in and pulled out some more bottles. 'Yeah. Bringing him down from these.'

Clover looked at him blankly.

'Our boy likes to party,' he muttered, putting them back again. 'Wingman and freeloader – playing to type so far.'

She walked back into the bedroom and looked around it with disdain. 'And supposedly he's the nice brother!'

'Oh good.' Johnny rolled his eyes. 'Here's a thought – let's *not* do this in Ari's room. I'd really rather not chance upon his exotic knife collection.'

They walked out into the hall and stood outside the door opposite. 'Ready?' she asked him. Johnny shrugged – he just wanted this all to be over as quickly as possible – and she realized she had been asking for her own benefit. She needed to take a breath before she stepped in here, into the most private space of the most hated man. 'Here we go, then . . .'

They went in. It was like stepping into a cathedral – the instinct to look up, to gasp. Beau's room could have been, *should* have been beautiful, but this was a whole other level. Three times bigger and decorated entirely in milky whites, it was like stepping into a cloud. The entire far wall was crittall and smoked glass, looking onto the main living area downstairs and beyond it, the picture window over Lake Zell. A giant freestanding copper bath was positioned front and centre, affording the bather wonderful views, but for the person having a cup of tea on the sofa downstairs . . . ?

The walls were papered with a hand-painted Fromental wallpaper of cherry blossoms. A sheepskin sofa sat against the end of the emperor bed with two matching armchairs opposite, should he want to host some kind of meeting or gathering in his bedroom. Clover felt certain no one had ever sat down on them.

She went over and contrarily sat on them each, in turn.

'Enjoying yourself?' Johnny whispered, looking amused.

'Oh yes,' she grinned. But she felt strangely disappointed, too.

This was their first indirect encounter with Kit Foley, a deliberate breach into his inner sanctum. It was supposed to speak about him without words, but as she looked around, she wasn't hearing much. The room looked exactly as it had been conceived – pristine, beautiful, calm. The bed had been made, the wardrobes were shut. No porn mags, no smokes, no dirty underwear lying about. She got up – not even a scummy waterline inside the bath.

She went over to his wardrobe and looked in. There were three white shirts, one black suit, a clutch of snowboarding jackets – all in solid, sober colours – with JOR in matt shadow along the shoulders. JOR: Julian Orsini-Rosenberg. The man behind Foley's comeback. Supposedly, Kit had designed this himself?

She checked the drawers – he was a Calvins man; clearly not much interested in socks – just black ribbed pairs. She checked the other drawers – base layer thermals, jeans, some merino wool sweaters in dark grey.

'Ugh, he dresses like a bloody architect,' she muttered. 'Where are all the Hawaiian print shirts and board shorts?'

'He gave it up, remember? This is Foley Mark Two.'

'Well, Foley Mark Two is . . . dull.' She stood by his bedside table and did a visual inventory: vitamin tablets, a phone charger, airpods, some paperbacks. He was a reader?

'Oh god,' she smirked, holding up the top one to show Johnny. '*Unfuck Yourself: Get Out of Your Head and Into Your Life*. He's a deep thinker? Please.'

She went to the second. '*The Power of Positive Thinking* . . . Maybe *he* should take the anxiety pills?'

Johnny chuckled.

'Obama's biography,' she murmured, holding up the copy of *Dreams from My Father*. She flicked through it idly. 'Oh, look at that. A signed copy. Friends in high places.'

'Not anymore. I bet he wouldn't get a signature for Obama's new book.'

Clover smiled, mollified by the thought. 'True that.'

She picked up some loose papers and glanced at them – architect's drawings for a house. Surprisingly twee, she thought, looking at the pillared porch.

She put everything back down thoughtfully. What did all this reveal about Kit Foley? He could actually read – fine, so he wasn't a complete moron jock. He liked to associate with the great and the good – she already knew all about his ego. He was building a house. Okay, where? Was it simply an investment, or for him? Did he want to put down roots? He was thirty, no longer the teen sensation travelling the globe, breaking hearts and catching waves.

Johnny followed her into the bathroom. It positively gleamed. Towels were folded and hung on the heated rails. Clover looked at the products in the shower – local supermarket brands, nothing fancy. He used an electric toothbrush, the bristles bright and upright, suggesting the rotating head had seemingly recently been changed. 'Looks after his teeth,' she murmured. 'Clearly likes his smile.'

'I don't think anyone would deny the guy's got a killer smile, Clo.'

Clover looked back at him with narrowed eyes. 'I would. He's a snake.'

The contents of the bathroom cabinet were unremarkable. Paracetamol. Aspirin. Muscle rubs. Tubed support bandages. Some herbal remedies – echinacea, ginseng, St John's wort . . .

'Ugh . . . it's all so . . . yawn . . .' she hissed irritably.

'We should probably shift and get back downstairs. They could be back any second,' Johnny said nervously.

She looked around the space, feeling increasingly frustrated. Nothing that she could see revealed anything about the man. It was all so . . . unremarkable. And that was odd, because

Kit Foley was many things, but unremarkable wasn't one of them. There was no subversive reading material, no dodgy substances, not even a glimmer of bad taste. If this was a glimpse inside his head, there wasn't much to see. Where was his personality?

'Clo?'

'Huh?'

'Let's not push our luck?'

'Oh, yes . . . coming,' she mumbled.

Johnny visibly relaxed as she walked silently over the plush carpet and he closed the bedroom door behind her with a soft click. Clover followed him down the stairs in pensive silence. If it had been a revelation, it had been for all the wrong reasons. She had spent the past half year studying this man; she knew his birthday, knew that he was a goofy-footer, allergic to shellfish, preferred blondes, idolized Bruce Lee, had a Hawaiian kākau tattoo on his left bicep , had torn his ACL in both legs . . . But having gone in hoping for added insight into a man she already knew so much about, she had come away somehow knowing less. He not only hadn't conformed to expectations – he simply hadn't *been* in there at all. It was troubling. If even in private he was hidden, how was she supposed to find him?

She had a sudden dread feeling that filming Kit Foley was going to be like getting a photograph of the invisible man.

Chapter Five

'. . . They send their apologies,' Carlotta said, pouring the champagne into tall flutes and handing them out. 'They took advantage of the fresh powder and lost track of time. They said to go on without them.'

'Well, when will they be back?' Matty asked. 'We could wait.'

'They said they couldn't be sure.'

Clover, Matty and Johnny swapped looks. This was becoming ridiculous.

Carlotta straightened up; her mid-length dark hair was held back in a low ponytail and she moved with a steady briskness. She was officious and seemingly not prone to smiling. 'Dinner tonight will be *tafelspitz.*'

'*Tafelspitz,*' Johnny echoed blankly.

'Yes. It is a traditional Austrian dish – boiled beef broth with root vegetables, horseradish and minced apples. Mr Foley thought you might enjoy a typical Austrian meal on your first night here.'

'Boiled beef broth? How kind of him,' Johnny said with a lightness that betrayed sarcasm.

'It sounds delicious,' Clover said quickly. 'Is Mr Foley always so considerate to his guests?'

'Mr Foley has never had guests here.'

'Really?' She couldn't keep the surprise from her voice.

'Well, I mean to say, his guests do not usually come for dinner.'

Matty caught Clover's eye and smirked.

Clover tried to ignore her. 'Have you worked for him long?'

Carlotta nodded with a note of pride. 'Since he arrived in Zell am See.'

Clover took a sip of her champagne. It was good stuff, vintage – biscuity, with a golden colour. 'So that's over a year now, isn't it? You must know him quite well.'

But Carlotta was clearly not inclined to chat; she briskly replaced the champagne in the ice bucket. 'If you'll excuse me, I'm needed in the kitchen,' she said, hurrying away.

Once she was out of sight, they swapped looks again.

'She's terrified you're going to interview her,' Matty muttered.

'She's right to be. She must have some dirt on them, surely?' Clover said, reaching for an olive.

'Well, I just wished I'd changed into my trackies,' Matty moaned, tugging at the waistband of her skinny jeans. 'I thought it was the least I could do to make an effort for the first meeting. But they can't even be arsed to show up?'

'So good of them to arrange for our dinner to be "boiled beef" though . . .' Johnny puffed his cheeks out, feigning nausea.

'It's all fine,' Clover demurred with a placidity she didn't quite feel. 'We shouldn't be surprised by any of this. Foley plays games. This is what he does.' She shrugged. 'He's simply showing his hand.' She took another long, slow sip of her champagne but inside, she felt rattled. This wait, wait, constant waiting, for him to get back . . . She felt like she'd been holding her breath all day. It was disconcerting being alone in the home of the man who was her friends' mortal enemy. They were expected, but not welcome.

'Well, he obviously hasn't read the sponsor's memo about

bringing us onside,' Johnny sighed. 'Which means it probably *is* going to be the arm-wrestling route.'

Matty and Clover both chuckled. Matty reached for a breadstick. 'So when do you think they'll show? Halfway through dinner, when we've got boiled beef broth dribbling down our chins?'

'Probably.' Clover looked around the impressive space again. It was going to take some getting used to. They were sitting by the fire, now lit and crackling away; Carlotta's return to duty had been efficient. The town was just a confection of lights below them, the lake an ink spot below a starry sky.

'Hey. Cool beats,' Johnny said, noticing a vinyl record player behind the billiards table and going over for a closer inspection.

Clover looked up at the glass wall of Kit's bedroom on the mezzanine, the copper bath gleaming even in the dark. She wished now they had taken their time up there, snooped with a little more purpose, instead of scuttling in and out within minutes.

She got up and began to wander, too restless to sit. A chess board was set and mid-play on a side table. She went over, assessed the state of the contest; moved a piece. It was weighty in her hand.

'You're a rebel without a cause, you know that?' Matty asked, an eyebrow arched as she watched on.

'Can't help myself,' Clover shrugged. 'Want to see if you can beat me?' She was teasing but it was a valid question. She was good. Her father had taught her when she was young and it had rapidly become 'their' game, her way of getting his attention when he came home from work. She hadn't played in years, though. She would be rusty . . .

'Bet I get you sub-ten moves,' Matty said as Clover brought the small table over so they could play in front of the fire.

Clover laughed. Her friend was the most competitive person Clover had ever met. 'Hmm, fighting talk.'

Matty sat forward on the edge of her seat, scrutinizing the state of play. 'I'll play white,' she said after a moment.

'That's not fair. You've already got my bishop.'

'I always play white,' Matty shrugged as Clover dragged over one of the giant sheepskin beanbags and sank into it.

Clover took a deep swill of her champagne and examined how the black team was doing, minus the bishop. 'Well,' she said finally. 'This is a jam.'

'Pretty tricky,' Matty murmured, scrutinizing the board too. 'Which piece did you just play?'

'Rook to F4.'

'Hmm.'

The Who started playing through the surround-sound speakers. The quality was excellent, Johnny sitting cross-legged on the floor and flipping through the stacks of records, head nodding as he sang along.

Clover sensed a tranquillity settle over the room as they stopped clock-watching, at least for a bit. The fire crackled lazily, champagne fizzing in their glasses, the quiet knock of the chunky chess pieces as they were moved around the board in a slow gliding dance.

'How the other half live, eh?' Matty murmured, moving her knight and taking another sip of champagne. She looked around the room again as if she could hardly believe it – living the good life in a millionaire's ski chalet. 'If only they didn't have to come back; then it really would be perfect.'

'Slight issue of paying the rent, though,' Clover murmured back, her hand hovering over her king.

'What are you talking about? Your flat's worth a fortune! You could sell that and easily buy half of this.'

'Half. That's helpful.'

Carlotta came through to refresh their glasses. 'Is everything
. . . okay for you?' She seemed to freeze momentarily as she
took in the sight of them all – Johnny cross-legged and playing
vinyls, Clover and Matty playing chess.

'Great, thanks,' Clover smiled.

'Chef has said dinner will be in fifteen minutes.'

'Wonderful.'

Carlotta hesitated, then nodded. She refilled their drinks,
poked the fire and threw on another log. She hesitated as she
turned to leave again and Clover saw her survey the tranquil
scene, as if confused.

'Is everything all right?' Clover asked.

'Yes. Yes.' Carlotta straightened primly. 'It is just you are
not . . . what we expected.'

'Oh?'

But Carlotta didn't reply as she walked back towards the
kitchen, leaving them all to wonder what exactly Kit, Ari and
Beau had been saying about them. And what exactly *were*
they expecting?

She stirred and turned over, her body falling back into dead
weight, happy oblivion . . .

The sound came again, startling her, making her limbs
twitch and her brain begin to spark, but not enough to push
off the blanket of sleep. Her breathing was deep and slow,
already lulling her back from this reluctant half-waking as
she opened one eye and stared blankly into the blackness. But
the sliver of light coming under the door in the opposite corner
wasn't where she expected it to be. The confusion roused her
further. What . . . ? Where . . . ? Everything felt unfamiliar.
She was disorientated.

Then she remembered.

She felt her muscles set with tension, her heart begin to quicken as she realized what she was hearing.

What time was it?

Her hand flailed for the phone. Three thirty-eight glowed in neon green light, creating a spectral radiance in the room. 'Mats!' she whispered.

Matty, her face half-covered by a silk eye mask and wearing a headband with Bluetooth that piped her dream apps straight into her ears, didn't stir. They had stayed up as late as they could, but the early start and long journey – not to mention the emotional trepidation of what awaited them here – had forced them to eventually file downstairs for bed just after one. It was clear their hosts had no intention of 'hosting'.

'Mats, they're back!' Clover whispered, half-heartedly kicking her leg out across the space between their beds. But it was too wide to reach. Matty, somehow sensing a disturbance, groaned and turned over onto her other side.

'Ugh.' Still half-asleep, Clover lay perfectly still, trying to make out what was happening downstairs. She could hear the rattle of equipment scratching along the floor, knocking against walls, sliding along racks. Someone dropped something. Someone swore. Someone laughed.

It was hardly a stealth mission. They were clearly hammered, the timbre of their voices carrying up the stairs and carelessly interrupting the night, not giving a damn who was disturbed. Or perhaps that was the point – another passive-aggressive act of defiance. It was almost four in the morning. They had stayed out all day and all night, making absolutely certain that there was no chance of meeting her and the others tonight. They had wanted the snub to be absolute, making their point in the most hostile way. And now this? She wondered if Johnny had been woken up too. Whether he was lying there, listening and waiting for Ari 'Eyeball' Jones to come and stand at the end of his bed.

She listened to the commotion with a slowly simmering anger. She turned on her side, her back to the door and staring at the wall; she could feel the reverberations of her pounding heart on the mattress. So this was it – Foley's first move. It was the kind of mind game Cory had described to her as they sat on his porch and stared out at a sea he could no longer surf. 'Anger makes people weak because then they lose control,' he had said. 'Foley's always looking for which buttons to press to make *you* lose control.'

Her anger was his aim. Was she angry right now? Yes. But she'd also been angry long before tonight. She was angry for Cory, for Mia, for those three little boys who no longer lived beside the sea; and if she was going to get what she had come for, then she had to be cleverer and calmer than that. She couldn't afford to lose control.

She closed her eyes, determined to sleep. She breathed deliberately deeply and slowly, concentrating on softening her muscles . . . This was how she would win.

She jumped as the door to Ari's room, beside theirs, slammed shut suddenly, with clearly no consideration for them – or Fin, or Carlotta – whatsoever. It was a 'fuck you' in door form. If Johnny hadn't been scared witless before, he would be now . . .

She sighed, trying again. Breathing deeply, breathing slowly, relaxing her muscles as a quietude began to settle over the chalet once more. Everyone was in their rooms now, at least, their petty point made.

. . . But something, an instinct, fluttered through her; she had that strange sense of being watched, and her eyes opened just in time to see a cone of light on the wall snip out of sight, like the closing of a fan.

She twisted and sat up with a gasp – but the door was already shut. She sat motionless for several seconds, breathlessly replaying the moment in her head. It had all been so fast, so silent, she could almost have believed it was a trick of her imagination. A middle-of-the-night delirium. Almost. But she knew someone had been standing there, watching them. She had felt it.

Anger propelled her as she threw the covers back and flung open the door – the hallway was empty. It was beautifully lit with dim pools of amber light shining up the stone walls but she wasn't interested in aesthetics at four in the morning. She stepped out in her t-shirt, straining to hear footsteps on the stairs, but everything was silent. Every door was shut.

She frowned, confused and muddled with sleep. Had she imagined it after all?

A tiny 'ping' came from the lift.

Useful on big nights when you can't manage the stairs. She sprinted down the corridor as the doors began to close.

'Wait!' she gasped, but the doors were already almost touching as she got there. She had just enough time to see his head lift at the sound of her voice and his famous blue eyes meet hers for the first time.

Then he was gone.

Clover fell back against the wall, her heart pounding. The waiting was over. Not a word had been spoken, but that one look had said it all. It had blazed with contempt. It told her everything she already feared, everything she already knew – that he wasn't going to go quietly on this. He was a world-class competitor, used to the fight.

He knew how to win. At any cost.

Chapter Six

'Good morning! You must be Ari.' Clover stood up from the table and turned to face him. 'I'm Clover. I've been so looking forward to meeting you.'

The rough-shaven man stood at the top of the stairs and stared at her suspiciously. In black board trousers and a black t-shirt, he looked much the worse for wear, his tanned skin more sallow than bronzed, with deep dark circles under his eyes. His head was as stubbled as his pitted jaw and she could see the tip of a tattoo snaking round from the back of his neck. After a moment's stunned pause, he walked over to the table and shook her hand. Could it be that he'd actually forgotten they were here? '. . . Clover.'

Clover smiled. 'And this is Johnny Dashwood, our camera-man and editor. And Martha Marks, our researcher and PR and marketing manager.'

'How do you do,' Matty smiled coolly from the other side of the table. Johnny, beside her, gave what he hoped was a manly nod of the head.

Ari shook their hands in turn, evident distrust in his every move. Fortunately, his hangover appeared to be his greatest problem right now and he was forced to sink into the nearest empty chair, beside Clover.

Carlotta came out and placed a brown malted shake on the

mat before him, along with two pills. It appeared to be a practised routine. 'Thanks,' he said gruffly, seeing how the others were midway through their breakfasts.

'Oh, I hope you don't mind that we started without you,' Clover said. 'We weren't quite sure of your timings.'

He glanced at her, as if checking for sarcasm. But she was still smiling easily, holding her teacup like an English duchess. 'Was yesterday productive?' she asked lightly.

He seemed wrong-footed by her breezy manner. 'Yes.'

'You were so lucky getting a bluebird powder day. We were madly jealous being stuck on the train. I bet it was spectacular up there.'

'. . . Yes.'

'It was such a shame our flight was delayed. I hope you received my messages?'

Ari glanced around the table at them, looking discomfited to be reminded of his lack of manners. He gave a short nod. 'What time did you get here?' Speaking seemed a struggle; his voice was hoarse.

'About three?' Clover asked the others.

'About that,' Matty agreed, digging her spoon into her pink grapefruit half.

Clover began buttering her toast. 'It's *so* beautiful here. The mountains, the lake, this place. Johnny's going to be spoilt for choice for link shots.'

'There's almost too much choice,' Johnny replied, immediately gulping his black coffee as if to cover for the fact that he'd spoken and brought attention to himself.

Ari didn't say anything. Small talk was beyond him. He stared at the shake for a moment, then picked it up, placed the two pills on his tongue and downed the whole lot in four giant gulps.

Johnny looked horrified.

Ari exhaled loudly, smacking his lips together. 'Aaaah.'

'Big night?' Matty asked with a wry tone.

'You could say that.' He looked back at her as if seeing her for the first time. 'High spirits at high altitude. We ended up taking it on to a club.'

'Sounds fun.'

A sound upstairs made Clover look up, but she was out of sight of the mezzanine at this end of the table, away from the window, a fact not lost on her when she'd been deciding where to sit. She would not be spied upon again. Once had been quite enough. She had clearly not been alone in wanting to get a preview of her new housemate, but if Kit Foley wanted to see her, he would have to do it face to face.

'How do you find being in the mountains?' she asked Ari. 'Do you miss being on the coast?'

'Is that a formal question? Are you filming already?' His tone was defensive, the atmosphere around the table instantly thickening.

Johnny paused, his fork speared with egg and bacon just inches from his mouth. 'Not filming.'

'Ari, I'm just making conversation. Nothing more.'

He looked at her with resentful black eyes. 'Good. Because before this goes any further, we need to have a frank discussion.'

'Okay, sure.' She took another sip of her tea, waiting patiently, although her heart rate had shot up to the low hundreds.

Ari's mouth opened—

'Woah! . . . Oh shit, I forgot.'

They looked up to find a lanky, dishevelled man again stopped by the stairs. Clover immediately rose to standing once more. Friend, not foe. 'Beau? Hi! I'm Clover.'

Beau's eyes slid over to Ari as he shuffled over. 'Hey,' he said, shaking her hand. Clover kept her smile fixed, hoping he had washed it. She couldn't help but remember his shoddy bathroom habits.

'It's really great to meet you. And this is Matty, our researcher and PR and marketing manager. And Johnny, our cameraman and editor.'

'Hey,' the others said, half-rising out of their chairs to shake his hand too.

'How come we're sitting this end of the table?' Beau asked, taking the next empty seat beside Ari and immediately pouring coffee from the pot. He missed the cup somewhat, dark stains bleeding into the ivory linen tablecloth.

Matty winced as she watched. 'Your chalet is amazing,' she said to him quickly as Beau glanced up at her again. Matty drew a lot of second looks.

Beau grinned. 'I know. Pretty rad, right?'

'You're so lucky. I'd sell my granny to live in a place like this.'

Beau looked at her with blue eyes that were less dangerous than his brother's, certainly less focused. His shaggy brown hair was still sun-bleached at the ends and around his face from their old life and he was deeply freckled. He had none of his brother's sharp edges. 'Well, I guess now you won't have to,' he said after a moment. 'Our casa, tu casa and all that.'

Matty smiled. 'Lucky me . . . lucky Granny.'

Beau grinned at the quip, then immediately looked warily at Ari beside him and began sipping his coffee, looking as though he'd said too much. Been too friendly?

Carlotta came back in with a tray. 'Eggs,' she said, setting down an egg-white omelette in front of Ari and a plate of hash browns, sausages and beans for Beau.

'Thanks Carlotta,' Beau beamed, looking truly grateful. He began to tuck in with appetite, Ari watching on disapprovingly for a moment. Beau's hangover was clearly nowhere near as bad as Ari's, though the manager was – as she recalled – nine years older than him.

Ari looked to be waiting for the housekeeper to retreat again, his eyes darting between her and Clover. 'We were just about to have a chat,' he said to Beau, but Clover knew the words were intended for her. Sure enough, a moment later, he pinned her with his black-eyed gaze. 'I'll give it to you straight here, as I did in our emails – Kit's not on board with this.'

She didn't reply, though she kept her expression open and neutral.

'For reasons that are perfectly obvious to us all, he doesn't want you here,' he said bluntly. 'He doesn't like you and he doesn't trust you.'

Ari paused, as if to allow her to make an objection. But Clover didn't stir.

'As far as he's concerned, the whole point of this new career is to close a door on the past and move on. Kit's an athlete, he needs to compete.'

Clover nodded, which seemed to confuse him.

'No. I mean, he *needs* it. It's not about money or glory for him. And he doesn't need the fame. Which is why he doesn't need you.'

Clover allowed his pause to stretch. She wouldn't be rushed. 'And do you think that's why we're here? To make him more famous?'

'I'm not sure you could. You've made him infamous.' Even with a hangover, his eyes were beginning to blaze. His manner was abrupt and coupled with his imposing size, it made him intimidating. Johnny had been right to worry. 'I told it to you

84

straight in the emails – this is a pointless exercise, you'll get nothing out of him. Once Kit makes up his mind about something, there's no turning him.'

'But it was his sponsor who first approached us. He's told us Kit will willingly engage in the project,' she said simply.

'Julian says a lot of things, but he doesn't know much about snowboarding, and even less about Kit.'

'I was also told it was written into Kit's contract that he must fulfil marketing and promotion obligations as stipulated by JOR,' she said calmly. Surely, as his manager, he had read that contract? Surely?

Ari was quiet for a moment. 'Look, Julian might have strong-armed him into doing this, but that's what I'm trying to tell you: Kit's only following the letter of his contract. You can be here if Julian insists on it, but don't think Kit will give you anything. You're on a fool's errand. This is a waste of your time.'

Clover tipped her head to the side contemplatively, as she began to run a finger around the rim of her teacup. It was true Ari had done his best to dissuade her from pursuing the project. If he couldn't stop Julian, he'd stop her? 'And do you agree that that's in his best interests? Us abandoning the project?'

Ari seemed surprised by the question. 'Huh?'

'Well, you're his manager. It's up to you to make decisions that will determine the best outcome for his career. Reputation is an intrinsic part of that. You're surely not disputing that he has a serious image problem at the moment?'

Ari's eyes narrowed.

'The way things stand, he's toxic – to sponsors, the public, other competitors . . . he won't ever be able to fully move on until he addresses the past.' She tapped the rim with her index finger. 'I do understand why Kit's resistant to working with us. I do. It's not the easy choice.' She shrugged. 'And I won't sit here and pretend that I didn't become friends with Mia and Cor—'

Matty kicked her leg under the table, but Clover didn't take her eyes off Ari.

'—But this was never personal, Ari. We were never anti-Kit. We simply told Cory's story after the accident in which Kit was the catalyst.'

'Yeah, but it's the way you told it. And he's been demonized for it!'

'So then if he's got a side to give, now's his chance to give it.' She shrugged. 'We'll put it out there and people can make up their own minds.'

Ari watched her in defensive silence, the muscles of his jaw balling.

'Ari, you're his manager. I know you're old friends and you want to protect him, but you need to look at this dispassionately and advise him frankly. Kit needs a rebrand. Fast.'

Ari shook his head stubbornly. 'He won't listen. As far as he's concerned, you ruined his life.'

'Fine. Then let him say that. Get him to talk to me and he can say whatever it is he wants to say. However angry he is. However much he hates me. I've come here to listen to him, and I will. I promise.'

Matty cleared her throat in an exaggerated fashion and this time Clover looked over at her. Matty's eyes were wide and darting towards the stairs.

Clover twisted round in her chair to find Kit himself leaning against the wall, his arms folded over his chest. It was like coming face to face with a tiger.

There was a long, uneasy silence.

'Your promises don't mean jack shit,' he said finally. 'I don't need to explain myself to you.'

With a calmness she didn't feel, Clover got up from her chair and walked halfway across the space to where he was leaning. Standing closer now, she was reminded of that first glimpse of him last night; he radiated an energy field that felt like a sonic pulse, causing everything within her, at an almost atomic level, to gather and press – and then drop. '. . . You'd be explaining yourself *through* me. Like I just said to Ari, this was never personal.'

'Felt pretty damned personal from where I was standing.'

'Then I'm sorry about that.'

His eyes narrowed. They were burning like wildfires; she could see the fury in him as he read her. 'No you're not. Don't stand there and throw platitudes at me. You got yourself trophies on the back of destroying me. You made your name by trashing mine. And now you think you can undo what you did and *save* me?' His voice was low, more like a growl. She could feel the bass in it reverberate in her own chest. 'Fuck off,' he said simply. 'You're the last person I'll ever talk to.'

'I honestly believe that would be a wasted opportunity for you.'

He looked at Ari. 'Could I care *less* about what she believes?' he asked him.

Ari didn't reply. He looked like a man caught.

Clover cleared her throat, determined to keep her voice steady. 'Your sponsor—'

'Fuck him.'

'But—'

Kit pinned her with a look that made her want to whimper. 'Pack your bags. Get back on that plane. And get out of my face.'

Clover stared back at him, trying to think of the words that would calm him down.

'I said go. Fuck off.'

'Kit. Mate,' Ari said in a placatory tone.

Clover looked at Ari, but it was clear he held no real power here. Kit was the sun around which they all revolved. She looked at Beau, who was sitting silent, his head hanging down and his elbows splayed, not meeting anyone's eyes. She gave a small sigh and looked back at Kit. Clearly no one was going to stop him from throwing them out. 'No.'

She felt the menace rise off him like a heat. Cory had often told her what it had felt like being in combat with Kit – *he's relentless, a street rat, he won't ever surrender, he'll die on his feet* – but words couldn't describe what it was like to finally be in his shadow. He had a range of weapons at his disposal – physicality, skill, intellect – to cow and intimidate.

'Julian invited us here and as I understand it, you have a contractual obligation to go through with this. So we're not leaving.'

His eyes blazed. It was like staring into an inferno. It made her eyes water, her throat close. 'You've got twenty minutes to pack your things—' His voice was a low growl.

'No,' she said again, ice to his fire. 'You don't need to like me. You just have to work with me.'

His mouth curled into a sneer. For someone so beautiful, he could be grotesque too. 'You're not listening, Clover Phillips. I don't give a damn what Julian Orsini-fucking-Rosenberg wants. I don't need his sponsorship that mu—'

She heard the scrape of a chair and suddenly Ari was standing beside them, between them, his hand on Kit's shoulder. 'Mate, you're hung to hell. We all are. Now's not the time for discussions. Why don't we all just take a minute and work things out when our heads are clearer? Hey?'

He looked at Clover and subtly jerked his head towards

the stairs, in a gesture intended to convey her immediate departure.

'That's probably best,' she said quietly. She didn't want to run from him – with Cory she'd needed to establish a position of trust, but with Kit she saw she had to establish a position of strength from the start. But Ari was throwing them both a lifeline here. 'We'll leave you to enjoy your breakfast in peace.'

At the mention of 'we', Johnny and Matty pushed their chairs back too and came over to her, standing around her in a huddle. There was a brief silence as their opposing parties faced off, then Clover turned and walked away.

She was amazed her legs supported her and as she rounded the corner, out of sight in the stairwell, she put a hand to the wall for support.

'Fuck!' Johnny whispered, catching up with her. 'That was savage.'

But Clover wouldn't say a word until they were safely back in the bedroom. She waited for the door to be closed as she began to pace, her hands on her hips and her face upturned to the ceiling. Her heart rate was at triple time. She had never encountered someone so stridently aggressive before. He had only used his words, his voice, his bulk, yet she felt like she'd been roughhoused. She'd never been in a physical fight in her life, but her nervous system was telling her it felt just like *that*.

'That was intense,' Johnny said, watching her with a concerned expression. 'He looked like he wanted to burn you to the ground.'

'He does,' Clover muttered.

Matty put out a hand to stop her pacing, to force her to look at them. 'You okay?'

'. . . Sure,' she lied.

'You were amazing up there. You didn't give an inch. First

Ari. Then Foley. I don't know how you held it together. They were brutal.'

Clover shrugged. 'I was braced for it. After yesterday's warning shot, there was always going to have to be a confrontation. They were never going to welcome us with open arms.' She didn't bother to mention the near miss in the middle of the night too.

'I know, but still – that was something else.'

'Well, they've got a lot to lose.' Clover straightened her back and stretched her neck, trying to calm her nervous system. She didn't want them to know how shaken she felt.

'Damn,' Johnny sighed, rubbing his face in his hands. 'I have a bad feeling this project is going to make doing solitary with Cory seem like a walk in the park.'

'Mmm.'

'Is he what you expected?' Johnny asked her.

Clover bit her lip. 'Worse.'

No one spoke for several moments.

'. . . I was impressed he knew the word "platitude",' Matty offered.

Johnny stared at her in disbelief. '*That's* what you took away from it?'

'What?' she asked back. 'At least it means he's not a complete animal.'

'That's like saying psychopaths can appreciate fine wine!'

'Well, can't they?'

A knock at the door made them all jump. Hesitantly, Johnny – as the alpha male – walked over to open it.

Ari stared back at him darkly, then his gaze searched for Clover. '. . . Are you okay?' he asked, finding her in the far corner, leaning against the desk.

She gave a half nod, half shrug.

90

'Look, I'm sorry. The way he was just now . . . he never should have spoken to you like that.'

She didn't reply.

'He can be . . . intense, when he's angry. And when he's hung over on top . . . well, he wasn't seeing straight. But I've just read him the riot act . . .' Clover sincerely doubted that. He gave a weary sigh. 'The simple fact is, Kit's got no choice in the matter. You know it. I know it. He'll have to come round, whether he likes it or not.'

'I'm going with *not*,' she said simply.

'No, maybe not,' he agreed. 'But like you said, he doesn't have to like you. We'll all just have to find a way to work together.'

'That would be good.'

'So in that spirit, can we just start slow and not freak him out with anything too intense? Give me a chance to make him listen.'

'Do you really think you can do that, though?'

'I've known Kit pretty much my whole life. I know he's his own worst enemy sometimes but I'll get him on board somehow, I will. Just give me a little time . . . Don't jump right in?'

Clover looked back at him steadily. 'Fine,' she nodded. 'We'll give him a little time. No jumping. These feet will stay firmly on the ground.'

Chapter Seven

Clover swung her legs, marvelling at the drop beneath them and feeling a giddy sense of freedom. The grass was hidden beneath thick snowy blankets, but some of the trees still had their leaves and the sun felt warm on their faces. She had never skied in such balmy conditions before.

It felt like they had the mountain to themselves. There was hardly anyone on the ski lifts – the wide, cruising pistes not yet open – but the glacier glistened and shone ahead, and as they drew closer they could make out bodies as small as ants dotting the pristine landscape.

It had been Ari's idea that they come up here, 'as an icebreaker, no pun intended'. They had received a cautious welcome when they'd finally come back upstairs at the chalet, Beau greeting them with a casual 'hey' as though they'd popped out for milk; Kit had glanced up from the table with a black look but said nothing.

Ari's hunch was that it was better to start off by doing, rather than talking; just let Kit get used to them being around him, so Johnny had left the cameras behind as a deliberate show of 'no weapons'. Still, Clover could see he was instinctively scanning the landscape and making note of places that would work in cinematography terms.

It had been a ten-minute drive from Zell am See to the

neighbouring town of Kaprun, and the base station lift for the Kitzsteinhorn glacier. Clover, Matty and Johnny had caught a cab behind Kit's Range Rover. Now the three men were two chairs in front of them – with no one in between – their snowboards dangling from one foot each as they chatted easily. Or rather, Beau and Ari were chatting easily; Kit didn't seem to be moving at all, his brother and best friend flanking him, handling him with kid gloves. 'The star', she supposed, getting the special treatment; his ego being constantly stroked. Their livelihoods and lifestyles depended, after all, on his performance and successes.

'Smile.'

Clover looked up to find Matty angling her phone screen on them both, taking a selfie. Clover automatically stuck her tongue out of the side of her mouth and scrunched her eyes shut. Within a minute, it was on Matty's Insta grid and within two, it had thirty-nine likes. Matty had over sixty thousand followers; most people assumed she was a model.

She was certainly looking like a goddess in the new Perfect Moment skisuit she had bought at a sample sale – a slim-fitting navy all-in-one with red and white details at the shoulders, waist and knee. Johnny was looking a true powder hound in baggy teal-coloured trousers and a mustard jacket. Clover, trying to be as inconspicuous as possible, had chosen plain black trousers and a white jacket that she was now convinced made her look like a mum dropping her kids at ski school.

They were approaching the top station quickly and she could see the others pushing the safety bar over their heads, getting ready to disembark, shuffling forward in their seats. She watched as they stood in unison, allowing the chairlift to nudge the backs of their knees and send them gliding down the short slope, where they swished to a stop and buckled up their boots.

Kit was impossible to identify to a casual passer-by, his distinctive sculpted bone structure and those famous flashing blue eyes hidden behind a helmet and goggles. Clover only knew that he was in a khaki and pale blue colour combo, and Beau in all orange. Ari was dressed all in black – 'like a fucking Ninja,' Johnny had muttered worriedly.

Matty began pushing up the bar, bringing her attention back to the fact it was time for them to disembark too.

'Hey,' Clover said a few seconds later, coming to a careful stop beside Ari who was waiting – alone – for them. She looked around, her smile faltering. 'Where'd they go?'

'They've gone for a few runs to warm up first. You may as well do the same, enjoy the views. They'll make their way over to the snowpark shortly; there's not a whole load of places to go at the moment anyway. So go have some fun and I guess we'll catch up with you at some point.' Ari gave a shrug and, pulling his goggles down, carved away before she could protest.

'So petty!' Matty muttered, watching him bear right and soon disappear from sight. 'First they don't show. Then they run away. Are they men or mice?'

'It's no bad thing,' Johnny demurred. 'I don't want to board alongside those guys when they're in that mood. God only knows where we'd end up. And a free snow session on their watch? Don't mind if I do.'

'Johnny's right,' Clover agreed. 'Foley's sulking and trying to give us the bird whenever he can. Let him have these petty wins if it makes him feel more powerful.' She looked at her friend. 'It doesn't change a thing. We're still here.'

'God, when did you become so endlessly patient? It's like you're an adult,' Matty groaned.

Clover smiled, glad it wasn't obvious she was also feeling

pushed to her limits. She had to maintain the illusion of composure; she couldn't react. Cory, without meaning to, had schooled her in how to deal with Kit Foley and right now, it was Kit who was angry and losing control. That meant she had the upper hand . . .

Clover allowed her gaze to roam over the landscape. Lake Zell wasn't visible from here; they were cupped in a jagged bowl, almost three thousand metres above sea level. According to the piste map, the snowpark was a couple of chairs away to the right, out of sight from here. The run they were on was marked blue; nice to warm up on, it was wide and not too steep. She was going to need several practice runs to find her ski legs after so many years of not skiing, and she felt a frisson of nerves as she felt her skis want to run down the slope.

She realized her friends were watching her.

'Well? What are we waiting for?' Matty asked, her head tipped to the side, hands held up questioningly. She was facing them uphill and beginning to ski backwards. She looked like she'd been skiing her entire life. 'Last one to the lifts buys drinks.'

Immediately forgetting her nerves, Clover poled off; she was spending quite enough money on this trip as it was. Johnny and Matty both assumed Liam was still backing them and she didn't want them knowing otherwise. She believed in this project, even if their producer didn't. It was all about demonstrating confidence and leading from the front. As long as she had a film to submit for the Cannes deadline, she could make this work. They were here and now all she had to do was get Kit Foley to talk.

'Hey!' Matty shrieked, unprepared for Clover's sudden flight and chasing after her. Johnny was only a few metres behind them, his board slicing through the snow in loud carves that told the girls exactly where he was, making them scream.

Matty, for all her verve and long legs, lost the race to the lifts, but no one cared. They were off, skiing with abandon, whooping and laughing as they tried one run after another, cruising along with the sun in their faces, arms outstretched or crouched low into tucks. Matty and Clover completed one run alternately skiing between each other's legs, Johnny showing off around them with dramatic carving turns that showered them in snow. They did little jumps and spins, short turn races, trying to kick up moguls. After all the tension leading up to coming out here and yesterday's frustrations – not to mention this morning's shocking confrontation – it felt good to blow off steam.

Conditions were perfect. They were high above the tree line and the air had a whistling purity to it. There was very little wind even at this altitude and under the fast-clearing skies, shadows were hard-edged and dark, every contour of the snow visible.

They had been skiing for almost an hour when they stopped at the edge of a snowfield that dropped sharply between two pistes. It was the size of a couple of football pitches and had not a single track upon the pillowy snow. They all shared a conspiring look. First tracks were every skier's dream.

'We'd better go one at a time,' Johnny said sensibly as they scanned it for rocks or sudden drops.

'Yes, Dad,' Clover said, getting into a tuck and laughing and shrieking as she zipped down the face. At first, the momentum and speed meant she flew across the surface, but as the gradient lessened and she naturally slowed down, the fluffy powder snow began to gather on her skis, slowing her further until eventually, wobbling wildly . . .

'Whoooooooooaaa!' She went down face-first, much to the others' hilarity.

Lying on her tummy, she had to lift her head to call out to them. 'I'm stuck!' she cried, howling with laughter and unable to move. The tips of her skis had been pushed well below the powder surface but her slow stop meant the bindings hadn't released, keeping the skis on. The angle she was lying at meant it was difficult to reach back and exert the force needed to release the bindings herself. 'I'm properly stuck!'

'Serves you bloody well right!' Johnny hollered over. 'I got that on my Go-Pro, by the way!'

Clover groaned at the thought of it ending up on Matty's grid later. She could hear her friends laughing, still standing at the drop-in point by the side of the piste as, with a lot of tugging and grunting and a strong gratitude for those hours spent doing hamstring curls in the gym, she somehow lifted her legs enough to free the tips. Through an ungainly scrabble to keep them clear of the snow, much like a beetle trying to get off its back, she tried to get *onto* hers. All while laughing uncontrollably. She was in god knew how many metres of powder snow and every time she tried to push against the surface to help herself move, she plunged up to her armpit, face-first again. She couldn't take her skis off and stand, much less walk out, when she didn't know the depth. She was either going to have to slide out of here on her stomach till she got to the next piste – *not* a good look – or get onto her back and get up on her skis again.

'Oh god,' she wailed, laughing breathlessly. She was still stuck on her stomach with her legs bent, her feet in the air, in parallel. Carefully, without pushing with her arms so as not to 'drill' the snow again, she rolled onto her side, trying to keep her skis from crossing – but she must have over-rotated because the outer leg, weighed down by the ski, continued going over until she was on her back, her feet – and skis – angled outwards. 'Argh no!' she wailed, sliding into hysterics again. This was even worse!

'Oh! Bloody brilliant,' she cried, looking up and seeing that a chairlift crossed immediately above where she was lying. If this had been an ordinary day's skiing in high season, several hundred people would have witnessed her escapade by now. She gave a prayer of thanks that the resort was still mainly closed and the chairs passing overhead were empty and swinging. This wasn't her most graceful moment. 'I'm still stuck!' she yelled to the others.

'Don't worry, I'll save you, Clo!' Matty called, setting off dynamically and matching Clover's tracks. But she too was in carving skis . . .

'Oh-my-god!' she wailed as the powder covered over the tops of her skis, slowing her down and bringing her too to a comical, flailing stop. She lifted her snowy face and blew out a mouthful of powder.

Clover collapsed into hysterics all over again. Had she looked like that?

Johnny, filming it all on his helmet, was in no rush to come over and help them. His board – wider and therefore with better spread over the snow – would handle these conditions with ease, but this was comedy gold.

Matty grunted with effort, swearing furiously, as she tried to lift her ski tips free, but every time she tried to plant her hands in the snow to sit up, her hands disappeared into the powder, up to her armpits too. Watching it at close quarters was the funniest thing Clover thought she had ever seen and when finally Matty managed it, lying spreadeagled in the snow like her, they lay there together laughing like they hadn't laughed in years. They felt childlike, silly and free. So much for being an adult.

'Johnny, help us!' Matty yelled. 'We can't . . . we can't get up!'

'I'm just off for a beer!' they heard him yell back. 'Won't be long!'

'Bastard!' she giggled.

The two women lay back in the snow, laughing so hard tears were streaming down their cheeks and seeping into the foam seal of their goggles. Clover looked up at the sky, feeling weak and helpless as she listened to Johnny making his way over to them, approaching in easy looping turns. She watched the empty chairs pass over her as if in a delirium. It was so strange to be skiing with the mountain almost to themselves.

Almost.

'Oh no . . . you've got to be kidding me,' Matty groaned, her laughter fading as they saw a group of snowboarders sitting on an approaching chair, their arms on the safety bar as – faces obscured by goggles and helmets – they stared down impassively. It was a moment before Clover recognized them.

All orange. All black. Khaki and blue.

They passed over in silence, with not a word nor a glance back, leaving the two of them lying like rag dolls in the snow and feeling like utter fools.

'So this is where everyone's been hiding,' Johnny said as the girls joined him on the shoulder of the drop. Below was the snow-park, and it was positively heaving compared to the empty motorways they had been cruising on.

Clover looked down at the landscaped vista. It was so groomed and manicured, the snow glistened like white velvet. Two rows of rollers, rising and falling at alternate lengths and heights according to grading, were followed by a huge kicker slope that would send anyone going over it up towards the moon. Tens of snowboarders and freestyle skiers stood patiently along the lines, obeying the unspoken rules and etiquette and clapping others' skills with heavily gloved hands. Occasional 'whoops!' carried into the air, sudden gasps too when someone got it wrong. There was, if not quite a party feeling, certainly a tangible sense of camaraderie.

Clover, Matty and Johnny made their way down the neighbouring piste in single file, going slowly as they scanned the park for their 'team's' colours. Where were they?

Johnny found them first.

'There.' He pointed towards the superpipe. It differed from the usual halfpipes she'd seen before in that it was much bigger – with sheer vertical walls twenty-two metres high – and wider too. The projections and angles were deliberately engineered to promote big air jumps and ever more intricate tricks. It was the very reason Foley had chosen Kaprun and Zell am See as his base – the superpipe and this glacier meant he could train nine months of the year.

The pipe glistened menacingly in the bright sunshine and had a vast airbag set up at the bottom corner. A group of boarders were lining up along the top, waiting their turns to drop in. Beau's distinctive and bright all-orange kit was easy to spot. He was standing behind Ari, who was standing behind Kit.

'Quick. Let's get to the bottom and watch them come down,' Johnny said, taking off before they could argue.

They were there in twenty seconds, pivoting to a stop just as the guy before Kit launched into a languid zig-zag down the chute, his jumps becoming bigger and more complicated as he went. Clover gasped as he performed some sort of corkscrew twist at the end, flying through the air and landing on the giant airbag with a floppy, playful demeanour, like it was all just a game.

Several people cheered and shouted praise as he let the

airbag settle around him. Whatever he'd just done, it appeared to be a big deal and he seemed pleased with it.

Clover looked back up the chute, waiting to see, finally, what Kit Foley could actually do. It had been one thing watching him on her laptop for months on end, getting to recognize his signature style on water. He was known for his aggression, those powerful clipped turns, his effortless 360s, superb balance . . . But the mountain – all rock, snow and ice – was a different beast. Was he the competitor here that he had been out there? Back then?

He was standing on the top lip, seemingly ready to go, but there was something even in his stillness that was intense; he was inanimate, but not inert. Even under his baggy layers, she could still tell his body was coiled and primed. He stared ahead in unseeing concentration, oblivious seemingly to the fact others were waiting, before he suddenly dropped in, tipping down the nose of the board. His body assumed the warrior-like pose she knew so well – knees bent, arms out for balance – as he went down the sheer drop. It wasn't just the height and gradient that made the pipe so challenging, but the buffed slipperiness of the surface, the snow almost polished to a shine. There was no stopping once on it; as with a rollercoaster, the rider had to commit to the ride.

He took the first line modestly, executing a whiplash sharp turn and coming back down and over to the next side. This time he caught air – a lot of it. He landed well and Clover caught some people nodding in admiration as he went into the third pitch. He took off, grabbing his board with one arm and stretching his body in a backward arc as he hit peak altitude. Then he was coming back down again, his arms wide and squatting low to absorb the impact from the jump as he looked ahead towards his final ascent . . .

KAREN SWAN

'Ooooof!' Johnny looked away, a collective sucking of teeth whistling audibly down the chute. Foley was on his back and sliding down the ice. He kept his legs in the air, protectively, as he began to slow, spinning in small revolutions. 'Shame,' Johnny said, clapping him supportively.

It had looked like a nasty fall to Clover but Foley popped up on his feet as soon as he could get his board down safely and arced his way to the bottom of the pipe. He snaked right past them without giving any sign of having seen or recognized them. Another blank. Another bird. Clover hoped he had seen them. She hoped he realized they'd seen him fall. She hoped he had hurt himself.

She watched as he went over to a guy standing in a navy jacket with red piping, and sunglasses. They began talking intently, the other man using his arms expressively to explain something. 'Is that Tipper McKenzie?' she asked Johnny.

But Johnny was watching Ari coming down the pipe. He executed a series of serviceable turns and a tentative board grab, but there was no innate flair. Clover suspected his hangover was keeping him on mute; he was here in a backup support capacity only. He probably couldn't wait to get back to the chalet.

'. . . Huh? What d'you say?' Johnny asked, clapping Ari out.

'Tipper McKenzie?' She pointed to where Kit was standing down the slope, by the top of one set of rollers.

'Oh – yeah, looks like it.'

'He doesn't look happy,' Clover said.

'He shouldn't be. Rookie mistake. Foley's weight was too far back. He's not surfing now.'

'Holy cow!' Matty exclaimed, prompting them both to turn back. Beau was coming down the pipe, relaxed as a ribbon and pulling out a series of intricate aerials. 'He's good!'

'. . . Yeah,' Clover agreed. 'He really is.'

They all watched as he finished off with a Cab 180, landing perfectly, braking and doing a couple of celebratory 360 spins as everyone watching cheered.

'Go Beau!' someone yelled.

'Thanks man!' he yelled back before turning in to a set of simple arcs and heading straight for them. They all stepped back again as he went to pass them on his way out of the pipe. They braced for the Team Foley snub.

'Oh, hey guys,' he panted as he slid past.

Matty, Clover and Johnny swapped surprised looks. They'd got an 'Oh, hey guys'?

The day hadn't been a complete write-off, then.

By the time they caught a cab back, their hosts had been home for twenty minutes, the snow already melting off their boards and boots in the boot room. She could tell Foley got off on being driven about everywhere effortlessly – making sharp exits at whim – while they had to deal with bus queues and taxi ranks.

Matty and Johnny had gone straight to their rooms for hot showers. Clover had been tempted to lie on her bed and wait her turn for the shower too, but she had forced herself to go upstairs to show her face. Tempting though it was to hide in their rooms, they had to start normalizing the fact for Kit that they were living here with him. He had to get used to it – they all did – however painful it might be.

She walked up to the living space. Ari was on his phone, pacing past the table. She could hear Beau's voice in the kitchen. Kit was sprawled on one of the sofas, scrolling on his phone. He looked up, his thumb pausing momentarily at the terrible sight of her.

'Hey,' she said lightly, offering a head nod and half-smile. He didn't react. He just stared with a repressed anger that

made her feel her skin would blister. It was highly intimidating. He wouldn't even blink.

'You're back,' Carlotta said, behind her.

Clover wheeled around with relief. 'Oh. Yes.'

'Did you have much fun up there?'

'Oh. Yes.'

'Would you like some *gugelhupf*?'

Clover looked at the tall marbled ring cake on the plate
Carlotta was holding. 'Oh. Yes.'

'With tea?'

'Thank you,' Clover nodded. 'That would be lovely.'

'And the others?'

'They're just having their showers. They'll be up shortly.'

'Very good. Then I will bring it out in ten minutes.'

'Great.' Clover watched the housekeeper go and wished
she wouldn't. There was safety being in conversation with
her. She didn't dare to turn back and deal with another face-off
from Foley. There was zero chance of small talk with him;
he clearly couldn't even countenance being in the same room
as her.

She wrung her hands lightly and went over to the chess set
which she and Matty had played last night. They hadn't been
able to complete the second game before dinner was served
and she looked down at it now. She went to move a piece.

'Don't!'

The command made her jump and she looked up to see
Ari crossing the space in a hurry. He threw his phone on the
sofa. 'Sorry,' he said, holding his hands up apologetically as
he saw her alarm. 'I just meant . . . Kit and I have been playing
this one game for . . . what, a couple of weeks now, mate?'

He looked over at Foley, but Kit didn't respond at all. Ari
looked back at her with a grimace.

'You play chess?' She couldn't keep the surprise from her voice.

'There's a lot of waiting around on the pro tour – sitting in airports, hotels. It's a good way to pass the time.' He gave a shrug. 'Anyway, we're playing a twenty-move game, but with no time limit. We've just moved into the middle game and it's been tight as hell . . .' He stopped talking as he took in her expression. 'What?' He looked down at the chess set and saw how the pieces had been moved. '. . . Oh shit.'

Foley was on his feet in a flash. 'What is it?' he demanded.

'We didn't know,' Clover said quickly, to Ari. 'If we'd had any idea . . .'

Foley charged over to where they were standing and stared down at the despoiled game. His chest heaved and Clover, standing inches from him, felt a frisson of genuine fear. 'I'm sorry.'

'You're sorry?' In a whirl, he had turned and caught her arm in a vice-like grip. 'You're *sorry*? You come in here and just casually destroy something that had been going on for weeks? Something you knew nothing about?'

'No one was here. We didn't kno—'

Ari stood beside him and put his own hand over Kit's, on her arm. 'Mate, calm down. Let go of her arm.'

But Kit was still glowering at her. 'When are you going to realize your apologies are worthless? The damage is done. Nothing you say can make up for what you've done. Don't you get it?'

Clover stared back at him, her breath held. Was he still talking about the chess game?

'Her arm, Kit. Let it go.' Ari's voice was firm, his gaze steady. '*Now.*'

Kit looked down at her arm; he seemed surprised to find

himself holding it. He released his grip on her bicep, a sneer on his mouth.

'You okay?' Ari asked her.

Clover nodded, but she knew she was visibly upset; she couldn't hide *this*. She felt scorched by his contempt, frightened by his fury. She was aware her face was flushed and that she was breathing heavily, her body in panic mode.

'What's going on?'

They turned to see Beau standing in the middle of the room. He was holding a bowl of water and another of cotton wool balls. He had taken off his all-orange outer layers and was wearing only his dark grey base layers and socks. He was so tall, all gangly arms and legs . . . Matty hadn't been off the mark with her Pluto reference.

'Nothing,' Foley snapped, pulling his t-shirt and long-sleeved thermal over his head in one movement as he walked towards the sofa. Clover saw his muscled back was streaked with bruises and vivid red weals. They were nasty, running from his shoulder blades to his hips. From his fall earlier, she supposed. The surface of the halfpipe was so compacted it shone like glass, but small balls of hard crud formed at the top of the walls where the boarders carved and sliced turns, and they ran straight back down to the centre of the pipe. Skidding on them on exposed skin would be painful, like rolling on gritty marbles.

Beau gave a quizzical look to Ari as he passed, but the manager just shook his head in silence as if to say 'not now'. Clover watched as Beau joined his brother on the sofa and began dabbing the wounds with salted water.

She felt a light touch on her arm. 'Clover, I'm sorry . . . Can I ask you to forget that ever happened?' She looked to find Ari addressing her, his voice barely more than a murmur. 'Please.'

Ari jerked his head towards the other side of the room, and she followed him. 'That was bang out of order,' he said in a low voice. 'But he's not himself at the moment. He's stressed.'

Stressed? Clover stared at him. How much of Ari's job involved damage limitation for Kit's behaviour? This was the second time in twelve hours he had had to physically intercede. 'This is unworkable,' she whispered. 'I cannot do my job if I'm going to be physically threatened, Ari.'

'I know. And I'll tell him that if he so much as lays another finger on you, I'll pummel him myself.'

She looked over at the brothers. Beau was dabbing Kit's cuts, Kit hissing and jerking like a scalded cat at every touch.

'He's dealing with a lot of shit right now,' Ari murmured, glancing over to check they weren't being watched. 'Although I appreciate he doesn't present *sympathetically*.'

Clover looked back at him. 'How's he going to be able to talk to me, if he can't even look at me?'

'Just give him time. He's a good guy – underneath it all.'

How far underneath? She was an interviewer, not a miner.

'Look, even if you don't believe me, from a purely selfish perspective, I've just come off the phone to Julian. Again. He rang me seventeen times today. There's no fricking coverage at the park.' He gave an irritated look. 'Anyway, he heard we hadn't been around yesterday and he's made his feelings very plain. It's no more Mr Nice Guy . . .'

Clover frowned. Who exactly had told Julian they weren't around yesterday? Not her or the others.

'Look. *I* don't want Kit to be dealing with a lawsuit after all the shit he's already been through so I promise you, I'm dealing with it. Kit will play ball. I just need a few days to make him see sense. Can you give me that?'

Clover sighed. She could see Ari was doing his best. And

he had just stepped in between her and Kit, which was more than he'd done at their morning confrontation . . . 'Well, I guess we could do some B-roll shots while we wait,' she said finally.

'B-roll?'

'Backdrop shots. Stills. Panoramas.'

'Right. Yeah, B-roll. That'd be good.'

She glanced over towards the brothers on the sofa. 'They seem close,' she murmured, watching Beau tending his brother's wounds.

'Yeah.'

She looked back at Ari. 'I really am sorry about the chess game. I didn't know.'

'How could you have?'

'It's not our intention to antagonize him. We'll stay downstairs this evening,' she said quietly, still staring at the angry marks on Kit's back. His head was hanging down, his muscles clenched. 'Hopefully it will help calm him down. I'll tell Carlotta that we'll have dinner in our rooms.'

'Oh but—' Ari said, as she went to walk away. 'Didn't Julian tell you?'

'Tell me what?'

'You'd better check your phone; like I said, there's no reception on the glacier . . . He told me he's meeting you all at the Orsini Hotel tonight at eight. He's booked a table for dinner.'

It was the very last thing she felt like. Her shoulders slumped. 'The Orsini . . . it's his?'

'Oh yeah, he's the big cheese round here.' Ari sighed. 'You'll like it. It's the swankiest place in town.'

She tried not to show her despair. This had been a very long and not great day. 'Does that mean there's a dress code?'

Ari rolled his eyes. 'You'd better believe it. Julian doesn't do casual. That man was born in a three-piece suit.'

Chapter Eight

'What? No one said I would have to dress up out here!' Johnny protested as Matty rolled her eyes again at his outfit. Clean was the best he could offer: jeans, a new pair of trainers and a long-sleeved vintage Guns N' Roses t-shirt (the sleeves being the distinction between that and his non-formal clothes).

They were standing in a smart wood-panelled lobby with large country house rugs and library chairs in warm, smoky velvets. It was undeniably grand but the low-level lamps and squashy cushions gave the space a welcoming feel. Matty certainly looked very at home in a vividly patterned silk drawstring midi dress – bought pre-loved on Vestiaire – and slouchy black suede boots. Clover had had to borrow her pair of black Isabel Marant pirate trousers and a cornflower-blue blouse. Like Johnny, she had packed for action and adventure, not dinner with her grandparents.

'Agh, no! I had hoped to beat you to it!' an exuberant voice said.

They turned and were surprised to see a tall blonde man, early thirties, striding towards them. His legs must have been six foot tall alone, and he had incredibly deep-set dark eyes. He was wearing a slim-cut navy suit but with a jacket of the Austrian style – worn open – with a Nehru collar and brass buttons that closed to the nape of the throat.

Clover hadn't given a moment's thought to what their newfound ally might look like but she had automatically assumed grey hair, late fifties, paunch. And clearly, so had Matty; a small squeak escaped her.

'Oh sweet Jesus. It's Tom bloody Hollander,' Johnny groaned.

'You mean Tom Hiddleston, you berk,' Matty said under her breath, making Clover choke with unexpected laughter.

'Martha?' Julian asked, looking just as happily surprised, stopping in front of them as Matty stepped forward. As their marketing person, she was the only one to have had direct contact with him, calling him back just the once after his preliminary approach to confirm they were going ahead. Any communications since had been on guarantees of access to Kit and logistics in Austria when Ari's emails suggested otherwise. Julian had been very keen to discuss everything further but Matty had politely but firmly demurred; for reasons of integrity, it would be 'inappropriate' to confer, she had said. Judging by the look on her face, though, it didn't seem so inappropriate now.

'Julian, finally – a face to the voice,' Matty beamed as they shook hands and a moment passed that felt longer to Johnny and Clover than it seemingly did to them.

Johnny gave a not-so-subtle cough.

'And Clover, the famous, the remarkable Clover Phillips,' Julian said, turning to her next. 'I'm not sure whether I should be excited or terrified that I've managed to get you to come for dinner.'

'Oh, I hardly think I merit either of those responses.'

But he made a small sound of disagreement. 'You've got a way of making people talk, Clover. I know that only too well. I wonder if I should stick to water tonight.'

Clover laughed. 'We'll keep it light, I promise.' And hopefully quick, she thought to herself.

'And Julian, this is Johnny Dashwood, our cameraman and editor,' Matty said, staring again at his t-shirt of a dagger dripping with blood and entwined with roses. 'As you can probably tell.'

'Johnny.' Julian shook his hand vigorously, appearing oblivious to his attire. 'You are as discreet as Clover is direct. That footage of Cory at home, when he was having a dark episode . . . You handled it with great respect.'

'Thanks,' Johnny said appreciatively. 'Not many people notice.'

Clover spotted a hotel manager hovering at a discreet distance. He was holding a navy blazer.

'Ah,' Julian said, turning towards him slightly and discreetly waving the jacket away with a tiny movement of his hand. 'Thank you, Otto. It looks like our table is ready. Come, let us get out of the draught and into the warm. You must be tired after your busy first day, yes? Was the snow good?'

'Amazing!' Matty trilled, walking beside him as Otto led them through to a dining room that was again both grand and gracious, yet cosy: pale oak panelling, dark European School oils on the walls in gilt frames, white linen napkins with scalloped sage green embroidered edges. Almost every table was taken, people sitting in pairs and talking quietly, dinners that looked like artworks served on Meissen plates, tall arrangements of flowers bursting from Medici urns.

Julian went straight to a table in the far corner of the room and did not sit until the others were all seated. Matty and Johnny sat on the inside, along the wall, Clover and Julian on the other, with their backs to the room.

Moments later, a waiter came over with a chilled bottle of

Bollinger. Julian accepted with an almost imperceptible nod of the head. 'You have been blessed with good weather since your arrival,' he said conversationally, as the waiter popped the cork and began to pour. 'Last week it was all rain, rain, rain. Snow up top of course, but down here . . .'

'Don't worry, we're English,' Matty said with a smile. 'We can do rain.'

'Well, that is good. Because the forecast for the next week is not so desirable.'

'Dammit. I knew I should have taken the camera up today,' Johnny muttered.

'Why did you not?' Julian asked.

Johnny realized he'd spoken without thinking. '. . . Well, we thought we should tread lightly to begin with. We didn't want to scare the horses, so to speak.'

A frown came onto Julian's brow as he inferred Johnny's meaning. 'Yes. I heard Kit has been behaving very badly. I am sorry you were treated that way.' He looked at them all sincerely. 'But I have had a long conversation with his manager this afternoon and I can assure you, he will co-operate with you now.'

Clover's mind whipped back to the way Foley had exploded at her, manhandling her even as Julian had been on the phone to Ari. She forced a smile. 'Ari's been surprisingly helpful.'

Julian sat back in his chair so he could face her beside him more easily. 'Well, he understands the situation in a way that perhaps Kit does not. Do you feel comfortable there, in the chalet?'

'How could we not?' Matty asked, misunderstanding Julian's point. 'It's stunning!'

'Thank you,' Julian nodded.

Matty's eyes widened. '. . . It's *yours*?'

'My family's. We have a lot of different investments in the town.' He looked at Clover again. 'But if Kit should continue to behave like a child, please know there are always rooms here you can use.' He gestured vaguely to their grand surroundings. 'It is early still in the season so we are not at capacity. I'm afraid I cannot guarantee the best rooms but I am adamant Kit will not bully you away. That tactic has served him well in the past and he thinks it will work here too. I fear he's not yet learned from his mistakes.'

Clover regarded him as he spoke. Julian was cultured, sophisticated, mannered. His English was flawless, his manners those of a gentleman. He was an old-school European, used to moving among women in furs and men with cigars. So why had he chosen to associate his family's – clearly illustrious – name with a disgraced sports star who was synonymous with scandal?

She smiled as she asked him exactly that.

Julian laughed. 'Wow. And there it is – the steel fist in a velvet glove. Straight to it.' He tapped a finger around his champagne glass, bemused. 'Okay, well, it is a good question. And not one I can easily answer.'

Clover's smile widened. The best questions never were.

'I suppose I would have to say it's because I believe in second chances. We've all become so censorious, quick to judge, to condemn, to troll. We are not so good at forgiving or showing compassion, I think, but everyone makes mistakes.' The smile climbed into Julian's eyes. 'But listen, I am a businessman too. I will not pretend this just comes from the heart. I know market forces and Kit Foley is a champion. He has got whatever "it" is. He's insanely talented, driven. Very handsome too, of course – he's got the classic "men want to be him; women want to be with him" thing going on. And that translates into commercial gold.'

'Except Burton passed on him. Oakley. Salomon. They clearly didn't agree.'

'Because they are too big to be associated with him,' he shrugged. 'They need to keep their noses clean. The risks are not the same for us; sometimes, it can be a good thing to be a minnow in a sea of sharks. But that doesn't mean they wouldn't have liked to pick him up. They know his sporting pedigree! He might be new in this field but he's got the transferable technical skills, the experience, he knows the pressure of elite competitions; he's going to be right up there when he debuts this season.'

'But is medal glory enough to undo what he's done?' she pressed. 'To Joe Public, he's a dirty player. Perhaps they don't want to see him win! A lot of people hold him responsible – albeit indirectly – for Cory Allbright's death.'

Julian looked at her. 'As you do.'

Clover shrugged, not denying it. 'Cory became my friend, yes. I got up close to the consequences of Kit's actions that day. It was hard to see.'

Julian's smooth brow furrowed. 'Should I be worried? Will you give him a fair hearing?'

'Kit's not exactly helped himself so far,' she said frankly. 'Yes, I'll listen to him, but I'll go where the story takes me, and you should know that I can't make any assurances that you'll like what I find.' Clover shrugged. 'This' – she gestured to the beautiful dining room – 'is glorious, and I thank you for your hospitality, but . . .'

'You can't be bought. Yes, I can see that,' Julian nodded. 'And I respect you for it. But for what it's worth, I have full faith that no such compromises would even be required. I would not dream of trying to bribe you; Kit will redeem himself. At the moment he's face-down in the mud, but he's too much of a fighter to stay down there. It's in his DNA to fight. He will come back and his stock will rise again.' Julian's eyes sparkled. 'As my accountant likes to tell me, he is an appreciating asset.'

Clover smiled. 'Do you think he'll reward you with loyalty if his moment of glory comes again?'

Julian laughed again. 'Oh, I sincerely doubt it! If he starts winning and your film shows him in a sympathetic light, then of course, he'll sign to one of the big boys.' He clicked his fingers. 'He'll be gone. No regrets . . . But he'll have done what I needed by then.'

'Boosted your profile?' Matty said, trying to get in on the conversation.

Julian looked at her with an even warmer smile. 'And fur-lined my pockets. Early termination of contract comes at a price.'

'How long is he signed to you for?'

'Three years.'

Clover quickly calculated. 'So he'd be thirty-three before he's free to sign a new contract. That's getting on in the snowboarding world isn't it?'

'Well, the average age of his competitors is twenty-two, so . . .'

Clover's eyebrows shrugged up. 'You really do believe in him.'

'Or perhaps I am as mad as everyone has been telling me I am,' he grinned. 'The feedback on my new ventures wasn't exactly favourable.' He gave a lackadaisical shrug.

Clover wondered how many millions he had invested in signing Kit and delivering on the production capabilities for the clothing and snowboard ranges. The prospect of losing it didn't appear to be unduly worrisome. From what Ari had told her – that Julian had rung him seventeen times in an afternoon – she had expected him to be driven, but the man before her had an almost studied languor. Unless that was just part of his mannered mode of behaviour?

'How have *you* found Kit? On a personal basis, I mean?' she asked, watching him closely. 'It's obvious why he's hostile to us but your sponsorship bestows your family's good name upon his *besmirched* reputation—'

'Great word, besmirched,' Matty nodded appreciatively.

Julian chuckled, his eyes lingering on her for a moment.

'You've given him and his team a beautiful chalet to live in, a base where he can hone his new craft pretty much all year round. And I'm guessing the big shiny car is part of the package too. You must be best buddies, surely?'

Julian was not fooled. He knew the question was rhetorical. They were patently opposites: an aesthete and an athlete; old world and new money. Julian took a cagey breath. 'Well, Kit has his demons still. It is true he is not a man at peace with himself, and that can make him . . . difficult. But he is trying to rebuild his life and start over. We must all be patient.'

'So that's a no, then,' Clover grinned, calling him on his diplomacy.

'It's a . . .' Julian hesitated. 'A "not yet". But first and foremost, of course, this is a business relationship. It helps to get on, of course, but we do not *have* to like each other.'

'Funny, that's what I said too.'

'Then we are similar beasts.' He was smiling at her but she could see the assessment behind his eyes. They were neither of them quite what the other had expected.

'There's something I've been wondering about,' she mused. 'It's clearly incredibly challenging for Kit to have to deal with us, work with us. He absolutely does not want to do this film – but you've made it part of his contract.'

'I had to. His reputation is in tatters. Winning medals will not be enough. He must commit to every effort to win back the public's trust and forgiveness.'

'And make your brand look good.'

'Of course.' Julian didn't deny it.

'And yet, I think he's up there in the chalet right now, debating whether twenty years in jail for shooting me when I get back tonight would actually be completely worth it.' Julian gave a shocked laugh but Clover was perfectly serious. '*That's* how much he's hating this. Why is he putting himself through it? He's already a rich man. He self-funded his last year on the world surf tour. He could have done the same here and not shackled himself with marketing obligations that are clearly anathema to him.'

Julian was quiet for a moment. 'Well, perhaps it's because he self-funded his last year surfing that he wanted a sponsor for this. I suppose it bestows a certain . . . authenticity and respectability upon his efforts?' He hooked up a single eyebrow. 'More likely, though, his manager did not read the small print in the contract.'

Had Ari messed up? she wondered, not for the first time. Got his client into a situation with no easy way out? Ari was Kit's old friend and he undoubtedly had Kit's best interests at heart, but he was a former pro surfer himself, with no experience (that she knew of) in legalese. It would explain Ari's desperation for her to give him time to bring Kit round—

Julian laughed suddenly. 'What is it about Kit Foley? That man has a knack of dominating a room, even when he is not in it!' Julian lifted his glass and raised it towards them all. 'Come, let us dispense with business for the evening. Tonight is for us to get to know one another. I propose a toast – to new friends.'

Matty straightened up, sensing her 'in' at last. 'To new friends,' she said, clinking his glass first and not looking at all inclined to impartiality.

*

Owner, Slatterdorf Sports Yeah, I've seen him around town a bit.

Clover Phillips Is he settling in? Do you think the residents of Zell am See are happy to have him here?

Owner I don't see why not. He's come in here a few times and is always polite. Not overly chatty, but I think he's just wary.

C. P. Why do you think he's wary?

Owner Well, everyone knows what he did surfing. That film that came out did him no favours . . . Hey, is that why you're filming this?

*

Dog walker . . . Who?

*

Supermarket worker I think he has something to prove. Good luck to him. I like him.

*

'Yes, that's good. Along there,' Clover said, peering through the lens. She stepped back to let Johnny continue working his magic. He had set up a wide-angled shot above the snowpark.

The latest position he had found – involving an arduous trek up an unpisted slope – allowed for a panorama shot that swung from the magnificent glacier's peak to their right, bearing left until it looked straight down the superpipe, with the rollers behind. From this distance, with the industrial-looking rails and boxes too faint to discern, the park looked rather beautiful, like a highly stylized landscaped garden.

Snow was falling gently, fat flakes fluttering past the lens, a low-lying sky blocking the town of Kaprun from sight. Perched in their isolated position, Clover felt almost like she and Johnny were sitting on their own cloud. It had taken an hour to get up here and get into position; a further twenty-five minutes to set up the cameras and fine-tune the exposure settings. They were waiting for the sun to peep from behind Kitzsteinhorn – every so often, the clouds thinned just enough for hazy bright spots to emerge, casting the north faces into deep shadows and silhouetting the dramatic jagged skyline.

Clover hugged her knees to her chest. It was quiet in the park today, with just a few huddled groups of boarders and skiers left out there. Kit, Ari and Beau were down there some-where too, of course.

She and Johnny had spent the past few days immersed in this 'soft start', scouting locations, using the drone and filming holding shots in different weather conditions and at different times – dawn, sunset and today, late afternoon. They had done as Ari asked and kept their heads down, circling Kit and the athletes without ever drawing too close (although word had apparently still got out that Foley had his own film crew; '*The ego has landed*,' someone had shouted at them from a distance yesterday).

But their tiptoeing appeared to have little effect. Far from Foley's mood improving, familiarity seemed only to breed yet

more contempt. When they'd come back from dinner with
Julian on their second night, Kit, Beau and Ari had already
been in their bedrooms and all left for a training run 'off site',
according to Carlotta, before the others were up for breakfast
the next day.

The next couple of days had followed much the same
routine. It was childish behaviour but Clover refused to be
riled. She reminded herself she was playing a long game; she
could afford to let a little time slip between her fingers. Besides,
they always had to come back to the chalet sooner or later,
and when they did, she made sure she was on the sofa, greeting
them with a relaxed smile and asking how their day had been,
as if they were in fact friends, as if her plans had not revolved
around them at all.

Beau was always friendly, if somewhat sheepish, like an
overgrown puppy put on guard duty when he just wanted a
cuddle. Ari was brisk and noncommittal in Kit's presence, but
Clover sensed he was doing what he could behind the scenes.
Kit still wouldn't even look at her. He would come up the
stairs, look into the kitchen to speak to Fin about whatever
he wanted to eat and – if she was around – retreat to his room.
She always watched from a distance. If she wasn't yet getting
in his face, she was making sure she was in his space.

'Yes!'

She looked up to see Johnny jump to his feet and get his
face to the camera. The clouds were breaking momentarily to
the west and the early winter sun was suddenly dazzling,
bright shafts of light blasting towards the glacier like flashing
swords. She jumped up and grabbed the giant light reflector,
holding it at the angle Johnny had wanted, watching as he
carefully, expertly moved the camera round. Not too fast, not
too slow. He knew exactly how this shot had to read when

they were editing the documentary and splicing it together, early next year.

He looked back at her. 'Got it,' he grinned.

'Worth waiting for?'

'Oh yes.'

'Worth that trek though?'

'Oh yes.'

'Good. My thighs are killing me,' she groaned. 'I think I'll have a swim tonight.'

'You should. It's pretty cool. It's got a resistance motor so you can swim against it.'

'Of course it does,' she tutted. 'What doesn't that place have?'

'A lady of the manor?' Johnny grinned, lifting the camera off the tripod and into the padded bag. 'Although maybe it'll get one of those sooner rather than later.'

'Quite.'

Johnny crouched and collapsed the tripod. 'She was practically dribbling into her soup the other night.' He zipped up the bags and stood. 'What d'you think they're doing right now?'

'Uh, *working*, I hope!'

Julian had arranged for Matty to travel to Salzburg with him today to meet the PR and marketing chief at the headquarters of their parent company, O-R Holdings. Their portfolio was mainly luxury hotels with a few high-end domestic developments, and there wasn't any good reason that Clover could see why they should need to explore 'synergies', as Julian had put it. On the other hand, Julian was a valuable contact for them. As the only person in a position to wield any power over Kit Foley, it didn't hurt to keep him close for the moment, and Matty had been more than happy to step up. Delighted, in fact.

They lifted the bags onto their shoulders and began

trudging down the steep, unbashed slope. It was difficult with the bulky equipment to carry. 'Shall we do a drive-by?' he said as they got to the piste and he strapped on his board.

'Yeah, why not?' she shrugged, clipping into her skis; they had to pass by the snowpark anyway on their way back down. They traversed in easy turns, taking care not to drag the equipment, stopping at the point where a path ran off the piste down to the park.

A short line of boarders were waiting their turns. She saw Foley immediately. He was taller than most of the others and wearing a pale beige camo set. But that wasn't what marked him out – it was his isolation in the pack that made him easy to recognize. While everyone else was giving each other high-fives and sitting in the snow in groups, there was a distinct clearance zone around him.

If he had noticed, he wasn't showing it. He was waiting for the guy in front of him to drop in, but he looked distracted, his head turning towards the far edge every so often. Clover looked too and saw Tipper McKenzie, his coach, standing by the side, giving him encouraging nods in return. Ari and Beau were standing beside Tipper, their boards off.

'Go Mikey!' someone shouted. 'Whip it!'

'Schultzy!!'

Johnny, beside her, looked suddenly alert. 'Oh shit. Is that Mikey Schultz? He's Team USA. Just knocked Shaun White off the team for the next Olympics.'

'Really?'

'Yeah. What's he doing here? He's based in Utah, I thought.'

Clover thought for a second. This was an American Olympic squad member, riding right in front of Kit?

'Get the drone out, quick,' she said, shuffling the carry-bag off her shoulder so Johnny could unzip it.

'The light's not great,' Johnny said, moving quickly.

'Doesn't matter. Just do the best you can . . .'

The small crowd on the lip of the pipe cheered loudly as Schultz shuffled into position.

'Quick, he's about to go.'

Johnny got the drone up, its eye looking down upon the action as he fiddled with the remote. Clover kept her gaze pinned on the rider but in the next instant he was gone from her sights, the nose of his board tipping down and sending him flying into a vertical drop before scooping him up and sending him up and above the other side. He disappeared back down again, popping up another second later.

The onlookers were whooping and yelling as he got bigger and bigger air. From Clover and Johnny's vantage point, he was only in sight when he breached the pipe's walls, but even from a distance they could see the athletic dynamism of his aerials, his bravado astounding. Every jump required micro-precision and utmost control; to land two degrees front or back could be catastrophic.

He finished with a complicated trick that made Johnny stand bolt upright in response, his mouth hanging open, forgetting he was operating the drone. The onlookers too were on their feet, whomping the ground and sending their cheers out over the valley.

Seemingly something momentous had just happened.

'Did you see that?' Johnny cried. 'He just pulled out a Switch Backside 1260. Like, practically *no one* can do those. White did it once, I think, at X Games.'

'Oh?' Clover watched the cacophony with vague bemusement. Snowboarding was opaque to her. See one twisty jump, you've seen them all, was her feeling. 'Watch! Foley's up.'

They waited as Kit slid into his starting position. He kept

looking over at Tipper . . . Clover frowned. Did they have some sort of code? A Bluetooth connection that enabled them to speak to one another? Because Tipper suddenly stiffened. His hands came out of his coat pockets. He shook his head firmly. Took a step forward, shook his head again.

But Foley looked away. For a few moments, he readied himself and then he was gone – out of sight down the drop that made Clover's stomach pitch. Two seconds later, he emerged high on the other side.

It was astonishing to her that people could do these things. That *he* could. Standing in front of him, having him tell her to get the hell out, and now watching him down there, flying and free . . . how could he be both men?

Wait . . .

Clover frowned as she waited for his next trick. And then the next. Was she imagining it? She glanced at Tipper and saw how he was standing – as erect as if frozen. The crowd's murmurs confirmed it for her too.

Johnny's mouth was hanging open again as he positioned the drone. 'You've gotta be kidding,' he breathed.

Clover looked back at the pipe. At Tipper's rigid stance.

'Isn't he copying Schultz?' she asked Johnny. 'He's doing exactly what Schultz just did?'

'Yeah. But he won't do the last trick. There's no way he's experienced enough yet—'

But he did. For his last aerial, Foley took off. She watched as his body exploded upwards like a rocket, doing exactly what he asked it to do . . . twisting, arching, reaching . . .

Clover's hands flew to her mouth.

He landed perfectly on the airbag at the end, not even trying to land it. But it was abundantly clear that if he had gone for the hard landing, he'd have made it. It had been stroke perfect, his point clear – he had just matched Mikey Schultz, trick for trick. He had shown his cards.

Beau and Ari were standing at the sides, bear-hugging each other and roaring delightedly in each other's faces. Even Tipper was moving more freely, pacing in small figures of eight and clapping quietly.

But no one else moved. All along the pipe, on both sides, the spectators were perfectly still, utterly quiet; arms hung limply in silent protest. Clover watched on, clearly able to see from this elevated position the passive-aggressive vibe coming from a community that was famous for its bromances. There was no camaraderie here, not for Kit Foley. Among snow-boarding's band of brothers, he was a lone wolf.

Chapter Nine

She was back on her spot on the sofa by the time they returned a couple of hours later. Beau was clutching a magnum of champagne and singing at the top of his voice, one arm draped around Ari's shoulder.

'Come on, mate,' Ari said, staggering with him over to the sofa opposite Clover and unceremoniously dropping him on it. 'He's pissed outta his head,' he chuckled to her, in case she didn't recognize what she was seeing.

Kit was right behind them and sat beside his brother's slumped form. He slapped his shoulder affectionately. 'You okay, buddy?'

Beau gave him a gappy grin. Seemingly he had drunk most of the magnum himself.

'Don't puke, all right?'

'A'ight,' Beau nodded, closing his eyes.

'Celebrating something?' Clover asked lightly, setting her laptop off her legs and onto the seat cushions. She looked at the three men's assorted ranges of happiness. Ari, animated. Beau, paralytic. Kit, while hardly falling-down drunk, nonetheless in a better mood than she had ever seen if he was allowing himself to not only remain in her presence, but actively sit across from her.

'You better believe we are!' Ari said. 'Kit pulled it out of the bag today. He executed a Switch Backside 1260 – to perfection.'

'A Switch Backside 1260?' Clover echoed. 'They're pretty out there, aren't they? Didn't Shaun White do one at X Games?'

Ari and Kit both looked over in surprise.

'How do *you* know what Shaun White did at X Games?' Kit asked, pinning her with an intent look.

'Research,' she said simply.

'You research snowboarding jumps?'

'I try to understand the world I've stepped into,' she shrugged.

'The world you've stepped into,' he echoed quietly, mocking her; his sardonic gaze drifting over to Ari, and back to her again. For a moment he didn't say anything. 'Guess you must've been pretty bummed then, when you heard I'd moved into this. All that time you spent watching Cory, learning about goofy-foot and frontside riding.' A sneer curled his lip. 'And now you've gotta start all over again.'

Clover felt her heart beat faster as Cory's name fell from his lips. It felt like a slander, a deliberate taunt. Did he see the shock of it upon her? He was watching closely, no problem with eye contact. He was an apex predator and he used it as a weapon, like boxers going nose to nose before a fight. He seemed barely to move and yet with every breath, Clover felt like she was being squeezed, tighter and tighter.

Beau giggled beside him, breaking the deadlock. 'Goofy-foot,' he slurred.

'More than anything, I was intrigued,' Clover said simply, answering a question they both knew had been rhetorical, refusing to be baited. She would counter his heat with coolness – she would be water upon his flames, mist upon his steam. 'It's a big move, switching sports. It can't have been an easy decision to take.'

'Who said I took it? Perhaps it was forced on me.'

Blame blazed from his eyes. He held her responsible for his Faustian fall. 'I don't think so,' she said evenly.

'Oh. *You* don't?'

'No. I don't think you're the kind of man who ever does something he doesn't want to do.'

'You don't know me.' He seemed bemused by the very suggestion.

'Don't I?' She didn't elaborate. Her assuredness lay in her brevity, but her heart was pounding away, deep in her chest. This was the longest conversation they had had in the five days she and her team had been here. It was the most he had looked at her – and she didn't like it.

The curl on his lip grew as, for the first time, it seemed to occur to him that she had made studying him her business. 'If you think you know me from what you read in those pissy interviews my sponsors made me do – or from Cory's trash-talking me – you don't.'

Clover started again at the mention of Cory's name, coming from him. 'He never trash-talked you.'

He gave a snort of contempt. 'Now I *know* you're lying. He hated me. He hated me more than he loved his own family.'

'What?' Clover felt outraged by the statement, her determinedly calm demeanour dropping like a wet rag. 'I don't know if that's the most egotistical thing I ever heard or the most pathetic! What does that even mean? He hated you m—?'

'Guys, guys,' Ari suddenly walked in between them, blocking them from one another's sight. 'We've had a great afternoon. Let's not spoil it. The adrenaline is still running high. We still need to come down a bit.' He looked at Kit.

'Mate, why don't you go soak in the Jacuzzi? Or I can book you a massage?'

Kit said nothing for a moment. He was still glowering at Clover – or trying to, but Ari's legs effectively blocked her from his sight. 'Nah,' he said finally. 'I'm going to work out.'

'Now? But you've been going at it all day. You heard Tipper – you're taking hard knocks out there. Just take your foot off the pedal and relax.'

But Kit got up with a shake of his head. 'I need to box.' He looked down at his brother, now asleep on the sofa. 'You'll keep an eye on him?'

Ari sighed. 'Of course, mate,' he replied, slapping Kit's shoulder reassuringly. 'You go box then.'

Kit walked off without another glance. Clover watched him go up the stairs, saw the light go on in his room.

Ari was watching her. 'He just needs to—'

'Punch the bejesus out of something?' Clover finished for him.

'Look, that was progress. He actually talked to you.'

'I wouldn't exactly call it a meaningful conversation, but if you mean he was able to tolerate being in the same room as me for more than three minutes, then yes – I guess that's progress of a sort.'

Ari's shoulders slumped, his elated mood all but gone, and she felt almost sorry for him. She didn't envy him, having to negotiate around Kit Foley's ego all day long. 'Where are the others?'

'Johnny's chilling downstairs. Matty's on her way back from Salzburg.'

'Salzburg?' He sounded surprised. 'What was she doing there?'

'Julian wanted her to meet their PR and marketing guy at the head office for all the Orsini-Rosenberg ventures.'

Ari stiffened. 'Why?'

She shrugged. 'They said something about synergies. I don't really know.'

'But why? It's JOR Clothing sponsoring Kit – not any of the other O-R businesses. He's not got the name of Rosenberg Hotel on his back – thank Christ! Why's he bringing in their head office team?'

'You'd have to ask him. Mats will give me a full debrief when she gets back but I imagine she's just had a nice lunch and a day trip. We're not exactly busy here.' She gave him a pointed look.

He got it. 'I'll keep working on him. I *have* been working on him. You can see what he's like. What makes him a winner also makes him . . .'

'A nightmare?' she finished for him. 'Ari, look. We've done all the B-roll and we've spent the best part of our first week here lying low. But that, just now, was the first time he's literally looked at me, talked to me, shared a space with me – and only then because he had a good day at the office. But as a result of sharing air with me, he's now knocking ten bells out of a punch bag. If you keep waiting for him to "come round", we're both going to be sporting impressive facial hair.'

Ari gave a surprised laugh, but Clover straightened up, getting to her point. 'So we start rolling the cameras tomorrow.'

'Tomorrow?' Ari looked horrified. 'But—'

'It's that or we walk.'

Ari gave a defeated sigh.

'We'll begin by trailing him low-level.'

'What does that mean?'

'Fly on the wall stuff. Daily life – meals, training, him on the slopes, coming back here. Everything that makes up his day. Only bedrooms remain private spaces – we won't go into those unless invited, which I don't see as necessary on this project. At this stage, we'll just run the cameras, no one needs to look at or talk to us. They can carry on pretending we're not there and go about their lives as normal. We won't start the talking heads' – Ari frowned – 'sit-down interviews', she clarified, 'just yet; those can wait a little bit longer, till Kit's further "acclimatized" to the situation.'

'But—'

'We need to start getting footage. On average, forty hours of film will give us five minutes of edited footage. We can't lose any more time. Our exec producers want this film to debut at Cannes,' she said, no word of a lie. She was now the executive producer and she needed it to get to Cannes or her flat was gone. 'That means we need to wrap by Christmas. And even then, Johnny and I will need to work around the clock to make it.' She picked up her laptop and stood up. 'So will you tell him? Or should I?'

Ari looked drained. 'Better from me.'

'I agree. Thanks.' She smiled. 'Listen, I'll tell Carlotta we'll all take our meals in our room again tonight. We can at least give you a last evening without us.'

'You really don't have to—'

'Yeah. We do.'

He sighed and nodded, knowing there was no point denying the blatant truth. Kit Foley was no further down the road to accepting this project than he had been a week ago. Tomorrow was going to be the start of a war.

She walked across the room towards the kitchen.

'Clover?'

She turned.

'I know there's no reason for you to believe this, but Kit's not the guy you think he is.'

Clover hesitated. 'Jeez . . . I really hope not.'

*

Clover Phillips How do you feel about Kit Foley making his debut this season?

Snowboard girl Kit Foley? He was the surfer, right? Oh yeah! He's hot!

C. P. Did you know he's based locally now?

Snowboard girl Is he? *(Twists around)* I hope I see him around!

*

Lift operator I think everyone's excited to see what he can bring. From what I've seen, he's pretty focused. I think he's gonna surprise a few people.

C. P. Do you think people will care about his past?

Lift operator Nuh. You gotta live in the moment. Let shit go.

C. P. Even though a man died as a consequence of his actions?

Lift operator *(Shrugs)*

*

'How's it looking?' she asked Johnny, throwing herself onto his bed and staring at his back. He was working at the pale oak desk where he had set up his laptop and editing equipment.

From here, she could see he was cleaning up some of the footage they'd taken yesterday. Johnny had managed to get an arty shot of a front of rain racing across the lake, the droplets striking the glassy water like bullets on tin.

'Okay. Hardly groundbreaking. I've imported everything we had on the B-roll and now I'm setting up my folders,' he murmured. 'I want to keep up to date with the house admin if we're going to have any chance of getting this done in time for the March submission date.'

'Well, I literally just finished explaining that to Ari, and you'll be pleased to hear we are all stations "go" from breakfast tomorrow.'

Johnny turned on his chair, looking impressed. 'How'd you pull that off?'

'I gave it to Ari straight. He just witnessed Foley giving me both barrels again, and then implied I was supposed to be grateful that at least he was talking to me!' She sank back into the pillows, staring up at the ceiling. 'He's such a dick.'

'Ari?'

'No, Foley.' She straightened her arms up in the air and examined her nails. 'I reckon Ari's actually halfway decent.'

'Ha, if you say so,' Johnny said with a disbelieving laugh, turning back to his screen. 'He's not spoken to me yet. I'm obviously not worthy. Don't you reckon he looks like an actual photofit of a psycho. I mean, what are those knife scars on his face?'

Clover pushed herself up on her elbows, bored. 'I said we'd eat down here again tonight.'

'Suits me.'

'Have you heard from Mats?'

'Yeah. She says they got delayed and are getting back late so to tell Carlotta she'll have dinner at the hotel.'

'Oh.'

'Yes. Oh . . .' Johnny murmured. 'She's definitely shagging him. And if she's not yet – she will be by the end of the week.'

Clover groaned, falling back into the pillows. 'God, how bloody depressing. We've been here almost a week and Matty's pulled the local *lord*. Meanwhile we haven't even had a drink, much less a shag!'

'I'm always available,' Johnny shrugged.

'Hey!' Clover tossed a small cashmere scatter cushion at him.

'I meant for the drink,' Johnny tutted. 'Obviously.'

Clover laughed, getting up from the bed. 'I'm going for a swim. If I can't get laid here, then at least I can get fit.'

'Okay.'

'Drink afterwards though? We could walk into town.'

'Okay,' he murmured, already distracted. She had lost him to technology.

She slipped out of the room and crossed the corridor towards her own room. She supposed if Matty was having a fling with Julian, it would mean more space for her, at least – and privacy. She changed into her bikini and grabbed a towel, throwing it over her shoulder and skipping quickly downstairs to the ground floor before she saw anyone.

She pushed on the door and— 'This isn't the pool!' The words leaped from her, almost as a cry.

Kit stopped punching the bag, his gloved hands up by his face. He let them drop as he stared back at her, panting. 'Evidently.'

He was wearing a pair of black shorts, his skin glistening with sweat. Clover felt frozen in her confusion. 'Sorry, I—'

Time seemed to bend; like glass being mouth-blown, it slowly turned and oozed away from her. His eyes travelled slowly down her. With a start, she realized he wasn't the only one half dressed.

Kit frowned. 'Is that . . . ?'

But with a gasp of horror, she was tugging the towel around her and already backing out of the room. The door slammed shut in her face and she stared unseeingly at it, her heart hammering in embarrassment and anger at her *utter, utter* stupidity. She stood there for several seconds, cursing herself.

How could she have been so mindless, walking into the gym in her bikini? When he was in there. Him, of all people.

On the other side of the door, there was an equally baffled silence. Then she heard a pounding start up again. One-two. One-two. One-two-three-four-five-six-seven.

She turned away and hurried across the corridor, pushing on the correct door and walking into the swimming pool area. The lights were dim – consciously considered again along the rough stone walls – and set at intervals along a twelve-metre black-bottom pool. But she didn't give a damn about its tranquil beauty. She was furious with herself. She dropped her towel on one of the loungers and stepped into the water. It was warm and silky, a languid embrace of her weary body. She sank up to her shoulders and immediately began to swim, face-down, a regular paced front crawl.

She went up and down the lengths without bothering to count, perfecting her tumble turns and wanting only to wear herself out. She felt discomfited and agitated. Everything felt out of sorts and jarring. It had been a hard week.

She didn't know how long she went for. The stress of the project seemed to propel her along, her legs kicking, hands reaching, her face only half rising from the water. But when she finally broke the surface, her hand reaching for the shallow end wall, she was panting hard and she felt purged somehow. Empty, again, of the anger he brought out in her.

She stood up and swept her hair back from her face, smoothing the water off her skin. She opened her eyes.

Kit blinked back at her. He was sitting on the lounger, her towel in his hands.

Clover stared at him in disbelief. How long had he been there?

'I won't interrupt. I just need to . . .' He cleared his throat.

'I need to apologize. For that.' His gaze flickered down her again and this time, following it, she saw what he had seen earlier: several vivid bruises on her arm, perfect imprints of fingertips. Her mouth parted in surprise. She hadn't even noticed them. She'd not looked in many mirrors lately.

'I was angry but I never should have . . . It doesn't excuse . . .' His mouth was small, his face pinched with tension. 'Look, I know what you think of me. And I'm many things. But I'm not that.' He swallowed. 'So I'm sorry.'

She blinked, stunned that this was happening. Kit Foley was apologizing to her? On account of a tiny *bruise*? '. . . Okay.'

He got up, saw the towel was in his hand. He held it out questioningly.

She took it blindly. 'Thanks.'

He stood there for another moment, staring at her, and everything in his being – his posture, his energy – was different to what she'd seen before. She waited for him to say something else, but then he turned.

'Kit—' It was a half call, notably tentative. She had no idea what she was going to say but this had to be the opening, surely, she had been looking for?

He stopped walking but didn't look back at her. 'This changes nothing,' he said tersely over his shoulder, reading her mind.

She watched him go, seeing the marks still on his back from his fall the other day.

The door closed definitively and quietly behind him. It was a fire door, to stop fires from spreading, and she felt the tiny spark of a truce that had glinted between them – a promise of a different way of communicating with one another – extinguish again.

*

'What time do you call this?' Her whisper in the dark was like a firework in the night sky.

'Holy shit!' Matty hissed, almost falling on the bed in shock. 'You gave me a heart attack. I thought you were asleep!'

'I was. You're not as quiet as you think you are. Or perhaps you're not as sober?' Clover reached for the switch on the table lamp between their beds. Light bloomed like a midnight flower.

Matty grinned back at her. Her eyes were bright, a little mascara smudged around her eyes. 'Whoops.' A small hiccup escaped her too, proving the point.

'Oh god,' Clover groaned, unable not to grin back too. She'd seen that expression before. 'You didn't?'

'No, no. I didn't. I'm being really good,' Matty said, tucking her legs up on the bed and settling in for a gossip. 'But it was *so* hard.'

Clover hesitated. 'Being good?' she clarified.

Matty spluttered with laughter. She was clearly very drunk. She lay back on the pillows, her arms spread wide as she stared up at the ceiling. 'God, he's gorgeous.' Her head turned to look at Clover. 'Don't you think he's gorgeous?'

'I hadn't thought about it at all.'

Matty wrinkled her nose. 'You don't think anyone's gorgeous. All you think about is work. You're dead from the waist down.'

'Thanks.'

'I mean it! When was the last time you went on a date? 1982?'

'I wasn't even born in '82, much less dating. And besides, I can't date. I have a baby.'

'*Baby?*' Matty's befuddled brain stalled. 'Oh,' she said disappointedly. 'You mean Honest Box. You know, there is more to life than work.'

'Is there, though?' Clover tried to remember when exactly she had last gone on a date. Henry? That runner guy she'd met in the park? That had been . . . August? 'Well, maybe once I've got an Oscar.'

Matty sighed, sticking one slim leg into the air and examining it. She was wearing navy tights with a little cream skirt. Clover sensed the look would have worked well in Salzburg.

'So, how was it, anyway? What did you do all day if not *that*?'

'Well,' Matty smiled, stretching like a cat. 'We began with breakfast on the train.'

'A breakfast *meeting* on the train, you mean.'

'Sure,' she shrugged. 'Why not?'

'What did you talk about?'

'His family mainly. I had no idea they had such . . . reach.'

Clover knew that this was Matty code for 'rich'.

'They've got *seven* five-star hotels! Two in Salzburg, one in Innsbruck, three in Vienna, Zell am See obvs, one in Lech—'

'That's eight.'

'Is it?' Matty frowned. 'Oh . . . well anyway, they've got *lots*. Julian's brothers run the ones in the cities but he says he's always loved being in the mountains. That's why he's so focused on developing the winter sports sides of things. His grandfather set up the first hotel here in Zell and then his father expanded the portfolio into what it is now; but Julian's determined to branch out into other ventures altogether. He doesn't want to do hotels.'

'He wants to be a fashion designer.' Clover couldn't keep the wry note from her voice.

'No! The clothing range is *nothing*. He's got such big plans, he's been hiding his light under a bushel. Did you know he was the person behind getting the snowpark built at Kaprun?'

'No,' Clover sighed, not really that interested. Julian's other ventures didn't concern them. He was Kit Foley's sponsor, that was all that was relevant. 'I did not.'

'Oh yeah. He's invested in all the machinery and equipment for building it. And he brought in these famous *parkitects*.' She giggled. 'Isn't that a great word? Parkitect. They design the snowparks especially for you. He said it cost a bomb but he's so focused on really getting the area on the map.' She dropped her voice to a stage whisper. 'He's even in talks with the World Snowboarding Federation about the town becoming a sponsor.'

'Why are you whispering?'

'Because he said it was a secret.'

'Well if it's a secret, then why did he tell you?'

Matty grinned. 'Because he *trusts* me.' This was code for: 'and therefore must love me'. 'He's such a blue-sky thinker. He has these massive ambitions and just . . . goes for them. No hesitations.'

'Yeah, you can do that when you have money to burn,' Clover muttered, rolling onto her back. 'And what about Salzburg?'

'*So* pretty!'

'I mean, the contact he introduced you to. The entire point of the trip?' Clover's hair rustled on the pillow as she looked over at her friend.

'Oh, him.' Matty's giddy smile faded. 'Yes, fine. Dull.'

'What were the "synergies" they wanted to discuss?'

Matty's brow wrinkled as she dug into her champagne-soaked brain. 'He mainly wanted to know about our marketing channels for the film: what festivals we were entering it into; our publicity plans; whether you're doing a promotional tour.'

Clover considered for a moment. 'Visibility, in other words. They want a good return on their investment in pretty boy.'

'Pretty boy?'

'Foley,' Clover tutted. 'Who else?'

Matty's mouth opened. 'You've never called him pretty before!'

Clover stared at her incredulousness, incredulously. 'I didn't actually mean it! It's a saying! And hardly a complimentary one, either.'

'Who *doesn't* like being called pretty?'

'Um, a guy who's eighty-five kilos of solid muscle and has made a career out of chasing adrenaline rushes!' She pointed a finger warningly as Matty's mouth opened again to say something else. Clover could see from the gleam in her eyes that she wanted to pull her into her overblown fantasies. They could fall together! 'Oh my god, stop! Do *not* insult me with any stupid comments. You're very drunk right now. In the morning, you'll remember exactly what he did and what it led to and why I find him utterly abhorrent. Okay?'

Matty bit her lip. '. . . Then you're not going to like this.'

'Not like what?' Alarm flexed through her voice.

'Julian wants us to have dinner tomorrow night.'

'*Again?* But we just had dinner with him the other night.'

'No. This time it's just the four of us: you, me, Julian and . . . Kit.'

'What?! . . . Why?'

Matty shrugged. 'Why not? He just wants us all to get on.'

'No.' Clover's eyes narrowed. 'He wants to influence us and make sure we turn Foley back into a hero.'

'He does not.'

'Of course he does! He is love-bombing us, to make it impossible for us to present his pet in anything other than glowing terms. He's manipulating us – with a smile.'

'It is a lovely smile.'

'Ugh, you're in lust. You're not thinking straight,' Clover groaned. 'You're no good to me.'

'It'll be *fun*.' Matty somehow managed to thread the word out over several syllables.

'It will be hell on earth!' she cried impatiently. 'Thankfully it's entirely academic. We can rely on Foley to be his usual charmless, obdurate self and refuse to go.'

'It's just so we can all bond properly.'

'*You* two can, you mean. Have you kissed him?'

'No.' The daft smile spread over Matty's beautiful face again and she gave a sigh of happy anticipation. The words *not yet* hovered, unspoken, in the air.

'This would just be some glorified double date to legitimize you two being together! Keep me out of it.' Clover reached over and switched off the light again.

'Hey!'

'Go to sleep. It's almost two and we're filming from breakfast.'

'Huh?'

Clover turned over and faced the wall, making it clear the conversation was over. She heard Matty sigh, then get up and stagger into the bathroom, the door clicking shut behind her. She closed her eyes wearily. Matty and Julian getting together really was a complication she could do without. In the cold light of day, Matty knew full well they needed to keep the boundaries clear. No matter what he liked to think, Julian was not a main player in this film; he was a facilitator and nothing more, and this charm offensive could become obstructive. Affairs always got messy and they had several weeks here yet.

But Clover also knew trying to stop them would be like shouting into the wind. The ball was already rolling down the hill, momentum starting to gather, and she knew perfectly well that the laws of attraction couldn't be stopped. Only ignored.

Chapter Ten

'Ignore us,' Clover said quickly, as Beau staggered downstairs into the living room. He was wearing just a pair of Supreme stretch boxers. He stopped mid-stride, his hands still pulling down on his cheeks as he saw the camera trained upon him.

Johnny had set up a tripod along the far library wall opposite the stairs. It gave him an easy panorama of the room, from the sofas and fire by the picture window on his right, panning round to the dining table, the lift and staircase, over to the kitchen and the door leading into the cinema room and snug. In other words, it left nowhere to hide.

'Just ignore us. Go about as if we're not here,' she said breezily.

Beau's hands swung down from his cheeks. 'Ah man! I'm wrecked though.' He did look less than well.

'I sincerely doubt this is going to be interesting enough to make the cut,' she smiled reassuringly. 'We're just letting the camera roll.'

'Have I gotta do the interview with you now?'

'No,' she smiled.

He relaxed again. 'Oh good.'

Clover watched through the lens as Beau sauntered over to the table and collapsed into the chair opposite Ari, who was already at the table, eating toast with a taciturn expression. He looked like a little boy who'd been scolded by his mother, his eyes skating towards the camera every thirty seconds. Clover knew he was waiting – and bracing – for Foley's appearance. She wondered what he had said to Kit last night about the filming beginning in earnest, and how Kit had taken the news.

'You okay?' Ari grunted to Beau as Carlotta came through from the kitchen and poured his black coffee.

'Yeah mate,' Beau nodded repetitively. From here, Clover and Johnny could only see him from behind, but he still had a bouncy puppy quality; he was never down for long.

'Up for getting out there today?'

'For sure!' Beau reached for some toast too and tore into it, dry, seemingly unable to wait. 'Umpf,' he moaned as he chewed. 'I just need to load up on carbs.'

Ari glanced towards the camera.

'Reckon Mikey'll be up there again?' Beau asked, his mouth full.

'No. Tipper had a chat with him after the session yesterday. He's heading to Saas-Fee.'

'For the camp?'

'Yeah.'

'Doing both weeks?'

'Yeah.'

'Huh,' Beau nodded. 'Guess we'll see him there then.'

'Yeah.'

'. . . You okay?' Beau asked.

Ari dragged his gaze off the camera and looked back at him. 'Yeah.'

Johnny pressed his thigh against Clover's in amusement. Beau was a natural, Ari was not.

They all heard the footsteps coming down the stairs, Foley rounding the corner a moment later. He was wearing a pair of orange board trousers, hanging low on his hips – quite possibly the ones Beau had worn the other day – and a grey thermal base layer.

His gaze went straight to her and Johnny sitting opposite, against the far wall, training the camera's cyclops upon him. He didn't so much as break stride at the sight of them but she saw the anger ripple through his eyes as he passed by. Last night's apology felt like a distant, distorted dream.

'Bro,' he said, slapping his brother on the shoulder as he went straight to the table. 'You went hard last night.'

'We had some celebrating to do,' Beau said, looking up from his breakfast and meeting Kit's hand grip.

'It was only a training session.'

'No. It was a sign of what's to come. Mikey was *so* pissed.'

'Don't know why. He landed it. I didn't.'

'You didn't try. But you would'a and he knows it.' Beau shook his head and laughed. 'You threw down the gauntlet, man. You're coming to get them and they know it. They act pissy to you now but just like on the water, they're all gonna have to fucking bend the knee to you.' Beau was jabbing his finger excitedly.

Kit gave an amused grin and Clover realized it was the first time she had seen him so much as smile. 'Well, that I'd like to see.' He slapped Beau's shoulder and sat down at the next chair beside him, pointedly offering his back to the camera.

The first snub of the day.

Clover didn't care. 'Did you get that?' she whispered to Johnny.

He nodded, and she sat back and smiled. It was the first bit of decent material they'd shot.

'. . . gone on to Saas-Fee,' Ari was saying.

'Oh yeah?' Foley sat back in his chair as Carlotta again

144

came over with the coffee and his daily protein shake. 'Thanks, Carly.'

Carly? Was the nickname a flirtation? Or a sign of affection? Either way, Clover was sure the housekeeper was blushing on her way back to the kitchen. Johnny nudged her foot with his. He'd seen that too.

'. . . be lots of eyes then. We'll have to be careful what we show them.' Foley had lowered his voice but she knew the mic was picking it up.

She watched Ari catch Foley's eye and tilt his head warningly in their direction but Foley just shrugged with his usual contempt and looked out of the window. The sky was hanging low and soft today, blocking the mountains on the far side of the lake from view and setting the town in gloom. 'The light's pretty flat out there,' he muttered, clasping his hands behind his head and stretching.

'Yeah. There's supposed to be a dump tonight but I think it's coming in faster than they expected,' Ari said, looking out too.

'I've got a rad idea – why don't we take a day off from the park and just go catch some pow?' Beau suggested as Kit got up and walked over to the window. He looked out, pressing one hand to the glass, his body silhouetted against the light.

'Lifts are still open,' Ari said, checking the app on his phone. 'But the winds are picking up from eleven.'

'We could make some fresh tracks, head back early,' Beau chipped in.

'Mmm.' Kit's finger tapped the glass restlessly as he considered the idea. He didn't seem enthused. 'I'm not feeling it. It's gusting already. By the time we get up there . . . Do we really want a day of chewing on ice?'

'Oh c'mon!' Beau cried. 'Don't be such a pussy!'

Kit ignored his brother, looking back at Ari. 'We could go to the ball pits.'

'Yeah sure; whatever you wanna do. It's all there, ready.'

Kit pushed away from the glass, nodding, looking more convinced. 'Yeah. Let's get in there then. I want to embed the 1260, get some muscle memory fired up. I can't do that in these conditions. The wind's just gonna whip in our faces.'

'Or we could just free-ride,' Beau argued. 'If the weather's against us, let's just chill and enjoy the mountain.'

'Enjoy the mountain?' Kit frowned.

'How's your brother gonna do what you're so sure he's gonna do, if he loses a day to that?' Ari suddenly snapped, making them all jump. 'Kit doesn't get to arse around like you, Beau. He has to train. People *expect* from him. Saas-Fee's in a few days and we already know all eyes are on him. You saw how it was out there yesterday! Your job is to help keep him focused, not encourage him to take a day cos you're hung.'

There was a moment of silence, tension billowing, before Beau pushed his chair back sharply and got up. 'Yeah, yeah.'

'. . . So are you coming?' Kit called after him as Beau strode from the room, taking the stairs two at a time.

Four seconds later, his bedroom door slammed. A silence bloomed in his wake.

'He'll come,' Kit said to Ari.

Ari nodded, his gaze glancing over her and Johnny again. She sensed from his expression that he had forgotten they were there. That they all had.

Ari glanced at Kit and cleared his throat. 'So we're going to do an indoor training session today,' he said to them, as though the point may have been lost on them.

'Okay,' Clover smiled. 'Thanks for the heads up, we'll bring some lighting then.'

Kit frowned, his hands on his hips. He shot a 'seriously?' look at Ari, but Ari merely gave a small shrug.

'We'll start getting ready now. Anything else we should bring?' she asked.

Ari's mouth opened, but Kit spoke first. 'You'll be fine. It's been all set up for us. It's pretty sweet down there.'

'Great,' she replied, looking back at him uncertainly. His glower had suddenly gone. She smiled and patted Johnny on the shoulder. 'We'll get the equipment ready.' Johnny lifted the camera – still on its tripod – and they left the room together, not saying a word until they were on the floor below.

'No, your room,' she whispered. 'Beau's not the only one who'll have a sore head today. Sleeping Beauty's still snoring.'

They went into Johnny's room and shut the door. 'Did you see that?' she asked.

'What?'

'He didn't shoot fire from his eyes at me. He was almost helpful.'

'Well, I'm not sure he was falling over himself to be helpful,' Johnny grinned. 'But yeah, he wasn't picking a fight. I expect it's too early, even for him.'

Clover didn't say anything. Johnny had no idea about her altercation with Kit regarding the chess game; he didn't know she was sporting bruises as dark as tattoos on her arm. He didn't know about the apology.

'That was odd though, didn't you think? With Ari and Beau, I mean. The way Ari lost his rag at him like that. It just seemed to come out of nowhere.'

'Well, he's bound to get frustrated by the situation, I guess. He's trying to keep Kit focused – not helped by us being here, naturally – and Beau's just freeloading, trying to distract him.'

'I guess.'

'I mean, Kit pulls off a Switch Backside 1260 and Beau's the one who goes out and gets hammered? Come on! It's bound to lead to tension.' Johnny walked over to his wardrobe and unzipped an equipment bag, collapsing the camera and tripod and putting them in.

'Mmm. That was a decent start though – the comment Beau made about everyone bending their knee to him? That'll go down like a lead balloon. It's all supposed to be fraternity and brotherhood out there. And Foley wants to be king?'

'I know,' Johnny agreed, pulling out some lighting filters. 'It just confirms what we all already know – Kit Foley's not a team player. Never was, never will be.'

'And it's clearly not lost on them he's being ostracized.'

'Do you think he cares?' Johnny asked.

'No. He just keeps his eyes on the prize.' Clover sank onto the bed, looking out of Johnny's window. The view towards the mountains was largely lost in the low, gathering clouds today. It looked cold out there, and ominous. She was glad they were spending the day indoors. '. . . I wonder if he misses it.'

'What?'

'Surfing. The ocean. Sun. Sand. His old life . . . It's all so completely opposite to this.'

'And yet the sport has so many overlaps. Just a different surface.'

'Mmm. Do you think he *loves* it, though?'

Johnny thought for a moment. 'I don't really get the impression he loves much, to be honest. We've been here nearly a week and . . . he doesn't smile, tell jokes, chill out. He didn't really celebrate that trick last night, he doesn't go free-riding, much less muck about in the snow . . .'

'Unlike some people,' she grinned, remembering their first day on the slopes. 'God, that was so embarrassing.' She ran her face through her hands at the memory of Kit, Ari and Beau passing directly above them in stony silence. 'He's such a fun sponge.'

'Yeah, exactly,' Johnny grinned. 'He seems sort of frozen. Or hollow, or something.'

'Maybe that's the mindset of a winner. That's what it takes to be a champion – you can't react to the little things.'

'Or maybe – whisper it – he's just incredibly *dull*?' Johnny murmured, eyes wide with the scandal of it all. 'He might look like a Roman god but maybe, underneath the tan, and the muscles, and the hair and those fricking *unbelievable* eyes . . . maybe there's nothing else.'

'Mmm, maybe. I've not seen anything to get him going,' she mused.

Johnny gave a sudden laugh and straightened up. 'Well, apart from you, of course. He really fricking hates you.'

Clover's mouth opened in protest. '*Us*, you mean! He hates *us*!'

Johnny considered for a moment. 'Yeah . . .' His face broke into a delighted grin. 'But mainly you. This goes out in your name. It's your face on the screen. Your company. I reckon if he had us lined up against a wall and only one bullet in his gun, he'd shoot you.'

'Johnny!' she laughed.

'What? You don't agree?'

She shook her head, laughing harder. 'No, I do. That's the problem. You're absolutely right. He'd so shoot me. He's a . . .' She sighed.

'He's a monster.'

She remembered his apology by the pool last night. The words almost choking him. *I'm many things. But I'm not that.* 'Yeah,' she murmured. 'He's a monster.'

*

149

Clover stopped, shivering, in the hallway as Matty darted down the stairs, looking panicked. 'Oh my god, finally! Where have you been?' she hissed.

'Filming. We decided to show you some mercy and let you sleep in.' Clover looked her up and down suspiciously. 'Why are you wearing that?' Her friend was in heels and a cream Zara trouser suit that looked like a Valentino, a slip of caramel silk peeping past her revere collar. She looked ridiculously modelesque.

'I told you last night. Dinner! I've been trying to get hold of you *all day.*'

Clover rolled her eyes. 'Well, we had no mobile signal. We've been in an industrial unit outside Kaprun. Julian's set up a soft play zone for him—'

'Excuse me,' Ari grumbled, walking past with a stony expression.

Clover stepped out of the way, biting her lip apologetically. 'Whoops.' She lowered her voice; Beau and Kit would be following in from the car any second. 'He's got a load of ball pits and giant trampolines set up in a unit for them. They've been practising jumps all day. And when I say *all* day . . .' Clover rolled her eyes. 'Problem is, there's no heating. Or anywhere to get a hot drink or some food. So while *they* were keeping warm jumping about . . .'

'Oh no.'

'Oh yes,' Clover nodded, shivering. 'And guess who deliberately didn't tell us that – on purpose? I didn't even bring a jacket because he said we were going to be inside. I am *frozen.*'

'Your lips are a bit blue . . . Oh hi Beau,' Matty smiled as Beau loped past.

'Hey Matty, you look hot.' He stopped and corrected himself. 'Sorry, I mean . . . nice?'

Matty gave a bemused smile as he got into the lift. 'Not a clue,' she mouthed.

'None.' Clover gave another shiver. 'Look, I think I've caught a chill. I need a hot bath. Could you be a pet and ask Carlotta if I could possibly have a hot chocolate? I'm too tired to walk the extra steps.'

'Clo!' Matty cried, looking appalled. 'You can't have a bath *or* a hot chocolate!'

'Is it really too much to ask?' Clover sighed. 'We gave you a free pass today. The least you could do is—'

'Julian's going to be here any minute.'

'Okay. And you're all ready. It'd only take you a minute to nip upstairs for me. Pretty please?' she said over her shoulder as she began walking down the corridor.

'Clo,' Matty called after her. 'Julian is expecting you and Kit to join us.'

'Ha! As if!' Clover laughed, turning back. 'I am almost hypothermic because of him!'

'But he's made reservations.'

'And I already told you no. Over my dead body. I cannot think of anything worse—'

'Worse than what?'

They looked back to find Kit standing in the doorway, his board under his arm.

'Nothing,' Clover said quickly.

His eyes narrowed. He could easily read a lie. He looked straight at Matty instead with a quizzical expression.

Matty swallowed. 'Kit, I'm sorry if no one's told you this – I thought Clover at least might have mentioned it today.' She shot Clover a cross look. 'But Julian's expecting you to come out for dinner with us tonight. He's made reservations at eight.'

He digested the news in silence, looking slowly back at Clover. '. . . Why didn't you mention it?'

Her mouth dropped open in surprise. 'Because I knew you'd say no.'

'Oh. Because you know me so well?' The question was a taunt. 'Just because *you* can't think of anything worse . . .' he replied, quoting her words back to her. He looked back at Matty again. 'What time?'

'. . . Now-ish?' she grimaced.

Clover saw Foley droop fractionally. He had been training for eight hours solid, refusing even to stop for them to get lunch somewhere – all to punish her, she knew it. But he wouldn't go straight out to dinner after such a gruelling session, just to spite her. Surely?

'Fine. Give me ten. I need to shower,' he muttered, leaving his board propped against the wall.

Clover looked on in horror as he stepped into the lift and pressed for the fourth floor. The doors closed.

'You have got to be fricking joking!' she hissed at Matty. She had been fantasizing about her hot chocolate and long bath for the past four hours.

Matty winced, seeing her quiet fury. 'I'll make it up to you, Clo. I promise.'

'How?' she hissed. *'How?'*

Chapter Eleven

The door closed behind them with a swish and Clover felt eyes being raised as they walked up to the reception desk.

'Linz, how are you?' Julian asked, one hand casually slipped into his trouser pocket.

'Mr Orsini-Rosenberg, always a pleasure to see you. I have your usual table ready for you.'

'Very good.' He turned and looked at them all. 'You'll like it.'

Foley said nothing. He was wearing the black suit she'd seen in his wardrobe, no tie, and was staring at Linz like the poor man was the source of all his troubles.

'May I take your coats?' Linz asked, as Matty wriggled slinkily out of hers, Julian rushing to help her.

Clover was resistant to taking off her ski jacket at all. She was still chilled from her day effectively sitting in a fridge and her three-minute shower hadn't cut it in warming her up. She gave a shiver as she reluctantly wriggled out of it, Foley making no attempts whatsoever to help her get her arm out.

'Won't you follow me?'

Linz led them through the restaurant. It had old fir planks on the ceiling and slate walls, with an open fireplace and contemporary rugs. The fawn-leather chairs were handsome and spare in the 1930s style, set around large tables draped with curtain-quality cloths. Church candles flickered on every surface, sculptured bronze plaques adorned the walls. The overall effect was intimate and grand, arresting and timeless.

The clientele was distinctly younger than in the hotel and a couple of well-heeled young families were already eating.

'It's so beautiful here,' Matty breathed, her eyes shining as her chair was held out for her.

'It's very special,' Julian agreed. 'We may be out in the mountains, but we do not have to be savages, I hope.'

Matty laughed readily. Clover forced a smile. Kit didn't bother with either. He was glancing around the room as if making a mental note of everyone who was staring at him, rounding up his enemies. He flicked his napkin open, somehow managing to infuse a note of aggression into the gesture.

'Kit, would you like to look at the wine list?' Julian asked him graciously as the menus were handed out.

Kit looked up. He seemed in no hurry to speak. 'No,' he said evenly. 'I'm sure you've got a much more nuanced opinion on that than me.' His gaze flickered over Clover, who had been forced to sit opposite him. Matty had once again bagged prime position opposite Julian. All the better for gazing into one another's eyes . . .

Clover wondered if Kit knew what was happening between his sponsor and her researcher; he'd not seen them together yet.

They listened in polite, stiff silence as Linz ran through the specials. Clover caught almost none of it. She didn't want rich, fancy food served over four courses. A bowl of chilli, eaten in the bath, would have been her idea of heaven this evening.

Julian ordered the wines as Clover looked down and smoothed the fabric of the deep cranberry-red silky viscose dress Matty had lent her – again. It was a constant wonder to her that what had seemed like such a wildly unrealistic wardrobe for a working trip in the mountains was actually on the money. Aside from her ski kit, Clover had brought leggings and a single pair of jeans.

'You look really good in that colour, Clo,' Matty said, seeing her evident discomfort and still trying to win back her good favour.

Clover frowned. '. . . Thanks.'

'Yes, it really sets off your hair,' Julian agreed. 'You should wear it often.'

'. . . Okay.' She wasn't quite sure how to respond to that.

'You are going to go more easy on me tonight, I hope,' he smiled, before looking over at Kit. 'Has she begun with interviewing you yet? Don't be fooled. She's a smiling assassin.'

Kit's frown became an outright scowl.

On Clover, too. How exactly did it help their cause to have the one man who wielded any power – and therefore control – over this renegade, tell Kit Foley that his interviewer was a smiling assassin?! 'I hardly think—' she began.

'Dear god, just don't go on camera about that night in Monaco!' Julian laughed.

Clover caught sight of the profound change in Kit's expression.

'What happened in Monaco?' she asked, looking between the two men.

'Nothing,' Kit snapped.

Julian, who had been laughing, immersed in the memory, seemed to cotton on to Kit's profound displeasure. His smile faded at the faux pas. 'Nothing interesting, Kit is right. It was just an old joke from when I was trying to sign him up. Nothing relevant to what you are here for,' he said blandly.

But Clover wasn't buying it. Everything about Kit Foley's life was up for grabs in this documentary. *Monaco*. She made a mental note to get Matty onto finding out more. Frankly, it didn't look like it would be difficult for her friend to elicit quite a few secrets from their handsome host.

'Excuse me, Mr Foley.' The alto tenor of the voice made them look around as one. A young boy, maybe seven or eight, had come over to the table and was standing beside Kit. 'Please could I have your autograph?'

Clover watched Kit, not the boy. He looked astonished by the request. Surely he was used to signing autographs? Or had he simply not signed any lately? '. . . Sure,' he said after a moment, sitting up straighter. 'Have you got something to write on?'

The little boy looked panicked suddenly, as though he hadn't got as far as thinking of that. He twisted around to look back at his parents, who were discreetly watching from their table at the other side of the room.

'Don't worry. Here, this'll do,' Kit said, winking at him as he whipped his napkin off his lap. He reached inside his jacket pocket and retrieved a fountain pen. Clover was surprised. She had fancied him a Biro man. 'What's your name, kid?'

'Elias.'

'Okay, Elias,' Kit murmured, writing a message and signing his own name across the heavy white linen in black ink.

Julian looked horrified.

'That okay?' Kit asked, handing it over to him.

The boy nodded, seeming overcome.

Kit watched him. The boy seemed reluctant to leave. '. . . You want a selfie too?'

The boy brightened. 'Yes please.' And he held out the phone that he'd been hiding in his other hand. Kit took it and activated the camera screen. He looked up at her, hesitating. She knew he didn't want to ask her for a single thing, not even on behalf of a fan.

'Here, allow me,' she said, reaching across the table for it and saving him the agony of asking.

'Like this,' Kit said, putting one arm around the boy's shoulder and holding his fist up for a fist pump with the other. The boy delightedly pressed his small fist to Kit's and they both looked straight at her through the lens.

Clover felt a jolt of the usual panic she was coming to accept as normal whenever Kit Foley looked directly at her. 'Say cheese.'

'Cheese,' the little boy replied obediently.

She took a couple of shots as quickly as she could. 'There you go.'

'Thank you. Thank you, Mr Foley,' the boy said quickly.

'No worries, Elias. Stay cool, buddy.'

They all watched as he walked as quickly as he could back to his table, his mother ruffling his hair affectionately as he took his seat and showed them his prizes.

'I think you just made his week,' Julian said, looking pleased. 'What did I say? Once a hero, always a hero! The people love you still, Kit. Just you wait, you'll see.'

Matty looked across the table at Clover, but Clover couldn't react. Kit was glowering at her again, as though Julian's words had just reminded him that it was Clover herself who had taken away his glory and good name.

She looked down with a weary sigh and began to study the menu. Their aperitifs were poured as an awkward silence stretched above their table. Even Matty seemed stilted, losing her usual dry, laconic wit in Kit's presence. He managed to convey his sullenness through body language alone and Clover could tell he was already regretting forcing this dinner upon them all. He had been too quick to try to score another goal against her, not stopping to think what it would ask of him too.

'Have you warmed up now, Clo?' Matty asked, desperate to keep the conversation going.

'The chalet is not warm?' Julian asked in surprise.

'Oh, no, the chalet is perfection,' Matty clarified. 'Clover just got a bit chilled today, that was all. She was hallucinating about having a long bath . . . then of course remembered that we don't have one!'

'Oh, yes, I am sorry,' Julian said, looking pained. 'The only bath in the chalet is in the master suite.'

'It's fine, really. A hot shower was just as wonderful.'

But Julian was looking so troubled, Clover wondered whether he was actually deliberating having baths installed to make up for the oversight. 'I'm afraid baths are a very British thing. In Europe, we prefer showers.'

'Oh, I know. Honestly, it was no problem. I didn't care that much.' Clover shot Matty a look. Why did they have to be discussing this? It simply underlined Kit's point-scoring against her today.

'Of course, I'm sure Kit would not object to making the room available for you if you really coveted a bath,' Julian offered.

The look Kit gave to Julian following this comment almost made Clover laugh out loud. Their mutual disbelief was the first thing they could finally agree upon.

Kit slowly looked back at her. 'Oh yeah. Any time, day or night. Why not?' The sarcasm was as thick as Chantilly cream.

Julian seemed oblivious to the pillorying. He chatted

away – about the weather, the wellness spa plans they had for the hotel. He tried to engage Kit in conversation about the training camp in Switzerland the following week but Kit shut down all possible threads on the matter, saying he'd never been there before so couldn't comment.

'Tell me some more about you,' Julian said, turning at last to Clover again.

'Me?' Oh god, no.

'Yes. Did you always want to become a filmmaker?'

'No. I spent most of my childhood convinced I'd be a fire-fighter or a zoologist.'

Matty spluttered on her drink. 'No way!'

'Oh yes. My big brother was obsessed with nee-nors and hee-haws, so naturally I copied him and was too.'

Matty laughed.

'You have a brother?' Julian asked. He was a master of small talk, seemingly interested in even the most mundane details of other people's lives.

'Yes. Tom. He's three years older.'

'Are you close?'

'Yes, but we don't get to see each other as often as we'd like. I travel and am away from home a lot and he lives in Geneva now, with his family.'

'Oh? What does he do there?'

'He's a corporate lawyer.' She gave a careless shrug. She didn't want to be sharing the minutiae of her family life in front of her interviewee. As far as she was concerned, the less Kit knew about her, the better.

'How does he feel about having a famous little sister?'

'I'm not famous,' Clover rebuffed quickly. 'But even if I was, he'd be distinctly underwhelmed. Tom doesn't care about stuff like that.'

'He doesn't like the perks of success? But he's in the world of big business!' Julian teased. 'Bonuses! Making partner!'

'That drives most lawyers, I know. But not Tom.'

'What then? Surely not the pursuit of justice?' Julian gave another laugh.

Clover sat very still. When he said it like that . . .

'Oh.' There was another awkward silence as Julian realized his latest blunder. She could see Matty wishing it had been dinner for just the two of them now. Clover and Kit were lumpen dinner guests. 'Well, then, that is very interesting,' he said, rallying, never down for long.

'Is it?'

'Yes. Your brother concerns himself with seeking truth and just reward.' He regarded her. 'As do you.'

Clover swallowed. She said nothing, but she could feel her cheeks colour.

'That is what you're chasing in your films, isn't it? Justice?' he posited. 'So perhaps you are still copying your big brother after all?' He grinned again.

Clover gave a tight smile.

'I wonder what made you both truth seekers?'

'Does there have to have been something?' she asked defensively. Too defensively, she realized as Kit's head – in her peripheral vision – tilted to the side interestedly. 'Besides, that's not how I'd describe what I do,' she said firmly. 'I'm just looking for good stories. Human interest features.'

'Well, you choose wisely. You appear to have an unerring instinct for what people want to see. Fallen angels, flawed heroes, struggles back to redemption . . .' Julian spoke almost as if Kit wasn't sitting right there with them. 'Do you enjoy it?'

'I love it,' she said simply. 'I can't believe I get paid to do it. Don't tell my producer, but I'd do it for free.'

Julian laughed and pressed a finger interestedly to his lips. 'Tell me why you love it so much.'

She thought for a moment. 'There's a moment in every project when . . . someone sees themselves truly. When they've come through a struggle and they . . . This sounds really pretentious but, you see them step into their power. In my Grenfell film, Bindi, this young mother, twenty-two years old, dared to apply for an Open University law degree so that she could help in the fight for their rights . . . We were with her the day she got the acceptance letter. It was amazing. After everything she'd been through, we saw the world open up for her.' She inhaled. 'I guess I'm saying I love those moments when "I can't" becomes "I can". When people defy their limits, and you see the surprise in their eyes that they could actually somehow be more.'

'That's what you're aiming for with Kit?'

Clover looked straight at Julian. 'No. Kit already knows what he can be.'

Julian leaned towards her, just a little. 'So then . . . ?'

Clover turned and held Kit's stare as he glowered at her, daring her to say what she wanted from him. 'In Kit's case, it's almost the opposite. When you already are more, where is there to go? What becomes of your humanity? The need to win comes at what cost? And are the sacrifices worth it? Because it seems to me that when we reach for the sun, we always get burned.'

'Ah yes, the allegory of Icarus – when mortals play at being gods.' Julian smiled, his gaze lifting over to Kit.

'So you think people should settle for . . . mediocrity?' Kit's voice was low. Cutting.

Her eyes met his. 'No. Not everyone, although I do think most people are happy with what mediocrity offers; it gets a

161

bad press, if you ask me,' she said evenly. 'A bigger life doesn't necessarily equate to a better life, but some people just seem to need more . . . intensity, feedback, whatever you want to call it.'

'And which camp do you fall into? Or shall I take a wild guess?'

'I don't think anyone would be surprised that I'm happy with a smaller life.'

'No,' he sneered. 'It's perfectly clear how your life's going to unfold.'

She stared back at him, hating him, as he sat back in his chair, enjoying himself. 'You'll do this for a bit. Then you'll meet a guy in a suit. You'll get a house, have kids, get fat. And spend the next thirty years having TV dinners.'

She felt stung by his withering prediction, but she wouldn't let it show. 'Well, only if I'm very lucky,' she replied pithily.

She dragged her gaze off him and back to the others. Matty was looking worried again, her big eyes wide at their unconcealed antagonism.

'Actually, I would have to disagree with you there, Kit,' Julian said, surprising everyone. 'I think Clover's future trajectory is far more aligned with yours than she's letting on.'

'Excuse me?' Clover almost choked.

'You both have trophies. You both prepare exhaustively for your goal, immerse yourselves fully in the lifestyle, commit to getting a win. Neither one of you would be where you are now without that singular vision and obsessive drive. I don't see you becoming a housewife any more than I do Kit.'

The pause that followed his pronouncement bloomed into a silence and Clover reached for her glass. She could feel Foley staring at her still. His scowl had deepened, his finger tapping intermittently on the table, one arm slung out in front of him idly, waiting to pounce on any perceived weakness he could find.

She forced herself to smile brightly. 'And I understand your trip to Salzburg was very successful the other day?' she asked, unapologetically changing the subject.

'Indeed it was.' Julian glanced at Matty. 'Martha helped more than she could know.'

'Oh?'

'Yes. In fact, it was the reason I was so keen we should all have dinner tonight. I have a rather special announcement to make.'

Julian glanced at Kit, who was looking back at him with outright suspicion; the relationship between the two men was distant to the point of out of sight.

'At ten o'clock tonight . . .' He checked his watch and tapped it. 'A little over an hour and a half from now, an announcement is being released to the press: Kaprun, and specifically the JOR snowpark, will from next year host a four-day tournament – covering Big Air, Slopestyle and, of course, Halfpipe – as an official stop on the World Snowboard Tour. JOR shall be the official sponsors and Kit, as our original signing, will be the face of it.'

Kit looked stunned. It was clear he had had no idea of these discussions. A small smile came into his eyes and as his defence weakened momentarily, Clover realized how walled up he was all the time. Now he looked like a seventeen-year-old boy being given his first car. 'Seriously?'

'The deal is embargoed until tonight, but I hope this indicates our absolute faith in you and what we believe you are going to achieve in your new sport.'

There was a protracted pause, Kit's eyes roaming over Julian's face as if looking for signs of a trick. But Julian simply waited. Kit gave a sudden bright smile, reaching across the table and grasping Julian's hand in an earnest shake. '. . . I'm stoked. Seriously stoked.'

Matty looked at Clover with bright eyes, relieved that for once, peace had broken out. Clover smiled too, but she was less taken in by Julian's extravagance. Matty had relayed exactly this scoop to her last night – and if Julian was readily spilling his secrets, was Matty spilling theirs? It was in Julian's best commercial interests to make sure they polished his star to a shine. What was Julian getting from her friend? And how?

Julian picked up his glass to make a toast – another one. 'To bright horizons.'

'Bright horizons,' Clover murmured, watching as Julian's gaze came to settle upon Matty again. New friends, bright horizons: he was having one hell of a week.

Clover watched the maître d' hand back Julian his card. She wanted to weep with happiness. It was after midnight and a seemingly endless day. The wine had gone to her head, the waiters pouring too regularly for her to keep up, and although the tension of the evening had dissipated after Julian's announcement, she still couldn't get to her bed fast enough.

Matty's nerves had dissolved too and if Kit had been oblivious to the flirtation between his sponsor and her researcher before, he wasn't now. Several times Clover had caught him openly frowning at them both when one gave the other an outright compliment or they lapsed into a seemingly private joke.

Once, just for a moment, before he caught himself, Kit had looked over at her in astonishment. Julian had just told Matty she had the eyes of La Joconde and – mouth open, his eyes burning with scorching ribaldry – Kit had automatically looked over at Clover as an ally, one of his team to banter with. Her own incredulity had matched his so that her return smile had been automatic and for a single, blinding moment, they had been united in shared disdain. In that one moment, he wasn't the guy who'd cut in front of Cory, forcing him into the water as the wave crashed down, but the hero she'd seen on the podiums and posters: dazzling, irrepressible, the world at his feet.

It had gone again in the next instant as he remembered himself, the flickering connection abruptly switched off as he turned away and demanded more wine. But it had happened and she knew they'd both felt it. For one fractional moment, he hadn't hated her. And if he could manage one, then he could manage two. The thaw had begun, she knew it had. She'd known it when Cory, after two weeks of staring at the wall in a blacked-out room with her sitting quietly on the sofa, waiting, had finally turned over and asked her the time. And she knew it now, too. Kit might never like her, but he was learning to tolerate her. She could work with that.

A waiter gallantly held out her ski jacket for her and she shrugged it on. Its pillowy warmth was an instant comfort; in spite of the rich dinner and toasty fire, the earlier chill had set in her bones and she could still feel it flickering up and down her spine. Julian had collected them earlier in his Panamera and was dropping them back at the chalet too. She would be in bed in under ten minutes.

'Oh! What's all this?' Julian asked as the door was opened onto the street.

A small crowd had gathered, some of them carrying banners. Clover, coming through, caught sight of Kit's name on one.

'It looks like your fan club has found you,' Julian laughed, looking pleased and turning back to Kit as he stepped out after them. Kit looked on with a suspicious half-smile.

It had been a surprisingly positive night, what with the young fan, Julian's news, and now—

Something, a bright, glossy streak, flew through the night and landed on them. There was a moment in which time contracted and everything held still, like a television on freeze-frame. Then Matty gasped and screamed as she saw her cream suit covered in blood. Julian looked stunned too. It had gone over his hair, his face.

What—?

He reached for Matty blindly, pulling her away from the small crowd that was beginning to encircle them. Kit. There were a dozen, maybe fifteen people, all suddenly baying at him, throwing buckets, pelting them all with . . . Clover couldn't tell what . . . old fruit? Rotting vegetables?

She blinked, trying to understand what was happening. She felt cold liquid ooze over her skin. As if in slow motion, she put her finger to it and stared at it.

She looked again at the banners. Her German was rudimentary but she could translate them well enough. *Kit Foley – blood on your hands! Kit Foley – go home!*

With a gasp of utter horror, she looked over at him. He wasn't moving. Ironically, the blood appeared largely to have missed him, landing mainly on Matty and Julian as they'd exited first. But then he moved – like a leopard leaping from a tree, he was suddenly upon them, in the very midst of the crowd, pushing them back. Several of the men staggered back, out of the way, but on others, fists were pulled back and punches began to fly at Kit. They swarmed him.

'Stop!' Clover screamed, unaware she was screaming. 'Stop!'

Several white flashes dazzled her, popping in the blackness of the night, and she saw people were taking photographs and filming them. Her hands rose automatically as she staggered towards them. 'Stop! Stop this!'

Several more people ran off, but it made no difference. Kit was still being attacked by four men. His suit jacket had ripped, his arms held back by three of them as the biggest of all punched him in the stomach, doubling him over.

'Stop!' Clover screamed, lurching towards them and into the melee. She felt the heat of the fight, the visceral tension like fibres binding them all together. Her flailing hands gripped the hair of one of the men holding him, and she yanked it back as hard as she could. The man buckled and twisted, opening up a space. A fist was heading straight for her.

'*No!*' The roar now didn't come from her. It was too deep for her body to contain. She felt the contact of bone upon bone, a terrible thrashing of limbs exploding like fireworks in the corner of her eye for several long seconds.

And then the world, closing down in diminishing circles. The last thing she saw was a pair of blazing blue eyes looking down at her. Until there was only black.

Chapter Twelve

'I think she's waking up.' Matty's voice sounded distant.

Clover tried opening her eyes but there was resistance, like pushing against a door with towels on the floor. 'Aah,' she gasped, wincing at the light.

'Clo, can you hear me?' Matty asked.

'Yes,' Clover mumbled. Her hands automatically went to touch her face but something – someone – applied pressure to her arms. 'Don't move. Try to be still.'

'Where am I?' Her words were indistinct, as blurry as her vision.

'In bed.'

Clover frowned. The voice was deeper. Johnny?

'Do you remember what happened?'

Did she? It hurt even to *think*. She felt battered. Bone on bone. The memory flashed through her, making her gasp. Startle.

Her eyes opened. Only one of them. The other—

Her hand flew to her face again before Matty could stop it. There was something soft – a dressing? – over her right eye. And her cheek came to meet her hand at an angle she didn't recognize.

She looked back at them with her one open eye. They were sitting either side of her on the narrow bed, looking down at her with concern. Matty's own face was puffy and pale, her eyes red-rimmed. Her hair was wet but her scalp had been stained red. Johnny looked sort of haunted.

'Jeez, how bad do I look?' she mumbled after a second, doing her best to reassure them.

Matty gave a laugh of relief that she could joke, but Johnny still looked dismayed.

'Mirror,' she commanded softly, looking at him.

'Oh, Clo—' Matty protested, her laughter dying in her throat.

'Mirror,' she insisted, still looking at Johnny.

'She has to see sometime,' he said pragmatically. He returned with Matty's make-up mirror.

'Well, not that side,' Matty hissed, turning the mirror around so she wasn't presented with the magnified side. Clover had difficulty looking in that thing at the best of times – and she had a feeling this wasn't the best of times.

Johnny held it up for her.

'Oh.' The word fell like a spirit leaving the body. An extinguishment of hope. She couldn't see the eye itself. It was covered by the dressing, but bruising was already seeping past its edges. Her cheek was a livid puce and badly swollen. There were a few specks of dried blood at her nostril. She hadn't thought it was possible to look worse than she felt. But apparently it was.

The image began to blur, tears gathering in her good eye.

'*That* was what I was afraid of,' Matty hissed, snatching the mirror from Johnny's hand.

'But you can't hide it from her,' Johnny whispered back.

'I'm fine,' Clover interrupted quietly, not wanting them to fight. 'It's better I know.'

They were all quiet for a few moments, as Clover tried to absorb what had happened.

'. . . I remember . . . eyes . . .' she faltered, feeling her body contract and tense as she tried to sink her mind back into the memories. 'Fighting . . .' She frowned. 'They had Kit . . . Blood.'

'Turned out to be red paint,' Matty said. 'I'm not sure what would have been better, though. Blood or paint? It's ruined the inside of Julian's car.'

'Seriously?' Johnny snapped with an anger that made both women flinch. Johnny never raised his voice. 'That's the concern?'

'No. No, of course it isn't,' she said quickly, chastened.

Johnny shook his head at her, looking like a disappointed father with his drunk teenage daughter. He turned back to Clover. 'Do you remember anything after you were punched?'

Clover concentrated, but nothing rose from the depths. Colours, but no visions, no sounds . . .

'Do you remember being in the car, getting back here?'

She shook her head. 'Should I?'

'You were in and out of consciousness.'

Clover processed that. In and out . . . 'How did I get in the car? Did I walk?'

'Julian brought the car round and Kit carried you. I called the doctor on the way up the hill. He was here within five minutes.'

'I don't remember any of that,' she whispered, feeling floored by the account of it.

'He says you've got a bad concussion. He'll be back in the morning.'

Morning? 'What time is it now?'

'Three. He told us to wake you every couple of hours.'

It was a lot to take in. She felt so groggy. Her eye wanted to close again. 'What about Kit?'

'He's fine.'

'They were all on him,' she mumbled.

'It broke up quickly once you went down,' Matty replied. 'It was horrific! What were you thinking flying into the middle of a punch-up like that?'

'I *didn't* think.'

'And you call *him* kamikaze!' Johnny shook his head despairingly again.

'I'm sorry,' she sighed, closing her eye.

'She's tired. Let her go back to sleep,' Matty said more quietly.

Clover felt a hand on her arm. 'We'll come and wake you again at five.'

'Please don't,' she mumbled. She was so tired. She just wanted to sleep and sleep and . . .

The thoughts drifted away, her body heavy, back into oblivion once more.

'Follow my finger, please.'

She did her best, but it evidently wasn't good enough. Didn't he know she was exhausted? Newborn babies had just had a better night's sleep than her, with Matty and Johnny splitting the burden of waking her in two-hour shifts.

'Hmm,' the doctor murmured, straightening up. 'I'll come back again this evening. She's to stay in bed and rest. Keep a window open; her temperature is elevated, which is concerning. Was she doing any strenuous activity yesterday, before the accident?'

'No. In fact, the opposite – she got really cold,' Johnny said, stepping forward from where he'd been standing in the bathroom door. Matty and Ari were both standing by the bedroom door. 'We were pretty stationary for most of the day and there was no heating. She thought she'd caught a chill.' He glanced at Ari.

'Hmm. Well, it's something that urges caution,' the doctor said, his English excellent but deeply accented. 'Hypothermia is known to create problems in moderate to severe TBIs; it is less well documented on mild cases. If her condition deteriorates in any way, you must call me immediately.'

The doctor looked at Ari too, standing by the wall, as he said this. Ari nodded. His arms were folded over his chest, his hands gripping his upper arms. He had been grim-faced throughout her review.

Clover wasn't quite sure why so many people needed to be present.

'When can I get up again?' she asked, surprised by how her voice sounded.

The doctor looked back at her sternly. 'You're not to get up without assistance. You're still disorientated and likely to fall. All bathroom trips must be accompanied.'

Matty grinned and winked at her.

'Depending on how well you rest today, you can start walking about tomorrow.'

'And getting on the slopes?'

The doctor looked scandalized by the question. 'Not for a week to ten days at the earliest. I would be more inclined to say two weeks.'

Her mouth parted in dismay. 'But—'

'Clo, don't worry about work for the moment,' Johnny said firmly, knowing exactly what she was concerned about. 'There's still plenty of time.'

Ari shifted his weight and looked down at his feet. Clover felt a wave of despair. They were supposed to be travelling to Saas-Fee tomorrow for the Stomping Ground training camp. It was where most of the elite athletes on the European circuit would be gathering in advance of the first event of the season

Midnight in the Snow

and it was a crucial opportunity for them to interview Foley's new colleagues: to gauge reaction to his debut into their sport and see how he was perceived. He was already ostracized here, in his 'backyard' park. They couldn't miss out on seeing how he was treated by the best of the best. What he saw as 'his' pack. There was no way she was going to miss it.

The doctor closed his bag. 'I'll be back this evening after six. Rest and stay hydrated.'

Clover nodded obediently, watching as he went out. Ari escorted him to the door. 'Fluffy bedside manner,' she muttered under her breath. '. . . I'm not missing Saas-Fee, Johnny.'

'You're not going if he says you can't.'

'Try and stop me,' she said stubbornly. 'You know as well as I do it's where we're going to get the meat for this film.' The sentence exhausted her. 'Ugh,' she moaned, sinking deeper into the pillows.

'We need to open that window,' Matty said, crossing the room and opening it a little. The cold air whistled in, chilled and pure.

'These just came for you,' Ari said, walking back in again, almost entirely hidden by a vast bouquet of flowers, elegantly potted in a pink and white striped pail.

Matty gasped, her hands raising to her mouth. 'Who are they from?'

Clover gave her a weary look. Even concussed, she knew they were from Julian. The extravagance was just his style. 'Open the envelope and read it for me, will you?' she asked quietly.

Matty happily obliged. 'They're from Julian!' she exclaimed, looking up. 'He says to get well soon.'

Clover smiled, her gaze meeting Johnny's. 'Well, that's very thoughtful of him.'

She watched as Ari settled the arrangement on her bedside

173

table, but they were so vast, there was no room for her jug and glass of water. He looked acutely uncomfortable. 'Uh . . .'

'Don't worry, Mats will sort them out,' she said quietly.

He gave her a grateful nod. He had seemed peculiarly muted throughout her appointment.

'Are you okay?' she asked him.

'*Me?*' He gave a surprised snort. 'I'm fine . . . It's just difficult looking at you . . . at what they did—'

'Honestly, I'm fine.' But their two expressions of being fine were clearly very different. 'And Kit's okay?' She hadn't seen him yet.

'He's fine.'

Fine, again. The word that said nothing, meant nothing.

He cleared his throat. 'The police were here earlier.'

'Oh?'

'I told them they couldn't talk to you till the doc had been. But they'll probably come back later. They just want to ask some questions.'

'Have they arrested the people who did it?'

'No. No arrests yet.'

Clover felt her heart beat a little faster. 'But they know who they are?'

'Not yet, I don't think,' Ari said, his mouth drawn in a thin line. 'But they're examining CCTV. Don't worry, they'll find the bastards.'

She looked back at him. She could feel his anger.

'How did they even know we were in there?' she asked, looking over at Matty. 'I mean, it's a tucked-away little place. It's hardly paparazzi central.'

Her friend could only shrug. 'Someone must have seen him going in and made a call? . . . Or maybe someone saw him giving that little kid the autograph and that attracted attention?'

Clover frowned as something else came back to her. '. . . They were taking pictures. They were filming it.' She paled at the thought of that footage being out there. 'Is it in the papers?' Clover looked at Ari. She knew the chalet received a delivery of the local and international newspapers every morning.

Ari looked away, clearly not knowing what to say.

'It is.' Clover's voice sounded hollow.

'Clo, don't concern yourself with any of that. It's irrelevant.' It was Johnny again, playing dad. 'You just need to focus on getting better.'

'I want to see it.'

'No.' Johnny was firm.

'You can't stop me. You know I'll be able to find it online anyway.'

Johnny stared at her with wide eyes. 'Fuck's sake, Clo! There's nothing to be gained from it!'

'I need to see it.' Her voice was quiet but insistent. They all knew it was impossible to stop her from finding it one way or another.

'Fuck's sake!' he said again through gritted teeth, striding from the room and barging past Ari without even thinking. The Johnny of last week would have been quaking in his boots at the prospect of just sharing space with Ari. How much things could change in a few days.

'I agree with Johnny that you shouldn't be looking at this yet,' Ari said. 'Your focus should be on your recovery. Looking forward, not back.'

'But that's just it – I don't remember much about it. There's just a hole in my mind, a few vague impressions that are more frightening without context. I have to see it in concrete terms.'

Johnny came back down the stairs and into the room. He was holding the local paper in his hand. 'It's only been reported locally so far. With any luck, it won't get picked up internationally.'

'Show me.'

Moving at what seemed like glacial speed, he shook open the paper to the front page. 'DISGRACE!' ran the headline, and below it, a large image of Kit in the middle of the melee. His arm was pulled back in momentum for another punch, his face twisted into a mask of fury, his teeth bared. He looked like an animal, the whites of his eyes making him seem crazed. On the ground, by his feet, a figure was stretched out; her face was turned away from the camera but her blonde hair fanned out over the pavement. Clover gasped to see herself, clearly out cold. Her whole body chilled at the sight of herself lying there, looking like a victim.

From the angle and – from what she could discern – the text, it clearly intimated that Kit had punched her to the ground. That he had started the fight. She couldn't remember the choreography precisely; she had only fleeting fragments, shards of images, glinting impressions that caught and then lost the light, but she knew he hadn't started it.

Clover looked up at them all. 'Has he seen this?'

Ari hesitated before nodding. 'Yes.'

'And what does he say about it?'

'Not much.'

Not much? '. . . Right.'

'I'll leave you to rest. I just wanted to make sure you were okay.' Ari's arm extended towards her awkwardly, as if he wanted to make contact but wasn't sure where. Or how.

He left the room instead.

'We'll leave you to sleep too,' Matty said quietly.

'Wait.'

Matty and Johnny turned to find her holding out a hand,

beckoning for them to come closer again. They gathered around, looking worried and anxious.

'You need to get hold of that footage,' she said in a low voice.

'What?' Johnny frowned.

'The fight. It'll need to go in the film. You've got to find out who took those pictures. Who was filming us?'

'Clo, have you lost your mind? You got knocked out in that fight!' Johnny hissed.

'I'm aware. But this is an opportunity we couldn't even have dreamed of. Kit's being mobbed in the street? How can we not include it?'

Her words were met with a stunned silence.

'Clo, he looked after you. He carried you to the car,' Matty argued.

'Okay. So he has *some* decency. No one ever said he's a psychopath. But this has to go in. This is his reality. This is how people feel about him and what he did. We can't ignore it.' Clover looked back at Matty with her one eye. 'And Mats – you are *not* to mention it to Julian. He cannot know it's going in. He's already interfering in things enough – fancy dinners, fancier flowers.'

'He's being kind!'

'He's manipulating us – keeping us on side, and you know it. But we can't be steered. This film has to be independent.'

'And is that what this is? Independent?' Johnny asked suddenly. 'Or are you just out to set him up?'

Mia's silvered face in the moonlight flashed through her mind.

'How would I even do that, Johnny? Showing that fight isn't telling a lie! It happened. We can't show something if it didn't happen, but it did and I've got the shiner *and* the t-shirt to prove it. Johnny, last night confirmed he's not welcome here – or anywhere. People don't *want* him winning medals again.' She looked back at them both. 'It's pure cinema gold. You have to get hold of that fight footage. I don't care what it takes.'

She sensed the gaze, like a prickle along her back. She turned, looking over her shoulder, and saw Beau peering in through the crack in the doorway.

He pulled himself back, but a fraction too late.

'Hey, Beau,' she said, heaving herself up and round. 'It's okay. Come in.'

'Sorry, I didn't mean to . . . Whoa.' He couldn't hide his shock as she lifted her head and he saw the scale of her swollen cheek and bandaged eye, the bruise seeping past the dressing like a shadowy nimbus. 'Fuck.'

'It's honestly fine,' she said quickly. She felt a peculiar pressure to somehow console others about her appearance. 'I feel fine.'

He looked unconvinced.

'The doc's only keeping me in bed because I've got a temperature, otherwise I'd totally be up and about. It's ridiculous really.' She saw how awkwardly he hovered by the door. 'Please come in. Sit. You're making me nervous.'

'I don't want to disturb y—'

'I'm going out of my mind with boredom. You'd be doing me a kindness, honestly.'

'. . . Okay.'

He perched at the furthest end and she saw how hesitant he seemed about being here – as if he was going against an order. Crossing enemy lines. 'Cheer me up. Give me some gossip. What's going on up there?'

'Nuthin',' he shrugged.

'Nothing at all?'

He thought for a moment. 'Well, I'm now top hundred in the Fortnite league.'

She looked at him blankly.

'It's a computer game.'

'Oh . . . You've not been riding?'

His face fell. 'Nup. Which is killing me, cos it's been dumping up there. Incredible pow.'

'So why don't you go then?'

He shrugged but didn't reply. Clover watched him. She couldn't understand why he . . .

The penny dropped. 'Is it because Kit's not going?'

He looked away.

'But he wouldn't stop *you* from going, surely? You're a free agent.'

'Just doesn't seem right, going without him,' he shrugged.

Clover stared, baffled. Why did Beau have to stay in, just because Kit was in hiding?

'Is Kit okay?'

'Oh yeah, he's totally fine.'

'So then . . .'

'He's just not wanting to be out at the moment. Doesn't want eyes on him.'

'Understandable,' she said quietly. But that made it even less acceptable to force Beau to stay in too.

'Especially when we don't know who those guys were yet. Who's the enemy, y'know?'

'Yes. It's so awful.'

Beau bit his lip, his eyes narrowing as he pulled at a hang-nail. 'Kit can't get over how they knew he was in there. He's convinced it was a set-up. Like an ambush.'

Clover frowned. 'I'm inclined to agree. It was very strange

that they found him there. *Someone* must have tipped them off. But why would anyone want to set him up?'

'To make him look bad. It's practically a sport at the moment, kicking a man when he's down.' He looked up at her sharply as he realized what he'd said. It was thanks to her that Kit's fame had become infamy. 'Sorry, I didn't mean that you . . .' He flinched at the sight of her injuries again. '. . . Ari said no broken bones?'

'No, I was lucky. Apparently!' She gave her best attempt at a grin. Winking wasn't an option. 'Lucky Clover.'

But he missed the joke. 'He could'a killed you. Kit said the guy was twice your size. If you'd hit your head going down . . .'

Her smile faded. 'Well, I'm trying to focus on the positives.'

'Are there any?'

She watched him. One of the very first things she had observed about Beau was that he was a conduit of his brother's moods: when Kit was happy, Beau was energized and relaxed. When Kit was stressed or distracted (which was almost all the time, certainly in her presence), he was jumpy and restless. 'Beau, is Kit really okay?'

'Totally,' he said quickly. 'He's just pissed off.'

'It was spectacularly bad timing,' she agreed, remembering Julian's embargoed press release. 'He's lucky to have you looking out for him. I can see you two are really close.'

Beau looked momentarily startled by her tentative foray into a more personal topic. But she kept her eyes down, as she picked lightly at the embroidery on her duvet cover, so as not to appear challenging. 'You're lucky. I miss my brother. I don't get to see him anywhere near as much as I'd like.'

'No?'

'He lives in Geneva so . . .' She smiled. 'Ironically, I'm

closer to him here than I have been in years and there's still no time to meet up.'

'You could get over there surely, for a few days? Or he could come out here? Does he ride?'

'He's a skier, like me,' she said with a rueful grin.

'Agh, never mind. I guess he can still have *some* fun,' he teased.

'You really love boarding, don't you?' she asked, watching him closely. 'Even more than surfing?'

He shot her a sly look from under his lashes. 'Don't tell Kit.'

Clover smiled, but she wondered why it had to be a secret that he loved the snow more than the surf. Moving into this arena had been Kit's idea, after all. Why couldn't Beau love it too? 'You do look completely natural up there. So in your element.'

'Feels like it's in my blood.' He looked around the room idly. 'Maybe it is. We boarded before we surfed. Our dad taught us.'

'Oh, really?' She mentally sifted through the profiles and timelines Matty had spent the summer preparing.

'Yeah. Everyone thinks we're Aussies but we're Kiwis, just with Aussie accents – did you know that?'

'I did, yes,' she smiled.

'Yeah. We were born in Queenstown, South Island, twenty minutes from Coronet Peak. We didn't move to the Gold Coast till I was five and Kit was ten—'

Clover quickly did the maths: that would have been straight after his parents' divorce.

'—and Kit ate up being an Aussie. He just went headlong into the surfing thing. Got so good, so quick. I always just followed him, of course – whatever he did, I did.'

'But snowboarding was really your great love?'

181

'Hey, I was just a toddler when I was first strapped on. What did I know? But there must have been some muscle memory there, I guess. It's felt so natural being here. Like it was always meant to be.'

'Well, maybe it was.'

'I dunno.' He looked down and Clover could see the guilt on his face. They were here because his brother's life in the surfing world had fallen apart, refugees from another sport. He wouldn't countenance the thought that his destiny to board came at the cost of Kit's destiny not to surf.

He stared into space and Clover wondered what a half-life it was for him, to be perpetually living in his brother's shadow. If he wouldn't even hit some powder without Kit . . . She remembered his unexpected blow-up at Ari the other morning, as his wishes had been subverted to Kit's training regime. He almost subsumed himself . . .

He jumped up suddenly. 'I should let you rest. I never meant to disturb you. I just wanted to check you were okay.'

'That's really good of you, Beau, thanks,' she smiled. 'I appreciate it.' It was more than his brother had bothered to do.

'Let me know if you need anything?'

'Of course.'

He gave her one last look and shut the door behind him.

Clover settled back into the pillows thoughtfully. Her mind had caught on something he had said – about Kit feeling he'd been set up. Ambushed. *Were* there people out to make Kit look bad?

Because if so, she wanted to meet them.

Chapter Thirteen

'No! You're supposed to be in bed!' Matty said, barring the door.

'And if I don't leave this room, I will go mad!' Clover argued, simply tickling Matty lightly on the waist to get her to drop her arms. She walked past and out into the hall, turning to go up the stairs. That alone felt thrilling. She felt like an escapee – to see another, different set of four walls! She had spent three full days in bed obediently following doctor's orders but her temperature was normal again and enough was enough. She had to move. She had to work.

The dressing on her eye had finally come off but the eye was still swollen shut. It was almost pleasingly gruesome – some of the swelling had gone down, but it was a very deep plum colour that bled into a curdling yellow at the edges. Clover was of the view that if she had to have an injury, it ought to look as bad as it felt; there was nothing worse than feeling grim while looking great. Matty could scarcely maintain eye contact, which she took as a good sign.

'Well, I'm walking behind you in case you fall,' Matty said sulkily.

'If I do fall, I don't fancy your chances for being strong enough to catch me. Maybe just leave a pillow at the bottom of the stairs?'

'Ha bloody ha. You know, your humour can be quite cutting sometimes. You're like the patient equivalent of an angry drunk.'

But Clover wasn't listening. A little of her gung-ho ebullience was leaving her as she realized how dizzy she felt. She put her hand on the wall to steady herself as she got to the top step. Carlotta was walking through to the kitchen with a vase of flowers that needed refreshing and she almost dropped it at the sight of Clover, battered and bruised, suddenly standing there. 'Sorry, Carlotta,' she said quietly. 'Didn't mean to startle you.'

Matty had been bringing all her meals down to her, so the extent of her injuries had been hypothetical to the housekeeper till this point. To Kit, too. He still hadn't seen her. Not once, in all the time she'd been lying in bed, had he had the decency to look in and just ask if she was okay. Everyone else had bothered; Ari, Beau, even Julian had dropped in . . . It was basic civility, but even that was clearly too much to ask. Kit Foley was fine and he didn't give a damn that she wasn't. He was probably even pleased. He probably thought she deserved it.

Carlotta gathered herself admirably. 'Ms Phillips, I thought the doctor said you were supposed to be resting still?'

'He did, but as I've just explained to Mats, I'll go insane if I spend another minute in bed. I thought I might sit on the sofa and enjoy the view for a bit instead? I can rest there.'

Carlotta looked, open-mouthed, back towards the other end of the room. 'Of course. Let me light the fire for you. It is ready to light.' Still holding the vase, she hurried back from whence she'd come, putting down the flowers and kneeling in front of the fireplace with the matches.

Clover followed her slowly, her hands held out, down low, not wanting to bump into any side tables or—

'Oh, hey!' she said, noticing Beau and Ari sitting at the

table, eating lunch. Beau's mouth dropped open now he saw her without the eyepatch.

'Fuck.' The word escaped him in a slow exhale.

'Don't worry, don't worry,' she said quickly. 'All fine,' she lied. The headaches for the past few days had been blinding.

No Kit, she noticed.

'Clover, you don't look like you should be up.' Ari looked concerned, rising from his chair.

She stopped him from protesting further with an outstretched arm and a smile. 'It was just one hit.'

'Yeah. That would've floored *me*.'

Matty chivvied her over to the nearside sofa, where Carlotta was arranging some of the cushions for her. 'I'm really fine,' she protested as Matty pushed down on her shoulder, forcing her to sit.

'I've seen octogenarians climb stairs quicker.'

'I was just a little dizzy, that's all, but it'll go now I'm moving about normally.' She was irritated that Carlotta had set her up on this sofa. It had a better aspect over the lake and she blankly registered that it was snowing – but it also meant she had her back to Kit's glass bedroom wall.

Lying in bed for three days solid, she had had nothing else to do but listen to the comings and goings of the chalet – and there really had been no goings. As Beau had told her – and Johnny corroborated – no one had gone outside once. No riding, no jumps. Not even a trip to the shops, a cafe, a bar . . . Beau and Ari had simply sequestered themselves in the snug, playing computer games as they waited for Kit to emerge from his room; but he was still lying low. Still sulking. Matty had told her there had been some journalists hanging around outside the gates for the first couple of days, but they had slunk off when it became obvious their quarry wasn't going to show his face any time soon.

Johnny had been taking full opportunity to 'get ahead' with the editing in his room, while Matty – unable to work in the bedroom where Clover was recovering – had followed up on Julian's offer of a room at the hotel. She had been spending most of her days working there, making the sensitive calls as she researched Kit's past that couldn't safely be made in privacy at the chalet.

If she had hoped working at the hotel might mean extra time with Julian, though, she had been disappointed. Following the fight, he had found himself in the midst of a PR fiasco. There had still been no arrests – the police were of the mind that the 'perpetrators' had come from out of the area, which only further begged the question of how they had known Kit was in the restaurant in the first place. Clover's money was on the restaurant – either a guest or a member of staff.

Unfortunately for both Julian and Kit, the news had leaked significantly further than the Salzburg region after all. The video footage had gone viral online, and the stills were being carried extensively in the Austrian national press and the British, Australian and American tabloids.

The timing couldn't have been worse for the announcement of Julian's collaboration with the WST. All embargoed press reports had been released just several hours earlier that evening, in time to make the morning headlines. Unable to get the genie back into the lamp, Julian instead was struggling to create a damage limitation strategy – but what spin could be put on his top-dollar signing and the face of his new venture, already a discredited public figure, brawling in the street, weeks before his new professional debut?

It crossed Clover's mind that perhaps it wasn't Kit they were trying to sabotage, but Julian. Was a rival determined to shut him down before he'd even got up?

The only mercy in the entire fiasco was that thanks to the way her hair had fallen, she hadn't yet been identified. No one had pieced together that she was the filmmaker responsible for the vehicle that had brought Kit's actions to the world's attention. And nor must they, not before she was ready . . . *She* needed to control the message. This collaboration was already controversial enough.

'Would you like a hot drink? Something to eat?' Carlotta asked.

Clover looked up in surprise. She had become lost in her thoughts. 'A coffee would be lovely, thank you.'

She watched Ari and Beau head back into the games room. It looked like Johnny hadn't been exaggerating when he'd told her there was nothing going on up here, that she wasn't missing out.

'I still don't think you should be up,' Matty said, watching her watch them. 'You're all spacey.'

'Stop. I'm fine . . . Game of backgammon?' She wasn't going anywhere near the chess set.

Matty tutted but retrieved the board for them. She beat Clover three times straight, then gave her a pointed look. 'I can never beat you that easily.'

'Well, now you have.'

Clover sighed in frustration. How long was he going to stay up there? She turned and looked straight up at the glass wall. There was no movement that she could see. Was he even in there?

'I'm going to go back to bed,' she said, agitatedly getting up again. Matty jumped up to help her but she held out a hand in a firm 'stop' gesture. 'Really – I'm fine. Just stay there. I'm going to take the lift, but if I need you, I'll call you.'

Matty gave up fighting with her and let her walk over to the lift unassisted. Clover stepped in – but she didn't press to go down. She felt a rush of blood to the head, sudden warmth in her cheeks.

The doors opened with a ping again twelve seconds later and she drew a steadying breath as she took in the sumptuous creaminess of the top floor. She stepped out, not sure what she was going to say. Not entirely sure why she'd even come up here. Yes, she was angry at him. She'd taken a punch for him and he couldn't even be bothered to check she was okay? She didn't even need him to mean it! The mere pretence of civility would suffice! But what was she going to do? Demand an apology? Demand he ask after her well-being?

She went to knock on the bedroom door but it was ajar and she hesitated, feeling an overwhelming urge to just look in and catch him – what? Sleeping? Sulking?

She peered around the doorway. The scene that greeted her couldn't have been any more different to the one she and Johnny had found when they'd first crept up here, a little over a week ago. The bed was a tangle, clothes everywhere, dirty plates and beer cans on the floor. The room smelled stale, and she could see blood stains on the carpet.

She stepped in and looked around in horrified amazement. If this private space was supposed to be an indication of his mental state, it wasn't looking good.

'What do *you* want?'

She whipped round at the sound of his curt voice. Kit was standing in the doorway to his bathroom, a long towel wrapped around his hips, steam escaping past him.

They both recoiled at what they saw. She knew how she looked after one punch, but he . . . he had been hit multiple times. He had not one but two black eyes, with a dressing across the bridge of his nose. He had a split lip, there were multiple bruises across his torso, his right hand was strapped up and a bright white bandage – freshly reapplied, seemingly – wound several times around his ribs.

She couldn't speak. He was the very definition of *not* fine. How could everyone have told her that he was? She stared, on and on in horror, realizing that she had come up here to shame him for not coming to see her; that at some level she had wanted him to see what had happened to her, in his name. She had wanted him to be appalled, disgusted, by what he made people do.

It had never occurred to her that he might have come off worse.

Her voice was a pale shadow. 'I came to see how—'

'Get out.'

She blinked at the harshness in his voice. 'But—'

'I said get out.' He took a step towards her and she instinctively stepped back. He saw it, her fear of him. He stepped back too. 'Get out!'

She rushed from the room, bumping into the side of a chair in her hurry. She gave a small cry of panic; she couldn't gauge width with only one eye, much less when it was filling with tears.

She fled the room and ran to the lift. There was no chance of taking the stairs. His roughness had undammed her belligerent defiance that she was absolutely fine, and the tears were flowing freely, unstoppable. The very sight of him had reminded her of the horror of it all – the heat, the energy, the hatred, the power. The feel of bone upon bone, one human crushing another.

She heard the lift open and she fell in, her hands blindly pressing any button, all the buttons. She didn't care where she ended up, just so long as it wasn't here.

Chapter Fourteen

Restaurant owner The waiting staff noticed he was very quiet at the table. He didn't seem to want to bring attention to himself, I think. Although a young boy asked for his autograph and he obliged. Not all stars do that when they're out for dinner.

Martha Marks Would you say he was intoxicated, or in any way agitated, when he left your restaurant?

Owner He was . . . more animated than he had been. But I wouldn't say he was intoxicated . . . It was a shock to see everything go off the way it did. One moment we were getting their coats, the next we were calling the police.

M. M. Did you see how it started?

Owner Not really. A diner near the windows had made us aware a small group of fans had gathered and was waiting for him outside. But we had no jurisdiction to move them on from the street, and after he had given his autograph to the boy, we assumed he would be happy with it anyway. He and his party paid and left, the door closed and then we heard shouting. I looked out and saw him start throwing punches. It was as fast as that.

*

Elderly lady He's a disgrace. He should be banned from the town. And the sport. All sport! Once a thug, always a thug!

*

Chairlift operator I dunno, it's like he's got some self-destruct button. Why get announced for this massive deal, and then launch a fist fight? (*Taps his head*) Ask me, he's got a screw loose.

*

Boarder Put him back in the water and point his board towards Australia. They can have him back. He's not welcome here.

*

Another week passed in quiet lethargy. The extent of Kit's injuries meant training, or even getting on the snow, wasn't possible and the Saas-Fee trip had had to be pushed so far back, it was now in doubt if they would even go at all. Clover had a feeling of being under house arrest. Only Matty and Johnny ever went out, to film – each time drawing looks of outright suspicion from Kit and concern from Ari – getting short interviews with people on the street about Kit's ambassadorship of their town. What they came back with was stunningly negative. The fight, and the resulting wave of sensationalist press, had stuck in the craw of this conservative town. Tourism was its lifeblood. Zell am See was known as the Megève of Austria; it couldn't and wouldn't become known for 'loutish behaviour' and 'snow yobs'.

But Clover was frustrated as she watched the playbacks each day, noting the questions that *weren't* being asked. Opportunities were being missed to get harder-hitting material. People were angry! Appalled! They should be capitalizing on that high emotion; Kit was living down to expectations, but Matty wasn't a journalist, and half the footage involved her admiring someone's coat or petting their dog. Johnny wasn't pushing Matty on it, either – he was purely a visuals man – and Clover still felt troubled by his reluctance the other night to go in hard on Kit and include the fight footage. If he would willingly leave that out, what other material was being missed?

Clover was itching to get back out there herself, but there was no way she could; her blackened, bloodshot eye was still too alarming for public scrutiny, not to mention it made a direct connection with the fight. Instead she spent most of her time with Johnny when he got back, the two of them working in his bedroom together editing the footage and cleaning up the files they did have, cutting them down to pithy soundbites.

Poor Johnny looked wrecked. He was pale from spending too many hours indoors and staying up late, working on screens. Clover couldn't keep up with him. Her bruised eye tired easily from the blue light, a low-grade headache niggled constantly and settled sleep was evasive.

Everyone was jarred, it seemed, and the atmosphere in the chalet was tense. Kit – leaving his room now, at least – was prowling like a wounded tiger, snapping at everyone and spoiling for arguments with Beau and Ari. He looked rough-shaven and moved stiffly. She supposed it would hurt too if he tried to laugh, but there was no chance of that. The fractional thaw she had sensed in the restaurant, as he had begun to relax into good news and even better wine, had frozen solid once more. He had scarcely looked at her since she'd intruded into his room and she could tell from his bristling hostility that he held *her* responsible for the fight, and its fallout. She could guess at his logic – her film had vilified him and therefore galvanized his attackers.

Clover was more than happy to keep out of his way. After the way he'd thrown her out, she couldn't muster the energy it took to put a smile on her face and pretend she was friend, not foe. She felt physically and emotionally beaten up and was beginning to feel worse as the days slipped by without a single arrest being made. Kit's face was all over the international press – but somehow these people had escaped as anonymously as they had arrived.

The only bright spot was that Matty had managed to get hold of the fight footage. It had been widely shared in the public domain, and whoever had taken it clearly had no intention of claiming copyright. But there was precious little else to be happy about; they had zero source material of weight, just some angry locals for B-roll filler, and now they had lost a key week of interview opportunities in Switzerland. They had yet to have a single sit-down taping with even Ari or Beau. Clover had been trying to establish trust with them first, but time was fast slipping away and no one was growing any closer.

Johnny and Matty had gone up to the snowpark after lunch to get some more material from the other local snowboarders. Clover was still pressing them hard to find out – now that the dust had settled a little – how Foley was regarded in light of the fight, and in view of the fact that his face was supposed to represent their town and sport on the world tour.

Johnny had gone out reluctantly, in a gloom of frustration, and Clover knew that whatever they came back with today, it wasn't going to bring any meat, any heart to this film. There was a gaping great hole at the centre of it – there were too many delays and too much tiptoeing around a hostile subject. There were only a few people whose opinions actually mattered and every time she thought she was inching closer, something happened to repel them again. But she couldn't go in too early. Regardless of the ticking clock, she knew she had to wait. She might only get one shot with each of them – Tipper, Ari, Beau, and of course Foley himself. There couldn't be multiple takes; to do reshoots and to repeat questions would be to give them time to rehearse and finesse their answers – the worst thing that could happen. She needed them firing off their instincts, she needed them to be raw and unguarded and shooting from the hip.

Clover looked at herself in the bathroom mirror. She had never – literally never – looked worse in her entire life. The swelling around her eye socket had now dissipated and the bruise had faded to a ghoulish yellow that was almost imperceptible in low light, but she looked drawn and worn down. At least she would be able to cover the shadows with make-up now, she thought, pressing the area gently with the pads of her fingers. Then she could get outside again and escape this gilded cage. Just to go for a walk, a coffee . . .

She closed her eyes, desperately wishing she was back in her London flat, wandering around in her underwear and over-watering her plants. She wanted to have brunch at Bluebird, watch a film at the Picture House, get plastered at the Duke of Cambridge. She wanted to be able to walk into a room and not feel despised by the people sitting in it. She wanted to go for a run in Battersea Park, go shopping on the King's Road, get her hair done and maybe – blow the doors off! – her nails too.

She bent down and splashed cold water on her face. It felt good on the bruise. Diminishing. She stared at her reflection in the mirror. Perhaps she should go for a swim? It would do her good to move her body. She could feel her inertia beginning to depress her mood.

She changed into her bikini and grabbed the towel, walking carefully downstairs. Her balance had fully recovered once the eye patch was off and she walked into the pool room, immediately feeling the warmth and humidity against her bare skin.

She dropped her towel on the lounger and—

She froze.

There was a body in the water, halfway along. It was face-down and floating, arms and legs limp, spread apart.

It was Kit.

Clover cried out in horror. She ran down the edge, diving in at a shallow pitch. The depth was less than two metres but there wasn't even time to jump and duck dive. Her arms reached for him, encircling his chest, as her feet found the floor and she pushed up towards the surface . . .

Even before she could take a breath, he tore free of her grasp; she saw him wince as the violent movement jarred his bruised ribs.

What? She stared at him in disbelief.

'*What the fuck?*' He was panting, breathless. But definitely not drowned. He hadn't inhaled any water.

'I thought . . .' She trod water in utter bafflement, trying to make sense of what was happening. Why had he been lying there like that if . . . ?

'Thought what?!' he demanded. He looked wild. Again. He was furious with her. Again. 'That I'd *drowned*?' The word was mocking.

She felt her anger burst through at last. She couldn't do it anymore – pretend to take the high road. He was insufferable. 'Yes! What was I supposed to think?' she cried. 'You were just lying there!'

'You actually thought I had drowned? In a fucking *pool*?'

he sneered, looking back at her. 'Yeah, well, I guess you would think that. Wishful thinking?'

'What?' She could hardly believe what she was hearing.

'Kit Foley found drowned! What a headline! What a fucking coup!'

'Don't be so ridiculous!'

'You could have got live footage! Brought Johnny down here with his camera! There'd be your ending! Got what he deserved in the end, right? What goes around comes around! First Cory, then me!'

'You're disgusting!' she cried, swimming away from him. She couldn't stand even to look at him. She tried to put a foot to the floor but it was too deep, the water closing over her head. She surfaced again with a gasp. It sounded like a sob.

'Is that what it'll take before anyone forgives me?' he shouted at her back, not giving up as she staggered away. 'I need to fucking die too?'

She stopped at the words and turned back at him. His voice had cracked and he was staring at her with a different look. The wildness, the anger, the contempt had shifted into some-thing else.

She stared at him. He wasn't joking. He wasn't trying to repulse her.

'Of course not.' Her voice was quiet and thin with shock. 'Kit, no. No one wants you dead. You can't honestly believe that?'

He looked away; she could see the tension in his jaw as he tried to draw back. To hold back. She could see he felt he had said too much, revealed himself. He shook his head just once and began wading back to the shallow end; he was unable to pull himself out at the sides, the bruises on his ribs still vivid on his torso, the shadows of the punches that had rained upon him.

'Kit!' she said, reaching for him with her arm as he went to pass her, but he shook her off like a fly on a horse.

'*Don't* pretend to give a damn.'

She lunged in front of him, blocking his way. 'I'm concerned! How can you think anyone would want that to happen to you?'

He stared back at her. 'Just admit it. You'd be glad.'

'No!' She shook her head. 'I wouldn't. Of course I wouldn't.'

He stepped closer to force her out of the way but she didn't move this time. She wouldn't let him bully her again, using his size to intimidate her.

She could feel the hairs on his leg against her skin underwater and a moment contracted as they processed their sudden proximity to one another. It felt dangerous to be that close to him. He was clearly not okay and experience had shown her he was unpredictable at the best of times.

He stared down at her. 'I know you're a *good* person, Clover.' There was a curl to his lip. 'You're everything I'm not. You want justice and rainbows. You tried to save me in that fight. You tried saving me just now. It's your instinct, you can't help it.' His voice was low and flat and sarcastic. 'But a part of you, deep down inside, also believes I'd deserve it. Just admit it.'

She shook her head again. 'No.'

'Just say it. You hate me.' He was completely still and she had that feeling of the ominous calm in the seconds before a calamity – birds flapping from the trees before the earthquake; the sucking back of the ocean before the tsunami's charge . . .

'No.' She could feel her heart clattering inside her chest, panic surging, confusing her.

'You hide it from the others, but I can *feel* it. You hate me.' He was so close now, their bodies swayed towards one another by the movement of the water. She could see the droplets on his eyelashes, the faint scar on his lip, the yellow bruises that matched hers. She could feel his heart pounding beneath his chest, as fast as hers.

'No.'

'You hate me.'

She couldn't stop staring at him, staring at her. What was happening? He didn't have a hand on her – not this time – but his gaze was on her mouth and she felt as caught as in a vice. She couldn't step back, move away from him.

'You hate me.'

He could see right inside her. Suddenly she knew it. She couldn't lie to him.

She nodded slowly. 'Yes. I hate you.' The words fell from her lips and they were like the springs on a gate, letting the hares run, because in the next instant, she was kissing him, or he was kissing her; they had moved in complete syn-chronicity, with an anger, an urgency she had never known. His lips were rough, his stubble harsh against her skin. She didn't care. She wrapped her arms around his neck to pull him closer, kiss him harder. It wasn't enough.

She felt his hands lift her easily and she wrapped her legs around his waist, gripping him as tightly as she could. He took two, three steps to the side of the pool, pushing her back against the wall, pushing against her. She felt his mouth on her neck and shoulders as she gasped for breath. Her entire body was trembling. She wanted to scratch him, bite him, consume him.

'I hate you,' she whispered as she felt his fingers move her bikini bottoms to the side.

'I know,' he breathed, making her cry out as he began to move inside her. 'I hate you too.'

'Honey, we're ho— Oh!' Matty's pseudo-American drawl died midstream. 'What's happened to *you*?'

Clover looked up from the end of her bed. How long had she been sitting there? She was still wrapped in her towel. Her bikini was almost dry but she couldn't stop shivering.

'Shit, Clo, what's happened?' she asked, dropping her bag as Johnny shut the door behind him.

Clover blinked back at them both. How on earth could she say it? She still couldn't believe it herself. She couldn't give what she'd done a sound, a shape, a body, a heft.

Matty crouched down in front of her. 'Clo? Do you need me to call the doctor? Is it your eye? The headaches?'

She shook her head, feeling so . . . stupid! What had she done?

'Clo, you've got to say something. You're worrying us,' Johnny said, sitting on the end of Matty's bed.

She stared at them both for what felt like an eternity. Johnny was right. She knew she had to tell them. She had to explain why they couldn't stay here now.

'What's that rash?' Matty frowned, brushing the back of her hand against Clover's jaw. She realized in the next instant. 'Wait—'

'I slept with him.'

A thunderclap of silence rang through the room.

Johnny gave a laugh. 'What do you mean you . . . you . . . ?' The laughter faded with the initial shock. '. . . Who?'

She blinked. They all knew perfectly well there was only

one 'him'. There was only one person with the power to blast her world apart like this. 'Kit.'

Matty's hands went to her mouth as she rocked back on her heels.

'There's a punchline . . . right?' Johnny asked, staring at her in abject disbelief.

Clover shook her head, absorbing their stunned expressions. They were right to be horrified. There was no other response to this. It was shocking. Unimaginable. How could it have happened? She still didn't know.

There was a long, long pause. Clover was aware her friends were thinking hard and fast, trying to process the bombshell. She'd had an hour and a half to think on it and it still made no sense.

Matty's hand found hers on her lap; she was looking at Clover with an expression Clover had never seen before. 'You need to be honest with us . . . What . . . what happened? I mean, did he . . . ?'

'No! He didn't force me, if that's what you mean,' Clover said quickly. 'It wasn't like that! I wanted it to happen. In the moment, I . . . I wanted *him*.' Her face fell. The words were incredible to her. How could she even be saying them?

Matty looked even more horrified.

Clover got up from the bed, unable to bear their stares. Her hands kept going to her head as if, if she just squeezed hard enough, sense would come to her. 'I don't know what happened! I just went to go for a swim.'

They looked back at her, waiting, and she realized she had begun.

Her shoulders slumped. 'I went to go for a swim and I found him lying face-down in the water.'

'*What?*' Matty yelped.

'I know! That was what I thought! I thought he'd drowned – slipped and knocked his head or something. It looked so awful.' She swallowed. 'So I jumped in. Obviously.'

'Obviously,' Johnny nodded.

'But he hadn't drowned. And instead he was furious with me. He was . . .' She frowned. 'Actually I still don't know what he was doing.' She looked back at them both. 'He really looked dead.'

Matty waved a hand dismissively. 'Fine. Go on.'

'Well then he started shouting at me. Said, didn't I think it was a shame that he wasn't dead? That I thought he deserved to be dead.' She looked back at them both. 'He was so . . .'

They waited for her to supply the word.

'So mad?' Matty prodded her.

'No. So sad. He sounded broken.'

Neither Johnny nor Matty stirred as she sank back into the memory of it. She could still see him forcing back the emotion; the forward set of his jaw, the heaviness of his brow . . . It had been a side to him she'd never seen. A side he'd hidden again in the very next breath.

She frowned. 'But then he . . . switched it onto *me* and started saying I hated him. That he knew I did and I had to say it. I had to say it. He just kept on, forcing me to just admit it. And the thing was, I couldn't lie because I could see that he knew the truth. Because I do hate him. I hate him so much. I hate everything he did to Cory and everything we've seen he is. I hate him almost more than I can bear.' She looked away, staring into space. 'And saying it to him . . . finally being honest at last after all these lies and this . . .' Her hands gestured hopelessly at her bruised face. 'It felt like a sort of release. We could just as easily have been punching each other.' She looked back at her friends. 'I hate him and he hates me.'

Her voice trailed off and no one spoke for several minutes. Johnny dropped his face in his hands and gave an exhausted sigh. Matty sank onto the bed and let her head hang, her elbows on her knees.

'Right, well . . .' Johnny said finally. His voice was barely audible, all of them trying to take in the afternoon's unexpected twist.

'I'm so sorry,' Clover whispered.

Johnny sighed again. 'I just didn't see this coming.'

'Nor did I! You have to believe that.'

He looked up at her. '. . . So how did you leave it with him?'

'Huh?'

'Well, was it all hearts and flowers? I take it from the way we just found you that he's not taking you for dinner anytime soon?'

Clover looked away, remembering his lips on her shoulder, his breath in her hair. The moment of perfect stillness immediately afterwards, just the hammering of their hearts, one against the other as madness gave way to sense. 'We didn't say anything. He just left.'

'Bastard,' Matty breathed.

'Well, what was there to say?' she said defensively. 'He was as stunned as I was. I didn't want to *talk* to him. It had happened before we knew . . .' She dropped her face in her hands. 'God, how could I lose myself like that?'

'Hate sex,' Matty said coolly. 'It's pretty much the best there is. Any girl can lose her shit over a guy she despises. There's nothing like it.'

Clover and Johnny's heads whipped up in surprise.

'What?' Matty shrugged. 'I had three months of the best sex of my life making and breaking up with my ex.'

Johnny stood up and walked over to Clover, giving her a hug. She was near tears. 'Look, cut yourself some slack. You said it yourself, it was a release, right? You've both been through a lot, what with the fight and everything. I dunno – it could have been some twisted moment of shared connection; a bit of PTSD? Strong emotions can slide into something else sometimes. Like you said, you could just as easily have been punching each other instead.'

'But I've betrayed Cory . . . and Mia! What do I tell her? How can I say that I ruined everything in a moment of madness?'

'Nothing's ruined.' He rolled his eyes. 'Well, so long as Liam doesn't get to hear about it.'

Clover stared at him. He still didn't know that there was no Liam. She felt another stab of longing for her flat; bought with her inheritance, it had given her a home when she'd lost her family. If this film didn't get made and find a distributor, there was no way she could pay back the remortgage. She would lose her home, their office . . . But how could she possibly make the film now?

Clover stiffened suddenly. '. . . Oh god.'

'What?' Johnny asked.

A terrible thought was running through her mind. 'What if . . . that was the plan?'

'What plan?'

'To get me to walk away. Make it impossible for me to continue.'

He frowned. 'You mean . . . he seduced you on purpose?'

There was a long silence as they all thought it through.

'He couldn't have planned it, though,' Matty argued. 'He didn't know you were going to find him in the pool like that and think he'd drowned!'

'No,' Johnny agreed. 'But it might have crossed his mind that sleeping with her – somehow, at some point – was an option; a tactic to throw her off her game and get the upper hand? It makes her position fairly untenable.'

Clover stared at him, feeling a rising tide of horror. 'Cory always said he would stop at nothing . . . Kit knew that by sleeping with him, I would be betraying Cory. He was my friend and I've just had sex with his enemy. With the very man responsible for . . .' She couldn't finish the sentence. Tears filled her eyes. 'It's the ultimate betrayal. Even if Kit didn't plan this outright, he'll know what this means for the film.'

Nobody rushed to fill the silence. She'd been played and they all knew it, for how could she sit opposite him and interview him now?

'Bastard!' Clover cried, beginning to pace, her heart pounding all over again. 'Bastard! That's why he did it!'

Johnny watched her walk in looping figures of eight. 'Okay, well look, even say it was – you don't have to let him get away with it. If he assumes you're just going to run out of here from *shame* . . . Then do the opposite. Call his bluff and face him down. Brazen it out. You can be sure that's what he'll be doing!'

She stared back at him. She knew it was true. He would. 'But I can't . . . He'll have told them – Ari and Beau.'

'So? You've told us.'

Was he right? Was this going to come down to a matter of nerve?

She looked at Matty. '. . . And to think I've spent the past couple of weeks trying to keep you and Julian on the right side of professional!' She gave a mildly hysterical laugh that looked like it might slide back into tears. 'And *I* ended up being the one to cross enemy lines!'

Matty and Johnny swapped looks. She was flip-flopping like a landed fish, not knowing which way to go.

'Okay, here's what you're going to do,' Johnny said, taking charge. 'You're going to go up there right now and act like it never happened.'

'What? N—'

'Yes. And if anyone says anything – either directly or indirectly – just shrug it off. Don't deny it, but say it was nothing. Heat of the moment. A mistake. Boredom. PTSD, whatever you like. Just don't invest it with *any* emotional significance whatsoever.'

She blinked. 'Well, that'll be easy enough. Because there wasn't.'

'Good. So we'll start now, then, and go up there.'

'No!'

'Yes. Just get it done. The first time seeing him will be the hardest – he'll be looking to see how you react, so give him nothing. Less than nothing.' He headed for the door. 'We'll ask Carlotta for some tea and cakes, then come straight back down here. Boom, done, the worst bit will be out of the way.'

Clover hesitated. 'I can't go up there . . . *right now.*' She needed more time, just to settle herself down. Her emotions were flying around like rockets, exploding unexpectedly and making her jump. 'I . . . I need to get dressed,' she procrastinated, looking down at herself. She was, thankfully, still in her swimwear.

'Just put this on.' Matty picked up a slouchy jumper and wrestled it onto her.

'But—' Clover tried to think of more reasons why they should delay.

'Come on.' Johnny led the way, but Matty grabbed her by the arm, stopping her.

Clover looked back.

'Was it amazing though?' Matty whispered.

Her mouth dropped open. '. . . What kind of question is that?'

'What kind of answer is that?' Matty shot back, an eyebrow arched. They both knew it hadn't been a denial.

Clover shot up the stairs as Johnny reached the top step.

'Hi Carlotta,' he said with forceful friendliness, striding into the living room. Clover had never seen him so assertive before.

'Ah you are back, good. The fire is all ready for you. Would you like some tea and cake?'

'God, yes! Matty and I are just in from a monster filming session in the park.' Johnny openly scanned the space to see who was around. No one. '. . . And Clover's done thirty laps in the pool so she's famished,' he murmured.

Clover gave a small smile as Carlotta glanced at her, seeing her strangely dressed, bare-legged and barefoot in just an oversized jumper.

'Of course. I shall let Fin know.'

'Thanks.'

Carlotta turned to leave.

'Carlotta, where are the others? Are they in the games room?' Johnny asked, jerking a thumb towards the far door.

'. . . No. They left an hour ago.' Carlotta looked confused. 'I assumed you knew.'

'Sorry?' Johnny shot Clover a panicked look. 'Left for where?'

The housekeeper shrugged. 'Why, Saas-Fee, of course. They've gone to Switzerland.'

Chapter Fifteen

'Now this is more like it!' Johnny said as they stepped down from the bus and looked around them. The streets were teeming with activity, snowboarders and skiers walking past in heavy boots and carrying kit. Everywhere was pillowy and white. The town sat another thousand metres higher up than Zell and snow-laden balconies and roofs were plumped up like cushions. Rows of wide-hipped chalets rippled down to a gorge and fast-flowing aquamarine river. Pretty lights crisscrossed the streets, a giant Christmas tree twinkled and shimmied in the full brightness of the day.

'I think Santa's come to town,' Matty said as a couple of guys walked past in oversized elf onesies. One of them winked at her. 'I'm beginning to feel pretty Christmassy. Aren't you?'

Clover stared ahead, seeing nothing.

'Earth to Clover.'

A hand was waved in front of her face, fingers clicking. '. . . Huh?'

Matty looked over at Johnny with a tut.

He put a fraternal arm around Clover's shoulder. 'Come on, let's go find the apartment. And we should probably do a shop on the way too for some milk and bread . . . There's no one to look after us here, more's the pity.'

Clover realized her feet were moving, that she was actually

going through the motions of being . . . fine. She looked like every other twenty-something here, but none of them could have done something as stupid as her. Who . . . who else could go against their own nature like that? The shock still sat within her body like a leprechaun, leaping about and making her startle as flashbacks played on a loop: his hands, his breath. *I hate you too.*

She looked up at the Swiss alps; they were rougher-cut than their Austrian neighbours, taller too. She could see the soaring beauty of the place but she couldn't feel much. She kept going over it in her mind, trying to find the schism, the exact moment when she had lost herself – but she couldn't. The two of them had seemed to fall towards one another like they were gliding on rails, coming from opposite directions and crashing violently, unstoppably. Her body kept shuddering involuntarily, goosebumps prickling her skin as she suddenly remembered that first feel of his leg in the water, his tongue in her mouth, his hands lifting her up . . .

Johnny's arm squeezed around her shoulder. 'Stop hating yourself,' he murmured, reading her mind. 'We've all slept with people we shouldn't.'

Matty's head whipped up. 'Have we?' she asked. 'Who was yours? . . . Johnny?'

Two hours later, they were settled. The fridge had been stocked with the basics – OJ, milk, cheese, ham, vodka – and they had made up their own beds. But the mood had distinctly flatlined, Fin and Carlotta already sorely missed.

Their expulsion from the garden of Eden was sharply felt. Matty kept staring in dismay at the orange pine kitchen and pale blue Eighties tiles in the bathroom. The lino floor was curling in the corners and the mountain watercolour prints on the walls looked like they'd come from a charity store. The bed linen was pale primrose bobbled polyester and had given Matty such a charge of static that her fine hair was standing on end.

'What? It was the best we could get with a few hours' notice,' Johnny said.

That wasn't strictly true. There had been other lets available, but this one was all Clover could afford. The prices in this town had been eye-watering and she'd had to come up with something about Liam rebalancing their expenses budget to advertising instead. The original plan had been for them to stay with Kit and the team here too, but he had deliberately walked out on her. Them. Her . . . She wouldn't go cap in hand, asking for their address.

'But why can't we just stay where they're staying?' Matty asked, sensing she was missing out on a five-star mini-break. 'We are supposed to be living *immersively*. If Julian knew—'

'But he doesn't, and he doesn't need to. It would only raise questions.'

'But we were always supposed to stay with them.'

'Yes. And now things have changed. Clearly,' he said exasperatedly. 'You can cope, Mats. You don't have to be such a bloody princess about it.'

She gasped, her eyes wide with surprise. '*Me?*'

'Yes, you. We're staying here for a few nights. Deal with it. We'll be back in Zell before we know it and you can go back to living in the style to which you've become accustomed, with Mr fucking Smooth.'

'Don't call him that!'

'I'll call him what I like,' he shrugged.

There was an indignant pause. 'What exactly is your problem?' Matty demanded. 'What's Julian ever done to you to deserve your contempt? He's been nothing but generous. Do you even know that he saved you from the humiliation of being publicly asked to wear a jacket in the hotel? He didn't have to do that!'

'I never asked him to!'

They glowered at one another, becoming slowly aware that they were waiting for something. That something was missing. *Kids!*

He glanced over at Clover. She was standing by the window, staring down at the street below. Seeing nothing.

A few seconds later, she felt a hand on her shoulder. 'Earth to Clover . . . ?'

'Oh yes!' Matty sighed with satisfaction as they walked out of the gondola station and threw their skis and boards onto the snow. 'I take it back. *This* is more like it.'

Clover stood beside her in silence. The snowpark was teeming with activity, music booming from giant speakers. Shouts and cheers pitched into the sky as people practised their tricks off the halfpipe and slopestyle runs. There was a big air jump with a giant airbag at the end and bodies were flying through the blue in various intricate contortions. There was an airbag by the halfpipe, too; it was the size of the one in Kaprun but seemed even sharper, more menacing, with edges that glinted like swords. The specialist pipe-carving machine, looking more like a weapon of war, sat parked to one side, ready to roll back in if repairs were required.

They watched for several moments, watching the boarders fly. It was more like aerial gymnastics than snowboarding, to Clover's mind. The riders made it look effortless, as though all bodies should flex and reach and spin like that, but she knew now – from having watched Kit and Beau – the hours and hours and hours of training and drills they had to put in on the trampolines and ball pits before they could progress to the hard surfaces out here. This was training camp for the best of the best – the snowboarding elite, the alpha pack. Kit Foley wanted nothing more than to beat them; he wanted their approval and respect. Would he get it?

She poled off and sped down the piste before the others could even get their gloves on. Not if she could bloody help it.

*

Clover Phillips Have you been impressed by what you've seen him do?

Xander Bergstrom *(Laughs)* Man. *(Laughs again)* I mean . . . what . . . how do I answer that? I don't wanna be a jerk but . . . I mean, he doesn't look like he's moving all that well . . . He's pretty old, right?

C. P. Would you be surprised to hear he pulled off a Switch Backside 1260 nearly two weeks ago?

X. B. . . . Seriously?

*

Nina Heikkinen Well, the women's tour's pretty psyched, if you get my meaning. *(Winks, sticks tongue out)*

*

Yuki Watanabe He's pretty quiet. He keeps himself to himself but I think he's just staking us out. He knows eyes are on him.

C. P. From what you've seen, do you think he's got what it takes?

Y. W. I've heard some rad stuff about him. I dunno, it's not like I've really seen him much. He doesn't move much off the pipe whereas I'm more about the aerials . . . But I've heard his brother is sick!

*

Mikey Schultz Is there any love for the guy? *(Laughs)* No.

C. P. Why d'you think that is?

M. S. He's not a team player. He chose the wrong sport.

C. P. You went riding at Kaprun a couple of weeks back. Did you know he was going to be there?

M. S. Sure. It's why I went. Why not? I was heading over here anyways so I thought I'd check him out. I'd been hearing some stuff.

C. P. And what did you think?

M. S. *(Shrugs)*

C. P. He rode straight after you; copied your ride trick for trick. Including the Switch Backside 1260. How did you feel about that?

M. S. It was a dick move. A flex.

C. P. Would you say the same if one of your crew had done it?

M. S. But he's not. That's the point. He's all about Number One. He doesn't give a fuck about anyone or anything and that's a fact. That surf film showed it for sure. He's not out here cos he loves it. He just wants to grind more faces in the snow.

C. P. Is that view shared by the other riders?

M. S. (*Laughs*) Hell yeah, it is! They know what he's about.

C. P. Do you think he can make his mark at the elite level in this sport?

M. S. He's an athlete. I guess he knows how to bring it. But if he's come here looking for glory, or forgiveness . . . No one wants to know.

C. P. So you don't think he deserves a second chance?

M. S. Nope. (*Grins*) I do, however, think I deserve your number for answering all your questions so good. I bet no one else has said it like it is.

C. P. You have been very candid. If I could just ask—

M. S. For my number? Sure. (*Grins*) Say, why you doing a film on him anyway? The guy's old, and he's old news. He won't stick around here for long. You should be doing something on me. I'm the one to watch. I'm the one pushing it.

C. P. I'll mention it to my producer. Thanks for your time today.

M. S. No worries . . . Seriously though, what are you doing later?

*

Annalise Shepherd I think, don't rush to judge, y'know? I mean, he's had some heavy shit to deal with.

C. P. Could you clarify what you mean by that?

A. S. Well, he got beat up the other week – you musta heard about that? And of course that's all connected to the whole Cory Allbright thing. He can't get away from it, can he?

C. P. Do you think he deserves to 'get away' from it? A lot of people hold him responsible for Cory's death.

A. S. (*Shakes head*) Nah, that's too simplistic. He made a bad call. But we all do. I bet Cory Allbright wasn't no saint neither. But Kit, he's been . . . branded with it; like he's the whipping boy for the whole shebang. And who can live with that? I feel sorry for the dude. Things musta got pretty bad for him if he felt he had to change his entire sport. I mean, he was top of that tree in surfing, making a mint. You don't just walk away from that.

C. P. Kit Foley had already left surfing before Cory Allbright died.

A. S. Yeah, but if you ask me, Cory Allbright had died long before his heart stopped beating. They were friends before. There's no way Kit wasn't affected.

C. P. You know a lot about his story.

A. S. We Aussies gotta stick together. Besides, I sorta used to have a one degree of separation thing going on with him. I used to get a bit of a scoop on his fiancée. (*Rolls eyes*) She was a peach.

C. P. Fiancée?

A. S. Yeah. Y'know, the model. Amy something. Does the swimwear catalogues. Blonde. Oh, you know the one – she's all teeth and tits.

C. P. When you say you got a scoop on his fiancée . . .

A. S. Well, my physio at the time knew her agent. Used to let things slip now and then. It draws you in more when there's that personal connection, doesn't it? But this was all way back. It's ancient history now. He's a free agent again. *(Winks)*

C. P. Have you ever actually met Kit Foley?

A. S. Not yet. But I hear he just got here so . . . this is a small town, you know what I'm sayin'?

*

'How can we not have known about this?'

'Clo, I have never seen the words Kit Foley and fiancée in the same sentence,' Matty pushed back. 'Don't you think I would have included it? It's absolutely basic for pulling together a profile.' Her french fries were getting cold but she couldn't look away from Clover's intense stare. 'I would have included it if the information was out there, of course I would!'

Clover sat back in her chair. 'There has to be *something*. This is the digital age! There is simply no way someone with his profile could have got away with a secret engagement.'

'I had noticed he seems to be very coy about putting his personal life out there. For a guy who looks like he does, he's very careful. From everything I've seen, he only ever turns up to events with Beau or another athlete. He had a few flings with some big actresses and did the red carpet thing a few times with them – but obviously none of those led anywhere. And yes, there's pap shots of him with different women on the beach, driving around, whatever, but they just seem to be a string of one-hit wonders. The women never get named or identified, seemingly cos they never last long enough to be significant.'

'Well, one did. Her name's Amy. She's a swimwear model. Aussie, it seems. Blonde. You've got to identify her. There *will* be a photo of her somewhere, probably taken before they got serious and he actively went to lengths to keep the relationship hidden. You need to look for what seems like a random pap snap.'

'Why hide her, though?' Johnny queried, biting into his burger.

'Obvious – he didn't want to risk losing his lusty fanbase,' Matty drawled. 'Look at any of the comp footage, those girls throw themselves at him.'

Clover felt sick to know that she had joined this dubious club. That she was one of the legion.

'Well, if he hid this relationship, then he could have hidden others too,' Johnny shrugged.

'Agreed,' Clover nodded, drawing herself back. They had a new lead on someone who could prove to be a prime character witness. Who else would know him better than the woman he had wanted to spend his life with? 'We'll start with her – Amy – and depending on when they were together, we can work back or forwards from there. Mats, just start going back through the photo files and look for anyone who matches her description.'

'I hate to break it to you, but "blonde bikini model" is pretty much half the Aussie population.'

'She also said white teeth, big tits.'

'Again . . .' Matty shrugged. 'Those women are hot.'

Clover sighed. 'Start making calls to the modelling agencies too, then. Try and get images of anyone called Amy on their books and cross-match them with faces in the files. Frankly, even just dropping Kit's name alone could be enough.'

'Unless this Amy doesn't want to talk about him. Or be

reminded of him. It could have ended badly between them.'

Johnny gave a small snort. '*Could* have?'

'Okay, I'll get on it. But why does she matter so much? She's obviously not in his life now. She's old news.'

'Perhaps, but she's one of the few people to know him intimately. His inner circle is pretty tight, so she could give us a vital new perspective on him . . . I also want to know *when* they were together. Does it overlap with the time of Cory's accident? She might even be able to throw some insight onto what happened between them.'

'Beau would be good on that, surely? He's Kit's shadow. The keeper of his secrets,' Johnny said, taking another giant bite of his burger.

'Oh, he'll know. Will he tell, though, that's the question?' Matty asked. 'Although he's not the sharpest tool in the shed. You could box him into a corner, Clo, I know you could.'

'I'm trying to build a rapport with him. I can't rush it, though – he spooks easily. But I do think possibly . . . he might be inclined to talk.'

Matty was quiet for a moment, her gaze caught on something across the room. She leaned in closer across the table. 'Clo, hot guy giving you the eye, two o'clock,' she whispered. 'D'you know him?'

Clo looked over in bemusement. She didn't know anyone here apart from them. A guy who looked familiar smiled back at her. She vaguely remembered those twinkling eyes. '. . . Oh. Yeah . . . We interviewed him earlier. He's the American – Mikey something.'

'Schultz. The twenty-five-year-old Olympian. It's just a small thing, but yeah, forget his name, why don't you?' Johnny quipped.

Clover laughed at his sarcasm. 'Hey! Just because you care

about this stuff, doesn't mean I have to.' She looked back at her plate, forgetting instantly about the flirty American. '. . . What were we talking about?'

'Beau,' Johnny muttered, dipping his fries into some ketchup.

'Oh yeah . . . Did I tell you he's convinced someone set Kit up? With the fight outside the restaurant, I mean.'

'Oh good, that'll help with Kit's paranoia.' Johnny rolled his eyes.

'Who would your money be on?' she asked them both, biting into a gherkin.

'You mean, who set him up? I guess it depends.'

'On?'

'What their intention was. Were they random Cory die-hards who took advantage of the opportunity to give him a good kicking?'

'Nup – they had banners. It was planned,' Matty said firmly.

'Well, then, if their intention was to make him look bad and get some bad press for him . . . who benefits most from trashing him?' Johnny murmured, before breaking into a small laugh. '. . . *You*, clearly. Like you said, it was cinema gold.'

'Not worth getting knocked out for, though,' Clover said, flashing a sarcastic grin.

'Well, there's obviously no upside for anyone related to him in a business or commercial capacity,' Matty said. 'Julian's been frantic trying to pick up the pieces. And Ari and Tipper must be spitting nails. What's bad for Kit is bad for them.' She gave a giant shrug as she ran out of ideas. '. . . So maybe it really was some Cory die-hards who knew he was in the area. Followed him. Planned the whole thing.'

'Or maybe it was Beau?' Clover posited.

The others looked at her with a frown. 'But you just said *he's* the one convinced it was an ambush,' Matty said.

'Yeah.'

'So then . . . ?' Matty looked confused.

'Oh, I don't know,' Clover sighed. 'I just wondered if he might be saying that to point suspicion away from himself. It's pretty obvious the ambush can't have been a coincidence. *Someone* orchestrated it.'

'But what would Beau have to gain from stitching up his brother?'

'Only everything! He's spent his entire life in Kit's shadow. He loves being in the mountains, he's a natural. Everyone here's talking about how good he is, I've heard some of them asking why *he's* not going pro. He's younger, more flexible . . . But all the time it's about Kit, Kit, Kit. Beau never gets a look-in. And we all saw that blow-up with Ari. The guy's frustrated. His life is passing him by. What does he have that's actually his?'

The others were quiet.

'No . . . that's not reason enough to get his brother beaten up!' Johnny said after a pause. 'My brother and I fought like rabid pitbulls but I'd still never let anyone else lay a finger on him.'

'So maybe it's someone from Kit's past, then,' Matty suggested. 'An old rival?'

'Who has access to his movements now?' Clover looked doubtful. 'That restaurant was down a back street. What happened wasn't an accident – they knew he was there.' She picked up her glass of wine and pressed her palm against it. 'I can't work out who, or why,' she sighed, 'but someone's out to get him.'

Chapter Sixteen

It was another bluebird day. The sky billowed taut above them, cloudless and bright, the sun making the snow dazzle so that not wearing goggles or shades wasn't an option. Everyone, it seemed, was out. The chairlifts were full and the mountainside felt more like a festival.

'Woooah!' someone yelled as the rider coming down the pipe pulled off a Method Grab. He landed it, throwing his arms up in the air jubilantly.

'Who was that?' Johnny asked, looking up from the camera. They were positioned just outside the bottom corner again, across from the airbag. Johnny had been getting 'epic' shots all morning – shooting straight up the chute – and Clover could practically read his mind, see him envisaging the montage he was going to pull together of all these athletes, airborne. A slo-mo composite arc, perhaps, of them twisting and spinning . . .

'I don't know, but I'll try to get their attention. See if they'll talk to me.'

Clover raised a hand up, the mic clearly visible in her glove, waving the rider down as he snaked his way out of the pipe.

'Hi!' she said, smiling widely as he swooshed to a dramatic stop. She could tell from his body language alone that he was pumping with adrenaline. 'Hi! Can I talk to you for a moment, please?'

'Clover?' The rider took off his goggles.

'Beau?' She froze.

'That was you up there?' Johnny cried.

'Yeah, man!' Beau laughed, nodding excitedly as the two of them high-fived.

'Oh my god,' Clover breathed, looking from Beau to Johnny again. But in all his excitement about the aerial acrobatics, Johnny seemed to have completely forgotten about what Beau's presence meant for her. Where Beau was . . . She looked around them apprehensively.

'I can't believe I just did that! But I was feeling so good, y'know? I just thought, fuck it, why not?'

'You cranked it!' Johnny laughed as Beau's body went rigid and he gave another long whoop.

'I am STOKED!'

Clover looked up the chute but there was nothing from here by which to identify the next rider. He was silhouetted against the sky. Besides, they'd been working here all yesterday afternoon and not caught sight of any of the three of them; Kit and Ari might not even be here.

'When did you guys get over here?' Beau asked them, fiddling with the chinstrap on his helmet.

'Uh . . . yesterday,' Clover said, looking back at him. 'Late morning.'

He frowned. 'So how come you're not in with us? The chalet's huge!'

Clover stared at him. Was he for real?

'We thought we'd get our own place for this bit,' Johnny said for her, seeing how she'd stalled. 'Give you guys some peace. It's been pretty full-on the last few weeks.'

'It's been pretty full-on here! You shoulda come out with us. We've had a non-stop *partay* since getting here.'

'Well, we've been really buried with work,' Clover said carefully. It was true. She and Johnny had been editing yesterday's interviews until long after midnight last night while Matty continued her deep dive into Kit's romantic history. 'But another time.'

'Clo, *any* time! Look, I gotta go. Tipper's calling me but I'll get Ari to hook you up with our plans. He's got your numbers, right?'

Johnny and Clover nodded, watching as he slid away.

'He doesn't know?' she whispered, looking back at Johnny. 'He *so* doesn't know.'

'But why wouldn't Kit tell him? I thought it'd be the first thing he'd do?'

A sudden slicing of snow made them both jump as another boarder came to a hard stop right in front of them.

'What are you doing here?' He didn't remove his goggles. He didn't need to. She'd recognize that contemptuous manner anywhere.

What are you doing here? So then, he had expected her to give up? Leave?

'Working,' she said quickly. 'You?'

The comment was pithy and bullish, a push-back against his arrogant expectation that she would walk from her job while he continued – uninterrupted – with his own. She stared at her own reflection in his mirrored goggles, hating that while she was plainly visible to him, she couldn't see him at all. She couldn't see what he was thinking, only the image of the last time she'd seen him, the last time he'd seen her . . .

For several moments, he said nothing. Then, with a single twist of his ankle, he was gone again, catching up with his brother, who was talking to the coach.

'Shit . . .' Clover stammered, visibly slumping from the

sudden ordeal. She hadn't realized she had become so erect in his presence, as if braced for the next onslaught – verbal, physical, emotional, whatever it might be.

'You okay?' Johnny put his hand on her arm.

'Of course.' She nodded, trying to let the adrenaline settle. '. . . It's good. It's done now. Like you said, now we've seen each other, we can move on.'

Johnny was quiet for a bit. 'Yeah. You did well, Clo. He never would have known.' He pulled his goggles down. 'I need the loo. Just look after the camera for me. I'll be back in five.'

Clover watched as he too sped off, frowning as his words sank in. 'Johnny, wait!' she yelled after him. 'He never would have known *what*?'

Clover shuffled forward in the lift queue, making way for the dozen ESS ski school mini tornadoes who had all passed her on the way down. She supposed falling didn't hurt so much when the very top of you was only two feet off the ground.

She was carrying back a very late lunch for herself and Johnny. After the hostile run-in with Kit at the pipe, they'd spent most of the day covering the big air and slopestyle fields, trying to get interviews with anyone they could. She'd spoken to passing ski instructors, more chairlift operators, coaches and almost every pro rider they could find on the mountain. They all had an opinion, which invariably fell into one of three camps: Kit Foley's a jerk/a victim/hot.

'Is that a baguette in your pocket, or are you just happy to see me?' a voice asked as she finally got to the front of the queue.

She gave a shocked laugh.

'Oh, it's okay, she's with me,' the stranger said as the lift operator went to tell her to hold back – the pro riders were entitled to priority use. He came and stood beside her.

The chairlift scooped her legs from under her and she felt the familiar swing into the air as they were whisked off together, just the two of them on a six-seater.

'I'm sorry, who are you?' she asked with a bemused smile.

'I'm hurt you don't remember.' He pushed up his visor.

'Ah. I guess the accent alone should have told me,' she said, looking back at Mikey Schultz.

'Yes it should. I'm a rare breed round these parts.' He grinned at her, cocky as hell. He knew he was a king on this terrain. Easy on the eye, too. 'So, I've been watching you all day. You've been busy.'

'Well, you know what they say – no rest for the wicked.'

'You're hotter than hell *and* wicked?' He looked delighted.

She laughed. She couldn't remember the last time someone had flirted with her.

'You realize I don't actually know your name,' he said. 'Makes you hard to find. Although most people knew who I meant when I said Camera Lady.'

'Catchy!' she grinned. '. . . It's Clover. Clover Phillips.'

'Of course it is,' he said, looking at her intently. 'What else could you possibly be?'

Clover laughed, hoping she wasn't blushing.

She felt the wind blow past them. She wanted to take her goggles off and feel the sun on her face but she didn't want him to see the vestiges of her black eye. In some ways, it looked worse now than it had at the beginning, withering into a sallow peakiness that made her look ill.

A flashback of Kit's bruised and cut face, his battered body, zipped through her mind again. She shuddered.

'Late lunch?' he asked, looking at the baguettes sticking out of her pockets.

'I'm starved,' she nodded. 'We've not stopped.'

'You're really after him, huh?'

She looked back at him. Mikey Schultz – Matty had done a brief biog on him for their files: twenty-five years old, two times X Games gold medallist, American Olympic team. He had sandy brown hair, freckles, a California smile. 'We're just trying to be comprehensive. We're not coming at it with any particular angle,' she lied. 'We'll gather the data, so to speak, see what it tells us.'

He leaned on the safety bar, looking down at the dramatic landscape below them. They were crossing a crevasse, deep rocky chasms overlayered with thick, bulbous skins of ice that glowed blue in the sunlight. 'I don't know the guy all that well, and I don't reckon I'm gonna either, but there's not much love for him that I can see; I know you can't be getting good stuff. So why's he letting you do this?'

'He's not. His sponsor is.'

Mikey's mouth opened in understanding. 'Ri-i-i-ght,' he said slowly. 'He signed up with Mr Moneybags . . . So that's the pound of flesh, huh?' He gave an amused exhale. 'Oh man.' He shook his head, chuckling softly. 'Can't you give the poor guy a heads up and tell him to go home? That film you're making is gonna be a shitshow.'

'Is it? Maybe you're just trying to get me to strong-arm off your competition for you?'

Mikey threw his head back and laughed. He had a good, easy smile. 'No. He doesn't bother me.'

'You're not threatened by him? You really don't think he could challenge you? He matched you stroke for stroke in Kaprun. I was there. I saw it.'

'Oh technically, sure. He'll be up there. But on the podium?' He shook his head.

'Because . . . ?'

'Because he's not got it here.' He gave a single thump to his chest, above his heart. 'Those are just shapes he's making out there. He's not got the love. He doesn't feel it. He belongs in the water.'

'What if I told you he was a boarder before he was a surfer? He was born in New Zealand, lived by the mountains.'

Mikey shrugged. 'Love is love though, right? You can't help what you love, or why. You just do. Don't matter which one he did first.' He looked at her skis. 'You ever tried riding?'

She knew that the boarders looked upon the skiers with, if not open scorn, at least pity. Johnny had told her they were known to the riders as 'plankers'. 'No. I'm perfectly happy with skiing. I know my limits. Thanks.'

'Fair enough.' He chuckled, unclipping the chinstrap on his helmet and taking it off for a few moments. He ruffled his hair, turning his face to the sky and enjoying the feel of the breeze. She could see that out here was *his* element. His entire body was relaxed, in harmony with greater rhythms.

He put the helmet back on again. '. . . So I didn't see you out last night.'

'You were looking for me?' She was bemused by the intimation.

'Anyone with eyes in his head would be looking for you, Clover Phillips.' He pinned her with a direct look, making his feelings plain. He had a confidence that was alluring. 'You should come out tonight. Penultimate night. It's gonna be big.'

'I can't. I'm really snowed under with work.' The rebuff was automatic, a knee-jerk response. It was true they'd been pulling especially crazy hours, trying to make up for the late arrival here after the fallout of the fight; but more than that – a party boy like him wasn't what she needed right now.

They were approaching the top station and he effortlessly

pushed the safety bar above their heads. They both stood and glided away down the exit ramp. He stopped beside her.

'Listen, it's not a big deal. There's a band playing at M+M Bar tonight. They're good,' he said, buckling his boot. He straightened up. 'You should come along. I'll put your name on the door – you know, in case all this snow you're under thaws.'

He grinned and gave her a wink, pushing his visor back down and setting off, leaning forward and back in languid arcs. He looked back once, giving her a salute.

Clover laughed, thinking how sexy he looked, how fun. She had completely forgotten that she was standing there, looking back at him with baguettes sticking out of her pockets.

'Anything?' Clover shrugged off her jacket and collapsed onto the sofa with a groan. 'Ugh, my feet. I've been in ski boots all day.'

Matty, sitting at the small kitchenette table, wiggled her cashmere-sock-clad feet in return. 'Actually, yes.'

Clover's head lifted up with a jerk. 'You have something?'

'Yup.' Matty got up and walked over with a sheet of paper in her hand. 'Her name's Amy Killicks. She's twenty-eight, lives in Sydney now but was in LA at the time she was engaged to Kit.'

Clover took the printout and stared at it. It was a model's bio sheet: height, 1.79 m; weight, 57 kg; hair, blonde; eyes, blue; measurements, 36–23–35.

She squeezed her eyes shut for a moment, not sure she needed or wanted this information.

'Biggest gig was the Pirelli calendar in 2016. She mainly does swimwear shows, catalogue shoots.'

Johnny came over to have a look, leaning on the back of

the sofa. He gave a bark of laughter. 'Holy cow! There she is – my dream woman! My future wife!'

Matty stuck her tongue out at him. 'Already taken, I'm afraid. She's married to some tech zillionaire now.'

'Course she is,' he groaned, pushing himself back onto the sofa.

'How did you find her?' Clover murmured, feeling sick. She was stunning. A regular doll.

'You were right. There was a picture of them walking – I assume – *her* dog. Little, yappy-looking thing.' Matty had grown up with German pointers. She had no time for *yipsters*.

She showed Clover another sheet. The image was grainy, mainly due to the printer quality: a tall woman in denim cut-offs and a black strappy vest, walking in Birkenstocks. Her hair was caught up in a messy bun, hoop earrings in her ears. Even 'undone' like this, she looked like a model. Kit was walking beside her, holding her hand. His grip was firm and he was smiling at her as she said something. He didn't look anything like the hulk of festering anger Clover knew.

She handed the sheets back, not wanting to look at them. 'And when was this?'

'Well, this shot was taken in 2016 but it looks like they were together just over a year. There's not many photos of them together because they were both always working – she'd be on location, he was on tour. You know, the usual tribulations of a power couple.'

'How do you know all this?'

'Her agent. *Fabulously* indiscreet, darling.'

'Why did they break up?'

'Pressures of work.' Matty shrugged. '. . . You look disappointed.'

'No, I'm not. I . . .' She sighed. 'I guess I was just hoping there was more to it. We have precious few inlets into his private life. None of the A-listers' PRs will let us within a country mile of their clients and we don't know who the other women are.' She bit her lip. 'D'you think she'll talk to us?'

Matty shrugged. 'I've asked, but the agent didn't think so. Amy's quite the lady these days. She's stopped modelling. Likes to be seen at all the right places now, and with the right people. Her agent didn't think she'd want to drag up her history with a surf rat, especially now – he's hardly riding high in the popularity stakes.'

'Well, keep on at her and see what else you can get. Even if it's just the name of the next woman he dated after her. One could lead to another? There must be someone willing to go on the record about him in a private capacity. Both his parents are dead and Beau is . . . Beau. All we've got so far is Kit Foley, the sports star. Nothing on the man.'

'Okay, I'll do my best,' Matty sighed, walking over to the small sofa opposite and sinking into it. 'And how did you guys get on? You've been gone all day.'

'It was great up there. Not a cloud in the sky,' Johnny murmured, scrolling on his phone.

'Ugh, don't,' she tutted irritably. 'You have no idea how painful it was being stuck indoors while you were out on the slopes.'

'We were working too! Werk-werk-werk and no play – Johnny *is* a dull boy,' he muttered.

Clover heard his weary tone. He never complained, never threw a tantrum, but the hours he'd been pulling for months now were unsustainable. She bit her lip, staring out at the town through the window. The stars were already out, Christmas lights flickering gently in chalet windows across the street. Life was happening on the other side of the glass.

People were settling down to watch a film, or eat dinner, or go dancing. While they busied themselves with poring over the minutiae of someone else's life, their own lives were being neglected.

'I don't suppose anyone fancies a quick drink?' she asked.

Matty's head whipped up. 'Speak,' she commanded.

'Well, there's a band playing tonight at this bar. My name's been put on the door.'

'Just yours?'

'We'd all get in, trust me.'

Matty frowned. '*Who* put your name on the door?'

Clover hesitated. 'Mikey Schultz.'

'Mikey?' Johnny echoed.

'Yep. I rode a chairlift with him on the way back from buying lunch, and we got chatting.'

'You got chatting? Or chatted up?'

Clover laughed. 'Look, it's no big deal. I didn't say we'd go.'

'But you wanna,' Matty said, peering at her more closely.

'Well, I could do with a little fun,' Clover shrugged. 'Things have been pretty shit recently.'

'Is this *in*cluding or *ex*cluding the hot sex with the target?' Matty held her hands up defensively even as she teased.

'Stop! I am not ready to joke about that. I mean it.'

'Well, in that case,' Matty drawled, '. . . you're going to need more than one drink.'

Chapter Seventeen

The queue was leading down the street, girls standing out in the snow and night temperatures in ski jackets over strap tops. 'Woah,' Matty murmured. 'Glad you got your name down. You're sure they'll let us all in?'

'Mm-hmm,' Clover said uncertainly.

She couldn't see in. The windows inside were misted, with illuminated Gösser beer signs on the glass, but the energy of the place could be felt even out here. Orange, red, purple lights flashed, music pulsing, the people inside singing along to fragments they knew of the songs.

They walked up to the doorman and Clover gave her name. They waited apprehensively as he checked the list. He had a tattoo and a carefully shaped beard.

'He looks like Max in Guess Who,' Matty whispered, making Clover splutter with laughter. They had shared a few vodka shots before coming out, 'to warm up'. Clover felt in need of courage.

'How do you even remember those things?'

'Well, *you* knew who I meant!'

'It says only one.' The doorman looked back at them.

'Really?' Clover queried, stalling for time. How could she talk him into letting them in, with a queue like that? 'That's so odd. Mikey told me to bring my—'

'Crew. We're his film crew. We're doing a documentary on him,' Johnny said, interrupting.

'Oh! You're Camera Lady?' the doorman said, a sudden smile breaking through his sternness.

'Yes!' Clover said brightly, having to suppress yet more laughter as she caught sight of Matty's expression. 'I'm Camera Lady.'

'I heard about you! Yeah, yeah, go right in.'

'What the fu—?' Matty grinned as the door was opened, just like that. They had to push their way through the immediate crowd, staggering through – less easy for Johnny, there was more of him to fold – until they eventually found a small pocket of space.

They looked around happily. So this was Saas-Fee's après-ski! The noise was deafening. The band was playing, the lead singer standing at the mic and giving it his all. There were tables set around the walls but they were mobbed. There would be no chance of sitting down.

'Shee-iit,' Johnny said, pulling a face as he looked towards the bar. 'That's some crowd. Could take a while.'

'You better load up then, Johnny-boy,' Matty said, pushing him into the melee with a wicked grin. 'At least they'll be able to see you.' He was almost a head taller than most people there.

Clover turned around on the spot, trying to find Mikey. There were so many people . . . it felt suddenly ridiculous to think that they could join him. How many people would he have asked along? Everyone he met? It was a full-on party in here; he wouldn't have given her a second though—

'Clover!'

She looked up. Mikey was waving to her from across the room. He was standing at one of the tables, beckoning her over. 'Get over here!' he yelled.

'Yikes!' Clover gasped, looking back at Matty. 'He's seen us.'

'Well, go on then. Lead on!'

Clover's hand flew up to her cheek uncertainly; Matty had put her make-up on for her, doing some intricate blending to lose the last shadows of the bruise, but she still felt insecure being out. It had been one thing being able to hide out in the chalet or behind ski goggles. In here, everyone was gorgeous.

'You can't see it, I promise!' Matty yelled, seeing her hesitation. 'Plus the lighting's so shit in here!'

'You're absolutely sure you're up for this?'

'He's got a table! Of course I'm up for it!' her friend said, pushing her onwards.

'We'll just stay for one drink!' Clover shouted over the noise.

'The hell we will!' Matty laughed back as they twisted, ducked and snaked through the crush of bodies.

'Oh my god,' Clover laughed as they finally squeezed up to his table, breathless from the crush. 'This place is mad!'

'Yeah! You made it!' He seemed genuinely pleased.

'Well, I thought . . . one drink.' She shrugged. 'This is my friend Martha. Matty. Mats. Smats, whatever you wanna call her. And Johnny's over there somewhere, at the bar.' She looked for him. 'The tall one.'

But Mikey didn't seem bothered about meeting Johnny. 'Hey Mats Smats! I'm Mikey. And these guys here are Logan, Ely, Kelly, Gretchen and Noah,' he said, introducing the others at the table. 'Guys, this is Mats – and Clover, who I was telling you about.'

Everyone nodded, waved, smiled back at them in turn. They all had a slightly glassy look. Clover wondered how long they'd been in here.

Mikey put a shot glass into Matty's hand. 'You look thirsty.' He put one in Clover's hand too. 'And you look *really* thirsty.'

Clover looked back at him and laughed. 'What is this?'

'Flügel. You gotta catch up.'

'Oh jeez,' she laughed as Matty clinked their glasses before she could refuse. They threw their heads back and downed them. The alcohol – red vodka – burned her throat and Clover gave a giant shudder. 'Aah. That stuff is lethal.' She pressed the back of her hand to her mouth and looked back at Mikey, who was grinning at her.

'I know,' he said. He sat back down and patted the seat beside him. '. . . So, the snow thawed, huh?'

Clover leaned in closer to hear what Logan was saying – something about a 'line' on the north face of a mountain in Breckenridge – her hand on Mikey's thigh for balance. She needed all the help she could get. The room was beginning to spin. His arm had been slung across the back of the bench seat all night and at some point, had come to rest on her shoulder; probably the same point as when dancing on the chairs had seemed like a good idea.

Matty had moved over to sit between Mikey and Logan, fed up with doing impressions of Her Majesty across the table. The band – if it was even possible – was playing more loudly than before and the heaving crush on the floor had become more of a jumping, stomping mosh pit.

Mikey passed Clover another shot.

'I can't!' she wailed, laughing.

'I will if you will.'

'You're bigger than me! And a lot more seasoned at drinking this stuff.'

He arched an eyebrow. 'Three, two, one . . .'

234

She downed it. 'Ohmigod,' she groaned. 'I did *not* need to do that.'

'But it's so much fun,' he said, leaning over and kissing her suddenly.

She was so taken by surprise, it took her a moment to close her eyes.

'. . . Don't ya think?' he grinned.

'Mm-hmm.' Clover felt her head swim. She could see Matty and Logan getting closer too; she sensed that with Mikey having made his move, Logan wouldn't be far behind.

Mikey kissed her again, more slowly this time, putting a hand in her hair to draw her closer. This time she kissed him back too. She remembered how good he'd looked riding away from her earlier, the way he'd been so pleased to see her. It felt good to be wanted, desired . . . Not hated.

The band started up a song that everyone seemed to know. Mikey pulled away, looking back at Logan and laughing. 'You remember last time we heard this?'

Logan nodded and began head-banging in time.

'I'm going to the loo,' Clover said to Mikey.

He laughed at the word 'loo'. 'But come straight back,' he said, holding her wrist. His pupils were dilated, his lips a deep pink from their kisses.

'I will.'

He kissed her again, releasing her.

She stood up, feeling the room lurch with the movement. Oh god, she'd been here before. She'd definitely drunk too much. She pushed feebly through the crowd towards the toilets, not making much headway. Everyone was flying, arms raised in the air, heavy-booted feet making the floor vibrate. She found an air pocket and squeezed into it, looked for another one and squeezed into that.

The toilets were near the front, by the main door, she knew that. If she could just get there, maybe get some air . . .

Someone dancing jumped on her toes suddenly, making her cry out with pain. It hurt like hell – and it would be a lot worse tomorrow, she knew. Inebriation was a great anaesthetic.

The man turned. 'Fuck! I'm sorry ma— Clover!'

She looked back at him in shock. 'Beau? What are you doing here?' she cried. Twice in one day.

'Same as you, I reckon!' he grinned, jerking his head towards a brunette in a beanie dancing slinkily against him. He winked at her, his expression dopey and relaxed.

Clover's stomach lurched. Did he mean he had seen her and Mikey? Did that mean—?

'Hey, you're not leaving, are you?' Beau asked as she looked around the bar. There were so many faces, the flashing lights . . .

'No! I—' Clover felt the room spin a little faster. She suddenly felt very hot. She had a vague feeling there was something she wanted to say to him. She could remember that he had been on her mind a lot. 'Listen, Beau, I really need to talk to you.' She could hear her words were slurring.

He dipped a little lower, still dancing. 'Sure? What about?'

'Amy. Kit's fiancée.'

His head jerked back as though she had burned him, a look on his face that suddenly made him resemble his brother. 'No.' The word was like a slap – hard and defined. He suddenly looked very sober. 'Don't even say her name.'

'But—'

'No buts, Clover. I'm telling you now, do *not* mention her name to Kit.'

She looked back at him, trying hard not to see two of him.

She had never heard Beau sound so stern before. He really meant it.

'I just want to know why they—'

'Never. Say. Her. Name.'

She swayed as the crowd jostled her. It felt like the walls were shuffling in, the ceiling dropping down. She felt confused, sick, hot, overwhelmed.

A hand appeared on his shoulder. Beau turned. 'Oh, hey!'

'We're lea . . .' Kit's voice trailed off as he saw who his brother was talking to.

'Oh man! You're not going, are you?'

'We're gonna take the party back to your place,' a softer voice said. Clover saw a petite black-haired girl standing in close to Kit, her body pressed against his arm, her hand clutching his. She had a nose ring and tongue stud, and the most beautiful eyes Clover had ever seen.

'We're leaving, yeah,' he said, his eyes on Clover as though she had asked the question.

Clover stared back at him, but she could feel her bruised eye begin to water. It was more sensitive to the smoke and lights. He didn't have the benefit of make-up to camouflage his bruises, of course, but he also didn't need it – he wore his scars and marks like a soldier. Clover could see how it would make the women flock, bring out their maternal impulses . . . Not that the girl hanging off him looked especially maternal.

It was the first time she had seen him properly since . . . since . . .

Because whatever she'd told Johnny to the contrary at the snowpark, their surprise meeting earlier *hadn't* counted. It hadn't moved them on. He'd had his goggles on. It had been like talking to a wall. Now, though, she could see into his eyes; and there was that look again, the one she'd seen in the pool. Not the one when he'd raged at her for trying to rescue him; nor the one where his taunts had spun into passion, like laughter sliding into tears.

This was the look when he'd asked her what it would take for him to be forgiven. Whether he would be better off dead. It was the look that had shown her he was broken somewhere inside. That had been the moment, she realized now, where everything between them had shifted, moving from their pantomime of contempt to something raw and vulnerable and hidden.

'Well, d'you want me and Stacey to come? I can get my coat,' Beau offered, breaking the seal on their vacuum.

'No.' The anger came back into his eyes again; still on Clover. 'This party's just for two.'

She stepped back as he pushed past, his date clinging on to his hand as the crowd seemed to open up for them. She felt the blast of cold air on her face as the main door was opened and they stepped out into the night.

For a few moments, Clover didn't move. It was as though her feet were nailed to the floor. She felt a whirl of emotions she couldn't even begin to unpick – bones shaking, muscles clenched – she was hot, she was cold . . .

She felt an ominous surge in her stomach.

'Oh god,' she moaned, slapping a hand over her mouth and running to the toilets to throw up.

Chapter Eighteen

'Ow! You're on my hair,' Clover mumbled.

'Ufff,' Matty groaned, turning over.

They lay motionless for several minutes, both of them breathing deeply and slowly, wanting to sleep for longer. But their legs were restless and they kept tossing about irritably.

'What time is it?' Clover murmured as Matty performed another one-eighty.

'Don'know, don'care,' Matty said, her face half swallowed by a ballooning pillow.

Clover listened to the sound of her own breaths. 'I think I might be dying.'

'I'm already dead.'

'. . . Thank you for holding my hair back.'

'Same.'

The sound of a door slamming shut made them both flinch. 'Wha—?' Matty moaned, barely able to lift her head.

Clover fared a little better. '. . . Hello?' she croaked.

Johnny's head peered round the door. 'Oh good, you're alive.' He disappeared again.

'. . . Wait . . . no we're not,' Matty wailed. 'We are clearly dead . . . Clearly.'

'You need to get up,' he called through from the kitchen. They could hear him filling the kettle.

'No. Never getting up,' Matty moaned, trying to turn deeper into the mattress and sheets.

He reappeared at the door again. 'It's the last day and the sun is shining. They're already all heading up. The queue's building fast at the lifts.'

Matty pushed her face deeper into the duvet. 'How?' she cried. 'How can they party like that and then get up and throw themselves—' She lifted her head as something seemed to occur to her. 'Wait a minute! Johnny, you've just come in!'

A loud silence came from the kitchen.

Clover opened an eye and stared at Matty, who was open-mouthed.

'Where have you been?'

More silence.

'Johnny, did you *pull*?'

There was no reply, though they could hear him moving around in the kitchen, opening and closing cupboards, setting down cups. He walked through a moment later, carrying coffees for them. Clover inhaled the aroma gratefully – that alone was enough to lift her up.

'Johnny, who did you pull?' Matty demanded as he set down the coffee on Clover's side of the bed.

He walked around and set down her coffee too. 'You don't still need this, do you?' he asked, picking up the washing-up bowl that had been left on the floor last night 'just in case'.

He went out again, leaving Matty staring after him in open-mouthed amazement.

'Why won't he answer me?' Matty hissed.

Clover reached an arm over and patted her. 'I think the question you should probably be asking is, why do you care?'

'. . . I don't! I don't care! I'm just . . . curious. Aren't you curious?'

'No.'

They heard the bathroom door lock click and the shower start up. They lay there for several moments more, feeling defeated by the prospect of getting up and beginning their day. With a sigh, Clover heaved herself to a sitting position and groaned, trying to remember quite how she'd got herself into this state.

'Oh god . . . those Flügels,' she groaned. 'I'm never drinking again.' She pressed the coffee mug to her lips and let the caffeine-scented steam mist her face. She felt worse than hung over. She felt humiliated. Matty had found her in the toilets, running in to throw up herself. What must Mikey and Logan have thought of them, bailing like that as they staggered out of the bar together, arm in arm and pale as death?

She closed her eyes and refused to think about the other thing.

Her eyes flew open as she remembered something else instead. 'Fuck,' she whispered.

'What?'

'. . . I spoke to Beau last night – about Amy,' she muttered, trying to force her mind onto work.

'Who?' Matty groaned.

'The fiancée.'

'Oh . . . *Why?*'

Yes, why? She wasn't sure herself. 'Because I was off my face and it seemed like a good idea at the time? I don't know why. I just saw him and . . . it came out. I guess I hoped that it's true what they say about drunk talk being real talk.'

'Who says that?'

'My grandfather.'

'Oh.'

Clover continued caffeine-steaming her face, trying not to

feel so bad. It felt better being more vertical. 'He was . . . strangely adamant that I should never mention her, never make contact with her, never bring up her name in Kit's presence . . .'

Matty turned over. 'So don't tell me – now you've been told that, all you want to do is mention her, make contact with her and bring up her name in Kit's presence.'

'Naturally.'

Matty scowled up at her. 'I don't understand you two,' she mumbled.

'What's to understand? We despise one another.' She bit her lip thoughtfully, her instincts beginning to push past her hangover. '. . . But you know, for Beau to overreact like that, there's clearly a story there.'

'Or maybe he was just as pissed as you were.'

'Possibly. But if she is a raw nerve for Kit . . . You've got to find a way to contact her.'

'How? I've tried. Her agent won't take any more of my calls; she says Amy doesn't want to know. Her social media accounts are all private. What can I do?'

'Be ingenious. *Find* a way.'

'Ugh.'

'Mats, I mean it. She could prove vital.'

'She's his ex,' Matty groaned. 'Probably everything she'll tell us is lies anyway.'

'We need to talk to her. Get a number for her, even if it's the *only* thing you achieve all day.'

Matty sensed an opportunity. '. . . If I do, can I go back to bed?'

'If you must.'

'Yay.' Mats snuggled deeper into the sheets, pulling them tightly around her neck. 'I've been so jealous the past few days, being stuck inside while you and Johnny get to be up there. But not today.'

'No,' Clover sighed, dreading what awaited her up there. 'Not today.'

It was instantly clear that yesterday's training had just been a warm-up for today's big finale. Every single rider was out there. The 'parkitects' had been working all night, refreshing the course, digging out and sharpening the angles. Coaches and trainers were standing to the sides, barking orders and swapping notes, watching intently as the athletes pushed themselves harder and higher.

Clover had been unable to rouse herself to move quickly, in spite of Johnny's pleas, and it was lunchtime before they got to the glacier and skied down to the snowpark. While Johnny scanned for the best sites to set up according to the light, she looked around for familiar faces.

Mikey. She was looking for him. She had to at least apologize for running out on him like that. She knew he'd be on the park slopes. He'd spent much of last night telling her he was going to the FIS World Cup event at Modena next week.

'Want to get some big air shots?' she asked Johnny.

He looked at her, puzzled. '. . . Why? Foley doesn't run that.'

'Yeah, but we could try and find some new faces over there. Get some more soundbites.'

'We did that yesterday. It's the last day, Clo. Kit's missed eleven days of this camp thanks to his drubbing. Don't you think we should focus on him now?'

She sighed. '. . . Yeah, you're probably right.' The last thing she wanted today was to see *him*.

'Hey,' Johnny said, suddenly jogging her with his elbow. 'You said you wanted to talk to Tipper McKenzie, didn't you?'

'Yes. Why?'

Johnny jerked his chin towards a figure walking down from the lifts, carrying a coffee. He was alone, for once, no sign of the others yet.

'Shit,' she said under her breath. There would be no better time. *Of course* her opportunity had to come when she could scarcely support her own head! 'Come on then.' She hastened forwards. 'Mr McKenzie?'

She raised her arm to bring his attention to her as he looked up. She jogged over.

'Yes?' he asked, seeming barely to move. He was white-haired and incredibly lean, his cheeks pinched by the biting temperatures. He was wearing a plain navy ski jacket with jeans – as he always did – with nothing at all giving away his esteemed status in this community.

'I'm Clover Phillips,' she said. And when he didn't reply, she said, 'Do you know who I am?'

'Of course I do. You're the reason my client has been a pain in my ass for the past month.' He didn't try to soften the words with a smile.

'Oh.' Clover nodded. 'Well, I'm sorry you think that.'

'It's a fact, not a matter of perception.'

She widened her smile. '. . . Have you been told what it is we're trying to do with this documentary? That the point is to offer an alternative viewpoint on Kit's story?'

'Does anybody actually believe that's what you're going to do? Kit's story is now inextricably linked with Cory Allbright's – and your position on that was clear.'

'We approach every project with a neutral stance. In this instance, we were contacted by Julian Orsini—'

'Yes. The less said about him, the better.'

'You don't get on?'

'He knows nothing about this sport and even less about Kit. If I were you, I would make a point of holding his opinions in the highest disregard.'

Clover sighed, not interested in their politics. 'Well, do you have a few moments to talk to us – on camera – about Kit?'

'My understanding from Ari was that I have very little say in the matter. Apparently we are all obliged.'

Long-winded way of saying 'yes', Clover thought to herself, forcing a smile as Johnny got busy beside her, setting up the camera.

Tipper took a sip of his coffee as he waited, watching her closely. 'How's your eye?' he asked.

Instinctively, her gloved hand rose to her face. She was wearing sunglasses but from the fact that he'd enquired, she knew the bruise must be visible again. 'Better, thank you.'

'It was reckless of you to get involved.'

'Yes, well . . . I didn't exactly think it through.'

Johnny cleared his throat, her cue that he was ready.

She smiled at him. 'Mr McKenzie, you've worked with Shaun White, Mark McMorris, Scotty James – some of the biggest names in snowboarding. What was it that made you decide to take on Kit Foley, when he's a relative rookie to the sport?'

Tipper gave a slow inhale; he looked like his patience was being tested already. 'Kit had won the World Surf Tour nine times by the time he retired and I don't doubt he would have continued to win if he'd chosen to stay in the sport.' His words were clipped, his tone flat, as though he was bored having to speak. 'When his agent made the approach, I made my decision based on the fact that he has a champion mindset and he knows how to win. He's an athlete at the top of his game: strong, agile and prepared to push his body to its limits. He knows how to commit to a training regime, he can cope with pressure. And more than anything, he's realistic about what is possible. Surfing has given him all the requisite skills for Halfpipe, but he knows that at thirty, taking up Slopestyle at this level would be . . . inadvisable.'

'Yes. Exactly how easy is it to switch from surfing to riding a halfpipe?'

'It's easier for a surfer to snowboard than the other way round. In surfing, besides actually riding the barrels, they must also perfect technique for paddling, timing the waves and getting up on the board. All on a moving surface. In essence, all Kit's had to do on the snow is learn to balance his weight through the centre of the board. In surfing, you ride with the weight on the back foot.'

'But it's a lot more involved than that, learning all the jumps. There's almost a gymnastic element to those.'

'Yes. But Kit's highly focused. He's probably spent as much time on the trampolines and airbags as he has on the snow. It was important to build his confidence with those moves before progressing to the hard-packed surfaces.'

'Does he have an innate sense for jumps?'

'No.'

'. . . Could you elaborate?'

'He's able to do what he does through sheer determination. It doesn't come naturally to him.'

'Is that enough, when his competitors are constantly pushing the boundaries?'

'My feeling – and I've told him this – is that he will get the high points by doing the basics very well – amplitude, style and rock-solid landings.'

She nodded. 'His brother seems to have a natural flair. You and I are standing here at the Stomping Grounds training camp in Saas-Fee and there's been much talk about Beau Foley potentially breaking into the professional circuit too.'

'Beau isn't my client. I focus solely on Kit.'

Clover was surprised. 'Isn't that . . . short-sighted?'

He looked surprised by her sudden bluntness. 'Kit is the star. He only has a couple of years to break through. He's my focus.'

She took a moment. 'You're very highly regarded in this industry. Did you think it might harm your reputation to become involved with Kit Foley?'

'No.'

'Do you think Kit Foley thought it might boost his reputation to be linked with you?'

'You'd have to ask him that.'

Clover bit her lip. Blood. Stone. ' . . . The snowboarding community is known for its camaraderie but Foley has been noticeably excluded, some might even say ostracized by the other riders.'

'People are too quick to judge. They believe what they read – or see.' His eyes narrowed accusingly.

'Has it never troubled you, Kit's role in Cory Allbright's accident?'

'No.'

Clover's eyebrows hiked up. 'He's never denied that he deliberately breached Cory's priority on the wave. He blocked his line and effectively forced him into the water. The wave picked Cory up as it broke and held him under . . . You don't find that troubling?'

He inhaled sharply. 'Kit and I have spoken privately, and at length, about what went on that day. I am satisfied with what he told me. I do not believe he is a danger to the other athletes.'

'So you hold Kit blameless?'

'I didn't say that.'

'But you don't seem to be holding him to any account. At the very least, he is guilty of gross gamesmanship.'

'. . . It's against the spirit of sport, but not the law.'

Clover had to look away; she could feel her anger surging. Johnny was watching her, a look of caution in his eyes.

'Okay, I just have one more question for the moment – do you believe he'll make it to the top?'

There was a long pause. 'I do.'

Her eyes narrowed. 'You don't sound sure.'

'He'll make it – but only if he wants it more than anything else.'

'You're not sure he does?'

'I'm not sure *he* knows yet.'

Clover looked at Johnny. He gave her the 'OK' sign and she pulled back. 'Thanks, we appreciate you giving us your time.'

He gave her a sceptical look with a half-nod, still no smile. He went to walk off—

'Actually, I have a question for you,' he said, turning back to them.

'Yes?'

'. . . Did something happen last night?'

Clover looked at him blankly. 'Last night?'

'Yeah. He's been like a bear with a sore head this morning.'

'We *all* have sore heads this morning,' Johnny said. 'There was a big night at the M+M bar last night and from what I saw, Kit seemed like he was . . .' He swallowed, as if his brain was finally catching up with his mouth, and gave her a side-long look. 'Having a good time.'

'Hmm.' Tipper frowned, his gaze swinging from Johnny back to Clover again. 'Well, whatever it was that riled him, we could do with more of it. He's been riding like a demon today.'

'I thought he was holding back,' Clover said. 'Because of his injuries?'

'Not anymore. Something's got him fired up and I wish I knew what. I'd pay to put it on tap . . . I thought it might be something to do with you.'

'*Us?*' Clover asked, looking at Johnny quizzically.

'Well, that's seemed to be the correlation lately.'

They watched him go. Clover felt her hangover bite at her again – she was hot, she was cold, she gave a shudder.

Johnny was already looking at her when she turned to face him. 'Well,' she said with a thin smile. 'That was . . . interesting.'

'Yeah,' he nodded, collapsing the tripod. 'That's definitely the word I'd use.'

*

Jay Kaplin, Team Canada Yeh, I've seen him ride a few times now but he's looking different today. He's really starting to bring it. It's like he was holding back before. *(Laughs)* I'm beginning to feel worried.

Clover Phillips Why do you think he was holding back before?

J. K. *(Shrugs)* I mean, he's had some injuries. He got beat pretty bad, from what I heard.

C. P. Do you think there's any truth to the rumour he was deliberately hiding his level?

J. K. *(Frowns)* . . . Nah . . . I mean . . . When you're out here, you've gotta bring it. There's no half measures on that thing. Snowboarding's a state of mind. I think he's just been slowly warming up.

C. P. He makes no secret of the fact that he's here for the trophies, not the homies. Can he ever be one of the crew?

J. K. I dunno, man. *(Sighs)* He's . . . he's not your typical park rat, for sure.

*

C. P. What do you make of the way Kit Foley's riding today?

Gabriel Beadeaux, Team France He's stomping it out there! I think he's forgotten he's not on waves! *(Laughs)* Can someone please remind him he's the rookie?

C. P. Do you think he'll be a serious contender this season?

G. B. I do now.

C. P. And does his past reputation for gamesmanship concern you at all?

G. B. Gamesmanship? *(Whistles)* Listen, you can see he's a warrior. He gets this different look in his eyes when he straps the board on. He goes from being chill to gnarly like that. *(Clicks fingers)* But I guess that's what made him a champion before, though, right?

C. P. So it doesn't matter to you that he'll fight at any cost?

G. B. Well, the pipe is solo riding anyway, so I guess it doesn't figure.

C. P. Would you want to share terrain with him?

G. B. *(Silence)*

*

Clover sat in the snow, her elbows draped over her knees. She tilted her face to the sun, relaxing into its warmth. Her hangover was receding. They had interviewed almost every rider. Almost.

'There he goes . . .' Johnny murmured.

She looked down at the pipe as Beau dropped in, his body looking supremely relaxed as he took flight. From what Clover could see, he had been getting better and better all day, growing in confidence as he put down tricks of increasing technicality.

'Hear that?' she murmured as he stomped the last jump, the onlookers cheering him madly; someone called him 'homie'.

'They love him,' Johnny agreed. 'But then he's one of them. They can feel it.'

His point was clear – *unlike* Kit.

To her immense irritation, Tipper McKenzie had been right; Kit was on fire today too, though not for the reasons he'd assumed. She remembered the girl with black hair and the nose ring. Kit hadn't had a bad night. He'd had a great night, and now he was riding with an energy that she hadn't seen before. He didn't have the poetic fluidity of some of the other boarders, didn't have a gymnastic flexibility that made the crowd gasp; but he had power and a sharp technical sense, making whiplash turns that pivoted on a sixpence. A few times he'd put a hand down as he landed a jump but almost every one was rock solid. He was balanced and focused, showing the crowd, finally, what he could do.

But the low-level buzz of resistance against him remained. Clover could see it in the muted response to his tricks. He might be grudgingly earning respect, but he wasn't loved; not in the way his brother was. Clover was no expert in the sport but it seemed to her that Beau edged his brother for flair – and sheer joy.

'Coffee?' Clover asked Johnny.

'No, thanks. I'm already buzzing . . . But don't you want to watch Kit? He's next again after this guy.'

'Nope,' she said tersely. She could scarcely bear having to look at him. 'You're the one with the camera.' She got up, clicked into her skis and poled off. It was only a couple hundred metres down to the Ice Bar, beside the chairlift, but it felt good to move her legs.

There was a short queue for the coffees and she took her place in turn, feeling in no rush. She turned around to look back up the slope – this position afforded an almost level-on view straight up the pipe – but she could see nothing as a spray of snow showered her suddenly, the furious froth of a board burning to a stop just inches from her. The snowboarder stared back at her, his chest heaving. With his helmet and visor on, for a second she couldn't tell . . .

'Mikey?'

He pushed his goggles up. His ski tan had deepened just throughout today, his freckles bolder and bigger across his cheeks. 'Thought it was you.'

It had been an aggressive stop. '. . . Hey,' she faltered. 'Where've you been all day? I was looking for you.'

'Yeah?'

She picked up the cool tone in his voice. He wasn't interested in chit-chat and they both knew she knew he'd been doing slopestyle runs all day, training for Modena.

'Listen, about last night—'

He shifted his weight on the board abruptly.

'I'm sorry. I don't want you to think I just ran out.'

'No? What am I supposed to think, then?'

She shrugged, feeling mortified she was going to have to admit this. '. . . I was throwing my guts up. Matty had to take me back. Really, I was in no fit state. I pretty much passed out . . . I'm really sorry.'

He was quiet for a moment, watching her as if trying to read her for lies. '. . . That last shot really got ya, huh?'

''Fraid so. It wasn't pretty.'

He nodded, looking away and watching as someone spiralled into the sky off the big air kicker. 'Well, that's a damn shame. It was shaping up into a great night.' She saw the warmth come back into his eyes a little.

She grinned, tucking her hair behind her ear. 'Yeah, it really was.'

'You all right now?'

'Oh yeah! Nothing three baguettes and twenty-five coffees couldn't sort out.'

He grinned back finally. 'This is twenty-six?'

'I don't know how you do it – partying like that, then throwing yourself around here all day. I've found it hard enough just to get by and I've been keeping my feet on the ground.'

'It's the life,' he shrugged. 'I'm used to it.'

She nodded, wondering what that translated into in real terms: how many different parties, how many different girls? Not that it mattered.

'We're flying out tonight,' he muttered, looking away.

'Tonight? You mean you're not staying for the last night?'

He looked back at her, hearing the disappointment in her voice. 'Olympics team sponsor duties.' He rolled his eyes.

'Oh,' she said, realizing the reason for his frustration as he'd barrelled up behind her just now. They'd lost their only chance last night. Time was up.

They watched another rider grind over some rails, Mikey giving a whistle of appreciation for his routine. He looked back at her. 'Y'know, I could see you from where I was over there. I watched you all day. You looked busy.'

'I wanted to get over to you to explain, but we had to make the most of the last day. We've missed so much time already and there won't be any other opportunities to talk to the pros before St Moritz now.'

His eyebrow twitched slightly. 'You'll be at that?'

'Yes.'

'Me too.' His grin widened, his message clear. Maybe they weren't fully out of time then, after all?

A wincing 'oooh' rippled through the onlookers as a rider on the pipe fell.

Mikey grimaced. 'Yuki Watanabe,' he murmured. 'Tends to over-rotate.' They watched as the guy lay dazed for a moment, before getting up again. People clapped him off, shouting his name. Clover remembered they'd got a soundbite from him before lunch.

Mikey's eyes narrowed thoughtfully. 'Hmm. It's looking sharp up there today.'

'Feeling tempted?' she asked, watching him closely. He'd been a good kisser, lots of fun to be around. St Moritz could be a date to look forward to. God knows she needed some of those at the moment.

'I thought I was done for the day, but I think maybe one last run . . .' He looked back at her. 'Especially if you're gonna be cheering me on.' He shuffled the board towards her. 'Especially if I get a kiss for luck . . . ?'

'If you think you need it,' she smiled.

'The luck? No . . . But the kiss . . . ?' He leaned in and kissed her, sending memories of last night – the lights, the heat, the noise – pulsing through her mind.

He winked at her, pulling his goggles back down. 'I'd better get up there then and start lining up.' He bent down and unstrapped his boot. 'Promise you'll cheer?'

'I promise. You go ahead. I'll only be a few minutes.'

He kissed her again, pulling her in tight with an arm looped around her waist. 'I'll see you up there, then,' he said, pushing himself off with his free foot and merging into the queue for the lift. She watched him go.

'*Ja?*' the man behind the counter asked.

'Oh. Sorry . . . *Milchkaffee,*' she said, turning away and pulling off her gloves with her teeth, to reach into her jacket for her card. She watched as the filters were tapped clean and reattached, levers pulled, steam billowing and roiling in the freezing air. Looking around, she saw a couple of riders take off into aerial tumbles, silhouetted against the sky.

The thick cream was poured . . .

'Hey! What are you fighting me for, man?'

Her head jerked up, along with everyone else's. The voice was fairly distant but the accent carried. It had come from the lift area; she saw Mikey's hands up in the air in a gesture of non-complicity as another boarder chest-bumped him aggressively. There were maybe a dozen people in the queue, not enough to warrant any sort of elbows-out, me-first queue-barging.

'What's your fucking problem?' Mikey demanded.

The other boarder didn't reply or look back. He just got on the chair with a couple of skiers and sat on the opposite end, like nothing had happened.

Mikey looked at some other boarders in the queue, who raised their gloved hands quizzically. 'Who was that?'

'A freaking asshole,' one of them said, with a baffled shrug.

'What was he even fighting me for?' Mikey asked again, to no one in particular, as the next chair swung round to scoop him up the mountain – leaving Clover staring on in silence.

Chapter Nineteen

'Welcome back,' Carlotta said, opening the door as the gate slid shut behind them.

'Ah, home sweet home,' Johnny sighed, his brown hair speckled white as snowflakes landed and settled on their heads. It was the first time they had seen snow right down in the town, and from the train they had been able to see all the pistes were now thickly covered. The resort was due to fully open from next weekend; the tourists would start arriving and the town would fill up, getting ready for Christmas.

'Ha, home? You wish!' Matty muttered, snaking past him through the front door as he stooped to pick up his bags. She stomped her snowy boots on the mat. 'Hi Carlotta, it's great to be back.'

'Your trip was successful?'

'It was . . . very busy. And varied, and interesting.'

'Your injuries look much better,' the housekeeper said, looking at Clover's cheek and eye.

'Thank you. The sun really helped.' The bruise was all but gone now; only in the brightest light could it be seen. 'I take it the others are back?' As on the way out, they had flown back. Clover, Matty and Johnny's journey had been more arduous – although arguably more scenic – by train.

'Yes. Kit and Ari arrived back this morning, although they are out at present.'

Not again? Clover resisted the urge to roll her eyes. It was like playing cat and mouse, chasing them across borders, staking out their own house. Wait . . . 'What about Beau?'

'He has stayed in Saas-Fee for a few more days. I believe heavy snow is forecast and he wanted to be there for it.'

'Oh.' Clover's gaze skated over to the others. Was this another thin crack opening up between the brothers? Beau beginning, finally, to reach for his freedom, his own future?

'You must be tired. We have drinks and canapes prepared for when you are ready,' Carlotta said, closing the door behind them and shutting out the cold.

'Yesss. I *love* this place,' Johnny murmured, smiling at her gratefully on his way to his room.

'Look, flowers!' Matty sang as Clover pushed her way into their room. She was already lying on the bed – beside a bouquet of red roses – and reading the accompanying card.

'Let me guess. Julian,' Clover said, dropping her bag on the bed and looking around with a sigh. These four walls again? Johnny might be glad to be back in staffed luxury, Matty happy to be back in Julian's orbit, but already Clover missed the freedom of the past few days, being able to fully relax and be herself once more, away from the slit-eyed scrutiny of Kit Foley. It felt like a backwards step returning here – to the scene of their crime.

She began unpacking her dirty clothes, reminding herself there were only a couple of weeks left till St Moritz, Kit's professional debut. They would be gone from here by Christmas but there was still a lot to do between now and then. They had amassed a solid bank of B-roll material – they had all the glistening panoramas, showy tricks and pithy opinions they could ever need, enough to make two films. But now they were coming to the nub, and the truth she had been trying not to face was that if she was going to get anything from Kit in his interview, she was going to have to somehow undo the damage she had done.

Because it wasn't sleeping with him that had been her greatest crime, but admitting that she hated him. As long as he believed that, he wouldn't trust her and she would get nothing from him. She had to find a way to dial it back and unsay those words. She had to make him believe – for just long enough – that she was prepared to hear his story.

She looked up, realizing Matty was talking to her. 'Sorry, what?'

Matty rolled her eyes. 'I said he's a class act. A man, not a boy, you know?'

Kit? Clover caught her drift. 'Oh. Julian . . . Yes.'

Johnny stuck his head around the door. 'Who wants a drink?'

'Yes,' Clover almost gasped. The last thing she needed right now was to listen to Matty bang on about how rich, handsome and thoughtful Julian was. They left her mooning over the roses. Clover didn't think Mikey Schultz was a red roses kind of guy, but they'd swapped numbers and he'd sent her some funny selfies en route to Italy.

'I want to make the most of having this place to ourselves for a bit,' Johnny said as they walked into the empty living space. Squashed cushions on the sofa suggested someone had been lounging around recently. A silver tray of assorted gins, vodka, vermouth and various spritzers had been left out on the table for them, along with bowls of crisps, breadsticks, olives . . . 'Whoa!'

They stopped in their tracks, looking up in amazement at the five-metre-high Christmas tree. It had been decked with what must have been miles of multi-headed white lights and was positioned in the far corner of the room, by the picture window. It occurred to Clover that Kit would be able to see it lying in bed. Or in that bath. She looked up again at the glass wall, trying to imagine him moving around up there – reading a magazine or one of his self-help books, blind to the sheepskin sofa or the thread count of the sheets.

'Carlotta did that all on her own?' Johnny asked.

'Fin must have helped, surely?' Or the fire brigade? The local school? How had they even got it up the stairs?

'I've said it once but I'll say it again: I bloody love this place,' Johnny said, walking over to the drinks tray and pouring them both a huge dirty martini, stabbing four olives on a single cocktail stick.

'Cheers!' They clinked glasses and she took an especially large gulp of her drink as he made a beeline for the record collection again.

'So that was interesting, what Carlotta said earlier, didn't you think?'

'What did she say?' he asked, glancing at her blankly.

'That Beau's stayed behind in Saas-Fee to do some free-riding.'

'Uh. Is it?'

'Johnny, he's usually Kit's shadow.'

'Yeah. Doesn't mean he's not still. He's just catching some powder.'

'But you heard how he was getting all the cheers out there, all the love . . .' Her eyes narrowed as she thought further, falling into scrutiny. 'D'you remember Beau got wasted when Kit pulled off that mega trick?'

'The Switch Backside 1260,' Johnny murmured.

'Yeah. That.' She took another deep drink from her glass. 'Why would Beau react like that?'

'Because he's a bum? He likes getting wasted.'

'*Or* because he knows his brother is about to do on snow what he did in the water? He's going to be a star again. It doesn't matter that Beau might be better. Tipper McKenzie won't even give him a chance. Ari just sees him as a freeloader. It will always be about Kit. It always has been and it always will be.'

'And so you think Beau staying back, riding with the homies, is an act of defiance?'

'Don't you?' she asked him back. 'He's being accepted by them in a way that Kit isn't. It's the one thing he's got over him. Perhaps, for the first time in his life, Beau is finally pushing back? He's taking something for himself?'

Johnny sighed, looking weary.

'What?' she asked.

'You got all this from Beau staying in Saas-Fee a few extra days?'

She blinked. 'Yes! Kit has dominated Beau all his life. He *has* to be the star. Everything has to be about him – where they live, where they ride, what they eat, whether they go out . . . I really do think Beau's finally getting to a point of having had enough.'

'Yeah. Maybe.'

'I reckon he might actually talk—'

Johnny straightened up abruptly. 'Clo, I'm knackered. We've been travelling all day. I worked like a dog on those slopes and the weeks beforehand.' He sighed. 'We've got this place to ourselves for a tiny window of time! Can't we just switch off from work and relax? For a few hours? Please?'

She felt bad. Every word was true. No one had worked harder or longer hours than him. 'Sorry,' she winced. 'Sorry. I'm finding it hard to switch off.'

'I'm getting that.' He winked at her, so easy in his bones, always ready to forgive and move on. She didn't think he could hold a grudge if his life depended on it. 'Come on,' he said. 'We need to get some music playing. This place might be stunning but it lacks *life*.'

Johnny was right; the chalet did lack life. It was beautiful, but in a sterile way. It had every luxury but the effect was somehow deadening rather than revitalizing. Clover helped herself to a breadstick and wandered over towards the gigantic Christmas tree as he began, again, to rifle through album covers. She could see her own reflection in the glass; it was already dark outside, lights twinkling from the town in the backdrop. She tugged up the waistband of her jeans and turned back into the room, sipping on the too-strong cocktail.

The fire was flickering away, giving contented crackles that brought some energy and sound to the house, at least. She drifted over to the chess set. It had been set up for a new game when she'd left the other day, but it was in play again now—

'Aha!' Johnny said, putting down his drink to get the record on. 'It's gotta be this one!'

Clover barely heard. She saw the black knight had been moved to E2 and that black had lost its bishop. She hesitated for a moment, remembering the fallout from last time when she had interfered with their game, but it was so clear to her what black's next move had to be . . . . She bent down and moved its queen as the first haunting strains of the Rolling Stones' 'Gimme Shelter' started up.

She looked over at him with a knowing smile. '. . . Ugh, my favourite.'

'I know,' he grinned. He knew very well that she could never sit still to this tune. She took another sip of her drink, the glass already half empty.

She instinctively closed her eyes and began to sway, immediately feeling her body relax a little more. A martini, some Stones, a fire and a Christmas tree . . . what wasn't to like? She took another deep sip of her drink, forgetting about the chess set again.

'Come on.'

She looked back to find Johnny dancing, his arms in the air. 'No!' she cried, laughing.

'Why not? They're not here. Let yourself go! Be *free*, Clo!' he joked, bending and looping like an air sock.

She laughed, slowly beginning to dance too as she felt the music run through her. She couldn't resist. It was her favourite song. She let her head tip back and her hair swing. She felt the stress begin to lift off her even more and she sipped her drink again, liking the weight of the tumbler in her hand. The melodies built up, the rhythm increasing as the drums came in.

Johnny did his best Mick Jagger impression, holding his lips at ridiculous angles, making her laugh.

She came in on the female vocals, leaning in towards him and rolling her shoulders. Their voices merged and blended; they had spent too many karaoke nights together not to break into song now. She spun away from him, arms above her head, swinging her hips and finally losing herself to the song . . . It felt so good. He was right. She had forgotten how it felt to let go, to not be constantly thinking about work, Kit Foley forever in her head.

The guitar solo came in and Johnny obliged with an enthusiastic air homage. Clover whooped and twirled around him, letting her arms fly wide as she spun in languid circles, her hair flying behind her, eyes closed. Yes, she felt free . . . free from the anger that had boiled in the pit of her stomach ever since Cory's death. Just for a moment she could feel light, effervescent, like she might dissolve into a stream of bubbles and lift skywards.

Johnny caught her mid-spin, so that she half twisted in his arms with the momentum. Her eyes opened as she laughed. '—Oh!'

'You were about to trip over that,' Ari said, indicating the low sofa table by their legs.

Ari?

'But don't stop, please,' he said, letting her go and stepping back, revealing Kit leaning against the wall, one hand stuffed in his trouser pocket. 'We were enjoying it. You're a great dancer. Very . . . spirited.'

Clover looked across at Johnny, who was looking even more mortified than her. Had they seen his air guitar?

'We thought you were out,' he said, clearing his throat.

'We were. But I wish now we'd come back earlier,' Ari laughed, going over to the table and pouring himself a drink too. He held up a glass to Kit questioningly.

Kit shrugged, still not moving. Clover felt her cheeks flame. How long had they been standing there?

'. . . So when did you get back?' Ari asked, letting the vermouth generously overflow the measures.

'Forty minutes ago? Something like that.'

'Long day,' Ari said. 'No wonder you were blowing off some steam.'

Kit pushed himself away from the wall and walked over to get his drink from Ari. Clover watched his back, knowing she had to compose herself, that this was the moment when she either began to win him over, or entrenched him in the belief that she was working against him. She had to be professional. Unbiased. Unhating. All those things. She needed to get water flowing properly beneath their bridge because until she did that, what had happened between them would continue to sit between them.

She downed her drink, needing the courage.

'Another?' Ari asked, holding his hand out, seeing her glass was empty.

'Sure,' she smiled, walking over too and standing close enough to seem relaxed. But her pulse told her otherwise. Standing by his side was the closest she had been to him since they'd been in the pool. *What are you doing here?* was the only thing he'd said to her since his last fateful words, *I hate you too.* The knowledge of what they'd done was as solid and immovable between them as a house.

The only saving grace was that Ari didn't appear to know. Like Beau, there was no knowing look in his eyes when he spoke to her, no smirk on his lips. As incredible and unbelievable as it seemed, she didn't think Kit had told either one of them.

'So did you enjoy Saas-Fee?' Ari asked.

'You sure looked like you did,' Kit said.

His tone was noncommittal but from that single comment, she knew he had seen her with Mikey at the bar. Nothing he ever did or said was careless. Everything had a point.

'Well, it helped that the weather was so great,' she managed, refusing to get drawn into an argument or even a defence. It was none of his business who she kissed; just like it was none of hers who he . . . She remembered the black-haired girl. '. . . And we even got a bit of a tan finally!'

Too late she realized she'd drawn attention to her face and she saw Kit's gaze settle on her cheek now, examining the dying traces of her bruise. His, too, had practically disappeared.

'Carlotta said Beau stayed back?' Johnny enquired, looking hesitantly between her and Kit as they examined each other's faces.

'That's right,' Ari said over his shoulder, pouring Johnny's drink too. 'You know what an animal he is for the powder.'

'Right . . . Who's he with?'

'Just some homies he hooked up with. He'll be back in a few days. Kit wants to get into the pits anyway and embed some of the tricks he picked up out there, so . . .'

'Ah.' Johnny's gaze flitted over to Clover, as if he'd got an answer for her. No great conspiracy after all.

Ari turned, the four of them standing in a loose square. 'Well,' he said, discerning something of the tension that knitted them together. '. . . Cheers.'

'Cheers,' Johnny and Clover said in unison.

'So what are you gonna play us next, Johnny?' Ari asked into the silence. The needle had come off the record and was back in its cradle, 'Gimme Shelter' being the last song on that side of the album.

'Hmm,' Johnny said, grateful for an excuse to turn away and walk back towards the records. 'What do you feel like? Something with some guitar? Drums?'

'It has to be something that will get Clover dancing again – and Kit smiling.'

Johnny froze momentarily before getting back down on the floor.

Kit glowered at his manager, looking suddenly furious.

'Relax, mate,' Ari said soothingly. 'I'm just teasing . . . But out of interest, before we walked in just now, when *was* the last time you smiled, huh?'

'It's a bit early for your bullshit. You've not even had a drink yet!'

Ari looked back at him steadily. Slowly he raised his arm and, without taking his eyes off Kit, drained his glass. He didn't wince or flinch as it went down. '. . . Now you.'

Kit mirrored him in stillness and mood, then drained his glass too.

There was a moment of complete silence.

Clover looked between the two of them, not sure if they were going to fight or do it again . . . She hoped to god they weren't going to expect the same from her!

'Better?' Ari asked a few moments later, one eyebrow hooked.

Kit broke into a half-smile. It was still like smashing open a rock and finding the sun inside. 'I guess it's a start.'

'Exactly!' Ari laughed, shoulder-barging him affectionately. 'Then we'd better get you another!'

Clover felt the room brighten. Even Johnny's shoulders dropped as he put on the Beatles' *Sergeant Pepper* album. Clover had to physically bite her lip to stop herself belting out *'It was twenty years ago today . . .'*

Ari dragged over the beanbags and they all collapsed into them, gathered in a semi-circle around Johnny as he trawled through the archive, putting on one song after another.

'No! I am *not* dancing,' Clover kept laughing, every time a new one came on and Ari urged her to get up and dance.

'Come on, Clover! Dance like we're all watching – again,' he joked, refilling her glass.

Matty came up after forty-five minutes to enquire 'what all the noise was'. Clover wished she could have got a picture of her face as she found them all drinking and laughing on beanbags on the floor. She was assimilated into the chaos within seconds. Kit even got up to drag a beanbag over for her too, while Ari poured her a drink.

'Hey . . .' Kit stopped as he went to pass by the chess board. 'Who made that move on white?'

Clover felt her smile wither and die. She saw Kit see it too and know instantly it had been her. She remembered the last time she had fiddled with the pieces.

There was a tense silence. She waited for the explosion. They all did.

'Fine,' he said finally, lifting the table and bringing it over. 'You want to play? Let's play.'

He set up a position opposite her. It was awkward; the beanbags were low-slung against the table's height and she had to shuffle around to get comfortable and be able to sit up. His legs were splayed out around the table, hers under it; his feet extending past her as he stared down at the board to see what her latest move meant for him.

Why had she interfered? What devil's imp had made her start all this up again?

Clover sat very still. The others were still chatting away, talking about songs, beginning to sing, drinking solidly. She could hear Ari asking Matty who the flowers had been from.

But they, she and Kit, they sat in silence. She could feel them settling into proximity with each other. She was acutely aware of the way his body enveloped her, their faces a metre apart, eyes downcast but always somehow in each other's peripheral vision. She sensed their very quietness, their still-ness, stood as a counterpoint to the passions that had unexpectedly rocked them that quiet afternoon downstairs. If they had lost themselves in the pool, they had found control again on the chess board and they were moving back into their correct positions once more: opponents, black and white, occupying opposite sides of the board.

They both wanted to win. They moved the pieces carefully, every play considered for all possible outcomes before a hand was reached forward. Neither of them rushed, savouring the battle. They felt evenly matched – his knight, her bishop. She captured a pawn but lost her rook.

She felt the silence envelop them. They might have been sitting in a cloud or under a duvet, drifting on a boat in the middle of the ocean. The drunker and more gregarious the others became, the louder their silence. It became too loud to want to speak through, something comfortable and easier to sit with. The forces that had repelled them so powerfully from the start – switching into catastrophic attraction for a few lost minutes – had begun to temper. They could share a house now, a room, a table.

It no longer astounded her that he played chess. It was actually obvious – *he's a tactician*, she told herself as he took another pawn, setting it down on the table with a satisfied look. *His whole life is a game of moves and power plays, intimidation and domination.*

But he couldn't bully her. She had her own strategy. His pawn on F3 was pinned to his queen on F6. If she moved her rook to F3, taking the pawn, he would have to play queen to C4, and she could take his queen with her rook to F4. She played aggressively, determined to hobble him—

'Check,' he murmured, moving his bishop.

What?

Her lips parted as she saw what he'd done. Or rather, what *she* had done. In moving her pawn to expose his queen, she had exposed her king on H2 to his bishop on D6. Her own pawn hemmed her in from H3 and she couldn't move to G3 without attack from his knight on E4.

'You were too busy going after me,' he said quietly, watching the blush stain her cheeks.

Clover knew he was right. He had deliberately lured her to F3 with the promise of his queen and, going on the attack like that, she'd left her own defences wide open. His ploy even had a name: attraction tactics.

'. . . Don't worry, you're not the first person who's wanted to beat me more than they've wanted to win.' His gaze met hers finally across the table, the first time they'd directly looked at one another during the play. She could see a thin navy rim around his pale blue irises, victory in his eyes.

She knew she had no one to blame but herself. She felt stupid. Humiliated. 'Congratulations,' she said, forcing a smile and extending her hand across the table. It was something she could do that he couldn't – lose graciously. He looked at it for a moment before clasping it in his and she felt the small shock of that first touch again as their palms pressed together, his fingers on her wrist. Close, too close, to her pulse.

'Good game,' he said quietly, drawing his knees up and resting his elbows on them as he stared at her.

They both knew it was a game they were playing on and off the chess board.

Come and get me . . . I hate you too.

'Well now, this is a sight for sore eyes!'

Everyone jumped as Julian suddenly appeared, coming up the stairs.

'Julian!' Matty gasped, very obviously gathering her legs in to run over to him – before remembering they had an audience. '. . . Fancy seeing you here,' she faltered.

'I'm just on my way to a dinner with the mayor,' he said, looking at Kit as he walked in. 'We're discussing the finer details of the WST sponsorship deal, now that the furore from the other week has died down.' His gaze swivelled between Kit and Clover, seeing their unbruised faces, noting their close proximity and the fact that they were *playing a game* together. 'I'm really very pleased everyone's looking so well.'

'Can you stay for a drink?' Matty implored. 'You don't have to run off yet, do you? There's so much to tell you about Stomp.'

Kit's gaze met hers again for a moment. A lot *had* happened in Saas-Fee, for them both. Other people, other lips, other bodies . . .

'I'd love to,' Julian said, unbuttoning the single fasten of his suit jacket and walking over to the drinks bar. He poured himself a gin and tonic. This was his house, after all.

Kit got up and removed the chess table, allowing Clover to move her legs and get up again. She rose, grateful for the opportunity to take a few deep breaths. Her loss at the game still stung.

Kit, on the other hand, was expansive in victory. 'It was a useful exercise, Julian,' he said, in the friendliest tone she had seen him use for his sponsor. 'Even if we did only have a few days there in the end, it was worth it.'

'Good! And the chalet? You liked it?'

'The chalet was great,' Kit nodded. 'Thanks.'

Julian looked at Clover. 'Did you like the water wall? I loved the way you could choose the colours. So much fun for dinners!'

Clover's mouth opened in an aghast smile. She couldn't tell him they hadn't stayed there after all, without revealing why. They were supposed to have been there too. That had been the plan . . . But if she lied to him and pretended they had, then Ari would know she was lying. And *he* would wonder why.

She could feel Kit's gaze upon her as he saw her difficulty.

'You sure you don't want some pink grapefruit with that, Julian?' he interjected. 'There's some pink peppercorns too. They're good.'

Julian looked down at his pale drink. 'Yes. Why not?'

Clover watched, her heart banging wildly, as Kit cut a thin slice for his sponsor, Johnny and Matty both shooting her 'WTF!' looks. Kit was helping them out?

She turned away, trying to calm herself. The blood was rushing but she knew this was the moment to keep a steady head, for she had a sense she could still turn this loss into a win after all. She had unwittingly drawn him closer to what she wanted: now that he felt he had the upper hand, he might relax and drop his guard. He might not be able to stop her filming, but he had had a slew of little victories at her expense: this chess win, mercifully 'saving' her in front of his boss, taking that woman home in front of her and reinforcing that their encounter had been as meaningless as brushing his teeth . . . he was relaxed and pleased with himself, beating her at every turn.

Ari had got his wish. Kit Foley was all smiles – and she hadn't even had to dance for it.

Chapter Twenty

'A bit more to the right?' Johnny murmured.

Matty moved the lighting softbox a few inches over.

'Yeah, great.' He looked up, squinting at the set. 'Just straighten the chair . . . No, the other way . . . That's it . . . Okay, I think we've got it.'

'Are we good?' Clover asked, coming over and looking through the screen herself. Her chair was positioned out of shot. The angle of the camera was off-centre so that her interviewee wouldn't be seeing its great black eye looking straight back at him over her shoulder. 'Okay.'

She straightened up and shook her shoulders out, running over her questions in her head. She had a crib sheet if she needed it but she preferred not breaking eye contact once the camera was rolling.

They heard Ari's footsteps on the stairs and turned as he came back in. 'Don't look so nervous,' Matty laughed. 'It's honestly only a chat. Clover's a pussycat, you should know that by now.'

They had caught him on the hop at breakfast, announcing they were interviewing him this morning. He had had a few minutes to get ready, but no chance to tell Kit. She had timed it deliberately, wanting to get him off guard while Kit was doing his usual morning training session downstairs in the gym, and the closer mood fostered by last night's impromptu gathering was still warm and beating.

Ari had changed into a collared shirt for the interview. Clover had never seen him look so smart; it had the effect of giving him no neck. He looked preternaturally uncomfortable.

'Just come and sit over here,' Matty said, ushering him to the chair on the far side of the fireplace. Zell am See and the lake fanned out beyond his left shoulder.

Clover, already sitting in the chair opposite, kept smiling reassuringly as he shifted position, tugging at his shirt cuffs, shrugging forward his arms, stretching out his neck. She half-wondered whether he thought he was here for a wrestling match.

Matty poured him a glass of water from the carafe. They had moved the small side table which had supported the chess set – not now in play, of course – to beside his chair; she found interviewees were more relaxed if they felt there was a facility by which they could take a break and look away from the camera.

Ari looked back at her, tense and hesitant. There was nothing now of the bon viveur of last night who had been pouring the drinks, calling out song requests, playing card games. He had shaved, but roughly, the scars on his cheeks still flecked with steel-grey bristles.

Johnny began filming, Matty snapping the clapperboard card between them.

'Okay then.' She looked Ari straight in the eyes and smiled at him as warmly as she could. 'So Ari, could you begin by telling me how you first met Kit?'

His shoulders loosened in reply. This he could answer. 'Sure. It was at a surfing competition in Byron Bay. He was twelve, I'd just turned seventeen. I'd heard his name about; I kept hearing about this tiny kid going up against guys four, five years older; how he was in everyone's faces, didn't give a fu—' His eyes opened wide. 'Shit, sorry, can you bleep that out?'

She laughed. 'Don't worry. Just be you. We'll deal with anything excessive in the edit room.'

He relaxed a little further. 'He just didn't *care*,' he said carefully. 'Didn't matter how big the other guy was, how old. I'm not sure he was even looking at them. Kit's eyes were only ever on the next set of waves. He was there for the ride, you know? The trophies just followed.'

Clover nodded, deliberately allowing a long pause before the next question, to give him time to settle. 'How was he with you?'

'It took us a while to gel. It pissed me off that he was so much younger and just as good as me . . . Actually, better.' He rolled his eyes. 'I guess we developed a respect for each other first; friendship came later. That first time we met, at Byron, he beat me in our heat. At the next comp, I beat him. It was like that for a bit, pretty evenly matched – but I knew the momentum was with him. He'd come into the sport pretty late, he was still learning so fast. Plus I'd pretty much got to this by' – he held his arms wider to indicate his stocky physique – 'fourteen, whereas he was a late developer; the skinny kid was only going to start getting taller, stronger . . .' He gave a small chuckle as he sank into a memory. 'The moment we actually became friends happened *out* of the water. We were at a comp in Philip Island and I got bored waiting around for the next heat. There was a skate park off the back of the beach where some local kids were hanging around. I started . . . I guess I started getting cocky. Next thing I knew, I was taking a beating. Then Kit showed up! He was smaller than all of them – half their size! – but man, his fists could fly.' He grinned. 'We were pretty tight after that. Hung around together at all the meets. I guess I saw him as a little brother.'

Clover smiled back, making a mental note that Kit knew how to scrap; it would edit well. 'Do you think what made him such a good fighter was also what made him such a fierce competitor?'

'Yeah, I mean, it's the same energy, right? . . . Different outcomes, but it's coming from the same place. At a certain point, especially when you go pro, you've gotta commit, you know? You have to want it. You're putting your body on the line. It's not for pussies out th—' His hand went over his mouth as he realized what he'd said. 'Sorry.'

'It's fine,' she laughed. 'Honestly.'

'I'm not used to being . . . like, formal.'

'This isn't supposed to be that. You're Kit's manager, his oldest friend. We *want* the vibe of how it was between you both.'

Ari nodded, looking ever more pleased. 'Okay then. I'm trying my best.'

'You're doing brilliantly Ari, seriously,' Matty chipped in. 'I'm loving these stories. You're giving us colour. Humanizing him. You're showing us how he became a champion.'

He seemed pleased by her words. ''Kay.' He looked back at Clover again.

'So going back to you two competing against each other as kids, what do you think his drivers were? What set him apart?'

He thought for a moment. '. . . I know his parents' divorce really hurt him and I think being on the water was where he could . . . channel his feelings.'

'What sort of feelings?'

'All the usual – anger, grief, frustration . . . He'd been through a lot by then. He'd grown up in New Zealand – most people don't even realize he's a Kiwi; he shook off the accent pretty quick when his mum moved with him and his brother over to the Gold Coast.'

'Was that deliberate, do you think?'

He considered. 'Not sure. Kit's never been the guy to worry about fitting in; it wouldn't have been that. But I guess he was at an age where he was still developing; it probably happened without him even noticing. By the time I met him, he'd been living in Oz for a few years and I mean, *I* couldn't tell. He'd cut all ties with the place.'

'Why?'

'Well, his relationship with his dad wasn't good. They weren't in contact. I imagine he didn't want to be reminded of him.'

'Did he and his father ever reconcile after the divorce?'

'No.'

'Not ever?'

'No.'

'Is his father still alive?' She already knew the answer to this question, but she needed it on tape.

'His dad was killed in a motorbike accident when Kit was sixteen.'

'That's terrible.'

Ari took a deep inhale. 'It was tough on him, but he'd never show it. That was the year he won the World Surf Tour for the first time. If anything, it made him push himself harder.'

Clover nodded, looking down at her sheet and pretending to read it. 'I'm sorry if this next question seems . . . intrusive, but it would be helpful for the viewers, I think, if you could answer it.'

Ari sat up straighter, bracing for it.

'Did Kit attend his father's funeral?'

Ari shifted position, looking down at his hands for a moment as he debated whether to answer. It was a moment before he looked up. '. . . No.'

She nodded sombrely. 'That must be a terrible burden on him. He's never really had . . . closure on what sounds like a deeply traumatic break in his family history.'

'No. But Kit is . . .' He sighed. 'He deals with things in his own way. He's not a talker. Like a lot of blokes, he takes his feelings and channels them into . . . doing. He processes emotion through his body.'

Clover stared at him but she didn't see him. She was remembering Kit's face in the pool. That moment of brokenness. How just a minute later he was lifting her, his face in her hair . . . *I hate you too.*

'. . . Sorry.' She gave a smile, tried to regroup. She looked down at her notes to regain focus, aware that her pulse had quickened.

'You okay?' Johnny murmured, behind her.

'Sure . . .' She took a breath, looking back at Ari. 'So, the estrangement with his father was never resolved. Do you know why they had no contact?'

Ari shrugged. 'Divorce is ugly, right? He was a little kid at the time. I guess he felt it came down to picking a side. And he chose his mum.'

'Is he close to her?'

'Was. She died – cancer – two years ago. But he used to talk to her every few days, no matter where he was in the world.'

'That's really sad. He must miss her.'

'Yeah. But . . .' Ari sighed. 'He just gets out on the board and works through it. It's like with every turn, he's slicing away at the pain and making it smaller.'

'What about in his personal life? Has he ever had any serious relationships?'

'No,' Ari said quickly. Too quickly.

'That seems surprising. He's attractive. Successful. Financially independent . . .'

'No time. He's always on the road and tour life doesn't work well with relationships.'

'Doesn't it? Plenty of other surfers make it work.' Cory Allbright being one. 'And tennis players, golfers . . .'

'Well, he doesn't want to lose focus, is the other thing. Relationships take too much energy. And I guess add all that in with being a child of divorce, you've got a guy who isn't especially invested in true love and happy endings.'

'Do you think he's ever lonely?'

Ari laughed. 'No. He lives a good life – he gets paid for doing what he loves. He's got good friends. And he's not stuck for company if he ever does get *lonely*.'

Clover knew what he was referring to – the groupies; the girl in the bar. But she was more interested in getting to Amy. Her name was on the tip of Clover's tongue . . .

She swerved. 'So his support system really is just you and his brother Beau?'

'Yeah, but that's solid. He and Beau, they're . . .' Ari pulled both hands into fists and bumped the knuckles together. 'Tight. They look out for one another. Always have.'

'Of course, Beau's a top surfer in his own right too.'

'Typical little brother, right? Does what his big bro does. If Kit was a rally driver, Beau would be as well.'

'Do you think Kit would be able to accept it, if his little brother was to ever outshine him in a sport?'

'Accept it?'

'Yes. I'm referring specifically to Beau receiving a lot of

attention at the pre-season training ground in Saas-Fee recently. Some people were even suggesting he might be better on the snow than Kit. Do you think Kit would ever step aside and support his brother in a wingman capacity, in the way that Beau does for him?'

Ari looked back at her with a first trace of uncertainty. 'I know Kit would always support Beau. And if Beau decided to go pro too, then he would treat him with equal respect as a fellow competitor on the snow; they'd always be brothers at home.'

That wasn't the answer she'd been hoping for.

She switched direction, wanting to hop about, keep him from seeing where she was trying to get to. 'Tell me about Kit's transition to snow. He's made it look effortless.'

Ari's shoulders softened again. 'Well, there's a lot of cross-over between the two sports. He didn't choose it by accident. And of course, he'd actually learned to snowboard back in New Zealand before he ever learned to surf, so he had some experience in the memory bank. But as I said, he's a competitor. If he puts his mind to something, he won't stop till he can do it.'

'Do you think he loves it in the same way as surfing, though?'

Ari's mouth opened but the words didn't come immediately. '. . . Honestly? No . . . I don't think anything could ever be for him what surfing was. I think he felt it saved him, at a time when things were falling apart. It was his therapy. As long as there was another wave, there was always another chance to transcend to that place where only surfing takes you . . .' He grinned. 'Look at me, getting all dopey on you. But it's true. Surfing has a spiritual element to it that you don't necessarily see watching competitions.'

'So then why did he leave it?'

Ari's chin lifted up, his eyes hardening suddenly as they found themselves, suddenly, in the territory they had all been skirting for the past month. 'You know why.'

'You mean the incident with Cory Allbright at Peniche?' she said, angling her head slightly to remind him to answer his questions for the benefit of the camera.

'Yes.' His body language was instantly closed, reminding her of their first morning here. 'He retired after the incident with Cory Allbright.'

'Although he didn't retire immediately, did he?' It was a rhetorical question. 'He went on to win the next season after Cory's accident. He got his ninth World Tour Championship title, the most ever. He broke the record and *then* retired,' she said levelly. 'I suppose the point I'm putting to you is that he didn't retire because of Cory's accident; he retired because he'd broken the record for most ever Championship titles.'

Ari looked down. '. . . It might look that way,' he said after a moment. 'But it wasn't the same for him after Peniche. When he won the Ninth . . . it really didn't mean that much. He'd lost the love . . . People forget that Kit and Cory had been close friends before.'

'So what changed between them?'

Ari gave a single swipe of his head. 'I don't know. Kit's never discussed it.'

'Not even with you? That seems hard to believe,' she pushed back.

'It's true.' He shrugged. 'I told you, he's not a talker.'

'But you're his manager, his childhood friend. When every jet ski was out there trying to get Cory out of the water, when the ambulances were screaming onto the sand, when he finally came out of the sea that day at Supertubos Beach . . . you're telling me you didn't ask him why he'd blocked Cory's line in the first place?'

Ari swallowed. 'There wasn't time for questions while it was all happening. Our concern was finding Cory.'

'And afterwards? In the hours and days afterwards when he was in an induced coma, the weeks and months later when the extent of his injuries became clear . . . you still didn't ask Kit *why*?'

Ari stared back at her. To her surprise, his eyes looked watery. 'Kit was in no fit state to talk . . . He barely said a word – *to anyone* – for two months after. I knew he'd talk when he was ready.'

Two months? She swallowed. 'And four years on . . . has he?'

Ari chewed his lip. He looked away, giving a tiny shake of his head. 'But I know he regrets it. I know there's not a day goes by that he doesn't think of Cory.'

'Do you think that would be a comfort to Cory's widow? Their three young sons?'

Clover watched as he looked from her to the camera – looking straight down the eye of it. She could tell he was at his limit – he would walk if she didn't change tack.

She modulated her tone, putting more questioning and less accusation in her voice. 'Kit's decision to change sport entirely – having to start from scratch, find new sponsors . . . That clearly has a major impact on you and Beau. Your lives follow his . . . How did you feel when he told you his plans?'

It worked. She saw his hands release and splay on his thighs. She wondered if his palms were sweating as hers were. 'Pleased. I knew he'd been searching for something that surfing couldn't give him anymore. I've been Kit's manager for seven years. This is my job now, so I don't mind where we go or what Kit does. And Beau will always be his brother.'

'Why *did* you become his manager? You were competing at the top level yourself.'

He raised a hand to his face, indicating the deep scars along his cheeks. 'I had a bad wipeout at Pipe Masters. The undertow dragged me over the coral reef, face-first . . .' She winced at the thought of it. 'It was a . . . humbling experience. I was just a rag doll in a washer. I'd had heavy drops before and you always know it's a risk, every wave you catch. But that day I knew, when I surfaced again, that I'd lost the edge I needed to compete at that level. You have to be utterly fearless out there. And after that, I wasn't.'

She watched him, deciding not to follow up with another question but to let him talk. It was often useful switching up the flow dynamics of the conversation. Sometimes, letting the interviewee ramble could throw up interesting nuggets that might have been kept from an initial response.

A quiet interlude blossomed.

'Kit knew it too,' he said, obediently stepping into the silence, falling into the memory. 'I didn't need to say a word. He may not talk much but he's good at reading people; and he saw it in me and understood. It was his idea for me to become his manager. He's a loyal friend. A good friend. He knew it was a way to give me skin in the game. I couldn't turn my back on the scene completely.'

'And yet, you have now,' she pointed out, indicating the alpine backdrop behind him.

He shrugged. 'I'm not twenty-five anymore. I'm older, helluva lot stiffer . . . The world has changed. We're neither of us the same people we were back then. Life happens. We have to know when to move on.'

She smiled. 'Would you go back if you could?'

'I don't deal in hypotheticals. This is my job. Kit Foley's a snowboarder now. He's committed and therefore so am I.'

Clover thought for a moment. 'What's been the hardest thing, would you say, about the switch up?'

'Well, getting used to wearing clothes, for a start!' he laughed, grateful for the steady easing up of the tension. 'I've never worn so many layers in my life. We antipodeans can never get used to the cold in the same way.'

'Do you think there's any part of Kit that misses his old life?'

'No. I think he's a hundred per cent focused on making the most of the opportunities that are ahead of him. That's the guy he is. He doesn't dwell. He's a doer. I honestly think he's excited about the challenges coming up.' It was a stock PR response. He was articulate, warm. She could see his confidence growing again.

'So you'd say he has no regrets?'

'None,' he said confidently.

'You said surfing was his salvation as a boy, following his parents' divorce. But surfing also became his downfall. Do you think he's looking for snowboarding to give him . . . redemption?'

Ari looked stunned by the question. She felt almost bad for asking it. '. . . No. I just think he was ready for a new challenge. There's other worlds to conquer.'

'Does snowboarding give him the kicks surfing used to? If that's where he processes his emotions . . .'

'Yeah. I mean, it's hard to find something that can compare. When you've spent your life pushing yourself to the very limits, as he has . . . There's not much that makes you feel more alive than screaming down a wall of water that's threatening to break on you with four hundred tons and is coming at you at speeds over a hundred kilometres an hour. Especially when you know that even if you survive the wipeout, chances are you're five metres underwater and gonna get stuck in a hold-down too . . .'

He seemed to realize what he'd said, the words fading on his lips. Clover didn't stir. They were back to Cory again.

She inhaled slowly. 'Kit thrived out there because he was driven. Driven by pain at his parents' divorce, driven by anger at his father . . . Is he reckless with life, would you say? His own? Other people's?'

'No!' Ari almost came off the seat of his chair. 'He's always been incredibly safety-conscious. He's an athlete, he knows his limits. He knows what the dangers are and he does everything he can to mitigate them.'

'But that's patently not true,' she said in a deliberately calm, slow voice. 'The rule of interference and respecting priority is based on water safety – and Kit deliberately ignored Cory's priority. He intentionally blocked his path, forcing Cory into the water, where the wave picked him up and slammed him down with those four hundred tons of force – and where he then got pinned under a *double* hold-down.'

Ari stared back at her. He didn't say anything for a long time. '. . . The double hold-down was . . . just a freak happening. Kit couldn't have known it was coming. If it had just been a normal set of waves, Cory would have been okay. All surfers breath-train. Kit, when he was competing, could hold his for almost four minutes. He learned to slow his heart rate right down. It saved his life more than once.'

Clover stared at him. '. . . Breath-training?' she frowned. 'Could you tell me more about that? How do you train for that?'

'The old-fashioned way – stick your head under water and hold your breath for as long as you can. In the ocean ideally, but in the tub or even a sink if you have to.'

'. . . Is there any reason why Kit would need to incorporate that into his current training regime?'

Ari frowned. 'For snowboarding? No, of course not.' He took in her quizzical expression. '. . . Why?'

'I found Kit breath-training in the pool the other day.'

'Seriously?' Ari gave a half laugh, half snort of confusion. '. . . Why would he be doing that?'

'You tell me,' Clover said, looking back at him coolly. '. . . Do you still think he has no regrets?'

'Ari, you did brilliantly!' Matty said encouragingly as Johnny gave them the sign he'd stopped rolling.

He didn't reply, his body held stiffly as she ran over and unclipped his mic.

'I told you we were prepared to listen,' Clover said, getting up and holding out her hand, forcing eye contact. 'Listen, you know I have to ask the questions about Cory. We can't avoid them. Everyone wants your side of things, that's what this whole film is about. We have to address the elephant in the room. But you did well, Ari. You really showed Kit in a sympathetic light.'

'You think so?' He shook her hand, seeming comforted by her feedback. 'I mean, this isn't my bag. I'm not used to being on that side of the camera. Kit's the star; I don't play the PR game. I just shoot from the hip.'

'And it's served you well. You've really helped draw up a different perspective,' Matty grinned encouragingly. 'See, it wasn't so bad, was it? Want some water?' She handed him his glass.

Clover could literally see the adrenaline beginning to wash through his veins. It was a different kind of rush than he was used to.

'It actually wasn't that bad.' He drained the glass, then smiled with relief.

'It was good!' Matty reassured. She was always great at the post-interview care.

He gave a nervous laugh. '. . . I was shitting a brick! Now I don't know what I was so worried about!'

Johnny, dismantling the lighting softbox behind him, looked over at Clover and smiled; they both knew Ari would now report back to Kit that there was nothing to fear. She'd gone in gently for specifically that reason.

'At least I can take this damned thing off now,' Ari said, already unbuttoning his shirt.

They all laughed as he headed downstairs to change, waiting for him to disappear from sight before they quietly high-fived one another.

'Pleased?' Johnny asked her.

'Yeah. I am. There's some good soundbites in there, plus some threads I want to develop with Beau and Kit. The stuff with his dad I want to work on with Beau. Ari calls it motivation, the rest of the world calls it anger management issues.'

Matty sighed. 'I'll have anger management issues if I don't get a coffee. Where's Carlotta?'

'But why didn't you go in on Amy?' Johnny asked. 'You teed it all up. I thought you were going to push him on it.'

'I know, me too,' she murmured. 'But right at the last moment, it just didn't seem right. I didn't want to spook him. Until we've made contact with her ourselves and found out what she's got to say . . . I didn't want him reporting back to Kit that we know about her.'

'But you mentioned it to Beau,' Matty reminded her.

Clover winced. 'I know. And I'm still kicking myself. But I'm just hoping that his overreaction to me even mentioning her name means he won't want to bring it up with Kit either. He's hoping he'll have scared me off.'

Johnny laughed. 'Yeah, right.'

'I want to keep treading lightly. They're all still jumpy as hell. I need to keep getting word back to Kit that these talks are okay. Not threatening.' She looked at Matty. 'Still nothing on Amy?'

'Not yet, but I'm finally feeling hopeful,' Matty said. 'I've made contact with my second cousin who lives in Melbourne.'

'But Amy's in Sydney.'

'I know,' Matty said irritably. 'There are loads of pics of her and her hub at races – the Melbourne Cup, the Queen Elizabeth Stakes – so I did some digging and found out the husband's got a few big-name racers. My cousin's a sports journo so I thought he might have an in. It's a small world, racing.'

'Yes, that sounds good,' Clover nodded. 'Keep pushing.'

'I'm doing my best but the time difference isn't helpful. I've basically got two hours every day in which I can reasonably hope to make contact.'

'Hmm.' Clover looked at Johnny. 'You don't happen to know anyone in Sydney? Someone who could go round . . . ?'

'And doorstep her?' he snorted.

'If you like. At this point, I'd consider the SAS going in from a Chinook. Time's getting tight and we've got to get some personal insight—'

The sound of footsteps on the stairs made them all turn. Kit came bounding up the stairs two at a time, turning in to the living room. His t-shirt was thrown over his shoulder, sweat shining under the lights.

He stopped dead at the sight of them in a huddle. 'Hey,' he said suspiciously.

'Hey,' Matty said brightly, as though he was exactly the person they'd been hoping to see. 'We just did Ari's interview!'

A scowl gathered on his brow. It was clear he did not regard that as a good news story, despite her tone to the contrary.

'He was amazing! And he actually loved it! You should ask him.'

Kit looked at them all, his gaze falling and sticking on Clover; she was the chief interrogator, after all. '. . . Funny that he didn't mention it at breakfast.'

'Well, we kind of sprang it on him,' Matty said in a confiding tone. 'Clo knew he was nervous and thought it was better not to give him time to worry.'

'Did she now?' he asked sceptically, still staring at her, and she could see daylight shining through holes that hadn't yet closed over in last night's skein of trust; it might yet tear into ribbons, leave them with nothing but rags. She needed to tread with fairy steps . . .

'But clearly that's not the case for you. When would you like to do yours?' Clover asked him. 'The sooner it's done, the sooner you lose the biggest obstacle to getting rid of us.' She shrugged. 'St Moritz notwithstanding.'

'Is that so?' he said coolly. 'Well, why didn't you say so? . . . Give me time to shower?'

Chapter Twenty-One

'Are you even ready for this?' Johnny whispered, setting the camera back up.

'I'm going to have to be,' Clover murmured, trying not to panic. Her efforts of bridge-building had backfired – there wasn't now time for her to develop the arc for questions, no time for Matty to transcribe Ari's interview. She would have to draw on the threads he'd set down from memory.

She walked over to the Christmas tree and closed her eyes, trying to clear her head. She knew what she had to ask – she knew the question that sat at the very heart of this film. It was just a matter of how she should get there. Should she go in early and catch him with the element of surprise? He might be expecting her to build slowly, in which case he would easily toy with her. On the other hand, if she went in too hard and fast, if she got the timing wrong, he might walk off and she'd have no interview at all.

She scraped her hands through her hair and gripped it at the temples. Oh god. Oh god. The moment she'd been waiting for for the past seven months was suddenly here, and *she* was the one caught on the hop? She tipped her head back and sighed.

She froze as she caught sight of Kit standing by his glass bedroom wall, staring straight down at her as he shrugged on a white shirt. Her hands dropped down as he buttoned it up, maintaining the gaze between them. They both knew how important the next hour was going to be for both their futures . . . She had to get him to trust her.

She smiled, but he turned and walked away, out of sight.

'Shit,' she muttered to herself.

He came down twenty minutes later as she was standing in front of the fire, glancing through a set of crib notes Matty had hastily compiled from the previous talking heads and printed up for her. Clover had sat down at the table and made some bullet points about topics she wanted to pick up on from Ari's interview. Amy's name was underlined, with question marks.

'Hey!' Matty said brightly again in greeting – and warning.

'Wow!' she laughed. 'It's always sort of weird seeing you guys in actual clothes. I feel like you should be doing this in swimmers.'

Clover turned. He was wearing jeans and the shirt, no socks, no shoes. His hair was still damp from the shower.

'Now I just have to clip this onto your shirt,' Matty said, squeezing the clips of the small mic so he could see them. But he had done countless interviews over the years; he knew the drill. He stood perfectly still, staring ahead at the Christmas tree as Matty clipped it on. '. . . Great. You're good to go.'

He glanced down at it, then across to Clover. He pointedly looked at the notes in her hand, as if they were a jury's verdict.

'Right, so if you're ready, you'll be sitting over there,' Clover said as brightly as she could muster, indicating the chair set by the window.

He looked at it, then at her chair. For a moment she thought he was going to say he wanted to sit in hers. She wouldn't put anything past him.

He walked over and sat down.

'Clo,' Johnny murmured behind her. 'Do you want any make-up on those?'

She looked across and saw that the light softbox – although it threw out a flattering warmth on a morning with flat light; the snow clouds were throwing down their confetti again – also highlighted the clinging traces of his bruises.

Clover squinted, walking over to him. 'Kit, your bruises are a bit visible under the lights,' she said, her gaze roaming over his face; his eyes tracked hers, suspiciously. 'They're not bad at all, but would you rather have some make-up on them? Matty's got—'

'No.' He stared back at her flatly. Where had yesterday's bonhomie gone?

'. . . Okay. Fine.' She straightened up again and went back to her chair. She clipped on the mic and settled herself.

Matty was holding the clapperboard. Ari's name had been wiped off and replaced with Kit's. She looked across at Johnny for the cue.

'I want a closed set.'

Every head turned in his direction.

'. . . What?' Johnny asked, his head bobbing up from behind the camera.

'I said I want a closed set. Just me and her.' His eyes were on Clover.

She was astounded. '. . . Kit, it practically is closed. There's only Johnny and Mats here, and you know them as well as you know me.'

It was the wrong thing to have said. He didn't move a muscle but she saw the contradiction flash in his eyes and she felt her cheeks immediately burn.

No one stirred.

Clover swallowed. 'We keep the team this small precisely so that it feels intimate,' she said instead.

'This isn't *intimate*.' A note of scorn fell upon the word.

She swallowed. Wrong again. 'Unobtrusive, then.'

He laced his fingers together, resting his elbows on the chair's arms. 'Closed set. That's my condition.'

Clover looked back at Johnny. Could it even be done? He exhaled, shaking his head. 'I guess . . . I could set the cameras to a timer?'

Kit nodded, looking satisfied with that.

Matty stared at Clover like she was mad, like she was willingly stepping into a starved tiger's cage. Clover forced herself to give a casual shrug in return. 'Fine. It makes no difference to me,' she lied. 'If it will make Kit more comfortable . . .'

They waited in silence as Johnny double-checked both cameras' settings, pressing various buttons to activate the timers.

'Okay,' he said finally. 'They'll start running in a minute. You'll see the red light come on. Clo, you'll need to hold up the clappers at the beginning. It'll be a bit awkward – make sure you reach into shot – but we can cut it in the edits obviously.'

Matty reluctantly handed her the board with a look of concern. Clover took it with a forcibly relaxed 'thanks', even though she knew that having to do just this menial task would be enough to break her focus.

'Thanks Johnny,' she smiled, swallowing as her two friends, colleagues, allies and protectors headed for the stairs. 'And can you tell Fin and Carlotta to stay in the kitchen until we knock? We don't want any unexpected intrusions or background noises.'

'They're both in town,' Kit said.

Clover looked back at him. 'Oh. Well, Ari too—'

'He's in the gym,' Kit said coolly, seemingly having all the answers. 'Don't worry. We'll be quite alone.'

'. . . Great.'

The others disappeared down the stairs; Clover wondered whether they would sit on the steps and try to listen in. She hoped not. She felt distracted enough.

They were alone, for the first time since that afternoon in the pool.

A silence bloomed as they waited for the red lights to flash. She twisted in her chair so that she could see the camera behind her, which shot full-length; the close-up camera, just off to his right side, would have been easier to watch for the timer, but this gave her an opportunity to escape Kit's gaze. She could feel him watching her, sensing her discomfort.

The seconds dragged past, seemingly in half time. She couldn't see the timer from where she was sitting; she couldn't tell how long they had to go . . . She held her chin up, trying to keep her breathing steady. She tried to think about her first question, but everything had gone out of her head. He had disrupted her routine, quite deliberately. She knew this was all part of his intention to throw *her* off-balance; these were the games he played, the ones Cory had told her about. Not just attraction tactics – if he couldn't win outright, he played dirty. He had done it back then and he was still doing it.

The red light came on. With a visible sigh of relief she held the board out so that it was within shot of the camera and clapped it shut. Slowly, gathering herself, she put it down by the legs of her chair and turned back to face him; she forced herself to meet his eyes.

'So,' she smiled.

'. . . So.'

*

'I know you're a reluctant interviewee,' she said with impressive understatement. 'So I thought we'd do some warm-ups, have a bit of fun with it.'

'Fun?' He frowned, his expression completely deadpan. 'I'm not sure I'm familiar with the concept.'

She smiled, but thinking about it, when *had* she seen him actually having fun in all the time she'd been here? Even last night, compared to everyone else, he'd still been muted. 'Let's start there, then. What do you do for fun?'

He arched an eyebrow, staring at her with a look that told her immediately. '. . . Are you sure that's the kind of material you want in the film?'

Flustered, she looked down at her notes. She could feel him smirking. It was the second time in this interview alone that he had alluded to their 'mistake', weaponizing it against her.

'Tell me something about yourself that the public wouldn't know,' she said instead, lifting her eyes to his again, knowing it was unavoidable. In spite of his games, she had to find a connection with him. Establish genuine trust. And fast.

He inhaled slowly. 'I'm good at chess.'

She blinked, seeing how the smirk had climbed into his eyes, like a cat at a window. 'Give me a contradiction about you.'

He thought for a moment. 'I like the smell of cigarette smoke, but I don't smoke.'

'What are you frightened of?'

'Fear itself.'

It was a pat response. Meaningless. 'Something else.'

'Spiders.'

Bullshit, she thought, smiling back. 'Tell me your earliest memory.'

He looked down for a moment, having to think more deeply. 'My mother's face.'

'What's the best thing about being on a board?'

'Going fast.'

'What was the best moment of your life?'

'Moving to Oz.'

Leaving his father behind? She was careful not to react. She had expected him to say winning the pro surf tour for the first time. Or the ninth.

'And the worst?'

'When my mum died.' His expression didn't change at all; he hadn't hesitated. Everything was presented as a fact – happy or sad, there was no emotion attached. These were simply words. He had a wall around him.

She paused. 'Okay, I'll ask you some either/or questions and you give me a reflex response. Okay?'

He shrugged, looking bemused.

'Tea or coffee?'

'Neither.'

'You have to choose.'

He sighed. 'Coffee.'

'Sofa or gym?'

'Gym.'

'Owl or lark?'

'. . . Owl.'

'Summer or winter?'

'Summer.'

Her head tipped fractionally at that. He saw it and straightened up a little.

'TV or book?'

'Book.'

'Book or film?'

'Book.'

'Lover or fighter?'

'Fighter.'

'Snow or surf?'

'Both.'

She shook her head. 'You have to choose.'

'. . . Snow.'

She stared back at him. They both knew that was a lie.

'Fine. Surf.' He shifted position slightly.

'Dog or cat?'

'Dog.'

'Aussie or Kiwi?'

'Aussie.'

Another rejection of his father. '. . . Blonde or brunette?'

'Brunette.'

Rejection of her. '. . . Love or hate?'

'Hate.'

Her lips parted in surprise; *no one* answered with that. Was he trying to be unlikeable? 'Glory in defeat? Or victory at any cost?'

His turn to be surprised. His eyes narrowed. He knew there was judgement in the wrong answer. 'Victory at any cost.'

Clover stared at him. It was the answer people expected him to give, the one now forever attached to his name. But she wasn't sure she believed it. He was answering from pure defiance. He was sticking two fingers up to her – and the wider world at large. His answers had told her he would lie with impunity, and that even when he told the truth, it would bring no emotion, no breakthrough. He didn't care if people liked him; he didn't care if they believed him. Unlike his sponsor, he had no interest in saving his own reputation.

She stared back at him, wanting just to hit him with it – drop Amy's name like a bomb and watch him scramble for cover.

'Tell me about your parents' divorce,' she said quietly, calmly. 'Why did they separate?'

'They forgot to love each other.' It was a flippant answer.

'From what others close to you have said, it seemed to have had a profound and lasting impact upon you.'

'Not really. You get used to it pretty quickly – especially when it's the best thing. I only wished it had happened earlier.'

'You wanted your parents to separate?'

'It was the best thing for everyone.'

She watched him, refusing to be rushed by his short, clipped answers. 'Yes, often it is. But that doesn't mean you didn't suffer. Witnessing the breakdown of your parents' relationship when you were just a young boy must have been traumatic.'

'If you say so.'

'. . . Do you feel surfing was a way for you to channel away any negative feelings, such as grief or anger?'

'Yes.'

'Was it somewhere you could be in control?'

He smirked. 'Anyone who thinks he's in control of the ocean is a bloody fool.'

'. . . Do you think you'd have become a nine-time world champion if you'd had a happier childhood?'

'How could I ever know? I am who I am because of the experiences I went through. I don't know any different to this. If my parents hadn't divorced, I'd probably have grown up in New Zealand and I might never have even got on a surfboard.'

'What do you think you'd be now, then, if that had been your path?'

'Nine-time world champion snowboarder.' She saw the arrogance shine in his eyes.

'So, you would always have been a winner? No matter whether your parents divorced, no matter where you lived?'

'Winning is fifty per cent preparation, fifty per cent mindset. You have to want it more than the other guy.'

'Victory at any cost, you answered just now. Do other people matter to you, Kit? Or are they just obstacles to beat?'

His eyes narrowed. '. . . It's not personal out there. It's every guy for himself. They're doing the same.'

'Are they? The snowboarding community is known for its camaraderie. There are plenty who think it shouldn't be an Olympic sport; that even just competitions erode the spirit of it.'

'. . . I meant the surfing world.'

'Do you still think of yourself as a surfer?'

His jaw slid forward slightly. 'Of course. I lived and breathed it for twenty years. How could I not?'

'Do you think you'll ever love snowboarding in the way that you did surfing?'

'I prefer the weather in surfing.'

He was being pithy but she smiled. 'Ari said pretty much the same . . .' She knew it would put him off his stride, just a little, to be reminded that other people had talked. He couldn't know exactly what they'd said, what she knew about him. 'Why have you come into snowboarding – *really*?'

'There was nothing left to win in surfing.'

'So you didn't feel driven out, then?'

'. . . No.'

'Have you felt welcomed by the snowboarding community?'

'. . . I'm not here to make friends. I've come to win.'

'To prove yourself?'

'*To* myself. I'm not interested in what other people think of me.'

'So you want to be Kit Foley – nine-time world champion surfer and world champion snowboarder – for you.'

'Yes.'

She could feel the questions beginning to gather a rhythm; as his answers became shorter, she knew she was nearing the nerve centre. She was skirting the main issue and he knew it. '. . . Why does it matter to you so much to be a winner? Is love of the sport not enough?'

'I like having targets. It focuses the mind.'

'So you would refute that you left surfing because your reputation was tarnished after the incident with Cory Allbright at Pipe Masters?'

'Yes. It was time to move on.'

'Tell me about your history with Cory. Most people don't realize you were good friends once.'

He didn't reply for a moment. She had dangled a carrot and he knew it – an opportunity to give another perspective on a story everyone believed they already knew. To her amazement, he took it.

'He was one of my best mates. Once I went pro, at fourteen, we basically toured the world together. We'd share hotel rooms to save money. Hang out together.'

'You were best man at his wedding to Mia.'

He shifted in his seat, looking openly uncomfortable. 'That's right. I was there the night they met.'

'You're godfather to his oldest son.'

He nodded. His fingers, interlaced, were blanched slightly at the knuckles.

'So what went wrong between you?'

'. . . Who says it did?'

'Everyone's seen the footage of that final at Peniche. They can see the body language between you on the beach beforehand; even paddling out, you looked to be scrapping . . . You were cutting in on his lines; you kept blocking his runs, running down the clock. Why?'

'To win.' He shrugged, as though it was obvious.

'But you couldn't.'

'Couldn't I?'

'He was leading the heat and the league. He had ten thousand points. You had seven thousand eight hundred. He only needed one more good run to win that event and secure the world title.'

'And if he didn't get the good run, it would push the world title back to Pipe Masters.'

'You couldn't have caught him up. You would have needed straight tens at all events.'

'Then I'd have been going for straight tens.' He shrugged.

'You were coming back from injury,' she pointed out. 'You were off-form.'

'Yeah. All of that – and I was still placing second. It's never over till it's over. Cory knew that.'

She stared at him, seeing the arrogance in his eyes. 'And would he have done what you did, if he'd been in your shoes?'

A sour smile sat on his lips. 'Oh yeah. Cory tried to do a lot of things in my shoes. He was a fighter.'

'When did his friendship become so meaningless to you that his safety was something you could just toss away . . . for a *win*?'

For a couple of moments, he didn't stir; the close-up camera would record almost nothing different in his demeanour, but Clover could see his breathing had become more shallow, that a sudden bleakness had come into his eyes. Then he sat forward in the seat suddenly. 'He chose to do what he did. He chose to ride.' He was speaking through gritted teeth. 'I didn't see the double set coming in. I was focused on the clock . . . When I saw him go down and stay down . . . I tried to get to him. I did what I could.'

'But it was too late,' she said simply. 'He was under the water for four minutes and thirteen seconds.'

He stared back at her with a blackness that made her feel her skin might blister. As though *she* was responsible for what he'd done. '. . . Could you hold your breath for that long?'

He blinked. 'No.'

'. . . Do you try?'

'I don't know what you mean.'

'You still train like a surfer. Even though you're now living in a country with no coastline.'

'I don't know what you're talking about.'

'In the pool, at this chalet here in Zell am See, you practise holding your breath, don't you?' Her stare was even. It was her turn to weaponize their mistake.

'. . . Yes.'

'Why?'

'Habit.' He shrugged.

'Not guilt?'

'No.'

'Not . . . trauma?'

'No.'

'As you said, you were out there trying to save him, to get to him. It must have been a horrific few minutes, dealing with those waves, trying to find him. Knowing that with every passing second—'

'Stop!' His jaw balled. 'Just stop . . . I was there. I remember.' He looked away, out of the window.

She waited for him to bring his attention back to her; she knew the footage on the close-up camera would be capturing his conflict.

'How long can you hold your breath for, Kit? What's your PB?'

His voice, when he finally spoke, was quiet. '. . . Four minutes, eight seconds.'

She let the silence lengthen, let the intimation become clear – it would have been five seconds too much for him too.

'Do you miss him?' Her voice was soft, gentle. His eyes narrowed, instantly distrustful of her sympathy.

She waited for his answer. Would he be snide here? Give an answer of defiance just to deny her the revelation she was pushing for?

'Yes.' His voice was different. The brittle hardness had gone.

'If you could go back, do things differently . . . would you?' It was the question Cory had never answered.

'Of course I would. I'm not a monster!' His voice cracked. He cleared his throat. 'But I can't, so . . .' He gave a shrug, the hardness coming back to his face.

She stared at him. 'People don't know the impact it's had on you, do they? In your heart and in your mind, you're still a surfer and yet you've turned your back on the sport you love. You lost sponsors. You lost the woman you love—'

His head whipped up. She could see the confoundment in his face. Clover hadn't named Amy, but her words had been specific. Targeted.

'What do you have left in your life . . . except winning?'

He stared at her; she knew she'd stunned him with her tactic – coming in hard like he was expecting her to, then pivoting and presenting as a sympathizer, a friend even . . . then turning again. There was a hard silence. '. . . Let me ask *you* a question.'

Her eyebrows lifted in surprise. She shook her head. 'That's not how this works.'

'Do I look like someone who gives a damn about rules?' he asked, leaning forward suddenly so that his elbows were on his thighs. 'You want me to open my soul to you while you sit there and judge me and give nothing back?'

'Yes. This film isn't about me. We're here for your story.'

'*I'm* not. I'm just minding my own business, living my life. I didn't ask for any of this. You know that.' He continued to stare at her, his weight on the front of his chair. 'It'll get edited out anyway. Why are you so scared of making this a two-way conversation?'

'I'm not.'

He stared at her, waiting.

'Okay, fine.' She gave as careless a shrug as she could muster. 'Ask me a question then.'

His gaze was steady. He didn't miss a beat. 'Why should I trust you? What's *your* driver for being here?'

'I want to hear your side of the story.'

'No you don't. You've already got the answers to these questions you're asking me. You got them doing exactly this with Cory. There's another reason why you're here.'

She stared back at him. 'Okay . . . Everyone knows what you did, but no one knows why, and Cory never said, no matter how many times I asked him. I want to know why you played dirty against an old friend.'

'But why? *Why* do you care why I did it?'

She frowned. 'Because I care about—'

'Justice?' His eyebrow arched; there was mocking in his tone and she remembered her conversation with Julian at dinner, the night he'd been attacked. She'd seen how he had registered her discomfort, how he'd somehow known it led to the very heart of her. 'What makes you qualified to decide what's just? What would you know about *anything* I might tell you? I bet the worst thing that's ever happened in your perfect life is . . . getting dumped. Not getting your hair done.'

'Don't be insulting.'

'Yeah? Tell me I'm wrong.'

'You're wrong.' She stared back at him but he was the one waiting now. And she could tell he wasn't going to speak, not another word – on this or anything else – till she'd given him the reason why he should trust her. Suddenly, this film – and her entire future – was resting on telling him about her past.

She felt her heart contract, hold and collapse into a gallop. Even just the memories of it were enough to put her body in flight mode. '. . . You make assumptions about me,' she began, her voice quivering with resentment. 'You think you know what I am. I look a certain way. I sound a certain way. And maybe I am everything you assume – but I'm also not. Yes, I grew up privileged: lived in an eight-bedroom house, went to a top school, had ponies . . . I was spoilt and lucky and sheltered. All those things – until I was fourteen and my father was accused of fraudulent trading. He was jailed for seven years and we lost our home . . .'

She saw a frown buckle his brow.

'. . . My mum and brother and I ended up living in a one-bedroom council flat on the nineteenth floor of a tower block. It was all we could get. Mum gave me and Tom the bedroom so we could sleep and still be able to study in our new school; she slept on the sofa; the walls were so thin you could punch a hand through them; there were crack dealers in the playground . . .' She stared back at him, refusing to show how terrifying it had been: the constant fear, the permanent cold, the light and noise around the clock . . . 'Don't think I expect or need your pity, because I don't,' she said quickly, her voice stony. 'We adapted to the change in circumstances quite well, all things considered.' Her mouth became smaller as her tension increased. '. . . What *got* me was that my father never had a fair hearing. The press had tried him long before the jury – they took pictures of our old house, the tennis court, the pool, the cars . . . Only when his former colleague was arrested, doing exactly the same thing, five years later, did anyone accept what my father had been telling them all along. That he'd been set up.'

He was watching her closely, like a cat tracking a mouse. 'Did he get out?'

She felt her eyes grow larger as the tears tried to gather; she wouldn't allow them to pool. She wouldn't allow her voice to shake. '. . . Not by walking out. He had killed himself in his cell three months earlier. He was broken by the fact that everyone was so ready to believe the worst. He must be corrupt! He must be guilty . . .' She took a tremulous breath. 'My mother died sixteen months later of a stroke. The strain was too much for her to bear.' Her voice faded into silence. She couldn't say any more. There was nothing else to say anyway.

He stared at her, unspoken words passing behind his eyes, unable to find a form.

'So, there it is,' she swallowed, her voice halved. 'That's why I do this. I make sure that people who've been victimized are heard.'

They stared at one another in solemn silence.

'Now I've answered your question, you answer mine . . . What happened between you and Cory that made you block his line?'

She watched him, seeing the words coming, building . . . Unspoken still, but she could actually feel the weight of them inside him. It was like a wave hitting the reef and surging up – an almighty, unstoppable power about to be released and spilled—

He stood up suddenly, breaking the trance. 'I'm not telling you, Clover. And I never will.'

She jumped up too. 'But we had a deal!' Her voice shook with disbelief.

'Yes. I asked why I should trust you – and now I know for sure that I can't.'

'How can you say that?' she cried, the tears pooling in her eyes at last as she forgot to keep them wide. 'I just told you something . . . something I never tell anyone! Johnny and Matty don't even know!' She had laid herself on the line. She'd revealed her past to secure her future – shown him they were both orphans. That they'd both driven into careers that salved their pasts. That they weren't as different from one another as they'd like to believe. He looked down at her. 'And I'm sorry you went through all that . . . I mean it, I'm sorry. I get now what your motivation is.' She could see the sadness in his eyes again, that fleeting melancholy that flashed unbidden from him sometimes. In the pool, in the M+M bar . . .

'So then what's the problem?' she demanded, grabbing his forearm, a feeble attempt to stop him from leaving. She could see the emptiness inside him as he saw her desperation.

'The problem, Clover, is that you've just told me you want to be the champion of the underdog.' Without even looking, he took her hand and easily prised it off his forearm. 'And we both know that's not what I am.'

Chapter Twenty-Two

'I really thought you'd got him,' Johnny murmured, pressing pause. The screen froze on Kit's face, the last look he gave her before he walked off.

They were all in his bedroom, Clover lying on her stomach on his bed. 'I know, so did I,' she whispered, scrunching up her face as she ran again through the conversation. She had thought she'd done it; she'd thought she was there. She'd broken past the act, got him to admit to feelings of regret, vulnerability, loss . . . And then he'd thrown it all back at her.

'It's almost like he *wants* to take the blame,' Johnny muttered. 'He won't play the victim, refuses any sympathy. He's a heartless bastard, guilty as charged, thanks? Everything we think about him is true?'

'Because it is. I guess this is what we wanted, right?' Clover sighed. 'Him admitting to that? He told us himself – he's no underdog.'

'Except we can't use that footage without including your admissions too. There's no way to edit it out and have the rest make sense.'

'No. I know,' Clover winced. It was attraction tactics all over again – *come and get me! Check mate.*

There was a silence.

'I just can't believe you went through all that – with your

dad, I mean,' Matty said quietly. She was sitting cross-legged on the desk chair beside Johnny. 'You never said.'

'Sorry.'

'Don't you be sorry! *I'm* the one who feels bad. I assumed your trust fund was because you were this rich bitch. You hung out with that crowd at uni . . .'

Clover shrugged. 'They liked to party. I wanted to escape.'

'So your flat . . . ?' Johnny asked tentatively.

'Was bought with my inheritance . . .' She took a deep breath. 'And quite possibly lost by my stupidity.'

'Huh?'

Clover bit her lip, knowing this was the moment she had to come clean. The film's viability was hanging by a thread. Without some sort of confession from Kit, all they had was what looked like a vendetta against him – further proof that he was the villain of *Pipe Dreams* in every way. His life had been left in ruins, yes, but he showed no remorse. What were viewers supposed to take away from that? She had promised Mia an answer, but she still needed to deliver a commercial message and so far she had neither.

She looked between her two friends. 'Liam didn't back the film. He wanted Angelina. He thinks this will undermine *Pipe Dreams*.'

Matty's and Johnny's mouths parted.

'So then . . . who's producing this?' Johnny frowned.

'I am. I remortgaged the flat.'

'But the budget—'

'I know.' She looked apologetically at Matty. 'Hence our Saas-Fee shithole.'

Matty's hands flew to her mouth. 'Oh god! I feel like such a cow!'

'Mats, you couldn't have known. I should have told you

both earlier. I just didn't want you to panic. Or feel under pressure. This is my decision. My risk.'

They stared at one another, all understanding the stakes. The question upon which the entire film pivoted was still unanswered and if he wouldn't give it to her after *that*, then when?

No one spoke for several minutes, all of them lost in thought. Was he worth it? Was Kit Foley's big secret – and Mia's right to know it – worth Clover losing her home?

'Y'know, Johnny's right that Kit seems determined to keep the blame, but there were definitely times when it also looked like he wanted to talk,' Matty said quietly. 'I really feel like .part of him *wants* to confess . . .'

'Just not to me,' Clover muttered, meeting her eyes.

'. . . Yeah.'

Liam had been right. If Kit was going to talk to anyone, it would be Oprah. Not her. *Never* her. She had come here for Mia, to finally get full disclosure in Cory's memory. Leaving with anything less than that would be a fail.

'So what do we do?' Matty almost whispered. 'Like you said, you've tried everything.'

Clover's head dropped back into the pillow. She had exposed her innermost pain and he had thrown it back in her face, leaving her feeling like she had exploited her parents' tragedy. For nothing. She had revealed more than he had. He'd been in control almost all the way thr—

She lifted her head suddenly.

'Johnny, just go back on the tight-shot camera to where I said all the things he'd lost – what was it . . . turned his back on the sport he loved . . . lost the sponsors blah blah . . .'

Johnny swung back round on his chair and scrolled back through the frames, finding the right one. They listened closely as Clover's voice filled the room.

'*You lost sponsors. You even lost the woman you love.*'

They watched his head jerk up.

Clover's own head tipped to the side thoughtfully. 'See that? See how quickly he moved? There wasn't anything else that made him startle like that.'

'Well, that's the first time you let it drop that you know about Amy,' Matty said, staring at the screen too. 'You've been keeping him from knowing that you know.'

'Yes. And I didn't even mention her by name. But look at his expression.'

'He's shocked.'

'No, it's more than that. He looks . . . worried.' She looked back at them, thinking harder. She scrambled up onto her knees. 'And right after that, he took all the attention off him and put it onto me . . . Suddenly he *had* to ask a question too! . . . That timing isn't a coincidence. His natural response – based on his behaviour to date – should have been to deny there was a woman he loved, or to deny that he loved her; or to ask me how I knew about her when he's gone to such lengths to keep it hidden? But to completely invert the conversation and put it onto me . . . ?' She looked back at them. 'He just didn't want any attention on her whatsoever. Nothing. Not a breath.'

Matty was looking at her. 'Meaning what?'

Clover arched an eyebrow. 'That she's not just an ex . . . We already know she was with Kit around the time of Cory's accident. For him to react like that . . . she must know something about what happened between him and Cory.' She looked at Matty. 'We have to get hold of her. If Kit's not going to tell us what went down, then we're going to have to make sure she does – even if I have to fly to Sydney and doorstep her myself.'

*

Clover and Johnny sat in the gondola with three others, the windows misting up as they were whisked higher and higher towards the peaks. Matty had stayed back to transcribe Ari and Kit's morning interviews. It had been cloudy in town and she'd been more than happy to change into her cashmere trackies and 'have the run of the place' for the day; Clover wondered if that also meant seeing Julian. Kit and Ari had left – naturally – while they'd all been 'in consultation' in Johnny's room, leaving it to Carlotta to confirm they were back up at the pipe, training.

Clover wiggled her toes in her ski boots, trying to shake off her agitation. It was after lunch and she felt restless. She hadn't been joking about flying out to Sydney. She would do what it took to get an answer to her question. She'd already lived in California with Cory, travelled to Austria for Kit; why not Australia too?

Johnny was reading the piste map, looking for an itinerary route. The recent heavy, relentless snowfall had brought over a metre and a half to the upper slopes and everyone wanted to play. The resort was fully open now and the town was fast filling up, with skiers and snowboarders walking through town on their way to the lifts; the car parks were full, coffee houses crammed and restaurants requiring reservations. Clover thought it was almost a shame that just as everything felt awake and came fully alive again, they would soon be leaving.

She could almost taste her escape. Her to-do list was getting shorter: Kit's debut at St Moritz was the week after next and he was coming into his final preparations, so they needed to capture those; they would also have to record some pre- and post-competition interviews. Beau's sit-down was still outstanding but would have to wait till he returned from Saas-Fee. She needed to get hold of Amy too – of course – and, as bruising and deeply unappetizing as it was, she knew she would have to somehow get another interview with Kit. But could she? He had fulfilled his obligation to the letter, if clearly not the spirit, of the contract: he had let her interview him, as Julian had insisted. Was it his fault she hadn't got what she needed?

The gondola rocked as it swung into the top station and the doors slid back. She waited for everyone else to disembark first. Johnny was holding her skis for her by the time she stepped out. 'All okay?' he asked, handing them over and sensing her pensive mood.

'Yeah.'

'Still pissed off?' he asked, patting her shoulder.

'Wouldn't you be? I feel like I got mugged.'

'You'll get the last laugh. He's the one with something to hide, remember.'

They walked out together onto the snow and threw down their board and skis. The brightness dazzled them both as the clouds parted temporarily and the glacier shone like a crystal bowl. Skiers and boarders speckled the white canvas in multi-coloured dots, like a Slim Aarons print. The Alpine Centre, a 1960s Bond-esque circular building with a medical centre, restaurants and shops, sat off to their left. Clover felt tempted to get herself a coffee and spend the afternoon just enjoying the view; the thought of watching Kit Foley laying down tricks, flexing his latest expertise, stuck in her craw.

They poled over to the chairlift that would take them to the runs above the park and then shuffled over to allow others to sit in the empty seats beside them. Johnny winked at her as they heard people speaking in German, French, Italian, English . . . The difference a week could make! Before they'd left for Saas-Fee, this place had felt almost like their own private playground, just them and a small group of pros.

She liked the feeling of her legs hanging as they soared up and away from the ground. The sun kept playing peek-a-boo with the clouds and she watched as their shadows scudded across the vast, unpisted snow plains. She looked down, searching for animal tracks in the off-piste sections, marvelling at the grotesquely beautiful ice swellings in sudden crevasses. The Ice Camp, on the plateau just down from the snowpark, was full of skiers making the most of the fleeting sunshine and lying back in deckchairs, their faces angled to the sky. They wouldn't have long, Clover thought, looking at the horizon; heavy clouds were coming in from the east. Yet more snow was on the way. This would be a short afternoon's work, and that suited her fine.

'Happy to follow me?' Johnny asked as they disembarked at the top, gliding down the exit ramp.

'Always.' She adjusted the wrist straps of her poles and checked the chinstrap on her helmet – or 'brain bucket', as she had heard Logan calling them in Saas-Fee.

They shushed languidly down some blue runs, staying clear of the ski school groups who could be . . . unpredictable with their turns. Johnny made it look easy, boarding with equipment bags over his shoulder even though a fall onto his back would be painful – not to mention costly.

Within ten minutes, even taking their time, they could see the snowpark below them, black dots flying off white jumps, sometimes successfully, other times not. Clover gave a weary exhale. She could already anticipate the smirking look of victory in Kit's eyes – he had not only made her confess her most shameful secret, but had taken it and used it against her. Try as she might, she could never beat him. Nothing worked.

'Come on, while the light's decent,' Johnny said, as if reading her mind.

They stopped at their usual spot just above the pipe, Johnny reading the activity and light situation. The park felt even busier once they were in it. Young kids and teenagers were throwing themselves over kickers and rails that parents knew better than to attempt and Clover discerned at once that the atmosphere had changed during their absence – it felt more playful, joyous. Only the pipe remained much as it had – the dimensions of the superpipe were too advanced for pedestrian riders – but a crowd had gathered to watch those who could take it on.

'Could be good for some extra talking heads?' Johnny said, seeing the number of teenagers watching on. 'The next generation – do they like him or no?'

Clover nodded reluctantly, skiing over to them and flatly making enquiries as Johnny unpacked his camera and tripod bags. She rounded up a few who were keen to see themselves on camera but their reactions were disappointingly positive: he's a legend; rad; a dude . . . The only one she remotely liked was Kit being called 'a bit old'.

'I'm not sure it's worth it,' she said to Johnny with a defeated groan, after an hour of pointless probing. 'They're impressed by anyone who can do a Cab. They don't give a stuff about something he did in the water four years ago.'

'Yeah, I know what you mean,' Johnny sighed, straightening up and rubbing his face. He looked worn down too. They'd been doing this for weeks. *This* wasn't what the film needed. They both watched as Kit himself dropped in again and flew up their side of the pipe, flying high above them and twisting into a Haakon Flip.

'He's on form today,' Johnny murmured, watching the technicalities with an eye she would never master. All she could see was Kit flaunting his extraordinary athleticism, showing off to an adoring crowd . . .

'Well, he's in a good mood, isn't he?' she said, turning away. '*His* morning went well.'

'Clo, stop beating yourself up. You'll get what you need. Amy's the missing link.'

'And she doesn't want to know.'

'She doesn't know *what* she wants yet. She probably thinks we're out here to blow smoke up Kit Foley's backside! But if things finished badly between them – and let's face it, they would have done – then if we can get her to see that we're not necessarily Team Kit . . .' He raised his eyebrows.

'Yeah. Maybe,' she sighed. 'I just want it to be tonight already so we can get on and ring Sydney.'

'Mats is fully on it.'

A huge cheer went up as Kit finished his run, punching the air delightedly. 'Wouldn't it be great if he just caught an edge and went flying right now, in front of all these people?' she murmured.

Johnny laughed. '*You* need sugar. I'm going to get coffee and chocolate. It's getting cold up here.'

He was right. The clouds had pulled over the sky already, losing light and making everything feel colder. The light was flat and the wind was getting up too. She had seen the temperature as they'd got off the chairlift earlier – minus twelve then, and it had to be lower than that now. It was after three and the sun was already beginning its rapid descent. Days were short in the mountains at this time of year. It would be dark by four.

'Look after the cameras, okay?'

'Alternatively *I* could go,' she suggested as he clipped in. Anything to get away from watching Foley show off.

'I need the little boys' room anyway,' he shrugged, swerving away.

315

Clover sighed and looked back at the pipe. The queue feeding into it was short, but a large crowd had steadily gathered. With the weather closing in, people were taking their last runs for the day, stopping to enjoy a quick show before heading back to the lift stations.

Her phone rang.

'Hello?' she asked distractedly as someone she didn't recognize went for a Front Nine, only to land badly on a Back Five. A loud gasp rippled through the crowd as he spun awkwardly, trying to hold his legs and board up from catching on the hard-packed snow.

The group of teens sitting just along from her cracked a few jokes that she couldn't quite hear. The boarder seemed to be okay, but as he unclipped and walked out of the pipe, Clover could see he was limping.

'Clover?' California crashed down the line: the sound of surf in the background, kids shrieking.

'Mia! How are you?'

Mia laughed, the sound rare. She had almost never laughed in all the time Clover had lived with them, and certainly not since Cory's death. 'You'll never believe what's happened to us, Clo! *I* can't believe what's happened!'

Clover grinned. Happiness was contagious. 'What's happened?'

'Hunter, get your brother! Look, the rocks there.' Her voice was muffled as she turned away from the receiver for a moment. 'Sorry Clo. We're at the beach . . . Guess which beach!'

'Uh . . .' Clover knew their new apartment was twelve miles inland.

'Mavericks!'

Half Moon Bay? Their old beach? Were they picnicking? '. . . Ah! Is it lovely to be back?'

'Oh, we're back! We're back-back, baby!'

Clover was confused. She watched blankly as another rider took off, soaring above her head moments later. Mia sounded almost high, she was so happy.

'We got the house back, Clo!'

It took Clover a moment to understand what she was saying. '*Your* house? The old one?'

'Yeah! Except it ain't old now!'

Clover remembered about the developer . . . Cory threatening to knock his teeth out. 'You bought it back?' Clover frowned. *How?*

'No! That's the thing. It was given back to us!' Mia gave a laugh of utter amazement.

Clover couldn't speak for several moments. *Given* to them? '. . . Mia, that doesn't sound . . . I mean, how is that . . . a thing?'

'Oh that's what I said! Believe me, you shoulda seen my face when my attorney called and said he had something for me! I went in expecting another fucking bill and instead there was a set of keys, and the deeds, in my name! It's ours again!'

'But why? Who . . . ?' Clover was stammering, worried about her friend.

'It's anonymous, he can't tell me. It's the one condition of the contract. But I know who it is. I mean, it's pretty obvious really.'

Was it? 'Who?'

'Razorfish!'

Clover strained to place the name. Eddie Kahale. The surfer who'd led Cory's memorial.

'You heard what he said at the paddle-out. He said he'd make sure we were supported and protected, but I never in a million years thought he'd come good like this!'

'But how could he afford it?'

'Not just him!' Mia laughed. 'It's everyone – the whole surf community! Everyone loved Cory. They've all pitched in to help us, but they're keeping it anonymous cos they know we wouldn't accept charity.'

Could it be true? She certainly remembered the numbers of people who'd come out on the water to pay their respects that day. And she vaguely recalled someone had set up a GoFundMe for them after the film had brought attention to their straitened circumstances . . . 'But you're quite sure it's all legal and binding? It can't be taken away from you?'

'My attorney quadruple-checked it. He said he's never dealt with a bequest like this before, but it's fully legit. Kosher. So we're back in! We moved in at the weekend. Honestly, I still didn't really believe it myself till I saw the kids' boards against the walls of the house again.'

Clover laughed, feeling reassured. 'Well, my god – send me photos then! I want to see it! . . . I just can't believe it! I mean, it's extraordinary.'

Mia sighed contentedly. 'It's so good to be back, Clo. I can't tell you what it was like, stuck in that concrete jungle. The boys just . . . faded. We were all really lost out there for a while.'

'You deserve this, Mia! You've had such terrible things to contend with. I'm so glad something's gone right at last.'

'I tell you – you don't know the meaning of home till you lose it.'

Clover felt her breath catch. '. . . No,' she agreed quietly. She shook her head, pushing away her own problems. 'Well, a lot of people love you very much. No matter how bad things got, you've never been alone.'

'Thanks to *you*, Clo. You helped make this happen. You made people see . . .' Clover heard her friend take a sharp inhale. 'Talking of which . . . how's it going with Foley? Where are you?'

'Well, currently Austria. And right this moment, I am sitting beside a very large, white, shiny halfpipe.'

'I can't believe he's still going for that.' Mia's voice was hard. 'Is he playing his usual games?'

Clover could see the man himself across the way. He had unclipped his board to walk back up and was standing with it lying across both shoulders, arms slung over it casually. Tipper was talking intently to him, gesticulating with animation, bending his arms and demonstrating an action he clearly wanted Kit to replicate. '. . . Yeah. I'm afraid he is.' This morning had been a prime example of that.

'I heard about the punch-up . . . Sounds like he's still an angry son-of-a-bitch.'

'Mmm, for sure.'

'You got any sense out of him yet?'

What she meant was, any explanations for why her husband was now dead. '. . . Getting there. It's been taking a while to establish trust.'

'Yeah. He's cagey as hell.' Mia's sigh whistled down the line. 'Brace yourself, Clo – it probably won't ever happen.'

Clover swallowed. 'I'm doing my best. If I can get that answer for you, I will.'

There was a silence, only the sound of the crashing waves between them; Mia's voice, when it came back down the line, subdued. 'Well, that would be . . . that would be the final thing to give us peace. And knowing that man as I do, he's probably made the fatal error of underestimating you . . .' A commotion in the background made her voice fade out momentarily. She sighed again, back in mummy mode. 'Clo, I've gotta go. Taylor's been stung by a jelly.'

'Ouch. Give him a kiss for me. Speak soon – and send me photos!'

'Sending now!'

They hung up. Clover looked back at the drop-in queue, waiting for the next rider to set off, but he was twisted back and talking to someone. The person behind was showing him something on their phone.

Her own buzzed with an incoming text and she clicked on it, her face breaking into a grin as she looked at Mia's newly restored, newly gifted home. A shiny glass cube it was not. In fact, it didn't look so very different to what had been there before. Had there been planning restrictions in place? She supposed it was a landmark plot. It had the same cottage feel as before, with the wraparound porch and louvre contrast shutters; the only difference was there were dormer windows in the roof, suggesting upstairs bedrooms now. She looked closer, smiling as she saw the familiar Allbright mess: skateboards on the grass, surfboards on trestles mid-wax. Towels and wet swimmers everywhere . . .

A sudden shout made her look up in alarm. Someone had thrown his board down the pipe and she blankly watched it slide up and down the walls in a slowing pendulum.

Huh?

She looked around. Everyone was looking at their phones. Kit was standing in front of Tipper, who was talking on the phone to someone, a hand on his head as if to keep his hat from blowing away. But he wasn't wearing a hat . . .

She looked up and down. Some people were getting upset. There was swearing. Everyone . . .

'Hey, what's going on?' she called over to the teenagers nearest her. But they didn't hear her. They were huddled over a phone, listening to something too. 'Hey!'

A boarder, maybe sixteen, seventeen, with blonde dreads and a gold tooth, looked back at her in surprise.

'Sorry,' she smiled. 'Don't mean to be rude. But what's going on?'

The boy leaned towards her, one hand in the snow. 'There's reports that Mikey Schultz has had an accident in training in Italy.'

She stared at him. 'Mikey?'

'Yeah. The American. Olympic team.'

'. . . Is it bad?'

'They're saying he's dead.' He shrugged. 'I mean, I dunno though. Nothing's confirmed yet. That's just the buzz.'

Clover realized she was standing; that at some point during his words, her body had moved of its own accord, pushing her away from such a diabolical lie. She felt her breath catch in her windpipe and just hold there, neither in nor out.

Mikey? . . . No . . . There was no way . . . He couldn't be . . . She'd only just seen him . . . She was supposed to see him in Switzerland . . . No . . . No . . .

'Hey lady, you okay?' the boarder asked her as she stepped back further. She stumbled against something and fell. The tripod. The camera stood inert and inactive, trained on the empty halfpipe, her skis on the snow. '. . . Did you know him?'

This wasn't right. It wasn't true. There was no way . . . he was twenty-five years old . . .

She got to her feet again, her limbs feeling strangely disconnected from her body. She looked around for Johnny. Where was Johnny? He'd tell her the truth. He'd tell her it was a vicious lie . . .

Coffee. It came to her, a distant bugle. She had to get

down to the Ice Camp. It would be all right once she was there . . .

Blindly, she clipped into her skis, her hands shaking as she grabbed the poles, not bothering with the wrist straps. She had to get to Johnny.

She turned her skis down the slope, sliding down the back of the pipe, coming out along the bottom and not seeing another skier coming down from the far side until they almost collided. There wasn't even time for her to scream and she fell awkwardly, crossing her tips as the other skier executed a sharp turn that covered her in snow.

'Fucking moron!' the skier yelled, continuing on.

She lay there, panting, realizing why she couldn't see properly . . . tears were stinging her eyes. Skiers and boarders zipped past her, telling her to get out of the way—

'Clover!'

Johnny? She looked up but she couldn't see anything clearly. Everything was a blur. She struggled to get up again, pushing up on her poles and just letting the skis run. Her heart was beating too hard; she knew she was panicking. Shocked.

'Clover!'

She just had to get to the Ice Camp and tell Johnny. He would know the truth. He would tell her it wasn't real, just a vicious, wicked rumour, someone's idea of a sick joke . . .

Mikey was not dead. No way. No.

Left, right, left . . . She let the skis traverse the piste in long meanders, not seeing beyond her own tips, barely seeing those. She was skiing badly, turning at the wrong points, going too fast.

The bar was just below the snowpark, a fifteen-minute walk back uphill . . . Coming into sight any second, surely . . . ? Where was it? She glanced up, scanning down the mountain for it. It had been easy to spot from the chairlift, in the sunshine, but now, in the flat light, with the wind skimming a crust off the snow . . .

Right, left, right, left . . . The pitch became steep, the snow softer . . . All she could see was the image of Mikey swerving away from her, saluting her. Cocky, charming, sexy as hell . . .

. . . Not dead. No way.

'Clover!'

The voice was so far away, a voice in her own head telling her to keep going. She had to get to Johnny.

'Clover, *stop!*'

She heard the sound of snow being cut, sliced, thrown into the air – and then she was tumbling. Rolling and rolling . . . She felt one of her skis release. Snow was flying in her face, into her mouth, against her eyes, in her hair—

'*Fuck!*'

The word tore her from her own head as she came to a stop. She was face-down in the snow, panting and sobbing, her body sprawled like she'd been dropped from a height. She opened her eyes and froze – a few metres downhill of where she lay was Kit. He was sitting back with his legs bent in front of him, with one arm hooked, at the wrist, around a sapling fir. He looked frozen into position, his body bracing with tension.

She stared at him in bewilderment. *What* . . . ? She could see his legs shaking, the ground beneath him shorn of snow to reveal yellow grass from where he'd pushed his board as a brake.

Slowly, her gaze sharpened and she saw the sheer drop in front of him. He was on a rock outcrop. Her eyes lifted to the view and she saw the escarpment of the mountain opposite . . . This was not the plateau of the glacier. She gave a whimper of fright. Where the hell was she?

He looked back up at her. He was paler than she had ever seen him. For several moments, he didn't seem capable of talking. He had been inches from going over that drop.

She couldn't speak either. She couldn't understand how they were suddenly here. What had happened . . . ? She lifted her head and looked back up the slope. It was steep, an unholy mess – her parallel tracks cut through by the blade of his board as he'd chased after her.

She'd missed a turn? Come off the piste? But where? When?

Moving slowly, his arm still wrapped round the tree, he lifted his legs into him and unclipped his boots from the board. His movements were jerky and clumsy, partly from the adrenaline, partly the awkward position, and the board slipped from his feet before he could grab it, toppling over the edge and disappearing into a whistling silence.

Still they didn't speak.

She went to get up but he heard the rustle of her clothes and turned back. 'Don't move. I'll come up to you.'

His voice sounded strange, as if hollow. Everything was happening in slow motion. She watched as he crawled towards her, going up to her feet first and pushing down on the bindings of her remaining ski with his body weight. The ski released and he pushed it over to the side, out of the way. 'Sit up.'

He held her arm by the elbow as she scrabbled onto her knees and sat back on her heels. All she could see now was the drop over his shoulder. She had been heading straight for it. She would have skied straight off it. In the flat light, against the white backdrop, she wouldn't have seen it till . . .

He pushed her goggles – now scratched beyond repair – up onto her helmet and unbuckled her chinstrap. He laid her helmet in the snow. 'You okay?' he asked, seeing the tears that had pooled on her cheeks.

She nodded, even as the tears fell. Suddenly faster as it all caught up with her – fright, shock . . .

'I know,' he said quietly.

'Mikey's not . . . ?' she whispered, pleading with him with her eyes.

He looked down. She saw his Adam's apple bob as he swallowed. '. . . Yeah. He is.'

A cry left her and the view was blocked out as his arms wrapped around her. She felt the tension in his muscles, not releasing, as she wept. She couldn't believe it. She couldn't . . .

Mikey Schultz was dead? Twenty-five years young – and a salute, a kiss and a smile was all she had to remember him by.

Chapter Twenty-Three

They waited for the helicopter. Kit's jacket had been fitted with an emergency transponder, pinpointing his position to within three feet. All they had to do was sit tight.

Which was easier said than done. Clover had never sat tighter as she stared into the abyss. She was shivering, in spite of her ski jacket and thermals and gloves. She wasn't sure there was any technical clothing that could counteract sitting still, unable to move off a rock, on a north-facing slope in the Austrian Alps, in the growing dark, in December. They couldn't even dig a snow shelter, the wind whipping around them in menacing gusts. Climbing back up wasn't an option; she'd realized that without having to ask. It was too steep and, below the fresh layer of powder, the snow here was hard-packed and icy. In their boots they could slip. They were safer waiting for help to get to them.

'I don't understand how I didn't see,' she said.

'You were in shock.'

'But how could I not notice the pitch?'

'Adrenaline,' he replied. 'The body steps up in flight mode. It can adapt to almost anything. I used to get it, surfing heavy water. I'd feel physically sick when I looked back at some of the footage of the stuff I rode, but when I was out there, in the moment . . .' He shrugged.

'I would have just skied over the edge,' she whispered, staring at it, the swirl of air where the mountain wasn't.

He looked back at her. '. . . Yeah.' He swallowed, looking away again. 'Lucky for you I'm a Kiwi . . .' And when she appeared not to understand, he added, 'Rugby? I can tackle?'

'Oh. Yes . . . I played netball at school. Not sure how much use that would have been if I'd been trying to save you.'

He gave a faintly bemused look. '. . . No.' It was growing so dark, so quickly, the snow appeared to glow ultra-violet.

'How did you even know I was down here?' She stared at him.

'I was talking with Tipper when he got the call from the US team coach. He told me, just a few moments before I saw you barrelling out past the pipe. I knew you'd . . .' He cleared his throat. 'Had a thing with him . . . so I realized you must have heard, to be skiing like that . . . Then I saw you miss the turn and go off-piste.'

'But you could have been killed too,' she said quietly.

He didn't respond for a few beats. 'Well, you dived into a fist fight to save me. I figured it was the least I could do.'

'Fist fight? Right, yes. Completely comparable to skiing off a cliff.'

He shrugged. '. . . I don't like being beholden.'

A small snort escaped her. 'I didn't have any sense that you felt you were.'

He looked at her but didn't reply. His arms were clasped around his knees as he looked out over the drop. He had made her sit cross-legged, clutching the sapling – 'in case there's an avalanche'; no word of what *he'd* do in that eventuality.

They were stranded in a couloir that faced deeper into the mountains. Kaprun and Zell am See were at their backs, and in the absence of any light pollution whatsoever, the stars were beginning to wink at them, peeping out, one, two, three, four . . .

'Jeez, it's cold,' she murmured, rubbing her gloved hands together. Snow had got inside her coat as she'd rolled down the slope; it had melted, leaving her skin chill and damp.

He looked across and saw how she was shivering. 'Take my jacket,' he said, beginning to unzip his coat.

'No!' She looked at him, horrified. 'No.'

'I'm fine. I don't get cold.'

'*Everyone* gets cold in minus twenty. Even polar bears get chilly in that.'

He gave a small grunt but zipped his jacket closed again. 'You're shivering.'

'I'll cope. They'll be here any minute.' Wouldn't they? How long had it been? Forty minutes? Surely they should be here by now? She suppressed a tremor of fear at the prospect of being stuck out here all night. They'd die of exposure on this rock.

They sank into silence. As much as they struggled with being in each other's company, for once she was glad of it. She felt grateful for the sound of his steady breathing, telling her she wasn't alone in the dark. She could still remember the feel of his arm swooping around her waist, knocking her sideways and pushing her into the lee of the slope.

'. . . I keep thinking of Mikey's parents,' she whispered.

'I know,' he murmured back. She looked over and saw that his head was hanging.

'Did you know him?'

'Not as well as you.'

She recoiled, taken aback by the comment, a sudden flash of his usual temper.

'Sorry,' he said quickly. 'Shit, I . . . I didn't mean that . . .

I really didn't.' She heard him inhale. 'I just . . . didn't behave well, the last time I saw him.'

She remembered the pushing and shoving between them at the chairlift, Mikey's bafflement. 'Why?'

He looked sidelong at her. 'I don't know,' he said after a pause. 'I don't know.'

A northerly gust rounded the cliff and hit them square in the face. She gave another shiver, which he saw. He leaned over and looked at her more closely. 'Your lips are going blue,' he murmured. He pulled off a glove and pressed the back of his hand to her cheek. 'You're freezing.'

'I'm fine.'

'Stop saying that.' He put his glove back on and carefully scooched over to her. 'You need to get out of the wind. Lean in to me.'

'What?'

He held his arms and legs out wide. 'You need body heat. Lean in to me.'

'No.'

'Fuck's sake, Clo. This isn't a *cuddle*. You'll suffer from exposure. Lean in to me.'

More than anything, she was surprised by him calling her Clo. But reluctantly, she let go of the sapling and scurried on her bottom over to where he sat.

'No. Face the other way.'

'So bossy,' she muttered. She changed direction, sitting side on to him, her back now to the wind. He lifted up his knees and brought his arms around her in a windbreak. He tipped her off-centre so that she was leaning against him. Immediately she felt warmer.

'That any better?'

She nodded, her hair rustling against his jacket.

'Good.' She felt him drop his head down, trying to keep warm too, his breath warm into her hair. She closed her eyes, trying not to remember the last time . . . 'Don't tense your muscles. It restricts blood flow.'

She tried to relax them. She could hear his heart against her ear, slow and steady.

They sat there quietly, trying to conserve heat as the evening grew blacker, the wind sharper.

'What if they can't find us?' she asked him.

'They will.'

'But they're taking so long.'

He paused. 'They'll come.'

She shivered again and he clasped her tighter, holding her so closely she could have been a baby in his arms. She felt herself warm against him.

'. . . You're being very kind to someone you hate so much . . . You could push me off this cliff and no one would be any the wiser.'

'Don't think it hasn't occurred to me.'

She lifted her head and looked up at him. He looked back at her, the whites of his eyes the only bright spots in the dark. He looked cold and haunted, incredibly tired – and she felt a sudden, inexplicable, urge to press her lips to his. As though it was the natural thing to do for warmth, human contact, body heat . . . A kindness she could give back.

She saw it run through his eyes too, a surrender of the hostilities that marked their every encounter. She watched his gaze roam over her face in that way it had in the pool, when acrimony had shape-shifted into passion, when suddenly shouting wasn't enough and the verbal had had to become physical. She felt it again now, the need for emotional conflict to find a physical form. They were both cold, frightened, shocked, grieving . . .

She heard a thud-thud-thudding and he lifted his head, like a wolf nosing the air, as a bright light suddenly rounded the mountain, heading closer. Almost instantly, his grip released her, his legs sliding down and letting the wind twist around her once more. '. . . They're here.'

She walked, her head tucked down against the wind and sleet. It felt strange to walk on the flat in trainers after weeks of trekking on slopes in ski boots. So many bodies, so many lights . . . The shop windows twinkled with extravagant displays – snow-dusted reindeer and life-size sleighs, giant wooden Advent houses and mannequins dressed in velvets and sequins, broadcasting that it was time to sparkle, to celebrate . . .

She kept her gaze averted, eyes fixed on the rubber-soled feet of the people coming towards her, stepping around her. Mikey Schultz was dead. That beautiful, vibrant man-child, on the brink of glory and success . . .

She kept putting one foot in front of the other, her hand on the strap of the backpack on her shoulder which was her only luggage. She had packed nothing more than toiletries, knickers and a couple of t-shirts. She didn't want *stuff*; she didn't want to wait. She just wanted to get away from there and from everything that had happened. She had caught the first train back to Salzburg this morning, only Matty aware of her plans and up to wave her off as the chalet slept. The plane had taken off and landed without her even noticing as she'd sat by the window, her head pressed against the glass.

The world felt like it had been pulled inside out; everything was inverted. Life felt chaotic and as fragile as glass. She had almost died. Blinded by shock and horror, she would have skied straight off a cliff if Kit Foley hadn't chanced to have seen her . . . If. Her life right now, today and for ever after, hung upon that singular *if*.

She'd barely slept, her body jolting violently with the sensation of falling. And when she did dream, her mind kept replaying the image of that solitary snowboard swinging up and down the walls of the pipe as the news about Mikey reverberated through the band of brothers. She already knew she wouldn't ever step foot up there, on that glacier, again.

She turned into the street. There was a playground and she could hear the sound of children playing; she realized how alien it sounded to her – unbridled laughter, sheer joy . . . When had she last heard laughter like that? When had she last laughed like that?

The slam of a car door made her look up. A little boy was scrambling out of the back of a black Audi estate, having to slide down the side of the seat till his feet touched the ground. His father stepped out too, reaching back into the car for something in the central compartment. His phone? Glasses? A beautiful dark-haired woman in a padded Moncler coat walked around from the far side and picked up a toddler from a car seat, kissing pink, chubby cheeks.

Wasn't theirs the life Kit had told her would inevitably be hers?

Clover watched as the father walked around and opened the boot of the car, pulling out a Christmas tree, still constrained in its net. The little boy was hopping on the pavement excitedly, clapping his hands as his father effortlessly hoisted the tree onto his shoulder and shut the car boot. She watched the locking lights flash twice as the young family turned towards the smart stone apartment building, the little boy charging up the steps first.

The mother clutched the baby close to her chest, shielding

her daughter from the cold and sleet, as she followed. The father went last, glancing around protectively before he turned in to climb the steps.

He stopped at the sight of her, standing there, watching them, crying.

'Clover?'

It was a moment before she could fully catch her breath.

'. . . Hi Tom.'

Chapter Twenty-Four

'Here?' Clover asked, dangling the striped bauble and looking back at her nephew.

'No! Higher!' Elliot squealed, pointing to the next branch up.

'Here?'

'Yes!' he cheered as she positioned it carefully just above her head.

'I feel like a superhero,' Clover grinned, glancing at her sister-in-law, who was sitting in the armchair, feeding the baby.

'Oh believe me, if it's appreciation that you want, get a dog,' Charlie smiled. 'Trixie makes me feel like a superhero every time I step into the kitchen! It's kind of depressing that no one will ever be as excited by my presence, as the dog!'

Clover laughed. She picked up a glass snowflake and let it spin as it dangled on its thread. Elliot stared back with starry eyes.

'There!' He pointed to a fir frond by her shoulder.

'Here?'

'No, there!'

She placed it three inches to the right. Elliot did his little skipping run on the spot.

'So Tom said you've been in Austria lately?' Charlie looked down at Bella, stroking her cheek.

'Yes, for the past month or so. Zell am See, do you know it? It's quite near Salzburg.'

'No. Is it nice?'

'It's beautiful! The town sits right on a lake, seven hundred metres up, in the middle of the Alps. You should go.'

'Maybe we will. What's the skiing like? Tom's keen to get Elliot on skis as soon as possible.'

Elliot's head lifted at the sound of his name. 'Which one now, Mama?'

'The pom-pom robin,' she pointed, without hesitation.

Elliot handed it to Clover and began scanning the tree for spaces. 'There!'

'There are some great nursery slopes in Zell am See,' Clover said, following Elliot's direction and hanging it on a higher branch. 'And it's linked to Kaprun, which has the Kitzsteinhorn glacier, which is where I've been spending most of my days lately.'

'Lucky you!' Charlie's eyes narrowed as she watched her son still dance on the spot. 'Elliot,' she said in a warning tone. 'Do you need the toilet?'

He shook his head, a little too hard.

'I think you do . . . Go on, quick, quick!' She grinned at Clover as the toddler broke into a sprint for the bathroom. 'There's such a thing as being too excited about putting up the tree.'

Clover chuckled.

'Sorry, go on. While I'm sitting here feeding and giving loo instructions, you were telling me about your incredibly glamorous life.'

'Ha. It's sadly not that! It might sound that way but it's been all work and very little play. The next film's about a snowboarder – that's why we're there.'

Charlie looked up. 'Oh. So are you specializing in sports documentaries now?'

'No, but this story is connected to *Pipe Dreams*.' Clover reached down into the box for another bauble.

'You mean a sequel?' Charlie looked confused. She knew about Cory's death, of course.

'No, more like . . . the other side of the coin. It's on Kit Foley, the guy responsible for Cory Allbright's accident. He's retired from surfing now and is about to make his debut – next week in fact – as a pro snowboarder.'

Charlotte's eyes widened. 'You're kidding?'

'I know. That was what I said. When I first heard he was switching to snow, it just seemed like the ultimate arrogance. Cory's life had fallen apart and the guy responsible was just cruising on like nothing had happened? Then when Cory died, it seemed even more grotesque.'

'So then why are you doing a film on him? I thought your USP was giving victims a voice?'

'It is. Kit's the villain of Cory's story. He's never issued an apology or even made a public statement about his actions that day. I want to know how someone does something like that and still sleeps at night. From the outside, everything's cool – he won the world title the year after Cory's accident – but his sponsors had dropped him, the crowds booed him, some of the other surfers refused to compete against him. He didn't retire from surfing, he was frozen out. Now he's trying to reboot his life but he hasn't exactly been welcomed with open arms on snow either. The guy's reviled. He's got trophies but no glory. Cory may never have had the luck, but Kit – who once had it all – now can't seem to get it back. Is that worse? Cory was a flawed hero, but Kit's a fallen one.'

'So this documentary is to show his fall from grace?'

'Yes. I think people should see he didn't get away with it unscathed. His actions have had consequences that didn't just hurt Cory. There's a public appetite for justice.'

'So what's he like?'

Clover gave a bitter laugh. 'He's hostile and aggressive. He's insular and aloof. Has almost no friends, it's just him and his brother and his manager, who he's known since they were kids. All he does is train, train, train. He never laughs, never smiles. He's a real peach to hang with . . .'

'He sounds depressed,' Charlie said, gazing down at her daughter.

Clover stopped in her tracks. Her sister-in-law, when she wasn't busy creating the perfect family, was a sought-after psychologist. 'Depressed?' She shook her head. 'No. He's arrogant. And angry . . .'

'Yes, but depression often manifests that way. People think it means being sad or teary, but often they present with hostile, isolating behaviours.'

Clover kept on staring at her. Depression? *He's dealing with a lot of shit right now. Although I appreciate he doesn't present sympathetically.* Ari had said that to her. And she remembered the self-help books by his bed, the anodyne bedroom.

'It must be hard for you having to deal with someone like that.'

Clover tuned back in to find Charlie smiling at her. 'He'd be hard work for any filmmaker – much less the person who made him public enemy number one! It's fair to say we haven't exactly hit it off.'

'Sounds gruelling! Is it really worth it? There must be other stories you could tell – with people who are less personally invested in you.'

'Honestly, if I could walk away, I probably would.' Clover

hesitated. 'But I have to stick it out. I made a promise to Mia, Cory's widow.'

'Ah.' Charlie looked at her like it all made sense now.

Clover shrugged. 'She needs to know *why* Kit did what he did. She needs it if she's to have any kind of closure.'

'Cory didn't know?'

'He had some amnesia after the concussion. Any time I tried to press him on it, he'd become incredibly agitated and stressed.'

'Who's stressed?' Tom asked, walking back in with the boxes of decorations he'd been unearthing in their basement store.

'Cory Allbright. Was. Not anymore, obviously,' Clover said quietly.

Tom frowned. 'No.'

'Clo's new film is about the lowlife who *caused* Cory's accident,' Charlie said, sitting the baby up and patting her back.

'What? *Why?*'

'He's about to relaunch himself as a pro snowboarder,' Charlie said, smiling with satisfaction as she got up a big burp.

Tom shook his head in bafflement, as though that made no sense. His expression changed. 'Talking of snowboarders, did you hear about the American guy, yesterday?'

Clover fell still.

'No,' Charlie frowned. 'What happened?' She got up another burp and kissed Bella on the cheek.

Tom lifted the lid on a box and pulled out a chain of paper links. 'Fell badly in a training session for a competition in Italy. Broke his neck . . . twenty-five years old.'

'Poor guy,' Charlie murmured.

'Yeah. Did you hear about it, Clo?' He saw her expression. '. . . Clo?'

She swallowed. 'I knew him, actually.'

Tom looked back at her. 'Oh, shit.'

'Yeah.'

'Did you know him well?'

'. . . Well enough that I was kissing him in a bar in Switzerland last week.'

'Oh shit.'

'Tom, stop saying that,' Charlie said, seeing her expression. But they both still stared at her in wide-eyed silence.

'Is that why you were upset outside?' Tom asked suddenly. '. . . Is it why you're here?'

'She's your sister! She doesn't need a reason to come and see you,' Charlie said, rolling her eyes. 'Ignore him. He has all the subtlety of a pig in stilettos.'

Clover cracked a smile. It was a powerful image – and accurate.

'Look, I didn't know Mikey well. I can't stand here and claim to be heartbroken. But he was a really good guy – fun and funny and charming . . .' She couldn't believe she was talking about him in the past tense. 'We'd made plans to meet in St Moritz next week. It's where Kit's competing,' she added as she saw Tom's eyebrows shoot up in a 'la-di-da' way.

Tom looked blank. 'Kit?'

'Kit Foley. My snowboarder. The one I'm making the film about.'

'Oh. Right.' He nodded. Recognition dawned suddenly on his face. 'Oh – Foley! He's the guy Orsini-Rosenberg's signed up.'

'That's right,' Clover said, faintly bemused that her own brother associated Kit's name with Julian and not Cory. 'Do you know Julian?'

'Julian? No.' Tom gave a smile. 'But I know his brothers. And his father.' He gave a low whistle.

'What does that mean?'

'Let's just say, you wouldn't want to be sitting around that family dinner table now. They are feeling the heat.'

'From what?'

'Fending off a hostile takeover bid. Noble Hotels Group has been circling them for eighteen months now. They're in scorched earth mode – selling off assets left, right and centre trying to stay alive; meanwhile Junior's wanting to play at being a snow mogul, thinking that's the answer to all their problems.' Tom pointed at her as he remembered something. 'Didn't this Foley get into a fight, right when Rosenberg made his big announcement about sponsoring some . . . tour?'

'Yes.'

Tom laughed. 'I mean, you couldn't make it up.' He shook his head. 'My advice, if that guy gives you a tip for the horses, do the opposite! Midas he is not.'

Clover rolled her eyes. 'Thanks, but my involvement with him is very limited. He's just been useful to me for getting Kit to play ball. If it wasn't for him, there'd have been no film.'

'Yes, I'm sure he can be very persuasive. He's well connected and charming – just no businessman.'

Charlie lifted up the baby and sniffed her nappy. 'Yep. Time for a change,' she said with a roll of her eyes. 'Back in a bit. Tom, get the fire going, won't you? And open that bottle of red. Clo must be dying for a drink.'

'I just made her a tea!'

'She didn't travel all the way over here for *tea*, Tom.' Charlie and Bella left the room, taking the distinctive odour with them.

'Is my wife who's always right, right?' Tom asked her. '*Do* you need something stronger than tea?'

'. . . Yes.'

He looked at her for a moment, seeing her paleness. He

walked over and gave her a long hug, the only person in the world who loved her. 'Come on then, sis. To the kitchen.'

She followed him through the beautiful apartment. It was all grey contemporary sofas and yellow curtains, mid-century lights and framed lithographs. The kitchen was an ode to minimalism with marble counters and white glossy units, not an appliance or even a handle in sight; Clover supposed it was as good a system as any for keeping the kids out.

'Is it the snowboarder?' he asked her, pressing a door and revealing a glasses cabinet.

'Yes. And also no,' Clover sighed. 'I guess I just needed to . . . breathe.'

Tom glanced back at her as he reached for a bottle of merlot. 'I'm glad to hear it. You *not* breathing would be an issue for me.'

'Ha.' Her smile faded again. 'Although . . . I almost skied over a cliff yesterday.'

She saw him pale like a cartoon character. 'What?'

'I'd just heard about Mikey and . . . I was upset and I missed a turn and ended up off-piste and . . .' She swallowed.

'How close was it?'

'. . . Within metres.'

He put the bottle down on the counter, his palms splayed flat, his arms locked. 'Christ. Clo! . . . I can't believe you stopped in time.'

'I didn't, that's the thing. I didn't even see it until after I was down.'

He shook his head. 'I don't understand . . . How did you stop, then?'

'Kit stopped me. He . . . tackled me.'

'He *tackled* you?'

'He was on a snowboard and he tackled me.'

'He tackled you, on a snowboard?'

'Yes.'

'. . . And he's okay?'

'He's fine. We were just both a bit shaken up. We got pretty cold waiting for the helicopter.'

'*Helicopter?* You had to be helicoptered off?'

She nodded, remembering how Kit had helped her into the harness that had been lowered to them, and clipped her in. She remembered the feeling of becoming weightless, spinning away from him, his upturned face below her feet as she was winched to safety.

'. . . Christ, you do need that drink!' Tom began peeling back the wrapper. 'And you owe *him* a drink, that's for sure.'

She gave a wry smile as he started pulling on the cork. 'Trust me, he wouldn't accept it from me.'

It gave with a satisfying *pop*.

'Why not?' He poured her a large glass. Very large. Then one for himself too.

'We don't exactly get on. We've got a bit of a hate–hate thing going on.' She saw his blank look. 'He's responsible for Cory's accident. It's because of him Cory's dead.'

'Oh, right.' He looked puzzled. '. . . But he also saved your life.' He held his glass out to her. 'And I'll drink to that!'

'Huh?' She stared back at him.

'Well, he might be why Cory's dead – but he's also why you're alive.' He shrugged and took a deep glug. 'That's worth cutting him slack, surely? At the very least, you've got to buy the guy a drink!'

'You don't understand, Tom,' she sighed, watching as he turned and pressed on another door. This time, the fridge was revealed. He reached in and pulled out a slab of manchego. 'He hates me. Like properly reviles me.'

'And yet, not enough to let you ski off a cliff,' Tom said,

placing the cheese on a board and beginning to cut it into thin slices.

'Well, no, but—'

'It sounds to me like perhaps *you're* the one who's taken this "enmity" too much to heart.'

'You're a lawyer, you would say that; your heart is made of ashes and straw,' she tutted. 'But this isn't about my feelings – Cory was my friend. I'm trying to defend him.'

'Against what, though? Yes, something went horribly wrong with Cory; that accident was terrible. But luckily it went right with you.'

'Why are you defending him?'

'I'm not, but you seem to have taken the position that this Foley's a bad guy – yet bad things can happen to good people, you know.'

'He's not good.'

'He saved your life.' Tom watched her carefully as she struggled for another line of argument. 'You know, there's a quote by Roosevelt that I've always liked.'

'Ugh, said the lawyer.' Clover rolled her eyes, aware she was reverting to her teenage self in her brother's company.

He grinned at her. 'Roosevelt said –"We consider too much the good luck of the early bird, and not enough the bad luck of the early worm."'

Tom let the words settle as Clover stared at him. 'Who's the worm in this?'

'He is.'

'*Kit?* You think Kit Foley's the worm?'

'He could be. Have you ever stopped to even consider it?'

'No!' she scoffed.

He raised his glass to his lips, watching her with a bemused smile. 'Well, don't you think perhaps you should?'

Chapter Twenty-Five

'Clo! You're back!' Johnny couldn't keep the relief from his voice as he twisted on the sofa to look back at her. She smiled from the snug doorway, surprised to find him watching a rugby match with Ari and Kit.

'Hey.' She had spent five days in Geneva in the end. It had felt so good to escape, she hadn't wanted ever to come back. There had been such a happy simplicity to being with her family – reverting to type, as Kit would have said: taking Elliot to the park, walking Bella in the pram . . . She and Charlie had baked mince pies and finished a bottle of red as they watched their from-scratch gingerbread house gently sag and collapse (too much golden syrup). She had sat at the kitchen table, making paper chains with Tom and Elliot, chatting about everything and nothing. She had surprised Elliot with a miniature Christmas tree for his bedroom, such had been his excitement about decorating the main one, and she had got him to teach her how to make pom-pom decorations and paper snowflakes. She had completely switched off, refusing to think about the film, or her flat, or the Cannes deadline, or how she was going to keep her promise to Mia, or whether Kit Foley was an early worm. That especially. She had spent a lot of time refusing to think about him.

If it had been left to her, she would still be in Geneva; but

Kit and Ari were scheduled to leave for St Moritz tomorrow and she knew she had to see this last bit through, even if her film was asking a question it couldn't answer. If nothing else, she couldn't leave Johnny to deal with Matty's packing. 'Have I missed much?'

'Not really,' Ari shrugged. 'Kit's just been training, training, training. We've been on the pipe, on the trampos. And watching the rugby every night.' He grinned. 'Making the most of having no women about the place!'

'Oh? Where is Mats?' She hadn't been in the bedroom just now.

'She's been doing some work in town,' Johnny said quickly, scrambling to his feet. 'D'you need a hand with your bags?'

She went to tell him she'd only taken a rucksack but something in his demeanour made her nod instead. 'Yeah, thanks.' Her gaze tangled with Kit's as she went to turn away; he'd not said a word.

'What is it?' she whispered to Johnny as he hustled her towards the stairs.

'Not here.'

They went down to her room and he shut the door carefully. 'Mats got hold of Amy,' he whispered.

Clover's eyes widened. 'And . . . ?'

'"She's no lady" were her exact words. Amy has quite a lot of anger, shall we say, that their engagement has been revealed. It's fair to say things between her and Kit *didn't* end well. She never wants to see him again.'

'Well, did she say why they split?'

'Matty couldn't get that far. It was a stream of expletives, threats about calling in lawyers and then she hung up. Mat's been trying every day since but . . .' He shrugged.

'. . . Why would she call in her *lawyers*?' Clover frowned.

'It's not a crime to know, or make public, the fact that they were engaged!'

He shrugged again.

'And why didn't Matty tell me she'd got hold of her? Or you?'

'We wanted to, but it's not like she's given us anything but an earful so far. We thought it was better to let you . . . rest. You've been stretched too thin lately. What with the stress of dealing with Kit, getting punched in the face, the news about Mikey, then almost skiing off the side of the mountain . . . ! No wonder you needed the peace and quiet of the city.'

Clover sighed, squeezing his arm gratefully. She still flinched every time she heard Mikey's name; his death had been widely carried in the news. 'So where is she now?'

'Well, that's the other thing. Her and Julian . . .' He arched an eyebrow. 'It's officially on.'

'Oh.' Clover's shoulders slumped.

'Yeah. He followed up the flowers with *more* flowers, then dinner, and . . . she's scarcely been back since.'

'What? So you've been up here every night on your own? With *them*?' She jerked her chin towards the ceiling.

'I know! How brave am I?' He flexed a bicep. '. . . They've actually been decent; let me continue filming, no probs . . . We've had a laugh.' He winked. 'It's amazing how nice Kit is when *you're* not around.'

'Thanks!' she chuckled. 'I told you it was personal.'

'Oh it's personal all right. I think he actually likes fighting with you.' He looked back at her. 'You should have seen his face when Matty told us at breakfast that you'd gone to see your brother for a few days! He was stunned. Like it hadn't occurred to him that you actually could act of your own free will.'

'Yeah. I'll bet he was gutted.'

'He has been pretty flat, actually. Beau's extended his stay in Saas-Fee; he's meeting us now in St Moritz.'

'*Really?*' she asked interestedly. '. . . It definitely sounds like he's finding his wings.'

'Yeah, I agree.'

She sank onto her bed and fell back, her arms outstretched. 'So, are you all set for leaving tomorrow?' she asked. 'It's gone by quite quickly, don't you think?'

'I'm certainly going to miss that view; and the gym. And Fin's cooking. And Carlotta's creepy instinct for appearing around corners unannounced.'

'Yeah. We've been spoilt . . . How did Kit look in training? Do you think he's ready?'

'Physically, yes.' He tapped his head. 'But I think the news about Mikey has definitely got to him. The vibe's been different up there this week. I don't think he's looking forward to tonight. There'll be a load of press there.'

'Where?'

'At the casino.' Johnny saw her blank expression. 'You don't know? I thought that's why you came back in time. There's a big charity fundraiser being held at the casino in town. Julian's a sponsor, natch. He's making Kit go.'

'Well of course he is.' She rolled her eyes. Where Kit went, she had to follow. Back five minutes and she was straight back into it. 'You know, talking of Julian, you should have heard the things my brother was telling me about his family's business . . . Things really aren't as rosy as Mats might like to believe.'

'No?'

'They're being eyed up for a hostile takeover, apparently. Julian's under pressure to start making a success of his side of things because absolutely nothing else is going right for them.'

'Mats won't be happy. She's bought into the whole Prince Charming thing.'

'Well, he is still that, I guess, just possibly with a smaller dowry,' she sighed. 'So what time is kick-off?'

'Eight.'

'*Eight?*' It was gone six now!

'And the dress code is black tie,' Johnny added casually.

'But you don't even have a collared shirt!'

'I can wear Beau's DJ, apparently. We're about the same size.'

'But I didn't pack for black tie in the mountains!'

'Chill, Cinderella.' Johnny walked over to the wardrobe and opened it with a flourish. Clover stared at Matty's jewel-like clothes. 'For you shall go to the ball!'

Yellow silk. Red suede heels. Clover stared at the combination draped over her bed. It worked – but what had ever made Matty think these clothes would be needed on this trip? Clover supposed she should be grateful that such exigencies existed in her friend's world.

Matty – already at the hotel with Julian – was meeting them at the casino.

Clover opened her door and called across the hall. 'Johnny, can you zip me in please?'

'Just a sec,' he called back through his door. 'It's a fight to the death between my cuff and a cufflink over here!'

She ducked back into her room and put in her earrings and stepped into the heels, slipping the heel strap on with her finger as she heard him come in.

'Thanks Johnny.' She straightened up and held her hair up, out of the way. She waited. '. . . Well go on. You've seen a woman's bare back before. Zip me up.'

There was a pause, then she felt him run the zip up slowly,

348

pulling the dress in to her body. 'Thanks.' She wiggled a little, getting the dress to settle. She turned.

Kit looked back at her as she let her hair fall. 'Oh.'

In her heels, she was only a couple of inches shorter than him. 'I just came to check you were okay.'

'. . . Me?'

'After the other day, I mean. When you left the next morning, I thought . . .' His words ran out and he shrugged.

What? What did he think? She could never tell. She could peel back one layer, only to find a hundred more. Who lay at the heart of him? 'I'm fine. I just needed to get away for a bit. Things were . . .' It was her turn to run out of words.

'I know.'

She couldn't understand why he was down here. He'd never checked on her after the fight, when she'd had far worse injuries. He'd got her off that ledge without so much as a split nail – so why check on her now? 'Are *you* okay?' she asked.

He looked surprised by the question, as though it wasn't something he'd ever been asked. He flinched, a defensive reaction. 'Of course.'

'Of course, because you're invincible? It's not every day you almost go over a cliff. You're allowed to feel shaken up, you know.'

He stared back at her, looked away. He stuffed his hands into his trouser pockets. He was wearing a dinner suit she didn't remember seeing in the wardrobe. '. . . I'm more shaken by the fact that I didn't push you off while I had the chance. What the hell was I thinking?' he muttered, before giving a brief, dark smile.

She watched him stare at his shoes. He looked as uncomfortable as Ari about to be interviewed.

'Well, my brother was very grateful you saved my life. He says I owe you a drink.' She gave a short laugh. 'Don't worry,' she added quickly. 'I set him straight on that score.'

'What do you mean?'

'That hell will freeze over before you'd accept anything from me.' She swallowed. 'But still . . . thank you.'

He stared back at her and for a moment, she remembered being on the ledge with him, his body a windbreak, saving her all over again. She tried to gauge the setting between them. Where did they stand now? In the hours before she'd almost skied off the mountain, he had thrown her interview – and secrets – back in her face. She had hated him more then than ever. Now she no longer knew what to feel about anything when it came to him.

He stuffed a hand into his trouser pocket. 'So are you coming tonight?'

Her eyebrow arched. Couldn't he tell? She was standing before him in heels and a column of yellow silk. 'Well, I don't usually wear a gown for a TV supper, so . . .'

'Right. Yeah. I mean, you look—'

'Right Phillips, breathe in . . .' Johnny appeared over Kit's shoulder. 'Oh!'

Kit half-turned. A small silence bloomed. The room felt airless and Clover felt strangely awkward, as though she and Kit had been caught doing something they shouldn't. Something other than talking.

'Sorry Johnny, Kit helped instead,' she said with a weak smile.

'I was just leaving anyway,' Kit said quickly, stepping past Johnny and patting him on the shoulder. He couldn't get away fast enough.

Johnny turned back to her, looking astonished by the rapid exit. 'Was it something I said?'

She listened frustratedly to the sound of Kit's footsteps on the stairs. How *did* she look?

Chapter Twenty-Six

Ari swung the car round towards the casino entrance. Even with blacked-out windows, the photographers' flashes were dazzling. Johnny was already filming from the back seat, his camera trained on Kit's profile. Kit's hand automatically went up to shield his face.

'Jump out. I'll meet you in there,' Ari said with a grim expression.

Kit's door was opened by a doorman and the outside noise – and freezing night air – leaped into their cream-leathered, climate-controlled sanctuary. Clover felt her nerves grate; she had had a taste of this at the BAFTAs and Golden Globes and it felt so abrasive, the press huddled in a scrum, voices yelling as they saw Kit emerge.

Johnny didn't wait to have his door opened. He had leaped out before the wheels had fully rolled to a stop, running around the car to continue filming Kit's arrival.

Clover's door was opened too, and she made a point of pinning her knees together as she swung her legs round to slide out. The skirt of her dress was narrow and the car was high off the ground. The doorman offered her his hand for balance.

'Thank y—' She saw the hand belonged to Kit.

Ari pulled away, withdrawing the car's protective shield, and Kit's eyes lifted off her onto the press again. He wore his distrust like a mask. There were no smiles, no waves (much to Julian's later chagrin, no doubt). Clover wasn't sure she blamed him. Only a couple of weeks ago, the same publications had plastered their front pages with images of him being beaten, with headlines that suggested he had started the fight; now, looking handsome in black tie – and he did, he really, really did, look handsome in black tie – they wanted him to smile and pose for them?

A man in a dark suit indicated for him to stand on the red carpet laid along the ramp that led up to the doors. Large placards highlighted the charity this benefit was in aid of, with Orsini-Rosenberg Hotels as one of the evening's sponsors, their name large and bold across the top.

Johnny got into a crouch, his camera's eye trained on Kit as he was led into position for the press. There was an explosion of light and noise, like fireworks bursting in front of their faces.

'Kit! Over here!'

'This way, Kit!'

'Look at me!'

'Can you smile for us, Kit?'

He could not. He wouldn't even turn his head; he stared dead ahead, looking like he wanted to jump into their melee and start another fist fight.

'Ma'am?'

Clover looked up. The man in the suit was holding out his arm, indicating for her to take her place beside Kit. She shook her head firmly.

He indicated again.

'No.'

She saw Kit's eyes graze in her direction, but he didn't move.

'Clover!' She looked up and saw Julian – and Matty – standing up by the doors into the casino. Julian had his hands pressed together in a prayer position.

Clover was amazed. Was he really so openly desperate? Had he no pride?

She looked at Matty, who was standing beside him in a tiered black lace dress and looking radiant. *'Please,'* Matty mimed, before turning her mouth into an upside-down smile and tracing a pretend tear wiggling down her cheek. Her friend certainly had none.

Clover looked at Julian again. He was still pleading with her, his hands in prayer, and she remembered what Tom had told her about his family's business worries.

'Ugh,' she groaned, allowing the man to shuttle her in front of the camera too, positioning her by Kit's side.

She heard her name mentioned by one of the photographers – then Cory's too – as the three-way connection between her and Kit was suddenly, finally, realized. Once more, the light cloud crackled and popped as everyone clamoured to get a photo of Kit Foley standing beside his nemesis.

'Oh my god,' she breathed, not moving her mouth. 'This is horrific.'

In response, as though they were still on the mountain, she felt Kit's fingertips at her waist, lightly at first but then becoming bolder. She felt his warmth through the thin fabric of her dress – she had no suitable coat, of course. The light pops doubled in frequency.

She froze. Was he trying to make her feel better? She glanced up at him in bewilderment, only to find him already looking straight back at her. The photographers went into a further frenzy as his eyes locked with hers like they were newlyweds on the church steps, like they had on the rock, in the pool . . .

No. She realized what he was doing. She knew he would kiss her right here, in front of them all, if it would give the press a controversial image. The two of them – *more* than friends? When just being friends was a big enough story? It was another game, a perfect way to undermine her.

She pulled back.

'That's your lot,' he said brusquely to the photographers, removing his hand from her waist. He turned to go in.

Clover walked up the ramp and into the warmth. She gave a huge shiver, rubbing her bare arms and feeling the goosebumps as Matty rushed over.

'Uh . . . what the fuck was that back there?' Mats murmured in her ear as they kissed cheeks. 'I thought he was going to go in for a snog!'

'Mind games,' Clover murmured back. 'Imagine *those* headlines.'

Matty just stared at her with a funny expression.

'Thanks for the dress, by the way.' Clover pinched the yellow silk fabric.

'Is that m—?' Her eyes widened. 'With those shoes? I never would have thought . . .'

'Meanwhile, you're looking gorgeous in *that old thing.*' Clover let her finger tickle the fragile webbed lace. 'Don't tell me he took you shopping?'

'He wanted to!'

'And when did things progress to this stage?' Clover asked, glancing across at Julian and Kit, who were deep in conversation; or rather, Julian was. Kit was standing there, hands in his pockets, his head bent and looking bored.

'Well, what did you expect?' Matty hissed. 'You buggered off for five days. There was nothing else to do!'

Clover arched an eyebrow. 'This is *not* on me.'

'Well, we're leaving next week anyway. It was now or never . . .'

'I just don't want you getting hurt, that's all.'

'I won't! Look, it's just some fun. No hearts will be broken in the making of this film, I promise.'

'Hmm.' Clover wasn't so sure her friend was as unentangled as she thought. She'd never been wooed like this before. She'd grown up with hand-me-downs and too-small shoes, and this world she now found herself in – with luxury hotels at her disposal and designer dresses being bought for her – was a childhood dream. But it wasn't real. Did she see that?

'Come on. Let's leave them to talk shop. You look in dire need of a drink,' Matty said, linking her arm through Clover's and leading her into the casino.

Clover could feel the men's eyes on their backs as they walked.

'Now here's some chips for you. Five hundred euros on the house, to get you started.'

Clover looked astonished as Matty dropped the tokens into her hand. 'Five hundred euros? For free?'

'Yeah, they're doing it for everyone. To get the juices flowing.'

'They've given five hundred euros to every person here?' Clover asked, surveying the packed room.

'Clo, that's nothing to what these people are going to splurge tonight! And thirty per cent of the takings goes to the charity.'

Clover looked at the other guests. She supposed Matty was right – a five-hundred-euro outlay per head was nothing. There were some serious jewels on display, lots of couture dresses and diamante-encrusted shoes. Clover suspected many of the guests must have come in from Salzburg and further afield; she could practically smell the money in here.

She scanned the room, her eyes skipping over the blackjack, roulette, baccarat, poker tables . . . Johnny wasn't allowed to film inside for obvious reasons – even Julian hadn't been able to swing that – but he planned on joining them later 'for a flutter' once all the guests had arrived. Clover was keen that they shouldn't miss any big names who might arrive and be prepared to be interviewed . . . though her hopes weren't high. She certainly didn't recognize anyone so far.

Matty swung them each a glass of champagne from a passing waitress. 'So . . . are you feeling lucky?' she asked, clinking her glass against Clover's.

Luck . . . The wise words of an American president drifted through her head. 'Mats, I think we can both agree luck has *not* been on my side recently.'

'Au contraire, it would have been unlucky if Kit Foley *hadn't* happened to see you skiing down the wrong side of a mountain.'

Clover frowned. 'Have you been talking to my brother?'

'Huh?' Matty pressed her glass to her lips, watching something intently. '. . . You've got to admit he looks good in that DJ.'

'No comment,' Clover muttered, trying to sound bored as she nonetheless followed Matty's line of sight and saw Kit and Julian standing beside the blackjack table. She remembered how Kit had paused before zipping her dress. Why had he paused? 'Tell me about Amy,' she said, turning away and changing the subject.

Matty's eyes widened excitedly. '*Right?* Did Johnny tell you?'

'He told me she threatened to set her lawyers on us. Why?'

'No idea. I didn't get beyond saying your name and that we were making a film on Kit and she went off.'

Clover frowned. 'How did you get hold of her in the end?'

'My cousin came good. He got me her email too, but I decided to call first – I thought it would be better to catch her off guard.' She sipped the champagne. 'That backfired somewhat, but I've sent her an email explaining what we're doing, along with a link to the trailer for *Pipe Dreams*. That'll show her which team we're batting for and should bring her onside . . . I feel good about it. She was just shocked, that's all, but she'll calm down, and when she does . . . A woman that angry has *got* to want to talk!'

'Well I hope so, because she's our last bona fide chance for getting any kind of insight into what happened with Kit and Cory.'

'You still don't think Kit will talk? Even though he saved your life?'

Clover laughed. 'He won't talk now *because* he saved my life! He'll see that as the ultimate Get Out of Jail Free card. How can I go after him and get him to incriminate himself, when he did the ultimate good deed? That's what I meant by my bad luck. Am I now somehow beholden?'

'No. You took a right hook for him. I'd say it's pretty even.'

That was what Kit had said too. They were entirely free of one another. Neither one of them was indebted.

She followed Matty over to a roulette table. The wheel was spinning fast, the ball jumping over the red and black pens, gilt numbers gradually becoming visible as it began to slow.

'I'm going red,' Matty murmured.

They watched the wheel stop. The ball on red.

Matty gave a delighted laugh. 'Yes! I am feeling it! Come on, let's play.'

They stood by the table. Matty put two chips on red 22. Clover put one across black 14 and red 9.

'You can be a bit more daring than that, surely,' Matty teased.

'Let's test the waters first.'

They watched the wheel spin round again.

Red 22.

'Yes!' Matty whinnied excitedly. Clover watched her chip – and one hundred euros – disappear; Matty received back six. She winked at Clover. 'Again?'

'Sure.'

They set down their chips at random.

'Oh my god!' Mats cried as her numbers came in again. 'I'm on fire.'

A much older man to her right side looked her up and down with a concerned look.

'Not literally,' she reassured him, laughing harder and drinking some more champagne.

Clover drank too. Two chips and she was already crashing out. She had never liked gambling. It didn't excite her to place her future in the hands of luck, or whim, or chance. She knew only too well what it felt like to lose everything at a stroke. It made her feel anxious and jittery. 'I prefer blackjack.'

'Then let's play some of that,' Matty said, gathering up her piles of chips.

They walked through the crowd, past heavily scented women and grey-haired men. There was a large crowd around the blackjack tables and they watched the action, enjoying the show put on by the dealer: the tapping of the table, flawless shuffling and breaking of the decks, hands as fluid as a magician's. There was almost a carnival atmosphere as the game was played, people gasping and cooing according to the whims of the deck. One woman placed fifty thousand on a play – just like that – and lost it, giving the merest of shrugs and a serene smile.

Clover took a read of the room. As the minutes were ticking

past and the champagne glasses steadily refreshed, she could see the tension gradually stiffening beneath sociable, good-natured smiles. Matty had been right – the house's largesse had whetted appetites and things were beginning to get more serious, as players dipped deeper into their own pockets.

They sat down as spaces finally came free. They had been here almost an hour now. Clover felt the pressure of public scrutiny, eyes on them as they sat under the lights before the dealer. It was too easy to lose and yet she was amazed at how everyone was so ready to believe that good luck would fall into *their* laps.

Clover was out in three hands. 'Ah well,' she muttered, feeling privately relieved to be done, as Matty cleaned up yet again. 'At least you're on a roll.'

'Cheer up. Your luck *will* change,' Matty said, handing her some of her own chips as they got up and wandered some more.

'Thanks – but I don't want these; gambling's just not my bag.'

'Hold on to them; a couple, at least. It's just Monopoly money,' Matty said breezily, behaving with an insouciance that belied a thirty-grand student loan and no imminent chance of getting on the property ladder.

'It's not, though, Mats. It may have started with a gift, but that's real money you're holding there. Keep it.' She smiled. 'Or give it to your boyfriend. I reckon he needs it more than me right now.'

Matty gave a confused chuckle. 'Yeah, right. Do you know how much this dress cost? It's Chanel! New!'

Clover shook her head, not interested in the dress. 'His family's business is in trouble. Big trouble.'

Matty looked over and watched Julian at the baccarat table. He was laughing, scooping in an armful of chips. 'Does that look like a man with financial troubles?'

No. Julian looked, to Clover, like the life and soul of the party. He seemed to know almost everyone here and he stood a head taller than most people in the room. His blonde hair gleamed golden under the lights; he was charismatic, dynamic, ebullient. He glanced up, as if sensing their scrutiny; his eyes brightened at the sight of Matty and he waved her over.

'Ooh, come on,' Matty said, going to pull her by the arm.

But Clover resisted. 'No, you go. I'm going to go check on Johnny, make sure he's okay.'

'You won't do one of your French exits, will you?'

'Would it make a difference if I did? Let's face it, we both know you're not coming back to the chalet tonight.'

A coquettish smile spread across her friend's red lips. 'Well, that is true,' she admitted. 'Tonight will probably be our last night together. He said he's hoping to come out to St Moritz but he can't guarantee it. There's so much to deal with here.'

'Exactly – he's propping up his father's ailing empire.' Clover patted her arm in goodbye.

She watched as Matty skittered over to Julian's side. Whatever Clover's misgivings, she couldn't deny they looked good – even right – together.

She scanned the room, looking for Johnny. Had he come in yet? A waiter stopped in front of her and she swapped her empty glass for a fresh one. It was beginning to feel stuffy in here. Her eyes fell to the terrace beyond the glass doors and she was tempted to step outside for a moment, but she knew even one moment would be all it took to remind her of just how cold it could be in a silk dress, beside a lake in the Austrian Alps, in December.

There would be nothing to see anyway. The lake was like a pool of ink, the mountains sleeping under their white cloaks. She went to turn back into the room, her eyes catching on its reflection in the windows. Someone was watching her. Instinctively, she knew who. She stared back at him in the glass, feeling suddenly lost. The world felt like it was pulling inside out again, like an old sock that she couldn't get comfortable with.

She turned. Kit was sitting at the poker table, looking down again, considering the deck.

Clover watched him, reading the body language at the table and sensing the tension between the players. Her eyes fell to the thick pile of chips in the middle of the table. Even a quick scan told her it was several hundred thousand euros. It showed up her own efforts as scant and paltry; then again, he liked taking risks. He had built his life around it.

She moved closer, feeling her own heart rate accelerate at the thought of playing for that much money. A woman in a rose-printed satin cocktail dress made space for her. She said something, which Clover didn't understand.

'I'm sorry, I don't speak German,' Clover apologized. Kit glanced up at the sound of her voice, seeing that she'd come closer and was now watching.

'He's just gone all in. Three hundred thousand. He's going to give it to the charity, if he wins,' the woman whispered in flawless English, jerking her chin lightly in Kit's direction, opposite. 'He's on quite a streak.'

Clover watched Kit closely as his fingers pressed down on his cards. She saw the corner of his jaw ball, eyes moving as the hand was dealt. He glanced at her again.

'Fold.' The man beside him threw down his cards, pushing them into the muck.

Kit didn't stir. Clover watched him breathe. It seemed like every set of eyes in the room was on him. 'I'll raise twenty.' He pushed a chip into the pile; his eyes rose to Clover again.

Twenty? Did that mean twenty thousand?

She looked at the man on the other side of the table. He was watching her too. Or specifically, he was watching Kit watching her.

Clover stiffened, suddenly aware of her every blink. What did any of it mean?

The silence lengthened, the tension growing heavier with every passing moment.

'All in.'

The man's words elicited a murmur around the table. Kit's gaze flickered up to her again, but this time there was heat in his gaze. She knew she had done something wrong again.

The other player showed his hand. A straight flush.

Clover looked at Kit in rising panic, watching as he bit his lip before turning his cards too. One off a full house.

A groan swept the crowd, hands flying to hair, faces scrunched in disappointment as the dealer swept away the chips.

'Oh what a shame!' the woman beside Clover cried.

Kit looked straight at Clover, pinning her with a dark stare that left her in no uncertainty that he blamed her for this loss. Without a word, tossing a chip as a tip to the dealer, he pushed his chair back and got up. Clover watched him stalk away, into the crowd. *What had she done?*

'Do you know him?' asked the woman in the floral dress in surprise.

'Yes,' Clover murmured.

'Clo! Christ, there you are! I've been looking everywhere for you!'

She spun round, to find Johnny heading towards her through the crowd. 'Johnny? Well timed. Kit's just lost three hundred grand on the poker table and supposedly it's all my fault.'

He frowned. 'Why?' he panted. Had he been running?

'Well, I'm breathing, aren't I?' she asked angrily. She looked at him. 'Why are you so out of breath?'

'I've basically had to fight my way in here! You haven't been picking up your phone. I've been texting you for the past half hour!'

'Well, why would I have been picking up texts? I'm in a casino! What's so desperate that you had to text me so urgently anyway?'

She was already opening her evening bag and pulling out her phone. She clicked on the texts.

Johnny watched her expression change as she read, saw how the blood drained from her cheeks. She looked back at him in horror. '. . . Are you sure?'

'You can see it yourself.'

'When did this happen?'

'Just now. It's breaking over there this morning. It's gone mad. The networks are all running with it as their leads. Her husband's a big noise.'

Clover ran over the sentences. 'Do you believe it?'

Johnny looked surprised by the question. 'You *don't*?'

'No, I'm not saying that. I just . . . I mean, we shouldn't assume—'

Johnny gave a surprised laugh. 'I thought you'd be over the moon. He'll have to talk now and *you're* the one with exclusive access to him. You are his only hope. If he wants to have any chance of surviving this, he's going to have to tell his side of things.'

'But he *can't* justify this!' she cried. 'He's ruined!'

Johnny shook his head. 'Then he apologizes. He goes on camera and throws himself on the public's mercy. He wouldn't be the first celebrity to have to prostrate himself.'

364

'There is no chance he'll do that!' she scoffed. 'You know him!'

'Yeah, but Clo, you haven't seen what it's like out there.' He jerked his thumb in the direction of the main doors. 'If he thought things were bad before . . .' Johnny whistled. 'One of the guys working for Reuters picked up an early ping from Sydney and went back to his bosses, told them he was standing right outside the casino where Kit Foley was playing poker . . . They're all waiting for him, Clo. He's going to be walking into an ambush.' He took a breath. 'You need to talk to him and convince him to leave *now*, by the back door. I can get Ari to bring the car round.'

She knew Johnny was right. They had to get Kit out of here before things escalated.

Clover looked around the room. 'Ari's over there,' she said, pointing to him standing by a roulette table, talking to a brunette with impressively sculpted triceps. 'You tell him. I'll find Kit. I just saw him . . .'

But where had he gone?

Johnny ran off, weaving past the bodies, as Clover turned on the spot. Had he gone to another table? She could see Matty and Julian laughing and talking intently with an older couple; they were having a perfect night. Her eyes lifted off them in the next second; this was no time for happiness . . .

She remembered the direction Kit had headed after leaving the poker table and she looked over that way, standing on tiptoe. It felt like a heavy weight was pressing on her chest as she scanned the room. Those headlines couldn't be true. Could they?

She saw him! He was heading straight for the doors.

'Excuse me,' she said, trying to get past a corpulent man in black barathea. 'Excuse me.' The man turned, feeling her hands pushing against him. She couldn't take her eyes off Kit.

'Kit!' she cried, but her voice was swallowed up, drowned in a cheer as someone won big on the baccarat tables. There were so many people. No wonder Johnny had been out of breath trying to get to her. 'Kit!' she cried again, reaching up with her arm.

This time he heard her and turned. He was right in the doorway now. Two more steps and he'd be out on the ramp, in front of the baying pack of photographers, ready to capture his latest shame.

He looked straight at her.

'Kit, wait! Don't go!' she cried.

He just stared at her with his usual inscrutable look, then turned again. Of course he would defy her! The doors were opened and he stepped outside.

'No!' she gasped, pushing now past the people getting in her way. She didn't care if she was rude, she didn't bother to listen to their indignant protests at her lack of manners. But even before she got to the doors she could see the furious glare from the photographers' flashes. It was like seeing an atomic bomb from the moon. White and silent.

She burst through the doors. The noise was like a wall. Kit was being surrounded by reporters, their microphones thrust in his face, all of them asking for a comment, any comment, what comment did he wish to make, on the allegations made this morning by his former fiancée Amy Killicks?

He looked stunned and Clover saw his face freeze as he registered what Amy had done, understanding he had been exposed at last. Slowly he turned, as if knowing she was there. He looked back at her standing on the ramp. He knew she knew.

He knew she was the reason Amy had gone public. They had squeezed her till the pips squeaked, with Matty's incessant calls and emails, asking for her side of the story . . . But Amy didn't trust them. By letting her know they knew about the engagement, they'd forced her to come out swinging. This was her only way to tell the story and control the narrative.

He blinked, three, four, five times, seemingly oblivious to the furore around him. He stood at the eye of the storm. He knew there was no coming back from this. She'd got what she'd come for after all. Kit Foley was done.

Chapter Twenty-Seven

Ari brought the car round and she and Johnny jumped in in silence. In all the commotion, their connection to Kit had been forgotten. The journalists were already filing copy to their editors. They had their backs turned. The big story of the night had already erupted.

They drove through the quiet town without saying a word and if Ari had worked out why Amy had sold her story, he wasn't saying. He was grim-faced, his fists tight on the steering wheel. Kit was already home – he had climbed into a waiting taxi – and they were back at the chalet within a few minutes of him. Clover looked up as they swept up the street – she could see the lights on, not in the drawing room, but beyond the glass wall – in his bedroom.

Ari swung the car into the drive, his hands flexing impatiently as they waited for the gate to slide back. Everything was taking too long . . .

'Leave him to me,' Ari said in a tight voice as they trooped into the chalet's reception hall. He shrugged off his jacket and undid his tie.

Clover's mouth opened.

'I mean it. You don't want to be around him like this.'

She closed her mouth again, seeing Ari's firm expression. She nodded.

'Clo, you need to chill. Go and have a bath or something,' Johnny said, pushing her on her back towards her bedroom, seeming to forget that the only bath in the chalet was in Kit's room.

Ari ran up the stairs in giant bounds.

She turned back to face him. 'Johnny – that was *bad*,' she hissed, her eyes wide.

'I know.'

'We should never have let him go out to that.'

'We did our best to stop him. There was nothing more we could have done.'

'But this happened because of us!'

'Maybe,' he nodded. 'But if what those things Amy said about him are true . . . then he's not really deserving of anyone's sympathy.'

Clover stared at him. 'Do you think they are?'

Johnny squirmed. 'I wish they weren't. But I don't think anyone would deny he's capable of it. Would you want to be Ari right now?'

She sighed. 'It's all such a mess.'

He looked at her quizzically.

'What?' she asked.

'I don't know,' he shrugged. 'I guess I thought you'd be more . . . pleased. This is a shock for us all . . . but it isn't a million miles from what we came out for, either. We may not have a confession of why he did what he did to Cory, but we can get the inside track on *this* story. You can bet your bottom dollar Ari's up there right now telling him to do a sit-down with you and get his story on the record, for once and for all. He'll never have a better opportunity than this. It's all out of his hands now. If he stays quiet, he's ruined. He won't be competing for anyone or anywhere – ever again.'

He looked back at her, seeing how wide her eyes were, how rapidly she was blinking.

'Julian's going to have to cut ties with him now, of course. He has no choice. It's been one disaster after another. He'll be a laughing stock if he continues to back him.' He patted the wall. 'Bye-bye lovely chalet . . . Kit's about to lose a lot of perks.'

'I think perks are the least of his worries,' she murmured. She pulled off her heels, feeling the burn in her feet, and paced anxiously. 'What do you think's happening up there?'

'Kit's going ballistic and Ari's trying to calm him down,' Johnny said flatly. He ran his hands through his hair and gave a weary sigh; Johnny wasn't cut out for drama. 'I could do with calming down myself. That was bedlam. Want a drink?'

'Yes. I'll get it—'

'No! You stay put. I don't want Kit seeing you yet. It'll only make a bad situation worse. I'll go.'

Clover stared in frustration as the door closed behind him. She stood patiently – as patiently as she could – for a few minutes, but she couldn't stand not knowing what was going on. She peered her head out and listened up the stairs. She couldn't hear shouts or the clamour of things being broken. She looked down towards the lift . . . She could get up there almost silently, see if she could hear anything from the top landing . . .

'Don't even think about it.' Johnny came back down the stairs again, drinks in his hands. 'Get back in there.'

She went back into the bedroom. 'Well? Did you hear anything?'

'Nothing specific. Raised voices, but not so loud I could make out what they were saying.'

'I should go up there.'

'No.' He thrust the tumbler into her hand.

'But now's the time to get him to talk. While he's upset. If he calms down—'

'No. He's angry and that'll make him erratic. And if those allegations are true . . .' He gave her a warning look. 'Let him just sit with it overnight . . . Now drink up.' And he threw his head back and downed his cognac.

Clover watched, then followed suit. She winced as it burned her throat.

Johnny was watching her. 'Better?' he asked after a moment.

She nodded, sinking onto the bed. 'Do you think we should tell Mats? She could warn Julian.'

'I imagine they already know. Word spreads fast with scandals.' He gave her a bemused look. 'At least she's there to comfort him.' His tone was flat.

Clover watched him as he wandered over to Matty's toiletry counter and began aimlessly fiddling with the bottles and potions. He looked baffled by the vast array. '. . . Why does she need all this stuff?' he muttered. 'It doesn't make her any more beautiful.'

'You think she's beautiful?'

He half-turned his head. 'I didn't say that.'

'You said "It doesn't make her any more beautiful." Not – "It doesn't make her beautiful."'

He groaned. '*Don't* start interviewing me.' He had his back to her as he absently picked up and put down the various different bottles and ointments on the counter. She watched him smell Matty's perfume.

'Why don't you tell her how you feel?' she asked quietly.

'And what would that be?' he asked sharply.

'That you're nuts about her.'

'Don't be idiotic! She drives me mad. I think she's a horrific snob. And she thinks I'm a horrific slob.'

'Perhaps you should tell her you've got a title, then.'

Johnny went very still. 'How do you know about that?'

Clover sighed. 'It was on a letter to you once – the Right Honourable Jonathan Dashwood.'

His cheeks flushed with a rush of anger. 'I don't ever use it and I don't want her to know about it. I certainly wouldn't want to be with anyone who was impressed by it.'

'Look, Matty only thinks she cares about that stuff because she had so little growing up. The truth is, she doesn't know what she wants.'

He gave a bitter laugh. 'Trust me, she wants what she's got! Prince fucking Charming.'

Clover shook her head. 'Julian's a rich, stupid playboy. He's not what she needs, we both know that. The two of you are always laughing together.'

'When you say laughing, I assume you actually mean "fighting"?'

Clover ignored his sarcasm. 'And she didn't stop going on about it when you went home with whoever you went home with in Saas-Fee.'

Johnny didn't reply.

Clover cradled the tumbler in the palm of her hand. Its weightiness felt reassuring. 'Opposites attract, Johnny. You ground her and she elevates you. It's so obvious. I don't get how the two of you don't see it.'

'Like you don't see what's right under *your* nose, you mean?'

'Huh?'

'I've been standing behind that camera, watching the two of you prowling around each other for the past five weeks. I've got over two hundred hours of footage through there, of you two.' He pointed towards his bedroom across the hall. 'You never take your eyes off each other – he watches you when you're not looking; and you watch him when he's not looking. Every room he walks into, he looks to see where you are in it . . .'

'Yes! Because I'm persona non grata; public enemy number one.' She gave a shocked laugh.

He stared at her. 'What exactly happened between you on the mountain?'

The mountain? '. . . You know what happened! I almost went over the edge and he stopped me.'

'No. There was more than that – because the very next morning you had run off to Geneva and he was left like a clockwork toy someone had forgotten to wind up!' He stared at her almost angrily. 'You maintain this hostility towards each other, but it fools no one but you two. Your problem isn't that you slept with him, Clover. It's that you only slept with him once!'

Clover stared at him, aghast. Where had this come from? Johnny couldn't possibly think—

The sound of a cough made them both jump.

Ari was standing by the door. Clover felt her cheeks flame. How much had he just heard? Had Kit's name been mentioned? Was there any way for Ari to have identified him?

'Hey,' Johnny said in a strangled voice. 'How's he doing?'

'Fine.'

'*Fine?*' Clover echoed.

Ari shrugged. 'He's upset of course, but he's taking it on the chin.' He looked at them both. 'So I just wanted to make sure you're still set for an ETD of eleven a.m. tomorrow?'

Clover blinked in disbelief. 'He's not still planning to go to St Moritz?'

'Of course. Why not?'

Why not? Was it just her or was the whole world going mad? 'But the story . . .'

'Will blow over. Amy's entitled to have her say.'

Have her say? She had destroyed him! Clover's eyes narrowed; these weren't Ari's words. 'But Julian . . .'

'If he pulls the sponsorship, Kit can go solo,' he shrugged. 'He can self-fund.'

There was an astounded silence as Ari looked between her and Johnny with a tight smile. 'Okay, so eleven then. See you tomorrow.'

'Yeah. Night, Ari,' Johnny murmured.

He glanced at her as they heard Ari's bedroom door click shut. Another fraught silence blossomed. Their argument lingered like smoke, Ari's dramatic downplaying of tonight's events bordering on farcical. '. . . I'm going to bed too. I'm knackered.'

'But Johnny—'

He set down his empty tumbler on Matty's dressing table and walked across the room without looking at her. 'Night, Clo.'

Clover stared at the wall. It stared back. She could hear the sound of taps running, toilets flushing in the others' bathrooms. The chalet was preparing for sleep and the quietude of night whilst she sat there, both motionless and frantic. Everyone was playing roles that wore a veil of normality but the truth lay two degrees to the side; almost superimposed onto reality, but not quite. Was she the only one who couldn't just sit there and take it?

She rose, not quite sure of what she planned to do. She only knew that they couldn't roll into St Moritz tomorrow pretending everything was fine; something profound and terrible had happened tonight. She peered into the corridor, her gaze drifting over the closed doors and low blooms of light on the walls.

Silently, she tiptoed out and crept up the stairs. The lift would be too noisy, a liability with its distinctive 'ping' alerting inquisitive minds to movement. She wasn't sure if she was more horrified by the thought of being caught by Ari or Johnny.

Within thirty seconds, her toes were burrowing into the cream carpet of the top floor and her breathing was heavier. To her left, Beau's bedroom door was ajar, the lights off of course. To her right, they were still on. She stood outside the door, looking for shadows criss-crossing the room, but it was too large for them to fall by the threshold.

With a steadying breath, she knocked and – without waiting for a reply, before she lost her nerve – entered. Kit looked back at her; his bow tie was dangling loosely either side of his shirt, the top button undone; he too had a tumbler of cognac in his hand. Everyone was needing something forti-fying tonight, seemingly.

'Oh god, no,' he moaned at the sight of her, half-turning away. 'I can't . . . I can't deal with you right now . . . Just please go.'

She arched an eyebrow. *Please?* His manners made her nervous; it must be bad if he was being polite to her. She stepped further into the room. 'I want to hear your side.'

His whole body slumped. 'If you think I'm sitting down and doing a fucking interview with you, in the middle of the night—'

'Not an interview. I just want to hear it from you. Is she telling the truth?'

He stared back at her in a long-held silence, as though astounded she was even questioning it. 'Well, she must be,' he said finally. 'It's in the papers, right?' He turned away, a hand on his hip. He sighed again, then knocked back his drink.

'Is she lying?' she asked again.

'What reason would she have to lie?'

'I don't know. That's why I'm asking you.'

'Well, from what I've read so far, she's given a compelling account,' he said evenly. 'I'd sure believe it . . . The timing's funny though, right?' He stared at her. 'After four years apart, her married to some rich dude . . . and suddenly she is struck by the urge to . . . come out with that.' He gestured blankly towards his iPad on the bed, opened on the newspaper reports.

She knew what his point was. 'We only contacted her as a matter of routine. As far as we knew, interviewing her would have been no different to interviewing Ari or Beau . . . she was someone who was close to you back then, someone who could give us insight into who you were, how you were feeling, what was going on in your life . . . How could we have known—?'

'That I pummelled her? Beat her up? Pulled her across the floor by the hair?'

She felt herself go cold at the words.

His eyes narrowed. 'How did you even know about her?'

She shrugged. 'Research. Leads come up in the course of conversations . . . We weren't looking for it . . . But why did you keep the relationship a secret?'

'Because I was beating her up! Why else? She couldn't leave the house with all those bruises now, could she?' Every word burned with scorn.

'This will destroy your reputation.'

'What reputation?' he scoffed. 'I lost that long before tonight.'

Cory shimmered between them, but she blinked him away.

'Kit, if she's lying, then you have to say so. By saying nothing, you're condemning yourself.'

He shrugged, pulling the tie from under his collar. 'Well, that should please you at least.'

'You could get arrested! Why won't you defend yourself?' she cried, stepping towards him.

'Why are *you* assuming she's lying?' He threw the tie onto the floor and began unbuttoning his cuffs.

'I . . . I'm not assuming anything. I just don't know what to believe.'

He stared at her as he shook his head slowly. 'Clover, whether you believe it or don't believe it – it really makes no difference.' He shrugged off his shirt and let it fall too. He jerked his chin in the direction of the door. 'Shut the door on your way out.'

She watched as he walked into the bathroom, kicking the door closed behind him. She stared at it, her heart pounding against her ribs as she heard the sound of the shower starting up. There could be only one reason why he was being like this, why he wasn't fighting back – because he couldn't. It had to be true.

He was everything she'd ever said he was. She'd known it from the start.

He was the man who'd forced Cory Allbright into those waves. He was a man who used his fists.

He was a monster.

Wasn't he?

The door opened.

Kit stopped, silhouetted briefly, his hand already on the light switch before he saw her, lying there.

'. . . What the fuck are you doing?' His voice was a croak; it was a shock too far for his body tonight.

'What does it look like?' she asked calmly, even though she had no idea what she was doing. She was a stranger to herself tonight. 'I'm having a bath.'

The moonlight glinted on the copper as it fell through the glass walls.

'. . . I told you to get out.'

'No, you told me to shut the door on my way out. I haven't gone yet.'

'Clover . . .' There was a warning note in his voice. 'I can't deal with your games right now.'

'There's no games. You told me I was welcome to have a bath here, any time I wanted. Day or night.' They both remembered the sarcasm that had dripped from those same words the night he'd said them at the restaurant, all those weeks ago now.

He stared back at her, then closed his eyes. He looked done in. 'Fine. Have the damn bath then.' He switched off the bathroom light and let his towel fall, climbing into his bed. He turned off the bedside light and turned away from her.

Silence settled over the room.

Clover lay her head back against the copper bath and looked out – set now in darkness, she had a clear view through the glass wall and living room picture window, down to the town and lake. Lights twinkled prettily on the water. She could see the top of the town's Christmas tree down by the church. It looked almost like they could hop, skip and jump their way down there on the snow-festooned roofs of the chalets that lay in tiers below them.

She sighed, forgetting for a moment the absurdity – the perversity – of the current situation. She had acted before she'd been able to think, opening up the taps and filling the tub while he'd showered; he'd been in there so long, he wouldn't have heard anything at all of what she was doing through here.

In the silent pitch, they could hear only each other – the

sound of his body shifting restlessly on the sheets; the melodic rippling of the water as she stirred too. She listened to him breathing. He wasn't anywhere close to falling asleep. She moved her legs in the water, knowing he couldn't help but hear the sounds of her bathing. They both knew that at some point she was going to have to get out of this bath.

'. . . Why are you doing this?' His voice was quiet. Flat. For the first time ever, he sounded defeated.

'Because I don't believe you did it.'

He sighed but offered no protest. He sounded too worn out to argue further.

'. . . You couldn't even *look* at me when I'd been beaten.'

She heard the sound of his breathing pause.

'You apologized for bruising me just because you gripped my arm a little too hard – and you *hate* me, so I know how hard it must have been for you to do that, but you still did it. I remember what you said to me. You said, "I'm many things. But I'm not that."'

He didn't reply.

'Those aren't the actions of a man who did what she's accusing you of . . . She's lying.'

There was a long silence before he turned over to face her. The moon was shining high and bright in the mountains behind her, silhouetting her into darkness.

'Yeah? Well, I can't prove I *didn't* do those things. And who's going to believe me if it's my word against hers? I'm the bad guy, and everyone knows it.'

'Are you, though? Yeah, you once did a terrible thing.'

He waited for her to say something more. She didn't.

'. . . But?' he prompted.

'That's right, there is a *but* – you did a terrible thing but there was a reason why. I know there was. Tell me why you

379

did it? Why is Amy lying about you? Why are you letting her lie about you?'

'No, I'm not doing this,' he sighed, going to turn over, but the sudden sound of water splashing and trickling as she stood up made him pause. Unable to stop himself, he looked back to see her standing silhouetted in the bath.

He didn't move as she stepped out and towelled herself off.

'My brother said this thing to me when I stayed with him this week,' she said, taking her time, knowing she had his absolute attention. 'He said people consider too much the good luck of the early bird – and not enough the bad luck of the early worm. I didn't want to hear it at the time, but I think maybe he was right.' She looked straight at him. 'You're the early worm and Amy's lying about you. Tell me what happened.'

He shifted his weight onto his elbow as he looked back at her. 'Clo . . . I can't.'

'You have to. Her lies will destroy you.'

'Fine. That's better than—' He stopped himself but she could see he was struggling to maintain his reserve. She was getting to him.

'Better than what?' she frowned, taking a few steps closer. She was almost within touching distance. 'Kit . . . Better than what? What could be worse than this?'

He didn't reply.

'Let me help you.'

'No one can help.' He turned away from her abruptly. 'You need to get out of here. Right now.'

He wasn't going to tell her. She could see he wanted to, that the words were on the tip of his tongue. Something was stopping him . . . She stared down at him, seeing how his body was tense with anger and frustration, filled with words he wouldn't say, the duvet rising and falling with his laboured breaths. What motive could be so powerful that he would let his own ship sink and not reach for the life raft? Why wouldn't he save himself?

She stepped closer and slipped under the sheet, pressing her body against his.

She felt his sharp intake of breath. 'Clo . . .'

'I don't know why you're doing this,' she whispered. 'But I wish you would trust me.' She kissed his shoulder, once, twice, her arm caressing sadly down the length of his arm. 'Tell me what happened.'

He turned suddenly and grabbed her, rolling her around him into the middle of the bed in a single fluid movement. He stared down at her angrily. 'Why won't you ever listen?'

She looked back up at him. 'Because something . . . *unjust* is happening. You loved her once. And she loved you.'

'Yeah . . . ?' He kissed her with an urgency and passion and sadness that took her breath away. She could feel he wanted to subsume her, possess her, lose himself in her. The desperation of the lost man. He looked back at her, his eyes burning with confusion. '. . . Then why does hating you feel better than loving her ever did?'

She swallowed, taken aback by the question. 'Well, perhaps it wasn't love,' she whispered.

'Yeah.' His gaze roamed over her face. '. . . Or perhaps this isn't hate.'

Chapter Twenty-Eight

The wheels of the small jet touched down at St Moritz. Clover looked out through the window, feeling a sense of dread. As feared, the story had exploded in the international press. On almost every front page of note, Kit's face – chiselled and angry, handsome in black tie – had been placed mugshot-style beside pictures of Amy with black eyes and a split lip.

Kit was sitting in the seats in front, with Ari. Ari was briefing him on what to say and do – and more specifically, *not* do – when they arrived at Samedan, the private airport just outside St Moritz. Julian's generosity in chartering a private plane for this trip was a final act of kindness, if not mercy, before the relationship was formally severed; it meant they wouldn't have to travel in public (a blessing for Julian as much as Kit; the indelible link between their two names was toxic). No one thought it would be a good idea for Kit to be faced with people taking pictures of him in the airport. Not so soon after the exposé.

She, Johnny and Matty were keeping their heads low, trying to minimize their impact on a highly flammable situation that arguably they had helped create. None of them were talking much but Clover wasn't sure it could all be put down to the general muted mood surrounding Kit. Johnny was still angry with her for her comments last night, but Matty had been oddly quiet all day too; Clover didn't think she was finding it quite as easy as she'd thought to walk away from her sophisticated lover. Last night's scandal wouldn't have given them the romantic goodbye she had been hoping for.

Clover looked over surreptitiously at Kit again; he was sitting diagonally across from her in the row ahead. She could just make out his profile. He kept sitting back, pressing his head against the headrest and, his eyes closed, sighing heavily. He seemed exhausted – and not just because of their night together. She had been careful to get back to her room before Carlotta and Fin were up at six. No one knew about them and, this time, no one would.

She glanced at her friends. Johnny was already watching her. He looked away again, as if his point had somehow been proved. The camera was sitting in his lap, ready to go again. He'd filmed Kit getting into the plane, sitting in the plane, and he would capture him again getting off it and into the waiting car at the other end. Kit seemed not even to notice him now. He was in the midst of a scandal that was poised to finally shred his reputation beyond repair and they were perfectly placed to capture it from the inside. It was everything Clover had hoped for. Her film had a purpose now, a remit for Cannes.

So why did she feel sick?

She looked back outside as the steps went down and the cold alpine air rushed into their warm cabin. Johnny was first out to get into position on the tarmac, then Ari – checking no reporters had tracked them here, although there was clearly a high chance they would arrive via this airport. Kit glanced over at her before he stepped out. He hadn't shaved and his jaw was dark with stubble. She could see he wasn't the man he'd been yesterday – the look in his eyes was different; he

seemed if not broken, certainly fractured. Irretrievably weakened. But no matter how tightly he had held her last night,
whispering her name into the darkness and losing himself,
he wouldn't relent. His secrets were still his. They were still
on separate sides of the glass.

She looked out the window. Like him, she had to remember
herself. She couldn't allow herself to *feel* things. She had to
look at this journalistically. The events of the past eighteen
hours had changed everything; suddenly her film wasn't the
dead duck she had assumed. She had to retain focus. Amy
was alleging assault and battery, and Kit wouldn't deny it.
That meant she could take Amy at her word and confirm the
worst about him (something she would have paid for at the
start of this project). Or she could find out why he wasn't
fighting back. What was he hiding? Either way, her film had
legs. The pictures of her and Kit taken on the way into the
casino had created a white-hot frenzy of speculation for her
latest project and Liam had already left three messages for
her. She had yet to go back to him – he would think she was
keeping him hanging, but her head was as scrambled as Kit's.

The runway was clear with only their driver waiting for
them, and they filed into the blacked-out BMW X7 with relief.
Johnny sat beside the driver in the front, Kit and Ari in the
middle and Clover and Matty at the back. They swept along
the floor of the Engadin valley in silence, the mountains
soaring above them like gothic cathedrals. The light was pink-
tinted under a crystalline clear sky and the mountains here
again seemed more jagged and saw-toothed than in Austria,
the snow iced and peaked like a wedding cake.

In under ten minutes they were in town, passing the
famous frozen lake and horse-drawn sleighs. Clover wasn't
sure she'd ever seen more furs outside of the zoo. Posters

were up all around town, advertising the FIS competition with headshots of the biggest names: Scotty James. Mark McMorris. Everyone looked so healthy – tans, white teeth, bright smiles . . .

Clover felt a wave of relief that Kit's photo wouldn't have been included – he wasn't yet a big name in this sport and now he was a big name for all the wrong reasons. The lower his profile could be here, frankly, the better.

Kit frowned as the driver slowed and indicated to turn into the drop-off area outside Badrutt's Palace, in the very heart of the town. It was a vast, old-school European hotel, with arches, stone walls and turrets, a Swiss flag flying in the breeze and quite the most enormous Christmas tree Clover had ever seen.

'Are there squirrels living in that thing?' Matty whispered.

'What are we doing here? I thought we had an apartment,' Kit said in a low voice to Ari.

Ari nodded. 'We did. But the landlord bailed when . . .' He shrugged diplomatically.

'When he heard I was the client.' Kit looked out of the window, his jaw balling. '. . . Well, did it have to be here? This place is too . . . showy. I'm a snowboarder, not a banker.'

'It was all Julian could get at short notice. Everything's pretty much booked out for the comp. His family know the Badrutts. They're doing him a favour.'

'. . . Fuck's sake,' he muttered, looking back at Ari again. 'There's press outside as well. How could they know I was coming here when even I didn't?'

Ari shook his head, looking surprised. 'I have no idea. You're booked in under a pseudonym . . . Don't worry, mate. Just because you're paranoid doesn't mean they're looking for you. This place gets all the big names. There must be someone else of interest in town.'

'Hmm.' Kit reached into his coat pocket for his shades anyway. He was in jeans, trainers and his minimal JOR gunmetal grey snowboard jacket. He pulled on a beanie too. Everything was low-key; nothing about him stood out – apart from those cheekbones.

Ari leaned forward to the front seat and tapped Johnny on the shoulder. 'No filming here, mate. The last thing we want to do is alert this pack of hyenas to who's here.'

Johnny glanced at Clover in the rear-view mirror as he patted the camera on his lap, like it was a pet. 'Sure. Understood.'

The driver turned into the hotel's covered courtyard and stopped in front of the mahogany doors. Kit opened his car door and, with his head down, bounded straight past the uniformed doorman and into the revolving doors.

The photographers' flashes started up instantly, his name yelled out indecorously, asking yet again for comments. They were too late to get the shot, but they weren't too disappointed – at least they knew, now, that he was here and getting past them and up the mountain every day was going to be like running the gauntlet. He was clearly who they'd been waiting for.

Clover jumped out from her side of the car, pulling up the hood on her coat to hide her distinctive hair and keeping her face well away from the press pack – but she stopped suddenly as if hit by a bullet.

'What is it?' Matty asked, almost walking into the back of her. 'Oh.' She put a hand on Clover's shoulder, steering her away from the sight of the poster on the opposite side of the road. Mikey Schultz was grinning back at them. 'Jesus. Not exactly *responsive*, are they?' Matty muttered angrily.

Inside the hotel, there was no sign of the unpleasantness that lay on the other side of the stone walls. Marble latticed floors gleamed beneath vaulted ceilings, intricate wall sconces threw out lacy patterns, vast picture windows gave directly onto the frozen lake at the back, snow lying on the surface in several areas.

Kit was already standing at the reception desk, his back to the lobby as he tried not to bring attention to himself, waiting for Ari to come over and tell them exactly which pseudonym they were booked in under. People were staring nonetheless. There was just something about him that drew the eye – his athleticism, his dynamism. It was his posture, too, though: head down, shoulders rounded, as if he was trying to hide.

They each had their own rooms. Julian was covering the tab. It was supposed to have been his grand gesture for the big debut; now it was his swansong. Matty, Clover, Johnny and Ari had rooms with balconies looking onto the lake, while Kit had a suite. Kit had just rolled his eyes when told. His sponsor's ongoing generosity felt *de trop* when everything had gone so badly wrong.

Everyone retreated to their rooms with relief. The strange mood that had blanketed them all day hadn't lifted. No one was themselves. There were no plans for this evening. This was a working trip for them all. Kit had deliberately missed the warm-ups today for obvious reasons, choosing to go straight into the qualifiers tomorrow, and he needed to focus. Ari would be waxing and prepping the boards; Kit would have a massage, an early night . . .

Clover had a long shower and curled up on her bed, still wrapped in towels. The pillows felt silken under her cheek, the duvet soft and enveloping. She stared out across the lake, feeling the silence of the mountains steadily begin to slow her rushing blood and the questions in her head. She felt both drained and gripped by the urge to see Kit – to push him again on why he was protecting Amy . . .

Just to see him.

Suddenly the fact of leaving here – him – in a few days was feeling less and less like a promise. Johnny had been right. Whatever this tangle of emotions was between them, it wasn't as simple as hate. He repelled her in one instant and attracted her in the next. She had climbed into that bath, his bed, even as he continued to deny Amy was lying, because she believed – or wanted to believe – that he was something better.

It was a lie to pretend she was impartial or a neutral observer; she never had been that. She had come here clearly in Cory Allbright's camp, but at least her position had been unambiguous. Now, though, she had stepped inside Kit's story and she couldn't step out again. His life was like a massive avalanche and she had been caught up in the powder cloud. Who was she here for?

She closed her eyes, telling herself the sky would soon clear and she would find everything settled once more. She would know what to do. Things were already shifting. It was different here from the chalet; they were no longer sharing space, she didn't even know where his room was. He was a step removed, already drifting out of her orbit . . .

It was dark when she opened her eyes again, sitting up with a feeling of confusion. Where was she? She had slept in so many different beds recently . . . Her heart was beating far too fast, in the way it always did when she was roused from a deep sleep. But what had woken her?

The knocking came again. At the door.

'Wait,' she called, her voice muffled as she tried to co-ordinate her limbs into shuffling off the bed. Kit?

'Who is it?' She looked through the peephole before opening the door. 'I was fast as—' Her voice failed at the sight before her. Oh god. What had happened now?

Clover stared at the image on Matty's phone screen. They were sitting on her bed and it had taken Clover several minutes to get her calm enough to speak.

'The bitch *called* you? After she sold her story?'

Matty shook her head frantically, trying to make herself clear, but her thoughts and words were a jumble. 'No, not me. This is a photo I took. Julian was in the shower and his phone rang. Normally I'd ignore it but it had been such an insane night . . . people kept ringing him, wanting a comment. I thought I should at least look to see who it was, in case it was important.'

Clover put her hands up to stop her. 'Wait – so this is a photo of the lock screen on *Julian's* phone?'

'Yes.'

'. . . But why would Amy be ringing him?'

Matty's eyes widened again. 'That's what I've been asking myself! What possible reason does she have for contacting him? How does she even have his number? I've been going over it all day, trying to think of an innocent explanation . . . But I can't!'

Clover didn't reply. That was why Matty had been so distracted all day? She got up from the bed, needing to move to think. 'Okay, pause. Take a breath. Let's think it through. There'll be a perfectly logical explanation for why she's ringing Julian . . . hours after her story broke . . .' she murmured. 'Perhaps she was warning him that the story was coming out? She knew he could tell Kit for her.'

'But in that case, she would have rung Ari, surely? He's

Kit's manager. Or me! I was the one who'd made contact with her.'

'Yeah,' Clover agreed. 'Either one of those would have made more sense . . . But it's not completely outside the realm of possibility she called his sponsor instead.' Clover bit her lip. 'She might even know him. If her husband's that rich, they might move in the same social circles?'

'Clo, no . . .'

Clover turned at the tone of Matty's voice.

'I've been over every scenario. It's my fault. I know it is.'

'Your fault?'

'. . . I told Julian about Amy. The first night you were in Geneva, he took me out for dinner. I was really psyched; I hadn't seen him for a few days and I'd just made contact with Amy; even though it wasn't a good call, I felt certain we could swing her. I was convinced we'd finally got the missing piece to the story . . . I was excited about it and so I told him.'

'That you'd found Kit's ex-fiancée?'

'I know I shouldn't have said anything at all, but I figured where was the risk in telling him about Amy? She's just his ex, right? There was nothing to tell about her, beyond bikini model. I mean, that was all we knew! That and the fact he'd kept the engagement a secret.'

'And so that's what you told Julian?'

'Yes. I didn't think it was a big deal. I just mentioned it in passing.'

Clover tightened the towel wrapped around her. She was still 'dressed' from her shower earlier. 'So you told Julian about Amy, and the next thing we know, Amy's sold her story and is ringing him afterwards?'

'But that . . . I mean, that makes it sound so bad – but there has to be an innocent explanation!' Matty said, her words a gabble.

Clover frowned, thinking hard. 'Did you get the impression Julian had heard about Amy before you told him?'

'No. He was as surprised as I was.'

'Did you have Amy's number written down anywhere Julian could see it?'

Matty hesitated as she tried to think back. 'Uh . . . Well, yeah. I think it was written down on some papers on my desk.'

'On the desk in the hotel room Julian gave you to work in?'

Matty's eyes widened as she caught the intimation. 'Yes. But . . . ?' The word was an airy puff of disbelief.

Neither woman spoke for several moments. If Julian had been spying on her work, what else had he been doing? Clover began to pace. She had a gathering feeling of doom. Something was very seriously off about this.

'. . . It was Julian who first made contact with us, wasn't it?' Clover asked, thinking back to the start. '*He* got in touch with *us* about the possibility of the film . . .'

'Yes.' Matty's voice was quiet.

They stared at each other. Clover could see goosebumps on her friend's arms.

'All this time, I thought he was trying to influence us to go easy on Kit,' Clover murmured. 'But look at the timings of the things that have happened . . . the fight outside the restaurant: we were Julian's guests. Last night at the casino: Julian's guests . . . That's too neat to be coincidence, surely? Any time we've been with Julian, Kit has been stitched up. People with an interest seem to know where he is at the right time. That mob outside the restaurant, the press at the casino . . . And on each occasion, it's been timed for maximum exposure . . .'

'But that makes absolutely no sense! Julian wouldn't sabotage Kit! That would be shooting himself in the foot. No, more than that . . . it would be blowing his own leg off! Think about the money he's spent promoting Kit, setting up the clothing line especially for him, the boards, bringing the FIS world tour to Kaprun . . . The chalet, the car . . . He's spent an absolute fortune!'

'And yet hours after the story broke, he was taking a call from the woman responsible for obliterating his star signing?' Clover said. 'Why would he liaise with the woman who's undone all of it?' She looked at Matty as a thought dawned, buffering in her brain. '. . . Unless that's exactly what he wanted?'

'What?'

'You said it yourself, he's spent an absolute fortune . . .'

A whisper of old words flickered through her mind. *He'll have done what I needed by then.* Clover's eyes widened as she suddenly saw the whole picture. 'Oh my god – scorched earth . . .' Her hands pressed to her mouth, her heart escalating to a gallop.

'What is . . . scorched earth?'

'My brother told me about it in Geneva. It's a tactical business ploy, a high-risk, last-ditch strategy – selling off assets, acquiring debt. That's what Kit is to Julian – a running, spiralling debt: the tour, the sponsorship, the products . . . Everyone knows Julian's burning money; that he doesn't have the expertise – or frankly the interest – in snowboarding! He's just running up debt to make his family's company look unattractive to the hostile bidders' board.'

Matty had grown very pale. Clover was relieved she was sitting down. 'No . . . He wouldn't do those things to Kit.'

'Mats, it's precisely *why* he signed Kit. Look at the headlines he's garnered! The Orsini-Rosenberg name has been in the papers for all the wrong reasons. It's deliberate reputation *mis*management. Kit was already toxic – no one else would touch him! – and Julian's been pouring fuel onto the fire.'

Matty's hand was over her mouth now as they stared at one another in appalled silence. '. . . I feel sick . . . How could I . . . ?'

Clover reached over to her, sinking beside her on the mattress. 'Mats, you couldn't have known. He's been playing us all, every single one of us. *I* thought he was just a ridiculous, spoilt posh boy. I completely underestimated him too.'

Neither of them spoke for a few moments. It was a lot to take in. Even the flashy hotel room they were sitting in was part of his ploy to devalue the family brand, just long enough for the sharks to stop circling.

'There's something I don't understand, though,' Matty said flatly, staring unseeingly at the mirror opposite. 'If Julian did contact Amy after I told him about her, why would she spill the beans now? She's moved on with her life. That's all in her past. She's got a rich husband – it's not like he could have paid her to say those things, surely? She doesn't need the money. So what's in it for her?'

Clover thought hard too. 'It's got to be damage limitation,' she murmured finally. 'Whatever she thinks Kit might be saying to us about her, it must be worse than what she's flinging at him. At least in this, she's a victim and, thanks to those photos, Kit can't disprove it. His reputation is so tarnished, who will the world believe – her or him?'

Matty looked at her in surprise. 'Are you saying you think Amy's *lying*?'

'I know she is. Kit's many things, but he never hit her.'

'Has he said that to you?'

'Not in so many words.'

'So then . . . ?'

'He's being evasive,' Clover sighed. 'I can't put a finger on it, but . . . it's like he thinks this is the lesser of two evils. Or something.'

Matty gave a surprised, joyless laugh. 'How is *this* a lesser evil? Amy has kneecapped him!'

'I know. I don't understand why he won't come out fighting.' Clover shrugged helplessly. 'He's just rolling over and letting her beat him.'

'Which is *not* like him. We all know he's a fighter.'

If Matty's point had been to cast doubt on Clover's defence, it didn't appear to work. Matty watched her closely, seeing how Clover was studying her nails, biting her lip. '. . . I can't believe I'm going to say this—'

Clover looked back at her. 'Say what?'

'If I didn't know better, I'd say you looked like someone having doubts . . .'

'*Me?*' She watched as Matty stood up, as if to get a better look at her.

'You do still want to nail him, don't you?' Matty asked, staring down with a hard look. 'For what he did to Cory?'

Clover nodded, but her voice seemed lodged in her throat. '. . . Mm-hmm,' she croaked. She cleared her throat. 'Of course I do.'

'So then why do you look like a bride at the altar, gathering her skirts and getting ready to run?'

Chapter Twenty-Nine

Clover stared out onto the lake, the breakfast plates still on the table before her. A V-shaped flock of geese was flying low over the surface, honking loudly. The pine trees on the far side had been freshly dusted with snow in the night so that all the world she could see was shades of white – the soft pale sky, the freezing water, the craggy mountains. It was beautiful, the playground of choice for people who could play anywhere on the planet, and right now, high up on those slopes, people were already playing, making first tracks down groomed pistes—

'—Earth to Clo.'

She looked back to find Matty waving a hand in front of her.

'The waiter's asking if you want more coffee?'

Clover looked up to see the waiter standing expectantly with the pot. She gave a weak smile. 'Sure.' As though she was doing him a favour.

They watched as he poured. 'Thanks.'

'Are you sure you're okay?' Matty asked.

'I'm fine.'

'You're a million miles away.'

Clover looked back at her. 'I'm just trying to work out what to do . . . I don't know what to do.'

Matty sighed. 'Tell me about it.'

'Have you heard from him?' They both knew Clover meant Julian. They had agreed that Matty wouldn't let him know they knew what he was doing – or had done – until they had worked out some kind of plan. Privately, Clover was worried they had heard the last of him anyway. They had all served their purpose. If Kit went through with the competition here, win or lose, he would only earn more headlines that would circle back to Amy's allegations. Glory could never be his. Only Julian could keep winning.

'No.' Matty bit her lip. The longer the silence grew, the more it confirmed that she had been used. A pawn in Julian's game.

'We'll have to tell Johnny. We can't keep it from him.'

'I know.' Matty's grip tightened around her cup as she grimly stared into it. 'God, he'll laugh his head off.'

'Of course he won't.'

'Yes he will. He never liked Julian. He'll think I'm such a tool for falling for him. He always says I have appalling taste in men and he's right!'

Clover kept quiet. Voicing her thoughts with Johnny had only landed her in hot water with him; the last thing they needed was more arguments.

'Did you see the others before they left?' Matty asked, absently picking up a sugar cube with the mini tongs and dropping it into her tea. She didn't take sugar in her tea.

'Ari, briefly. I texted him, asking if he'd see me before he left.'

'So you told him about Julian?'

Clover nodded. 'He said he'll wait for the right moment before telling Kit.'

'Was he shocked?'

'Stunned. Furious and stunned. I don't think he could take it in that Kit had been used like that.'

Matty looked away sharply, her gaze on the lake. Not just on Kit. 'Did you see Kit?'

'No. He had breakfast in his room, apparently.'

'He really is hiding out.'

'Can you blame him? The world and its wife thinks he beats up women.'

Matty turned back to her. 'Why didn't you go up there with them?' She took a sip of her tea and grimaced at the sweetness. 'Eww.'

Clover didn't reply immediately. If she was going to get any kind of perspective on this, she had to keep her distance from Kit. 'I didn't want to add to the entourage and bring any further attention to him,' she said instead. 'It'll be distracting enough up there.'

She knew Ari would have arranged for the car to be brought so close to the hotel doors that no photos would be possible – again – but there was nowhere to hide on the pistes. Up there, Kit would be exposed at last. Every set of eyes would be upon him, for all the wrong reasons.

'But isn't that the point?' Matty asked. 'It'll be kicking off up there. Today's the first day he's appeared in public since the story broke. Everyone's going to have an opinion on him. This is manna.'

'Johnny's filming everything.'

'Yeah, but we need words as well as pic—'

Clover stopped her with a look. 'Johnny's on it.'

'. . . Sure.' Matty stared at her hands as a silence bloomed between them.

'Sorry.' Clover frowned as her gaze was distracted by something jarring and chaotic in the serene room. She gave

397

KAREN SWAN

a small gasp, rising from her chair and waving wildly. 'Beau?'

Beau's eyes widened as he caught sight of her and rushed over, almost tripping over a hostess trolley. Clover and Matty stared in bemusement as he staggered to the table. Was he still drunk?

'Thank god! I've been looking for you everywhere!'

'Beau, sit down, have a coffee,' Clover said, trying to calm him. 'You look . . .' He looked wild.

'No, I can't sit! There's no time!'

'. . . Did you just get here?'

'I couldn't get out before. The roads were closed. There was an avalanche down by Visp.' He seemed frantic.

'Oh . . . Well listen, I'm sorry, but you've missed them. They've already gone up. The eliminations start at eleven a.m. but Kit's not on till eleven forty or so. You might still make it if—'

'No.'

Clover frowned. 'Huh?'

'It's you I need to see. While Kit's not here. I have to do it now. If I see him, I'll talk myself out of it.'

Clover felt her heart rate switch into a gallop. 'Out of what?'

'I need to tell you what happened. What *really* happened.' He swallowed, his Adam's apple bobbing up and down in his throat; his neck was stretched with tension. 'If he won't say it, then I will.'

Clover looked at Matty.

'But Beau . . . Johnny's up with Kit and Ari. He's not here. We can't film.'

He picked up her phone from the table. 'Why can't you use this?'

Clover stared at it. Why indeed?

*

398

Professional it was not. Clover's phone was propped up on
the desk against a bottle of sparkling water from the minibar
and held in place by a Twix. Matty was using her phone for
the 'tight' shots on Beau's face, which was trickier than it
sounded – she had to hold the phone as still as she could,
without micro-tremors, whilst turning her head away on every
exhale so as not to blow on the mic.

Beau wasn't looking his best. He had grown a beard
since they'd left him in Saas-Fee and Clover could see
Matty was triggered by the fact his hair clearly hadn't been
combed in all that time either. He also had quite a sharp
ski tan, with the large goggles area around his eyes pale,
his lower cheeks and jaws a reddish-brown with wind and
snowburn.

They would both have liked to style and groom him but
they couldn't risk him having a sudden change of heart. If he
was acting on impulse, then they had to react accordingly.
Clover was just glad the hotel maids had already tidied her
room; that at least was presentable.

'Ready?' she asked him. They were sitting just a little further
apart than knee to knee.

He nodded firmly. She had never seen him look so focused
before.

She took a breath, reached over to the phone, set to video,
and pressed record.

'Beau, you're Kit's younger brother by five years. What was
he like, growing up? Were you close?'

'Yeah.' He nodded vigorously. 'He was my hero. He's my
first memory. I've never lived life without him. I couldn't have
asked for a better brother in this life. He's always been my
best friend. And protector – when we were kids.'

'Protector? You mean from other kids?'

'No. Our dad.'

Clover's eyebrows went up. 'Your *dad*?'

'Kit was the only thing between me and my dad's fists. He wouldn't let him lay a finger on me.' A look of relief washed over his face as the words hung in the space between them, as if they had flames.

Clover was stunned. They were straight in there? '. . . Can you expand on that for me please?'

'Yes. Our father was an alcoholic. He would regularly beat our mum; Kit too. And then he began starting on me.'

She swallowed, caught off guard by the casual ferocity of it. 'How old were you when the beatings began?'

'Four? Five?'

'So Kit would have been nine or ten.'

'Yeah. He was fearless. Clever, too. He used to pull the laces out of Dad's sneakers so that he couldn't run so fast in his shoes. It gave us time to get away.'

Clover stared at him in horror that they had needed 'escape' tactics. 'Is that why your parents divorced?'

'Dad broke Kit's arm. Threw him down the stairs. That was when Mum realized that if we stayed, he was eventually gonna kill us all.'

Clover was finding it hard to form her questions. Horror at Beau's blunt answers made her throat dry. 'And it's why she left the country. Took you both to Australia?'

He nodded. 'She wanted to get as far away as she could – a five-hour plane ride away. She had no money but our neighbour knew what was going on – he used to hear the screams – and he loaned it to her. Mum didn't know how she was going to pay him back when she had us to look after, rent to pay . . . Kit won the money in his first surfing competition eight months later and he mailed it over to him.'

Clover blinked at him. Her heart was beating so hard she felt sure they could all hear it. 'So . . . surfing became a way for Kit to help your mum financially.'

'Yeah. Within a year, he was the family breadwinner. A local surf company agreed to sponsor him and he went pro as soon as he could.'

'Did it also help him, emotionally, do you think? Being on the water?'

'For sure. It kept him from burning up. He had a lot of rage for a long time. He couldn't forgive my father for what he'd done to us.'

Clover was silent for a few moments. She didn't want to have to ask these questions. Not now. '. . . Beau, I'm sorry but I have to ask this. In light of the revelations that have been made by Kit's former fiancée in the press this week – doesn't your family history lend weight to her allegations? The abused becomes the abuser?'

'No.' Beau sat further forward on his seat. Clover could see his hands were tightly clasped together on his lap. She could see the self-control it was taking to hold himself together. He must have known she would ask this. 'It's because that happened to us, that he would *never, ever* do those things she's accused him of. He saw our own mother beaten black and blue. It simply isn't in him to do that to someone else.'

'But he was involved in that fight in Zell am See,' she said quietly. 'There's footage showing him—'

'He didn't throw a punch until he saw *you* get hit. I think it took him straight back there, to our childhood, seeing our mum with a black eye. He was a mess afterwards. I hadn't seen him like that in years. He couldn't bear to see what had happened to you.'

Clover looked at the floor. That was why he hadn't come

to see her? Why he'd thrown her out from his room, unable even to look at her? She could feel emotions pressing at the backs of her eyes, in her throat, a pressure in her chest . . .

'Beau, we've been living with you for weeks now and some terrible things have happened to Kit, directly and indirectly. And yet he hasn't released a single public statement defending or explaining his actions. People will say that if he was innocent, he would come out and defend himself.'

'No. He won't give them oxygen. Kit learned really quickly that the best tactic with our father was no engagement – no eye contact, no conversation . . . I guess that's carried through . . . His whole life he's had to be the strong one. He won't buckle now.'

'That sounds like a very . . . difficult way to live. You're saying he's emotionally shut-down.'

Beau shrugged. 'It works for him. He knows who to trust and who not. He doesn't let anyone close.'

'Not even Amy Killicks?'

Beau's eye twitched. They both remembered their brief conversation about her in Saas-Fee. 'Not *since* her. He cared about her. He protected her . . . Which is what makes what she did so disgusting.'

'You mean, her allegations that Kit beat her?'

'Kit tried to help her! He *never* hurt her. She knows that. She knows she's lying.'

'But there are photographs showing—'

'Her ex did it!'

'Amy's ex?' Clover felt as if he'd pushed her off the chair. She felt like she was staring up at the ceiling, the world suddenly the wrong way up.

'Kit took those photos himself, as proof. He kept trying to get Amy to take it to the cops. But she wouldn't. She was too scared. The guy was well known in the area back then – known for being easy with his fists. He did jail time.'

Clover was wary of asking his name. Unless the accusation was proved, they could be sued for defamation. 'And where is this man now?'

'Dead. OD'd.' He anticipated her next question. 'Which is convenient, I know, as now he can't contradict what she's saying. Not that he would anyway. He'd have had no problems letting someone else take the fall.' He gave a snort of contempt. 'But yeah, he's dead.'

Clover was silent for a moment. 'So then, if what you're saying is true. If those pictures showed the beating Amy took from her ex, I guess the question we should really be asking is – why would she do this to Kit? If he loved her and only ever wanted to look after her . . . why hurt him like that?'

Beau's jaw pulsed. 'I don't know.'

'. . . Her life has moved on. She's married. She's wealthy – she doesn't need the money . . . Why do this now?'

'I don't know.' His voice had a growl to it – frustration and anger beginning to surge.

'Do you know why they broke up?'

Beau sighed. 'No.'

'Beau, you can't seriously expect people to believe that.'

'It's true.'

'You've just told us you're his best friend, the person closest to him on this planet. You knew his girlfriend was a victim of domestic abuse but you don't know why they broke up?'

'I'm telling you, I don't. He never talked about it.'

'You didn't think that was strange?'

'Of course I did. I was worried about him. But you don't push Kit if he doesn't want to talk.'

Clover blinked. Ari had said the same thing and she knew all about it herself. '. . . When did all this happen?'

'2017. They'd been together for about a year.'

'When did they break up?'

He didn't hesitate. 'October.'

'October 2017?' She went still. It was a date she knew well.

Beau swallowed, then nodded. 'Yeah.'

'When Cory Allbright had his accident at Peniche?'

'Yeah.' He went very still as they both looked at one another. It was clear this was not a coincidence.

'Tell me what you remember about it.'

'That day specifically?'

'Yes.'

Beau was quiet for a moment. 'The conditions were heavy. There'd been a storm and they'd already delayed the competition by two days. The waves were big but there was a lot of pressure to get it done. Everyone knew Cory wanted it wrapped up and his title secured. He didn't want to wait for Pipe Masters.' He looked restless, shifted position.

'How was Kit?'

'Pretty relaxed, I'd say. The more wound up Cory got, the more he chilled.'

'How so?'

'Well, he's always had this ability to . . . take his opponent's energy and use it against them. It's a martial arts thing. Our mum put us in classes when we were little kids – looking back now it's obvious why, of course, but it taught us that the best defence was a strong offence. Kit liked that we had to combine defence and attack into one action.'

'His hero's Bruce Lee, right?' she asked, remembering Matty's biography notes.

Beau grinned. 'Yeah. He always loved his water quote

best – you know: "*Be* water. Be shapeless. Be formless. Put water in the bottle and it becomes the bottle. Put it in a teapot and it becomes the teapot. Water can flow, or it can crash."' He nodded. 'Kit's always been water. And his life has always been *in* water. Even now. Water can freeze, right? Fall as snow?'

Clover was quiet, considering this explanation of Kit's mind games. He had learned to shape-shift; to be what he needed to be to survive, to win. He could flow or he could crash.

'So that skill is what made him such a formidable competitor?'

'Oh yeah. Cory was never water. He was more . . . fire, you know? Too passionate. He could be his own worst enemy. He'd get too emotional, burn himself.'

Clover thought for a moment, trying to find the line between what Beau was telling her – and wanted her to believe – and what she knew from Cory. '. . . You say Kit was chilled. Relaxed. But when you look at footage of that day, you can see the tension between them on the beach, as they were waiting for the starting horns. In the paddle-out they even scrapped, hitting arms in the water.'

'Yeah.'

'So . . . not that chilled, then,' she mooted.

Beau faltered. 'Well, it's different once the game is on. Kit wasn't usually like that.'

She noticed his use of the word 'usually'. 'Could something have happened between them *before* they got in the water?'

He gave a shrug. 'Maybe. Like I said, Cory was getting up in Kit's face all season. He was desperate for the title; he was in the form of his life but the better he did, the more anxious he got. He was convinced Kit was gonna come back and steal it from him, like he did those other years.'

'And there was a chance, wasn't there, that Kit could still do that? If Cory didn't win at Peniche, Kit – in theory – could score enough to take the world title at Pipe Masters in Oahu two months later.'

'He would have had to have the ride of his life to get the score. But yeah . . . in theory.'

'So Cory was itching for glory. And Kit was desperate to stop Cory winning at Peniche. The stakes were high. There's half a million dollars' prize money at stake . . .' She arched an eyebrow. 'It sounds incredibly intense. Not chilled at all.'

'Look, Kit was getting steadily more pissed at the way Cory was behaving – making snippy comments in interviews, things like that – but Kit knew how to deal with him. He knew that even if it went to Oahu, his chances of scoring high enough to win were remote. It was Cory who felt threatened. The title was his for the taking. He just had to hold his nerve, go out there and do it one more time.'

'Which he did,' she argued. 'Cory *didn't* bottle it out there. Kit blocked his line. He stole his priority. He cheated.'

'Yeah, but it was just a moment of spite. Madness, whatever. That . . .' Beau looked flustered. 'That wasn't Kit's style.'

'And yet he did it . . . and the repercussions have been devastating.'

Beau didn't reply. Clover felt like she was kicking a puppy.

'Why did Kit compete in a way that was so – according to you – uncharacteristic?'

Beau shrugged. 'You already said it – the stakes were high. Things had gotten ugly between them, it gets that way some-times. But at the end of the day, Cory was his friend. They went way back. He never meant for him to get hurt! I know that the moment he saw the double sets and realized that

Cory was in a hold-down . . . No one tried harder than him to get to Cory.'

Clover sighed. 'How was he after the accident?'

'Devastated. He was completely cut up. Things got pretty dark. He wouldn't talk to anyone. He just retreated.'

She remembered what Ari had told her – that he hadn't spoken for two months afterwards. 'And Amy couldn't get through to him?'

'She wasn't there.' He shrugged.

'What – immediately afterwards?'

'It was all just chaos. I don't remember when exactly I noticed she wasn't there. But by the time I did, it didn't seem important. Everything had changed so much. We were just focused on getting Kit through it.'

Clover watched him. 'Why do you think Amy is saying these things about your brother now?'

'It wouldn't matter when she said them! They would always be lies. Kit never raised a hand to her, or any woman. It would completely dishonour our mother's memory. You've got to put that in.' He leaned forward, jabbing a finger towards her. 'That's what you've got to make them understand! Amy is lying. I don't know why, but she is. My brother is a good man and it's about time those that know him – I mean, really know him – stand up and say so. Because Kit won't do it for himself. He'll take the heat on this, just like he took my father's punches for me. He sees this as the price he must pay for the fact that he's alive and Cory's dead.'

Clover watched him for a second, then reached over and turned off the video.

Beau looked shocked. 'Is that it? Don't you want to ask me more?'

'Have you got anything more to say?'

He stared back at her, almost panicky. 'No . . . I guess not. I just wanted to explain about our dad and how that's proof he would never do what Amy said he did.'

'You did an excellent job, Beau. You were compelling and really believable. I think a lot of viewers will be convinced by what you've said.' She was. She could see Matty's eyes narrowing suspiciously at her over his shoulder.

'Is there anything else I should have said? I've got to help him. She can't get away with this.'

Clover leaned into him thoughtfully, her elbows on her thighs. 'Beau . . . you run Kit's social media accounts, don't you?'

'. . . Yeah.'

'So . . . you know his passwords?'

'. . . Why?'

She tapped her index finger against her lips. 'I may have just thought of a way you could help him.'

Chapter Thirty

They were sitting in the lobby area when the commotion outside and an explosion of flashing lights told them Kit and Ari were back. Clover sat erect in her chair as she saw Kit leap into the revolving doors.

'He's like Superman,' Matty muttered.

He pulled off the helmet and goggles that he had kept on as a further block to the photographers getting a clean shot. Snow sprinkled off him as he shook his hair out. Ari emerged behind him a moment later, then Johnny, his camera resting casually on his shoulder like a pet parrot.

'Bro!' Beau jumped up, wandering over to his brother, arms outstretched. If he looked incongruous with his baggy layers and tangled hair amid the polished marble and furs, he didn't seem aware of it.

Kit grinned as he saw him and they all watched as the brothers embraced; there was no doubting their bond. Everything Beau had told her was true, she knew that in her bones. For a moment she tried to see the two of them as little boys, running from a drunken bully, their own father . . . Kit flying down the stairs . . .

Kit looked up and saw them all, watching. His smile faded, his eyes snagging on her and staying there for a moment. Did he regret what they'd done – and said – the other night? She'd

scarcely seen him since she'd left his room and she knew he
was avoiding her. It had felt so natural at the time as they
wandered from their chosen paths for a few stolen hours . . .
He didn't trust her and she didn't know what to believe about
him, and yet the connection flickered between them like radio
static, voices occasionally coming clear through the atmosphere, before being carried off again in the next instant.

'Where's Tipper?' Beau asked.

'Still up there. Captain's meeting. We're having a debrief
with him at six.'

'So how was it?' Clover asked, looking between Kit and Ari.

'Well, a cautious first run, fell on the second . . .' Ari grinned,
slapping Kit so hard on the shoulder that Kit had to take a
step back. 'Nailed it on the third. Pulled a 95.8 out of the bag,
enough to get him starting position seven in the finals.'

'Yes!' Beau whooped joyously, oblivious as he almost
induced a heart attack in an elderly woman walking past with
her Maltese terrier. 'What did you put down?'

'Back-to-back 1620s and a Double Alley-Oop.'

'Sweet,' Beau nodded, raising his hand for his brother to
high-five. 'When's the final?'

'Seven tomorrow evening.'

'Under the lights? Nice.'

'I'm glad you got back here,' Kit said. 'I was getting worried
you were gonna stay in Saas-Fee.'

'Bro, I'd have been back yesterday but there was nothing
getting in or out. Major avalanche over the road.' Beau's eyes
narrowed as he looked at his big brother. 'You look all right
though. Could be worse. I wasn't sure what state I'd find you
in after everything that's gone down . . . You look chill.'

Kit gave a shrug. 'It's all good. They're just words she's
throwing around, right?'

Clover saw Ari's eyes slide towards her. She guessed he hadn't told him yet about Julian.

Kit shrugged his shoulders a few times. 'Anyway, I'm gonna get in the sauna, try and ease out the stiffness. There was a cold wind up there today.'

'You go up, mate,' Ari said, slapping his shoulder again. 'I'll get that deep massage booked for you for an hour from now, okay?'

'Be sure to ask for the happy ending, bro,' Beau laughed, pointing a finger at him.

Kit's eyes fluttered in Clover's direction but didn't quite meet hers.

'Later,' he nodded, heading for the lifts.

Clover waited for him to disappear, for the doors to close, before she turned to Ari. 'How was it really?'

Ari pulled a face. 'Chilly . . . And I'm not talking about the wind.' His expression was sombre. 'Put it this way, if he did win tomorrow night, I don't think anyone would be cheering.'

'Oh god.' She glanced at Johnny; his tiny nod indicated he'd got it all on tape.

'The only good thing is, the more they hate him, the more determined it makes him to win. He just takes the hate and feeds on it.'

'Right. Was there much press?'

'Fucking parasites,' Ari tutted. 'They were everywhere. Luckily they can't get into the competitors' area. Kit just kept his head down, went out there and did his job. He was completely focused; showed his class. That's what champions are made of – sheer grit.'

'That's great. Johnny, you'll show us, right?'

'Of course.'

'And you guys?' Ari asked. 'What did you do this morning?'

KAREN SWAN

Beau looked startled.

'Oh, not much . . . Hung out, chatted,' Matty said quickly. '. . . Clover and I went into town and did some window shopping.'

'Mmm,' Clover murmured.

'Sounds good. Well, listen, Kit's going to be doing his physio and stretching out this afternoon. He was scheduled to give a press conference today but I cancelled that, for obvious reasons. Then Tipper's getting over here later, so it's a full-on day but we'll keep in touch, yeah?' Ari gave them a thumbs up as he headed over to the lifts. 'Beau, you coming? Help me with the boards. You can tell me about the shredding that's kept you away so long.'

Beau cast them both a wink as he followed after Ari.

Clover looked at Johnny, then at the camera on his shoulder. 'Shall we?'

They settled in Johnny's room, where he'd set up the editing stations. Johnny kept glancing behind him as if to check they were still there, as the lack of conversation filled the room like smoke.

'Everything all right?'

'Yes.' Clover looked at Matty. She was uncharacteristically quiet again and Clover knew she was nervous about telling him about Julian.

They pulled an armchair beside the bed and flopped down as he pressed playback, bringing up the raw footage from that morning: Kit riding up in the bubble, staring pensively out the window; Kit stepping out of the top station and glancing warily around at the milling crowds. He had his helmet and goggles on, but his helmet was branded with JOR in black shadow letters; people who wanted to find

him would know what to look for. The superpipe lay in a
state of pristine perfection at the top of the shot as he walked
across the snow towards the competitors' tent. A couple of
guys walking across the frame stopped in front of him
suddenly. They eyeballed him, then one of them spat at the
ground by his feet.

Clover gasped. She saw Kit swallow, but not react. His face
wasn't visible but the corner of his jaw pulsed, just once. He
waited for them to move on. Point made, they did, but other
people had seen; Clover could see heads turn, whole groups
pivoting to watch as he walked. Ari, who had been getting
the spare boards from the gondola, caught him up and walked
with him, shoulders back, his chin up in a defiant posture,
daring anyone else to challenge them.

Johnny swung round, coming in tighter on Kit's face as he
went up to the competition marshals to register and get his
bib. He pushed his goggles up so they could see his face,
speaking quietly, his mouth pursed. He looked pale, with dark
moons cradled beneath his eyes. Clover wondered whether
he'd slept. *'They're just words she's throwing around, right?'* He
was playing it down as a flesh wound, but Clover could see
Amy had wounded him more gravely than that.

Johnny sped the tape up to three times normal speed. Ari
getting them coffees. Kit sitting alone in the tent, watching
the giant screens. The other competitors coming in, slapping
hands, ignoring him. The looks that came his way . . .
Everyone had believed what they'd read. They believed he
was a monster.

Clover felt sick. She felt a heat in her chest. This wasn't
right . . .

Kit getting up, doing some stretches. Picking up his board.
A high-five with Ari, then he was gone . . . Ari watching on

the screen, his fingers pressed anxiously to his mouth, his elbows on his knees. He looked sick too . . .

Johnny slowed the tape to normal speed. He had panned in on the other competitors. They were watching in silence, their lips curled with contempt. She could see them actively willing him to fail. Kit must have started his run because she saw their eyes narrow to slits, heads beginning to nod and smiles beginning to rise as the seconds passed. Ari had said this first run had been cautious.

'Fucking pussy . . .'

'Hasn't got the balls . . .'

'He's only good with his fists, not his feet . . .'

'Is it all like this?' Clover asked.

'Oh no. It gets worse,' Johnny said, running the tape faster and getting to Kit's second run. This time, he had moved position and pulled back so that he could capture both the action on the TV screen and the other riders. They saw Kit land a 1620, but his weight was too far back – surfer style – and he spun out. Clover instinctively gasped, her hands flying to her mouth as she watched him 'rag doll' down the sides of the pipe before he could slow enough to stop. She watched as for a few seconds he sat, dazed. A first aid marshal was already running up towards him to help, but Kit shook his head and – unstrapping his boot – slowly got to his feet.

She couldn't believe he hadn't broken something, and it was several moments before she tuned in to the rest of the scene and realized that everyone watching in the stands and inside the tent – they were laughing . . . Everyone was laughing. He could have broken his back and they just . . .

She got up and turned away.

'Where are you going?' Matty called after her.

'To the loo . . . Keep it running.'

She closed the bathroom door behind her, stood by the basin and ran cold water over her face, trying to cool down. She felt combustible. How could he bear it?

When she came out several minutes later, Johnny had teed the tape up to Kit's final run and pressed pause, waiting for her.

'He needed to score big here to get through,' Johnny explained, setting it running again. 'He was sitting tenth out of twelve at this point.'

Clover sank onto the bed with a sigh. Johnny was in the same position as before – getting a shot of both the screen and the riders. Ari was standing, too anxious to sit now, his arms wrapped tightly around him, chewing on a knuckle.

Clover stared at Kit's form on the TV screen in the tent. The quality of watching a screen on a screen wasn't great but she could tell he had greater amplitude in the jumps, and that his tricks were more complex.

She watched the riders instead, seeing how their eyes slitted and mouths opened.

'*Fucker . . .*' one of them hissed.

'*I don't believe it . . .*'

'*Man, he stomped that . . .*'

There were no high-fives this time; all that greeted Kit's triumphant run was a whistling silence. Tumbleweed could have blown down that pipe after him.

Clover watched as Kit unstrapped his board, reappearing in the tent several minutes later. Ari gripped him in an embrace that was part bear hug, part headlock. Clover laughed out loud at the sight of them – and of the other riders watching on in stony silence – prompting Matty and Johnny to look over at her.

'You seem quite . . . emotionally invested,' Johnny remarked, seeing that tears were shining in her eyes.

'No,' she demurred, implausibly. 'I'm just pleased he got through. It's better for the film if he makes the finals.'

He frowned, clearly not buying it. He turned to face them both properly. 'So what did you two do? Because I know you didn't go shopping.'

'No.' Matty pressed a finger secretively to her lips. 'We interviewed Beau.'

He frowned. 'First of all, why's that a secret? And second of all – *how*?'

'We did it with our phones.'

'*No!*' Johnny cried. 'The quality will be shit!'

'He was a cat on a hot tin roof,' Matty shrugged. 'He wouldn't wait! We had to let him talk before he lost his nerve.'

'Why? What did he say?'

'Mainly stuff about his dad. He was an alcoholic, used to beat their mum, threw Kit down the stairs . . .'

Johnny looked at Clover. '. . . But Kit never mentioned any of that in his interview.'

'Nope. And I don't think Beau would have done either, had Amy not made these allegations. Beau said their background is the reason why Kit would never raise a hand to a woman; that it would dishonour their mother's memory.'

'And he was really close to her. Ari said he'd always ring her, wherever he was in the world.'

'Yeah.'

Johnny thought for a moment. 'Well, I guess it provides a . . . sympathetic slant, but it isn't exactly binding proof that he's innocent. Beau's his brother. He's bound to stick up for him. I don't think it'll be enough to change people's minds.'

'You don't?' Clover bit her lip.

Johnny looked at her, seeing her anxious expression. 'That's a good thing, surely? I thought our line was Kit Foley's the people's enemy. Sympathy would be somewhat off message?'

Clover glanced at Matty. 'Well, things have become a little bit more complicated than we thought,' she said hesitantly.

'. . . How?'

Matty told him about Amy's call to Julian in the middle of the night; how it had unravelled his manipulation of the entire project from the start.

But it wasn't Julian's manipulation of Kit that was Johnny's principal concern. 'But you and he . . .' Johnny stared at Matty. 'He . . .'

'Oh, that doesn't matter,' Matty said lightly, forcing a smile. 'I'm a bloody idiot for thinking he could be what he seemed. As usual, my radar was way off. You must be super-happy to be proved right, right?' Her voice cracked on the last words, and she quickly got up and went to the bathroom too.

Johnny watched her go in disbelief. 'Is that bastard coming here?' he hissed. He was up on his feet, looking wild-eyed.

'No.'

'Then I'm going back there! He can't get away with this!' He looked like he was going to run back to Zell am See that very moment, in his Snoopy socks.

'Now who's emotionally invested?' Clover asked.

He stared back at her. 'But he used her like she was nothing . . .' His finger pointed angrily towards the bathroom.

'Johnny, she's okay. Wounded pride more than anything. She wasn't in love with him. He didn't hurt her.'

'Oh! So, what? We just let him get away with it, is that it? He's had his fun. Got what he wanted . . . *everything* he wanted . . . Used Mats, destroyed Kit, saved his empire . . . and there's no fucking consequences?'

He turned away, agitated and restless, his shoulders up by his ears.

'Johnny, I'm as angry as you are—'

'Oh, I doubt it!'

She blinked back at him. 'But this was never personal. It was a business tactic. Nice guys can play dirty too.'

The bathroom door opened and Matty came out again. Her face was freshly washed as well.

'You okay?' Johnny asked.

'Absolutely.' Her voice was as crisp as a green apple again but she didn't meet his eyes. 'I was just in there thinking we should actually be feeling grateful to Julian.'

'Grateful?' Clover frowned.

'Yes. He's an utter shit and he's played us all, but let's be honest – he has also actually done the spadework for us. We may not have realized it but, for very different reasons, we all wanted the same thing: Kit Foley on the ropes. And now he is.' She indicated the screen, paused on an image of Kit in the tent.

Clover swallowed. 'But what Beau said about their childhood. Their dad. I don't think we can just . . . underplay that. It's pretty heartbreaking. And it gives perspective on why he is the way he is.'

'Yeah, it does. To think of that man using his fists on his little boys,' Matty agreed. 'For what it's worth, I don't believe he did what Amy said he did either . . . ' She drew breath. 'But you still can't change the fact that he did what he did to Cory. He's still *that* guy.'

'Mat's right. We've all lived cheek by jowl with them for five weeks now,' Johnny said. 'I don't hate the guy. Far from it. We've had some laughs. I think he's pretty decent once he lets his guard down. But the simple fact is, we came here to get his side of the story. Like you said to me, we haven't got any footage that isn't true, or real, or factual. Kit hasn't done himself any favours making things so tough for you, and he sure as hell didn't pull his punches – forgive the pun' – he rolled his eyes – 'when you interviewed him. He had every opportunity to explain himself, get his side across, try to win back some public sympathy. Instead, he basically showed you the bird. And at the end of the day, that's on him. We can only show what he's given us.'

Clover turned away, feeling a jittery sensation she couldn't explain. Nervousness. 'But what he's given us *isn't* the whole story. He's keeping secrets. He never mentioned his father's abusive behaviour and that makes all the difference to how he's perceived.'

'Maybe he just doesn't want to be seen as a victim. You can see how proud he is.'

'So he'd rather live with being reviled? Publicly shamed? That makes no sense,' she cried, looking at their baffled faces and knowing they thought *she* was making no sense. 'I . . . I just feel we don't have all the story yet. The final piece of the jigsaw is still missing.'

'Clo, has it ever occurred to you that there is no final piece?' Matty sighed. 'That maybe it really was as Beau said – just a moment of madness. Sheer spite. The rivalry got out of control and a split-second decision ended in tragedy. No one's ever said Kit *wanted* Cory to be caught in a double hold-down. But he did play dirty to get him to lose. He went after him out there to win at any cost.'

Clover stared back at her, an echo sounding in her head, distant and foggy: *You were too busy going after me.* The words drifted through her consciousness like a bubble, holding something separate inside, something important . . . She squeezed her eyes shut, remembering his smirk as he'd checked her king. *You're not the first person who's wanted to beat me more than they've wanted to win.*

Not the first person . . . She frowned as the memories suddenly toppled like dominoes, the tip of one conversation tapping the end of another . . .

'Oh god . . . what?' Matty asked, watching the interplay of emotions on her face.

'Nice guys can play dirty too,' she murmured.

'Yeah, you said,' Johnny sighed. 'Julian—'

'Not Julian.' She was deep in thought, trying to make connections to frayed threads, half-remembered words . . . 'Our viewpoint all the way through has been informed by what Cory told us and what we could see on those tapes. We could see what Kit did and what it meant for Cory . . . Cory was the victim . . .' Her eyes met theirs. 'But that doesn't mean he wasn't *also* the aggressor.'

Johnny's eyebrows arched. Cory was the hero in *Pipe Dreams*. Cory was practically a saint.

She looked intently at Matty. 'Beau's gone on tape telling us Cory was agitated, acting up, getting in Kit's face.'

'Yeah. Tit for tat. Kit plays mind games,' Matty shrugged. 'We've seen that for ourselves.'

'Agreed, I'm not disputing it. But just reframe the story for a moment – consider it if everything was the other way round.'

'. . . You mean, if *Cory* started it?' Matty asked in a puzzled tone.

'If Cory started it – before they got in the water. If Kit was reacting to something Cory had done. But instead of being distracted or broken or defeated, Kit got angry . . .'

No one spoke as they tried to reverse the roles. To switch the world into a negative of itself.

420

Clover gave a small breath. 'Oh god, that's it . . . That's why he won't say a word in self-defence, because that would mean revealing what Cory did to him . . . and protecting Cory's memory – protecting Cory's family – is all he can do now . . .'

The silence spread as they all considered her words.

'Well then this film is screwed!' Matty threw her hands in the air. 'There's always going to be a hole in the middle of it if we don't know what went down between them. And we *won't*, because if Kit's not going to talk in the face of this insane amount of pressure, then he's never going to talk!'

Clover looked back at them as the dominoes in her head lay flat, exposed now, revealing themselves. 'Actually . . . I think he already has. I think he told me before I even asked.'

'What?'

'When?' Johnny and Matty asked in synchronicity.

Clover blinked. '. . . Pretty much the day we met.'

Chapter Thirty-One

Clover paced on the balcony. The wind was getting up, blowing loose powder off the uppermost surface of the handrail. She trailed a finger through the thick seam of snow; it went up to her knuckle, the freezing sensation delayed for a few seconds.

She stuck her hand in her pocket, counting back through the time zones. Midnight here meant it would be early afternoon over there right now. The boys would be at school. No doubt they'd have been in the water already . . . surfing from sun-up, like their dad used to.

'Hello?'

'Mia, it's Clo.'

'Clo!'

'Is now a good time? I can call back later if you're busy?'

'No, it's all good. The boys are at school and it's my day off. Cue six hours of me trying to get the house back in order before they come back and destroy it all over again!' She laughed lightly.

Clover gave a small smile. 'Endless, huh?'

'Definition of madness. Repeating an action over and over and expecting a different outcome.' Clover heard her pause and she closed her eyes. How was she supposed to say this? '. . . How's everything over there? Still in Austria?'

'Uh . . . Switzerland now actually. St Moritz.'

'Oh.' There was another pause, the sound of a soft snort.

'. . . Y'know, it doesn't matter how much I try and visualize it, I just can't see Kit Foley in the fricking snow. Wearing *clothes*. He practically had webbed feet.'

'. . . Yeah . . . It takes some getting used to.' She swallowed, feeling sick. How should she start it? How could she mitigate the shock? How could she say these words that needed to be said?

A silence buzzed down the line. Clover could hear the Pacific thumping down in her back garden.

'Is everything okay, Clo? You sound . . . strained.'

'I'm fine.' But her voice was strangled and weak.

'. . . Did you find something out?'

Clover's throat felt stoppered. Where were her words?

'. . . Should I be sitting down?' Mia pressed into the silence.

'. . . Probably.'

There was a long pause. 'Okay . . . I'm ready.'

Clover became aware of her rapid breathing, adrenaline flushing her veins. She had to say it. 'I know who bought your house.'

In the silence that followed, she listened to the sound of the faraway waves. On the lake in front of her, there wasn't even a ripple. Every day, every hour, the ice thickened, freezing the landscape into a static pose. She could see someone walking down by the water's edge, their footprints black depressions scowling behind them in the moonlit snow.

'. . . It's Kit, isn't it?'

Clover's breath snagged in surprise. 'How did you know?'

'Well, who else could it be to have you sounding so depressed?'

'Mia . . .' But what could she say?

There was a long pause. Mia's voice sounded altered when she came back on. 'Did he tell you?'

'No. I broke into his room the first night we got here and found some architect's drawings beside the bed. I didn't connect the dots till . . . well, today.' Her initial thought on seeing Mia's photo had been that the house looked familiar because it closely copied what had originally been there. It hadn't crossed her mind that it was what she'd seen beside Kit's bed – and she'd forgotten about it in the next instant anyway, as the news about Mikey had broken.

'Does he know you're telling me?'

'God, no!' Clover winced. 'I think he knows you would reject the house if you knew it was from him.'

'Of course I would! He already tried once before.'

'*What?*'

'. . . Straight after the accident, when Cory was still in the hospital, he made an approach. Said he wanted to make amends.' A bark of scorn split the word into two as Mia sank into the memory. 'I never told Cory about it. How could I? Kit Foley did this to us and now he wanted to make himself feel better? He'd taken away my husband's ability to earn! Can you imagine how Cory would have felt if he'd learned Kit fucking Foley was bailing us out?'

Clover closed her eyes, well able to imagine what Cory's response would have been.

A silence opened up as the truth was allowed to settle.

'I can't bear it.' Mia's words were almost whispers. 'I told myself he wouldn't be so arrogant as to pull that stunt again. I made myself believe Eddie had set it all up . . . How do I tell the boys we've got to go again?'

'Mia, no,' Clover gasped. 'You don't have to leave!'

'But how can we stay? This is guilt for what he did . . . it's a form of blood money!'

'No, that's the thing . . . I think it's a form of love—' Clover's own voice broke from the emotion. '. . . I think he's trying to make amends in the only way he can . . . Yes, he caused the accident, but Cory was his friend.' Clover's voice was quiet. '*You're* his friend. The boys . . . I know it isn't obvious, but he's been trying to . . . protect you, I think.'

There was another heavy silence. It stretched out like a mist on water. 'You sound sympathetic to him,' Mia said finally.

'I guess I am, a bit.'

'A bit? Or a whole lot?' Suspicion glinted off the words. 'Has he *turned* you, Clo? Have you fallen for his story?' She gave a gasp of surprise. 'Oh god, have you fallen for *him*?'

'It's not that!' Clover replied quickly, her words falling over each other. 'I just know more now. There was so much more than I knew.' She swallowed. 'More, I think, than even Cory knew. He didn't recover all his memories from the concussion.'

There was a long, loud pause. '. . . Didn't he?'

Clover frowned. What did *that* mean?

Neither woman spoke, but Clover could feel the connection between them begin to thrum, a vibrating guitar string intoning across the globe. '. . . Do you think I don't know why he lay in that room in the dark for all those weeks . . . ? Why he hated himself? Why he *raged*?' Mia's voice was low, ominous, like a faraway storm rumbling over the horizon.

Clover hardly dared to breathe. Her body felt as if made from glass, fragile, as though with one knock she might break. She had thought Mia knew nothing. That was the point – wasn't it – of this film? The reason why Clover was here?

'Mia, what exactly are you telling me? What do you know?' Her eyes were pinned to the lonely figure on the bank of the lake, standing now, staring out at the moonscape.

There was a long silence, then a distant sniff. '. . . I've been keeping up with the news. I've seen what Amy's said about

Kit beating her.' She gave a scornful laugh. 'She always was a scheming bitch. Never liked me because she knew I could see right through her little games.'

Clover swallowed. 'You don't believe her allegations?'

'They're bullshit!' Mia scoffed. 'Anyone who knows Kit knows he'd never hit a woman. Not after everything that happened with his father. But he's letting her get away with it because . . . well, he's our guardian angel, right? Silence, in this case, is golden. Better this than the truth.'

Another quiet spell settled over them, like a fresh sheet thrown over a bed. Clover didn't break the spell with words. She could imagine Mia picking the blades of grass and winding them between her fingers as she always used to do, when she was thinking on things.

'. . . Cory loved us, I know that. He just wanted that title too badly, that was the problem. To finally be the best . . . He wanted it too much and he lost sight of himself.' Mia tutted sadly. 'The rivalry had gotten out of hand; they'd gone from being friends to bitterest enemies. It was personal and it was getting worse and worse with every comp . . . It didn't matter what I said to him, that we didn't care about the title, we didn't care about being rich. We just wanted him . . . But Cory never had Kit's self-belief. He didn't believe he could do it by winning, only by Kit losing . . .' There was a long pause. 'I think he thought she was the only way to throw Kit off his game, the only way to hurt him – even if it meant betraying me.'

It was the confirmation she had dreaded. Clover closed her eyes, Kit's own words echoing in her head: *He hated me even more than he loved his own family.*

Neither of them spoke for several moments.

'Do you think Kit found them together?' Clover's voice was almost a whisper.

'I'm sure that would have been the idea . . . just before the final, to get Kit shaken up.' Mia's voice was flat. Toneless.

Clover felt sick at the thought of what it must have been like for him, walking in on them – but the plan had backfired. Instead of being broken, Kit had been angry. He knew how to translate pain into competitive edge. It was what made him a winner.

'But why would Amy have done it? She and Kit were engaged; he had rescued her from an abusive relationship—'

'Yes, and then she cheated on him too, because that's what she does! She's married to one of the richest guys in Sydney – do you really think that's a love match? She's clever; takes what she can get. Cory was on the cusp of becoming world champ and she was realizing she had backed the wrong horse – Kit was coming back from injury, some folk were saying he was past his best . . . He wasn't. Truth was, falling in love had just made him soft. He didn't have the same fire in his belly.'

Clover swallowed. She couldn't imagine Kit soft, or not on fire.

She watched the figure pick up a stone by the water's edge. He pulled his arm back and threw it far out of sight across the frozen surface. Faintly, the sound of it skipping over the ice – alone on the water – travelled to her ear. She felt a memory prick at the edges of her consciousness, a ghostly image trying to find form.

'Look, I'm not saying Cory was innocent in all this. I know it would have been his damned plan, but he paid for his mistake a hundred times over. But *her*? She gave him just enough to think she was the answer to his problem . . . and when it all went wrong, she walked away and never looked back. While we were left broken.' She began crying, angry, rasping sobs finally breaking through.

'Mia, I'm so sorry,' Clover whispered, feeling desperately useless. She was so far away. What could she do from here? 'I only wanted to help.'

'You did . . . you already did.' She heard Mia sniff and gasp, could imagine her wiping her eyes with the backs of her hands. 'When you first turned up here, he was lying in that room being eaten alive with guilt. But you went and sat with him, in silence and companionship for days on end . . . you showed him he hadn't been forgotten, that people still cared. You threw him a lifeline.'

'But what I put in the film, it wasn't true.'

'No, it was, Clo. It *was* the truth! Just not the whole truth . . . You acted in good faith. And if you . . . deified Cory, or vilified Kit, it was because we let you. Kit went straight on to win back the title the next year; he didn't miss a beat. The way we saw it, what did it matter if he copped a little bad press?'

Clover didn't stir. She'd been so ready to believe the best of Cory and the worst of Kit.

'. . . Thing is . . . all this time, I've been hating on the wrong person, haven't I? Kit got hurt the same as me, but I ignored that. It was easier to go after him and ignore what my gut was telling me. The whole world could see what *he'd* done . . .'

'Did Cory know that you knew?'

Mia didn't respond immediately. 'I'm not sure. I never mentioned her name, not once, in the years after the accident, even though her name was always there, right on the tip of my tongue. Every day I woke up wanting to ask him – was she the reason this had happened to us? I could see it in his eyes too, the need to confess what he'd done. He wanted to clear his conscience . . . But we were both cowards. We never said her name because then we would have to face what that meant for *us*.'

Clover sighed. She felt drained. Everything was a mess, nothing as it had seemed. Black was white and up was down. 'I'm sorry, Mia. I wanted this film to give you peace. An answer.'

'A *different* answer. I wanted it to give me a different answer to what I feared. When Cory died, all I had left was the hope that it *was* all Kit's fault. I needed him to be the bastard everyone believed him to be.'

Clover watched the man in the midnight snow as he walked back to the hotel. He looked up as he stepped into the pools of light from the windows and she felt her heart catch as Kit's eyes found her immediately, standing on her balcony. Instantly, she felt the gravitational pull between them. She wanted to run to him and tell him that she knew exactly what he was – and what he wasn't. That she'd been so wrong, about all of it.

But he kept on walking, disappearing a moment later into the hotel, and whatever instincts flashed between them, she knew he wasn't coming to find her. He had lost everything – if *Pipe Dreams* had amplified a perceived truth about what he had done, the new film had unearthed another truth, so much worse, about what Cory had done. Kit had kept his secrets for good reasons and now she'd blown his world apart. He had been right all along not to trust her.

The jarred memory fragment had bloomed now and she remembered him, alone on his surfboard at the paddle-out – apart from everyone, already on the outside. He'd been wronged by a friend, betrayed by the woman he loved, rejected by the sport he'd made his home, yet still he'd continued, quietly, trying to do the right thing anyway. He'd been everything Mia hadn't wanted. A good guy, with all the bad luck of an early worm.

*

429

Clover walked slowly, forgetting to look in the windows of the boutiques. She was supposed to be doing some Christmas shopping – there was a dress somewhere down here that Matty had spied and was coveting. She was going to need some cheering up. Julian hadn't returned any of her calls, all worst fears now confirmed.

The streets were busy; Clover had to step off the kerb numerous times as assertive couples strode past. Christmas was beginning to feel imminent, with children building snowmen in the playgrounds and carols playing in the shops. The competition had swelled the town's population, of course, but the sight of occasional snowboarders in oversized layers and drab colours was strangely jarring. The town felt not just frozen, but frozen in time. It was like being in the 1950s, as sable coats were clutched tightly against the bitter wind, the jingle of bells tinkling in the background as the horse-drawn sleighs were pulled through the streets, passengers bundled under blankets and against hides for warmth. Clover half-felt she should be 'promenading' in an opera coat and heels, not her jeans and Uggs.

She turned a corner, into a narrow side street. Matty had mentioned it was past the church and off to the left. Clover stared blankly at the luxury goods as she passed by the windows – Rolex watches on blue velvet pillows; cashmere jumpers in rainbow-hued stacks; glossy dragées and truffles in rows beneath giant chocolate angels; wooden toys and giant snowglobes on pedestals. Everything was the best, glittering and beautiful. Clover could buy what she liked. Liam had already come in with a negative pickup offer for a worldwide distribution deal that was six times what she'd got for *Pipe Dreams*. The full inside story of Kit Foley's fall from grace was hot property. She could name her price.

The dress – a flutter of cobalt blue silk – announced itself as Matty's even just on the approach. It was so perfectly her, Clover didn't even check the price. Whatever it cost, her friend must have that dress.

She pushed on the door and went in, pointing to it in the window. Within minutes, a new one was being tissue-wrapped for her, Clover still staring blankly out of the window, unable to feel any festive cheer. She felt numb, last night's conversation with Mia still playing on a loop in her head.

She watched an elderly lady walking on the other side of the street. She was hunched and taking tiny steps in her sheepskin bootees; Clover couldn't imagine how long it must take her to get anywhere.

'That will be six hundred and ninety euros, please.'

Clover's attention was back on the shop assistant in a flash. 'Six . . . ?' She dipped her head, rifling in her bag for her purse and trying to hide her shock. Was this something she'd get used to? Did she want to get used to it – a life of six-hundred-euro dresses?

She handed over the card just as a sound outside made her look up. The elderly lady had tumbled, Clover just able to glimpse a couple of kids sprinting past in the opposite direction.

'Oh god, that lady!' she cried, just as someone began running to her aid from the near side of the street.

'Oh. She's okay. Someone's with her,' the shop assistant smiled, watching the man crouch down beside her and begin talking to her.

Distantly Clover heard the buttons being pressed on the till as she watched the man reach over and gently lift the woman to standing again. She was so tiny, she couldn't weigh more than his leg. He was tender with her, clearly checking she had no pain.

She watched the old woman say something to him and

smile. Clover watched him watch her as the old lady took a few tentative steps; he had his arms outstretched towards her like an overprotective father, lest she should fall again.

'Ms Phillips?'

Clover turned abruptly. 'Huh?'

'Your PIN, please?'

'Oh. Yes.'

She punched in the number, checking she was pressing the right buttons for 'confirm'. By the time she looked up again a few moments later, the old lady and Kit had gone.

She turned in to the hotel, clutching enough bags to feel she probably now looked like one of their guests. After buying Matty's dress she had bought a high-end (and high-priced) remote-control Aston Martin for Johnny, a blouse for Charlie, some silver ski cufflinks for Tom, a wooden train set for Elliot and a toy elephant for Bella.

A group of carollers was gathered by the giant Christmas tree and singing '*Stille Nacht*' – much, it appeared, to the chagrin of the photographers still gathered on the other side of the road. Still awaiting their next opportunity with Kit, the man of the moment, the man everyone was loving to hate.

He'd be back sooner than later, she knew, setting them all off into a frenzy. It felt like a minor miracle that they weren't shadowing him down the streets. It had been a minor miracle too that she hadn't bumped into him. If she hadn't ducked into the boutique . . . But fate had had other ideas, conspiring to keep them apart.

She pushed on the revolving doors and stepped into the lobby. It was bustling, with a low hum of conversation and the muted tinkle of a piano playing somewhere, but she wasn't in the mood to people-watch. She just wanted to get to her room.

She went straight to the lifts and pressed the button. Through the windows, she looked back at the press pack, waiting like vultures. Did they ever stop to think what it must be like for someone to be doorstepped by them? Did they ever consider the vitriol that followed after their lurid headlines, the catcalls in the streets of passers-by, the trolling online . . . Was what *she* had done to him any better?

The lift doors opened and she turned back—

Kit was leaning against the back wall, his arms folded against his chest. He glanced up as she failed to walk in.

For a moment, she couldn't move. Lie low, she'd told herself. Stay out of his way. It had been the entire point of going out this morning . . . She hadn't wanted to even glimpse him before tonight. She had a plan and she had to stick to it. Now, for the second time in an hour . . .

'Quick then. Before they see me.'

She stepped into the lift's opposite corner, keeping as much distance as she could. He seemed to notice.

'How did you . . . ?' She glanced back at the photographers again, still waiting pointlessly out the front.

He reached forward quickly and pressed for the doors to close. 'They're letting me use the kitchen entrance,' he muttered.

'Oh.'

'. . . Which floor?'

'Uh, four.'

She watched him press the button, felt the lift begin to move. She could have bitten on the tension between them. It was the first time they had been alone since the night of the casino, since she had brazenly taken a bath in his room and climbed into his bed, pushing for secrets he had been right to hide. It didn't matter that she had wanted to believe the best in him; they both knew she had brought this situation to bear and, standing in opposite corners, their night together might as well have happened between two entirely different people than the two of them here now.

The lifts were polished brass interiors – anywhere they glanced, their eyes could meet. His gaze fell to her bags. To safety.

'Christmas shopping,' she explained in a quiet voice. 'Mainly for my brother and his family.'

'Nothing for me?'

She looked back at him but only a wry look flickered in his eyes as he looked away again. A joke. Small talk. He was locking her out; she was just another stranger in a lift.

'So what were you doing just now?' she asked.

'Outside?'

She nodded.

'Just went for a walk. Trying to clear my head.' He didn't mention helping the little old lady off the frozen pavement. Being a Good Samaritan. But she knew now that he never did.

'Are you nervous about tonight?'

'Not really.'

'Really?'

'. . . Maybe a bit.'

She caught his gaze but he looked away again, elusive as a fox.

His phone rang. He checked it with a sigh. '. . . Ari,' he muttered in a low voice. 'I'm just with Clover.'

He frowned as his manager said something to him. Clover watched the number three run past on the digital display. A few more seconds and she could be out of here. She had a desperate urge to get away as quickly as she could—

His arm shot forwards, pressing the stop button. The lift lurched, making her stagger slightly as he looked back at her.

'What is it?' she asked worriedly, feeling her heart begin to pound as she felt the full weight of his scrutiny.

'Ari says you have something important to tell me?'

She had hoped that Ari would break the news to Kit himself, but there was so much to explain . . .

She watched his expression as she told him what she knew: Julian's family's business troubles, their scorched earth plan, the ambush outside the restaurant, Amy's allegations timed to coincide with the press gathered outside the casino . . . Outwardly, he scarcely reacted. He stood still, breathing deeply and slowly as he listened. She saw him swallow at the particularly pertinent moments, he was blinking more rapidly than usual, but other than that, no one would have known he was hearing anything more than the weather forecast. She tried to imagine his face as he'd walked in on Amy and Cory . . .

'Is that it?' he asked finally.

She nodded, wishing the lift was smaller, that he would reach an arm towards her, catch her with his gaze, that he would say again the things he had said to her in the dark.

Instead, he leaned back against the far corner, his head tipped as he stared at the ceiling, absorbing the extent of Julian's manipulations.

Finally, he looked back at her. 'Thanks for letting me know.'

'Thanks—? That's *it*?'

'What is there to say? It was a business strategy.' He shrugged. 'Good luck to him.'

She stared at him, open-mouthed. His response was exactly as it had been the night of Amy's allegations too. He was Teflon-plated; bullet-proof. 'Kit, this isn't okay. What he's done to you . . . It's awful.'

His gaze slid across to her. 'I've had worse.'

She stared at him, seeing how he just absorbed the shock, the pain and moved on, never missing a step. He would take this betrayal and turn it into the will to win, just as he had after the split from his father, then his father's death, in the year after Cory's accident, he would keep driving onwards. Unstoppable. Uncatchable. Invulnerable now . . . No one could hurt him. No one could get close anymore. Amy had taught him – and she had too, in her own small way – that he could trust no one.

He reached forward and released the stop button. The lift lurched again, rolling upwards.

She wanted to tell him she knew about all of it, everything that had been hidden: Cory and Amy; what he'd done for Mia and the boys; the lies that had been endured as a secret kindness . . . But she would be doing it for herself. What did he care if she knew now he wasn't a monster? The damage had been done.

The number four appeared on the digital display. The doors slid open and she reluctantly stepped out.

'What are you going to do?' she asked, turning back to him.

'You know what they say: success is the best revenge.'

She hesitated. '. . . Isn't it happiness? . . . Happiness is the best revenge?'

He looked bemused. 'Success *is* happiness.'

'. . . Is it though?' He had won every trophy there was for him to win. He didn't seem happy to her.

He smiled – beautiful, broken – and for a moment, his gaze roamed her face like *she* was the conundrum. She sensed he was going to reach out and pull her to him. She felt the avalanche powder cloud clear around them momentarily, revealing blue skies and sunshine. But in the next heartbeat, he had drawn back. The doors began to close, preparing to take him from her. '. . . You've got some funny ideas, Clover Phillips. You'll be saying you believe in the Easter Bunny and happy endings next.'

Chapter Thirty-Two

Clover pushed through the revolving doors, Matty following her a few steps behind, nodding at the doorman who raised his hat to them. It was snowing lightly as they walked past the illuminated Christmas tree and crossed the road. It was dark now, but even without the mega-wattage thrown down from the giant tree, she could have found them by the glowing butts of their cigarettes, hovering in a cluster like fireflies.

'You're absolutely sure about this?' Matty asked her in a low voice as they drew closer.

Clover could only nod. She felt like her heart wanted to leap from her chest. She stopped in front of the press pack like she was standing before wolves. They were in off-duty mode, lens caps on the cameras. Sprawled in a loose band, they were smoking, drinking coffees, chatting on their phones. One of them noticed the two women standing before them, not passing. He gave a bored, faintly quizzical look.

Matty straightened up, impressively tall and intimidatingly beautiful. 'This is Clover Phillips, the BAFTA and Golden Globe-winning documentary-maker who produced the film *Pipe Dreams* about the surfer, Cory Allbright.'

Cory's name registered immediately; just like that, eyes were on them. The reporters knew exactly Cory's relationship and history with Kit Foley.

'Ms Phillips has come to make a statement.'

Suddenly, the slack band of men became taut and alert, hands reaching for lens caps, switching on voice recorders. Clover reached for her backpack too and pulled out the laptop. There were a few sheets of paper held in place beneath the cover and she opened it carefully, not wanting anything to escape before time. She looked back at the men. The cameras were already rolling.

She felt a spike of adrenaline, a sudden urge to run, but she knew if there was nothing more she achieved in her life, she had to stand perfectly still and see this through. She looked at the piece of paper in her hand and began to read.

'My team and I have been shadowing Kit Foley for the past few weeks for our new documentary, following up on the rivalry laid bare between Cory Allbright and Kit Foley in *Pipe Dreams*. If you've seen that film, then you'll know I have no bias or loyalty towards Kit. My alliances are pretty clear, in fact, to Cory and the Allbrights. However, allegations have been made in recent days that cannot be allowed to go unchallenged.' She took another breath, willing herself not to rush, her voice to remain steady.

'. . . Kit Foley is not responsible for beating Amy Killicks. He never raised a hand against her. The images first printed in the *Sydney Herald* were taken by Kit himself, after Amy had been attacked by her boyfriend at the time.' Clover cleared her throat, seeing the intense focus and incredulity in the reporters' eyes. They couldn't get a clean shot of Kit; even a terse 'no comment' from him would have been a result. To be getting this . . .

'Kit took the photographs as evidence. He had been trying to convince Amy to file charges against her former partner, who had been harassing and stalking her. I have further images here' – with a shaking hand, she held up the sheets Beau had printed for them to see – 'which weren't published, and which show Amy holding up her hair to display the bruises on her back. There would be no reason why she would do this for the person who had caused the bruises; nor would there be any logical reason for the person who had caused them, to document them, as they would act as evidence against him. Additionally, the digital paths of each image show the date and time that they were taken, and also the device used – Kit Foley's phone.'

She swallowed. 'You will, I know, ask two questions as a result of this revelation. Why is Amy Killicks lying? And why didn't Kit Foley defend himself against these allegations? . . . Well, Kit has been trying to protect the memory of Cory Allbright, in the best interests of Cory's family. His principal concern has always been for Mia Allbright and her three young sons, and he strongly believes that the events behind his much-publicized incident with Cory in the quarter-finals in Peniche, Portugal, were private and should remain so. Kit is *still* of this opinion.'

Clover steadied herself again. Everything in her wanted to run. Her voice sounded strained. With every word she knew she was throwing her film's exclusives – and her future career with them – to the wind. 'However, in light of the stories Amy has sold to the press, worldwide, Cory's widow has recorded this statement, which she has asked me to play to you . . .'

Clover pressed play on the MP3 file which Johnny had downloaded for her and turned the laptop towards the microphones.

'My name is Mia Allbright and I want to state on the record that in October 2017, during the Pro Portugal competition in Peniche, my husband Cory was unfaithful to me with Amy Killicks.

I knew Amy quite well back then, as she was Kit Foley's fiancée at the time. This event was the cause of Kit's separation from Amy, and of the subsequent incident on the water that day.

I want it to be known that I do not blame Kit for what happened. He and I were both victims of Cory and Amy's actions, and what happened in the competition immediately afterwards came from a moment of anger, justifiable anger, with unforeseen consequences . . . I think sometimes we confuse winners with heroes. They are not. They make mistakes, like anyone else. Kit did and Cory certainly did too.

I know Kit's tried to help us since in his own private ways and we thank him for that. It would have been easy for him to defend himself against Amy's lies but he chose not to. He chose to protect Cory's reputation for me and our boys. Which is why I am speaking out instead. Amy Killicks – now Mrs Robert Kesteven – is lying. She was contacted by Clover Phillips' team to contribute to the new film about Kit and I can only assume she believed Kit had gone on the record about what had happened between her and Cory just before the accident. I believe she has tried to discredit Kit with these unfounded allegations, in the hope that they might outweigh Kit's own revelations. It is for Kit to decide whether he wants to take legal action against her slurs but if he does, I'll say here and now that I'm prepared to stand up in court and act as a witness for him. We all need to find some peace and closure on this. It's been four years of suffering for us, and for Kit, and we need to move forward with our lives.

That is all I have to say. I will not be making any further comment on the matter and request you respect the privacy of my young family. Thank you.'

Clover pressed pause.

For several moments, there was an amazed silence. She knew that none of the reporters gathered could ever have expected they were going to land a scoop on one of the biggest stories in sport, standing here outside the hotel. Then they thrust their microphones towards her, their voices clashing and falling over one another in a rush of broken English.

'Ms Phillips, can you confirm if Kit will sue Amy for defamation?'

'Clover, are you the same woman lying on the ground in the photographs taken outside the restaurant in Austria?'

'Has Kit approved this press conference?'

Matty stepped beside Clover and winked at her proudly. She turned to the reporters, in her element. 'One at a time, please. Yes, you. What's your question . . . ?'

The music was pumping, lights strobing over the glassy super-pipe that was as precision-groomed as a Kardashian eyebrow; there wasn't a stray speck on the icy surface. The bleachers were packed, people waving banners and flags, their cheers rising into the night sky as they awaited the next rider. This was the third run of three and everyone was chasing a perfect ten.

Clover understood now what Beau had meant about competing under the lights. It gave everything a completely different feel. This was nothing like Stomping Ground, or their training runs on Kitzsteinhorn. Surfing had certainly never thrown up anything like this. Kit was in a brave new world up there – and he was loving it. The crowd had noticeably warmed up to him: a high score of 9.2 on his first run hadn't elicited much more than a tepid clap. But by his second run, which scored lower – 8.9 thanks to a hand down on a landing – the cheers had begun to crackle the night sky. And now, as he slid into the starting position for his final showing, people were on their feet, calling his name before he'd even gone.

Matty jogged Clo's elbow knowingly as the cameras caught

Kit's bewilderment, coming in tight and treating everyone to some close-ups. The crowd erupted again. Word had definitely got out. People were learning the truth.

But not him. Not yet. Clover knew he had his airbuds in. Like all the riders, he'd be listening to his own playlist, riding to his own beat, giving the spectators a show. He checked his goggles, his chinstrap, clapped his hands together a few times to get him in the zone.

The crowd picked up the beat, clapping him too. They were showing him in every way they could that they were behind him. On his side. Willing him to the win.

He dropped in—

'*And that's an aggressive start by Kit Foley,*' the commentator announced.

'Oh my god!' Matty whispered as Kit grabbed his board on the upswing and extended his body into a perfect arc. He landed it, cruised down and swung up on the other side, spinning through the air like it was the natural way to travel.

Down in the next instant, airborne again . . .

'. . . *There's the Switch Backside 1260 that Foley's beginning to claim for his own!*' the commentator cried.

Clover could hardly watch. She thought of Mikey. If he should fall too . . .

'*And he's coming in hard and fast! There he goes for the Double McTwist . . . beautiful execution, you can see his surfing background helping him here with those whip-smart turns . . .*'

Clover realized she was holding her breath again. She tried to breathe.

'*He's really using that up-draught to make the hits big and clean . . . Will he go for the Frontside Double Cork 1080? We've heard he's pulled it off in training, will tonight be the . . . Yes! Oh and it's good though! . . . He stomps that down!*'

Clover gasped as she saw Kit land cleanly on the last jump, his arms flying up and punching the air as he carved to a stop.

'And that's going to be a high, high score for the former surfer's final run! . . . What a debut! He made it look easy out there tonight . . . Is there anything Kit Foley can't do?!'

Matty squealed and threw her arms around Clover's neck as the crowds in the bleachers went wild. People were blowing on horns, chanting his name. The cameras came in close, seeing how his eyes were burning as he whipped off his helmet and goggles and threw them into the air.

Clover watched in amazement as the crowd's support wrapped around him as he pivoted on the spot, his arms above his head. She could see the disbelief in his face. She had never seen him look like this before. She'd never seen him *happy*.

'He knows it's good! He knows the crowd knows it too! That could well be the gold medal run of the night . . . !'

Clover's fingers pressed to her mouth as she watched him, drinking him in, tears pooling in her eyes as she watched him get his wish: Success. The best revenge.

The score flashed up suddenly on the giant board.

A perfect 10!

Everyone was screaming now! He'd done it! With only two riders to follow, there was almost no chance they could catch him with their aggregates, unless they scored tens too.

She watched as he sank to his knees, the emotion overwhelming him suddenly. His head dropped, his hands planted in the snow. She saw his shoulders heave from the emotion, the mental strain break over him like a wave, as for several moments he stayed kneeling on the snow. Every single person watching knew the pressures that had been bearing down on him. The lies that had been told.

'Foley! Foley! Foley!'

The crowd was chanting his name in perfect unison, showing him they were behind him. *For* him. Was this redemption? He looked up and the cameras caught the wetness of his lashes. The champion was mortal. He was flesh and blood and tears after all.

He raised a hand in acknowledgement to them all. He'd done what he'd come here to do.

And so had she, in the end – exposed the truth about Kit Foley.

Clover felt Matty grip her arm and rest her head on her shoulder. He was heading now for the press tent. In a few moments, he would find out why he was loved again. Why he had glory as well as gold. He would find out what she'd done, telling the world that his fiancée had slept with another man.

And he would hate her for it. He would never forgive her. She had told his secret to the world.

'Come on. It's time,' Matty said, jerking her head with a sympathetic smile.

Clover looked away from the TV screen. The boarding gate was now empty, 'Final Call' flashing in red letters above the desk. Heart pounding, with tears in her eyes, she picked up her bag and they walked over to the air steward.

'Good evening, welcome to Swiss Air,' he said, checking their passports and boarding passes before handing them back to them with a smile. 'We hope you have a pleasant flight.'

444

Epilogue

Two weeks later
Somerset House, London

'Now just hold on to me,' Johnny said, as they stood by the edge of the rink. It kept flashing turquoise and ultra-violet, Mariah Carey's 'All I Want for Christmas is You' playing seemingly on repeat. A ten-metre Christmas tree stood at the far end, the Palladian courtyard buildings picked out in golden lights. It was all formidably brighter and resolutely jollier than her darkened flat, with the curtains drawn, which was where she'd wanted to stay again tonight.

Her friends had had other ideas, though. They'd had this idea. And it wasn't a good one.

'Promise you won't let me go,' Clover said, her voice rising with nerves as she struggled to balance on the blades. She was clinging to the edges of the rink, feeling intimidated by the speed and ease with which everyone was whizzing past. Since when had *all of London* learned how to ice-skate? This wasn't Amsterdam!

'I promise,' Johnny grinned, looking thoroughly bemused as though it were her childish fears that were ridiculous and not his elf jumper.

'I swear, if you let go even for a second, I'll fall and break a leg.'

445

'Then I won't let you go for even a second,' he said calmly. 'Now hold my hands. I'll lead. All you have to do is glide. Get used to the feeling, okay? It's not so different to skiing.'

'Mats, you'll be behind me, won't you?'

'I promise, I'll be right here to catch you if you fall.'

Clover was aware of bemused looks being exchanged between her two friends as slowly she unfurled her fingers from their death grip, placing her hands in Johnny's and letting him pull her out onto the ice. She gave a squeal as she felt her blades run over the glassy surface. Why had she even let them talk her into this? They knew she'd had a lifelong fear of skating ever since Tom – aged eight – had terrified her with stories of blood-smeared ice and sliced-off fingers.

'Oh god, *please* can I have a penguin?' she cried as they moved out further into the slipstream.

'Clo, they're for children,' Matty laughed behind her.

'I don't care! I need a penguin!'

'You're too tall!'

'I'll go on my knees then.'

'That's not skating!' Matty chuckled.

'Now I know how men feel when their wives are in labour,' Johnny winced as Clover gripped his hands so tightly, they were blanched white.

'Johnny, this is probably the closest you'll ever get to that scenario,' Matty tutted. 'The chances of you ever convincing a woman to have your children is—'

'Dependent upon my openness to wearing a collared shirt?'

A silence opened up around Clover, looks she couldn't catch passing right by her. She was vaguely aware her friends needed her to adjudicate, as per, but she couldn't believe they were even able to conduct a conversation – much less an argument! – while doing this. They were holding her up!

Johnny was skating backwards! Was she the only Londoner who couldn't skate?

They did a few very slow revolutions of the rink. Clover wanted to get back to the safety of the drinks tent. She'd do anything for a high stool and a hot chocolate right now.

'Okay, now try this.'

'What? What?' she asked in panic, watching as Matty peeled off and away, skating past with a grace she could never achieve, even with flashing reindeer antlers on her head.

Clover felt ungainly and ridiculous by comparison and she was certainly regretting her Santa hat and tinsel scarf. 'Matty, come back! You promised!'

'Now I'm going to come round you and skate with you from behind,' Johnny said. 'That way you can transfer your weight a little and I can support you around the waist. Okay?'

'*What?* No! We have to keep doing this,' she insisted in a shaky voice, her eyes wide with terror.

'Progress, Clo.' And before she could stop him, Johnny released his hands from her grip with a wide smile. 'There you go!'

'Johnny, no!' she squealed as she continued to glide without him, past him, unable to turn or stop, wholly dependent upon him catching and steering her again. In the next instant, she felt one of his hands grasp her lightly around the waist, the other taking her by the hand as he came up alongside her. 'Oh my god!' she breathed, gripping his hand tightly. 'That was terrifying! You said you wouldn't let go for even a second! Promise you won't let me go again?'

'That is the idea.'

Her entire body stiffened. What . . . ? What . . . ? She wanted to turn her head, to see with her own eyes that it was true, but she couldn't take her eyes off the ice. Not if she wanted to stay upright.

Johnny glided past her with a wink, definitely not holding on to her, as he raced to catch up with Matty.

'Relax. Just hold on to me,' Kit said calmly. 'I've got you.' She could feel his eyes upon her profile.

'I . . . I need a penguin,' she stammered, feeling her panic rise again.

'I'll be your penguin.'

'. . . What are you doing here?' she whispered, terrified that even putting any kind of body into her voice might be enough to topple her over.

'Well, I figured I needed to get you somewhere you couldn't run from me again . . . This was Johnny's idea. He told me you couldn't skate.'

She could hardly speak from the shock. There was too much going on for her body and mind – and heart – to handle. 'Johnny's in on this?'

'Yes. Although it took some work. He wouldn't give me your address. Apparently he didn't think it would be in your best interests to see me again. Whatever that means.'

It meant she'd spent the past fortnight in her pyjamas, alternately crying and catatonic, while Johnny had been editing round the clock. Not that she was going to tell Kit that.

'So how did you convince him, then?'

'Ari and I had to get him hammered.'

'God, he would have been terrified.' She gave a tiny shocked laugh at the thought of Kit and Ari press-ganging him.

Kit's hand squeezed hers a little as they rounded the corner. *Of course* he was an expert skater too. He felt a lot more stable than Johnny had done. '. . . Where is Ari?'

'Back in Oz. With his family. He flew out this morning. Very hung.'

'Oh.' It was Christmas Eve Eve. With the twenty-two-hour flight, he'd get back only just in time, surely? 'And Beau?'

It took all her concentration to be able to stay upright *and* have a conversation with him. Her mind was racing, her heart even faster.

He sighed. 'Beau's back in Saas-Fee . . . Turns out it wasn't just the powder keeping him there.'

Her eyes widened as she got his meaning. 'He's met someone?'

'Apparently.'

They glided in silence for a few moments. She wished she could turn her head just to look at him, to get some reading of his mood. What exactly was happening? Why had he come here? To shout at her? Push her over? '. . . Exactly how mad at me are you?' she asked.

'Very.'

'Right.' She was quiet for several seconds. 'So you've come here for an apology?'

'No.'

'No?'

'No point. I know you'd do it again.'

'You do?'

'You were getting me justice, right?'

She heard the tint of sarcasm. 'Look, I'm sorry if it was a shock.' She couldn't imagine how blindsided he must have been, to come off the pipe with his gold and have to sit through the most bizarre press conference of his life as he was told about her roadside coup.

'*Shock* is putting it mildly.' She felt his grip tighten around her hand.

'But they couldn't just get away with it. Someone had to do something.'

'And it had to be you to do it?'

She swallowed. If she made him mad, he might let go of her. 'Well, I had to try and do something. It was my fault everything blew up the way it did.'

He didn't reply, didn't tell her she was wrong. They both knew she'd brought the sky crashing down on his head.

They glided in silence for several moments. Or rather he glided, she just held on. '. . . Have you heard from him? Julian, I mean.'

She heard him inhale at the mention of his old sponsor's name. 'No. Although I saw there's a bid for O-R Hotels. Their share price has increased twelve per cent in the past few weeks.'

'Yes. It's very . . . pleasing to see,' she mumbled.

His grip tightened on her hand again. 'Pleasing?' he scoffed. 'You *planned* it. It's why you pulled that stunt.'

'It wasn't a stunt!' she echoed indignantly.

'No? What was it then?'

'It was knowing that gold wasn't going to be enough on its own. You had to do more than win to beat him. You had to shine. People had to know those things in the papers about you were all lies.'

'I didn't know you cared.'

Was he being sarcastic again? She couldn't tell. '. . . It wasn't just for you. It was for Matty too.'

He was quiet for a moment. 'Well, from the things Johnny was declaring after ten pints last night, I think she's already got someone prepared to defend her honour.'

'Oh.' She gave a surprised smile as he led her into the next corner. 'Well, that would be . . .'

'Pleasing?'

'I was going to say, about time.'

She wanted so badly to look at him. It felt like an agony

to have her hand in his, his arm around her – and yet she couldn't see him . . . Then again, maybe it was better like this. It was easier talking to him if she didn't have to look into those eyes.

'So what about the film?' he asked. 'Do you still have one? Or did you give away all your best stuff saving me?'

A small sigh escaped her. Their only remaining ace was to film her talking about the fight outside the restaurant in Zell – hardly a clincher. 'Pretty much. Johnny's doing what he can, but we've effectively given away the punchline, so . . .'

Liam had pulled his offer again when word had reached him about her press conference and all its spoilers. It had been another compelling reason not to get off her sofa for two weeks.

Kit didn't say anything immediately. 'Sounds like you need an exclusive interview then.'

She waited for the 'but'. A silence spooled instead.

'. . . You'd do that?'

His grip tightened at her waist. 'I reckon it's the least I can do, all things considered. I might even behave this time.'

She gave a small smile as he led her round the rink, solid and sure, and she realized her fear of the ice was slipping away. It was beginning to feel normal through repetition, but she knew it was more than that – he made her feel safe.

'I spoke to Mia,' she said quietly. 'She says you've all been back in touch recently.'

'. . . Yeah.'

'You might be going over there in the new year?'

'That's the plan.'

'. . . She says Amy's husband's lawyers have come in with a pre-emptive settlement offer for damages. They just want this whole thing to go away.'

'. . . Yeah.'

She dared to snatch a glimpse of him, catching a fleeting glance of his profile. His hold around her tightened as she immediately wobbled. But he didn't. He was her penguin. 'She also said you're instructing your lawyers to have the entire sum put into a trust for the boys.'

'. . . That's supposed to be confidential,' he said tersely.

'Mia and I don't have secrets.'

The ball of his jaw pulsed. 'Clearly.'

'So then, all's well that ends well,' she said lightly. 'You've done right by Cory, setting up his family in their home, financially . . . You've got your gold and a new career. Success is happiness, right?'

There was a long pause. 'I used to think so.'

She swallowed. 'Not anymore?'

He didn't speak for several moments as he manoeuvred her easily around a couple who'd just fallen, laughing hysterically, on their backsides. '. . . I'm retiring from snowboarding.'

She gasped. 'But—'

His fingers gripped her waist more tightly. 'My heart's not in it. Tipper and Ari are going to work with Beau now.'

She couldn't speak for several moments. 'But after all that work you put in.'

'I'm going back on the surf tour. Thanks to you, I've got friends again. And sponsors. I reckon I've got a few more good years left in me.'

'Oh . . . Well, that's . . . great,' she said hesitantly. Her heart twitched like a caged bird.

'Yeah.'

'So you'll be travelling a lot then.'

'I'll pick and choose the events . . . but yeah.'

They did a whole circuit without speaking. She'd almost forgotten she was moving now. The feeling had become familiar, his rhythm beside her automatic. But the fear of falling was nothing to the fear of never seeing him again.

'Kit, why are you here?' The words burst from her, almost as a plea. She'd spent the past two weeks in a state that could only be described as grief. And now he'd come here just to tell her he was leaving?

'I needed to know something.'

'Okay.'

She waited, anxious, and he was quiet for a bit, as if gathering his thoughts. 'Why did you go? Why did you do all that stuff for me . . . and then just leave?'

'What? You thought I'd hang around and wait for your fury?' She felt shocked he even had to ask. 'What happened with Amy and Cory and you – it was private. And I went and told the world. It might have been the right thing to do, but I still knew you'd hate me for it.'

His hand gripped hers hard suddenly. 'I don't . . . *hate* you . . . You know I don't.'

'No, I don't know!' she cried. 'I don't know anything about what you feel. You don't trust anyone. You don't let anyone in. It's you against the world. Against your dad. Against Cory. Against me.'

She felt him speed up suddenly. She felt his hand let go of hers, both his hands on her waist, spinning her and then a sharp dig of his blades into the ice, coming to a stop. She bumped against his chest, facing him, his hands holding hers again. She wasn't sure what had just happened. There hadn't even been time to gasp.

He looked down at her. 'Because I can't find a centre with you.' His voice was low. 'I think you're against me and then I discover you put everything on the line for me . . . No one's ever fought for me before. I'm not . . . it's not what I know . . .' His eyes were burning. 'But then you were gone, without a word, and I was left with these . . .'

He didn't finish. But she knew what he couldn't say. Feelings scared him far more than the oceans or the mountains.

She stared at him, waiting.

'Nothing felt right without you.'

'. . . So then I won't go again,' she said simply.

He swallowed and she could see he hadn't expected that answer. That he really hadn't known, for sure, how she felt. 'No?'

She shook her head and a moment contracted between them as she saw the shadows leave his eyes.

'. . . God, I want to kiss you but I'm worried you'll fall.'

'Far too late,' she whispered, looking up at him.

With one move, he pushed off again, holding her effortlessly as she was glided backwards, his arm around her. She felt him brake, then the wall of the rink pressed at her back and his eyes glittered as they both remembered their first time in the pool – accidental, instinctive, inevitable.

She entwined her arms around his neck, no longer even aware that they were on ice. 'So you really don't hate me?' she asked.

'No.'

Her eyes narrowed. 'Yes you do,' she insisted. 'You hate me.' She felt him startle. 'No.'

'Admit it.'

His eyes burned as he realized her tease. '. . . No.'

'Just say it. You hate me.'

'No . . . I love you.'

She stared back at him, seeing past the layers at last. There he was, finally. Unmasked. 'I know,' she whispered as he pulled her into him. 'I love you too.'

Acknowledgements

I must start with a confession. Anyone who knows anything about either snowboarding or St Moritz will know that St Moritz does not have a halfpipe. And anyone who knows anything about competitive snowboarding will know that the FIS St Moritz event, whilst held in early December, is a ski event only. I try as much as possible to stick to 'real life' frameworks where I can but it's not always possible, especially when trying to write a Christmas book which, by definition, is somewhat inflexible on dates!

I had a great time researching this book – first learning all about surfing, then switching to snow and learning about snowboarding. As a skier, it was all new for me, but the thrill of playing in alpine snow is the same. The very first seeds for this story were sown almost ten years ago when I saw a documentary film called *The Crash Reel*, based on the lead-up to, and fallout after, an accident suffered by snowboarder Kevin Pearce when he was training for the 2010 Winter Olympics. It was profoundly shocking and upsetting to watch – although I'm glad to report Kevin recovered and, although he can no longer compete, has found fulfilment and success in lecturing about traumatic brain injuries and brain safety. The film made me realize, though, just how life-changing the risks can be when it goes wrong. This is a sport that looks like playing but the consequences of being one degree or one second out can easily be tragic.

Nonetheless, that was a long time ago and the film wasn't on my 'ideas' radar until I happened to watch a couple of other documentaries in quick succession – playing in the background, usually whilst cooking dinner – on two fallen sporting heroes: Lance Armstrong and Oscar Pistorius. Although their fortunes have been affected by very different fates, I nonetheless was struck by the similarities between them: a ruthlessness, perfectionism, and a ready willingness to be unlikeable in the pursuit of being the best. Is that what's required to be a winner? I was also intrigued by the idea of living with public disgrace, of being forever 'the villain'.

Bringing all these ideas and themes together of course requires a mothership of over-achievers to make it look like I know what I'm doing. Luckily, I was beamed up by Pan Macmillan many moons ago and, as ever, I owe the team all my thanks – from the art department for this stunning new-look cover; to the editorial SWAT team Lucy Hale, Caroline Hogg and Jayne Osborne for their precision edits and the deep-dive brainstorms that found us such a lovely title; my desk editor Samantha Fletcher and copy editor Camilla Lockwood for keeping the faith with all the random-ness that accompanies the early drafts – sometimes they laugh, sometimes they cry; Jez Trevathan, Stu Dwyer, Jonathan Atkins, Charlotte Williams, Elle Gibbons, Hannah Corbett, Jade Tolley, Rebecca Lloyd . . . Absolutely everyone places their own mark on this book's progress and I'm so grateful for all of it. To misquote the Instagram phrase – the book did *not* wake up like this.

As for my family, who have to live with me while I'm muddling through my tangled, knotted thoughts and trying to fashion a story . . . thank you for always repeating every three times for me and not leaving home when I haven't got time to restock the fridge. There's no me without you. You are utterly glorious.

Together by Christmas

'Stylish and compelling'
Woman & Home

Set in snowy Amsterdam, *Together by Christmas*
is a moving read of secrets, romance
and heartbreaking dilemmas

Lee arrived in Amsterdam with a newborn baby and a
secret. Years later, her career is flourishing, life is finally
approaching normal, and love is on the horizon.

But as the snow falls, the secret Lee has never told
resurfaces. Christmas is a time for being together – but
what if the truth means she ends up alone?

The Christmas Party

'Love, loss and reinvention'

Marie Claire

At an elegant country house party on
Ireland's rugged south-west coast, shocking
secrets and unexpected romances hide
just beneath the surface . . .

When the last remaining knight in Ireland dies, his estate
is left to his three daughters. The two eldest, Ottie and Pip,
get their share, but it is the baby of the family, Willow, who
inherits the castle. Having turned her back on her family
years before, Willow announces she is selling up.

At a lavish goodbye party days before Christmas, Ottie,
Willow and Pip must ask themselves which is harder:
stepping into the future, or letting go of the past?

The
CHRISTMAS
LIGHTS

'Epic books in dream destinations'
Woman's Weekly

Escape to the snow-fringed fjords of Norway
with *The Christmas Lights*, a delicious tale full of
drama and mystery, heartache and hope

Bo lives a life most people can only dream of. She and her
boyfriend Zac are paid to travel the globe, sharing their
adventures online. When he proposes, Bo's happiness is
complete, and they head to Norway to spend
Christmas under the Northern Lights.

But the mountains hold secrets from the past and, as
temperatures plummet and tensions rise, Bo must face
up to the fact that her picture-perfect life may not
be the one she truly wants . . .

The
CHRISTMAS
SECRET

'**Smart plots, brilliant characters and juicy romance**'
Heat

Set on the beautiful and remote coast of Islay,
The Christmas Secret is a gripping story of a love as
wild as the island itself . . .

Alex Hyde is an executive coach par excellence. With only a
few weeks until Christmas, she is given the task of getting into
the troubled head of Lochlan Farquhar, before he brings his
esteemed whisky distillery to its knees.

Lochlan, though charismatic, is unpredictable and destructive.
As she pulls ever closer to him, boundaries become blurred,
loyalties loosen, and Alex is confronted with an
impossible choice . . .

Christmas
UNDER THE
STARS

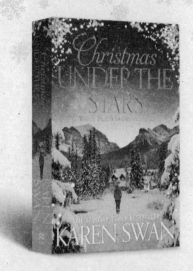

'The literary equivalent of a Richard Curtis movie'
Glamour

A heartbreaking tale of learning to love again, set amongst the dramatic, snow-capped Canadian Rockies

Meg and Mitch are living their dream – weeks away from their wedding and running a snowboarding business with their oldest friends. But when a storm hits, tragedy strikes and their perfect life unravels. As they try to cope with their loss, friendships are buckled by tensions, rivalries and devastating secrets.

Solace for Meg comes from the most unexpected place – a voice across the airwave, comforting her despite the distance between them. As Meg's future pulls away from her past and her friends grow more distant, can she take a chance on the unknown?